Cairn AND Covenant

August Li

DSP PUBLICATIONS

Published by
DSP PUBLICATIONS

5032 Capital Circle SW, Suite 2, PMB# 279, Tallahassee, FL 32305-7886 USA
www.dsppublications.com/

Cairn and Covenant
© 2015 August Li.

Cover Art
© 2015 Anne Cain.
annecain.art@gmail.com
Cover content is for illustrative purposes only and any person depicted on the cover is a model.

ISBN: 978-1-63476-121-5
Digital ISBN: 978-1-63476-122-2
Library of Congress Control Number: 2015901359
First Edition September 2015

Printed in the United States of America

This paper meets the requirements of
ANSI/NISO Z39.48-1992 (Permanence of Paper).

Readers love the Blessed Epoch series by AUGUST LI

Ash and Echoes

"The world of *Ash and Echoes* was incredible, and I loved how I adventured through a fantasy land."

—Queer Sci Fi

"The biggest surprise, for me, was near the end. I had a big smile on my face as it was revealed"

—Rainbow Gold Reviews

Iron and Ether

"I have to recommend this story if you love high fantasy, epic storylines, fantastic characters… and an ending that lets you know there is still more to come."

—MM Good Book Reviews

"Thanks, Augusta, for a heart-rending, intense, and uplifting experience."

—Rainbow Book Reviews

By AUGUST LI

<u>BLESSED EPOCH</u>
Ash and Echoes
Ice and Embers
Iron and Ether
Cairn and Covenant

Published by DSP PUBLICATIONS
www.dsppublications.com

Glossary

Abode of Shades—The realm of the Cast-Down, the unworthy dead, and all those rejected by the goddesses.

Bairn—The second highest title of nobility in Selindria, after "valen."

Baska—An obscenity in a language dead to all but the Order of the Crimson Scythe.

Cast-Down—A term used to refer to those gods and goddesses disowned by The Thirteen because of their wickedness. Most pious Selindrians will not speak of them. In some rare cases, a person can be referred to as Cast-Down.

Emiri—An ethnic group, or possibly a completely different race of people, who arrived in Selindria about 150 years ago. Their name is derived from *"Emir,"* the word for the sea in their language. Emiri have no formal homeland and are expert mariners. Their culture and values are quite different from that of Selindrians, and this leads to many misunderstandings.

Eru—The Emiri word for "wind."

Espero—A large and wealthy island nation to the southeast of Selindria, best known for the high population of mages and the arcane university there.

Estrella Lake—A huge freshwater lake in the northernmost corner of Selindria. Aside from providing most of the nation's water, it has a religious significance, is surrounded by shrines and temples, and is often visited by those on spiritual pilgrimages.

Everdale—A fertile valenny near the center of Selindria, which provides most of the kingdom's food, and sister province to Merryvale.

Eyrle—The third highest title of nobility in Selindria, after "bairn."

Fane—A legendary mage-emperor who ruled over a period of unimaginable peace and prosperity eons ago. Eventually he demanded his people worship him instead of the goddesses, and the ensuing war destroyed the known world. No one knows if Fane ever actually existed, but his story is told as a cautionary tale and given as the reason mages are forbidden to rule.

Gaeltheon—A powerful nation to the east of Selindria, across the Kanda River, almost equal in size and wealth.

Kanda River—An enormous river separating Gaeltheon and Selindria. The Kanda is fed by Estrella Lake and considered holy by association.

Lapir Mountains—A huge, impassable mountain range marking the eastern border of Gaeltheon. No one has crossed them in centuries, and what lies on the other side is a subject of speculation.

Lockhaven—An ancient valenny, ruled by the L'Estrella family for as long as anyone can remember. Because it houses the sacred Estrella Lake, Lockhaven is highly respected throughout Selindria.

Meritage—The oldest and largest city in Selindria. Meritage is a port along the Kanda River, and while it is held by the Selindrian monarch, the territory around it is unstable and ruled by barbarians and warlords.

Merryvale—A fertile plain, sister province to Everdale.

Mir—An Emiri ship's captain.

Mu-bo—A spicy Emiri dish made from shellfish.

Muri-ku—A very potent Emiri beverage made from fermented sea plants.

Narxium—A tree producing a fatally poisonous sap. It grows only in the Forest of Elwyd.

Order of the Crimson Scythe—A legendary and unstoppable cult of assassins. Thalil is their patron. While many people doubt the existence of the Crimson Scythe, their symbol, the red crescent, is still the most feared icon in the land. The Crimson Scythe are considered almost supernatural. When they have marked someone for death, that person has no chance of escape.

Selindria—The most powerful kingdom in the known world.

Shagiri—The Emiri word for "death."

Starmont—The highest peak in Selindria, marking the northern edge of Estrella Lake. In the past, many Selindrians believed the goddesses resided atop Starmont, but that belief has been abandoned by all but the most superstitious.

Syrai—The Emiri word for "friend," used to express a wide variety of relationships from casual acquaintance to intimate partner.

Tam—The lowest title of nobility in Selindria as well as a common expression of respect, similar to "sir."

Thalil—A very powerful Cast-Down god associated with seduction, subterfuge, murder, and deceit. He is the patron god of assassins, particularly the Order of the Crimson Scythe. Thalil, usually portrayed as a beautiful youth, is also associated with male beauty and homoerotic love. The Thirteen Goddesses forbid his name from being spoken, and his worship is punishable by death. Thalil is known by many epithets, some of which are: He Who Stands Just Out of Sight, The One You See at the Last, The Whisper Heard Too Late, The Dark One, and The Invisible Blade.

The Thirteen, or The Thirteen Goddesses—The main and most important deities of Selindria and Gaeltheon. They have many sons and daughters, both benevolent and Cast-Down. They are sometimes referred to as the sisters. Each goddess presides over a month, or moon, of the year.

Valen—The highest title of nobility in Selindria, second only to the royal family. Valens rule large holds of land known as valennies.

The Goddesses and Months

Both Selindria and Gaeltheon observe a thirteen-month lunar calendar. Each month, or moon, is presided over by one of The Thirteen Goddesses:

Fayelle, ruler of the first month—A virgin goddess of purity. While compassionate, she is a very demanding goddess who expects perfection from her devotees.

Sarmine, ruler of the second month—The goddess of romantic love and marriage. Most weddings take place during Sarmine's Moon.

Mother Goddess, ruler of the third month—The only goddess without a name, she is the matron of all living things. Her month is a time of devotion and celebration. The Mother Goddess is said to love all her creations, even the Cast-Down.

Myint, ruler of the fourth month—The goddess of warfare, battle, weaponsmiths, armorers, and martial arts. She is the patron goddess of all knights.

Diarana, ruler of the fifth month—The goddess of travel and transition. She is the patron of children coming of age. Certain worshippers of Diarana maintain that the goddess loves and protects men and women who favor the clothing of the opposite gender. This belief is not widely accepted.

Vestrafori, ruler of the sixth month—The goddess of truth and justice, protector of the blind and mute. Vestrafori's priestesses conduct all legal proceedings in Selindria and Gaeltheon, and their verdicts are absolute.

Laud, ruler of the seventh month—A mysterious goddess associated with fate, the passage of time, and abstract concepts. Her devotees live hermitic lives of deprivation and contemplation.

Jelsyn, ruler of the eighth month—The goddess of artisans and merchants. She adores handmade items, particularly woven cloth. Jelsyn is also said to protect the poor.

Berris, ruler of the ninth month—The goddess of farming, plenty, and the harvest. Her festival is one of the most joyous occasions of the year.

Ix, ruler of the tenth month—The goddess of the wilds and protector of forests and animals. Ix is well known to favor those who follow instinct over reason. Ix is also associated with the moon.

Strella, ruler of the eleventh month—The goddess of the sun, stars, and weather. Strella is also a liaison between humans and the goddesses. She carries prayers to the goddesses and guides the worthy dead to their rest.

Illira, ruler of the twelfth month—The goddess of music, poetry, history, and communication. She is the patron of all storytellers and scholars.

Pherara, ruler of the thirteenth month—The goddess of magic and arcane scholarship, and patron goddess of Espero. Most people feel Pherara values only her mages and turns her back on those without the gift. She is not widely worshipped outside Espero.

LESSER GODS AND GODDESSES

Helwyn—A goddess of solitude and a patron of lonely and abandoned women.

Ilverus—A deity (usually depicted as male) associated with the knowledge of healing elixirs and potions.

Keltha—A daughter of the Mother Goddess, patroness of pregnancy, childbirth, and nursing.

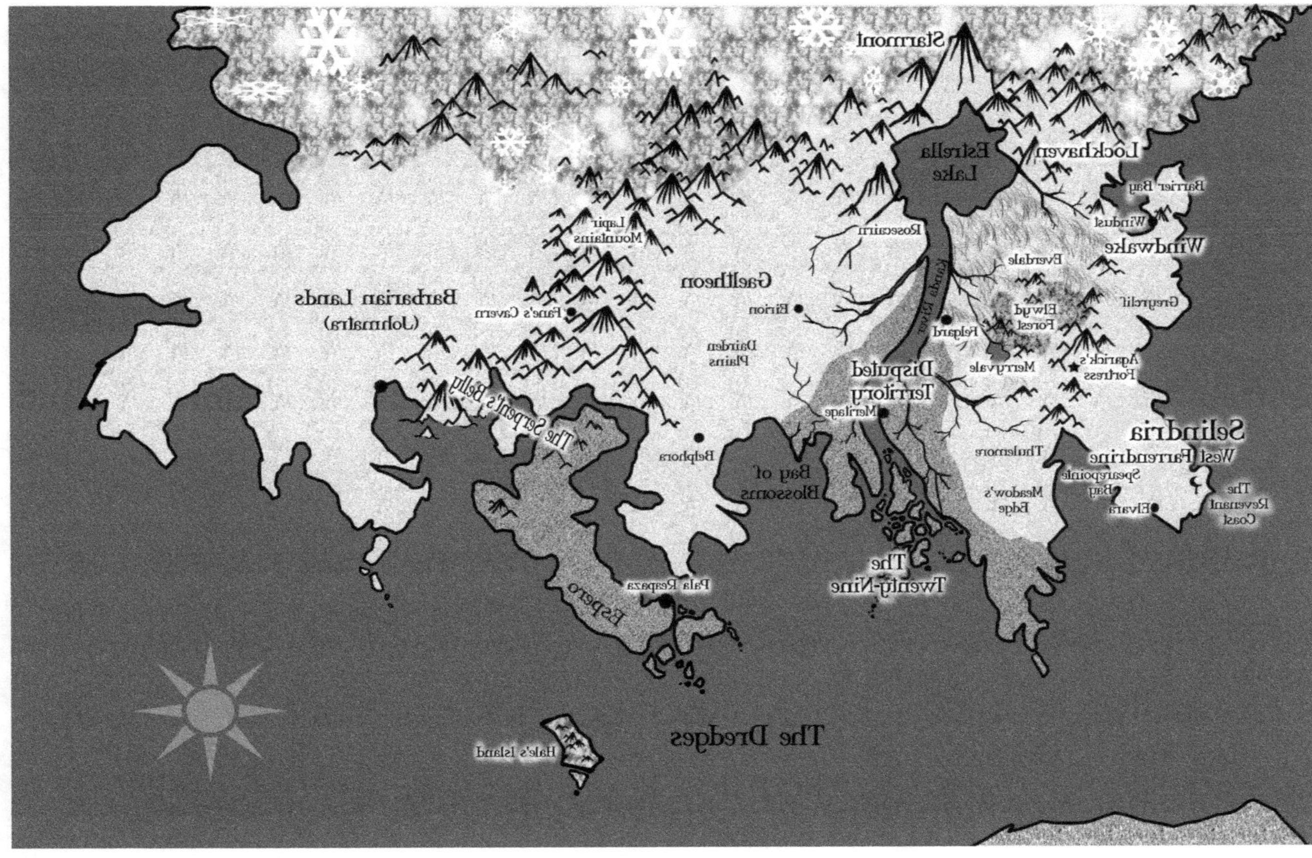

Starmont
Estrella Lake
Lockhaven
Barrier Bay
Windust
Windwake
Greyrell
Everdale
Elwyd Forest
Lapir Mountains
Gaellheon
Barbarian Lands
(Johmaira)
Fane's Cavern
Rosecairn
Kanda River
Birion
Bardain Plains
Relgard
Merryvale
Agarick's Fortress
Disputed Territory
Merritage
The Serpent's Belly
Belphora
Bay of Blossoms
Thalemore
Meadow's Edge
Selindria
West Farrendine
Speairpointe Bay
Elvara
The Revenant Coast
Espero
Pala Rapaza
The Twenty-Nine
The Dredges
Hale's Island

A Lesson and a Favor

This story takes place about eight years before
the beginning of *Ash and Echoes*.

AMONG THE dozens of candles burning within lanterns of crimson glass, the young assassin waited. As he had for the past week, he'd dressed in his snug leather armor and hidden his blades and poisoned barbs in the secret pockets. Then he'd come to the central chamber of his order's safe house and waited among the red velvet benches and lewd paintings of beautiful men fighting to the death, his red hood over his dark hair, sharpening his blades as he awaited his next mission.

Only the soft pop and crackle of the candle wicks and the subdued scrape of the assassin's steel against the whetstone broke the silence in the underground chamber. The young assassin neither anticipated nor dreaded the next time he would be called upon to spill blood for his Cast-Down god. He would take any life Thalil asked of him efficiently and without emotion. When he finished, he would fade back into the shadows and wait to be summoned again. His killer's heart held no room for passion, hope, or regret. Two types of people existed in his world: the successful and the dead. He planned to remain the first type for as long as his dark god would allow.

Though he had been trained from childhood to form no attachments—anything one valued could be used as a weapon—he did enjoy physical contact, particularly lying with other men. Perhaps tonight, if he wasn't given a mission, the leader of this house might take him aside for an informal lesson. The assassins of the Order of the Crimson Scythe learned much more than murder: they learned to manipulate emotion to the desired result with their words, their faces, and their bodies. The young assassin had been learning a great deal about pleasure from the lanky blond man in command of this particular safe house, and he could think of worse ways to pass the evening.

When the leader appeared, like a shadow solidifying at the end of one of the tunnels off the central chamber, the young assassin slid his newly sharpened dagger into its sheath and stood. The two assassins met each other's eyes in acknowledgement, both of their faces as cold and still as death masks.

"I have a task for you," the older assassin said.

"I look forward to spilling blood for our master," the younger replied.

The leader of the house nodded. "This mission will be difficult, especially for one so young and inexperienced. However, I have watched your progress, my brother, and I have been impressed. Of all the brethren currently residing here, I believe you have the greatest chance of success."

"What is the mission?"

"A group of thugs has kidnapped the son of a wealthy local merchant."

The young assassin let none of his surprise show on his features even as he said, "I don't understand. I'm expected to rescue this person?"

The other man's lips curled into a carefully honed and very pleasing smile. "Of course not. This is not an order of knights or defenders; it's an order of the world's most dreaded killers. This group of ruffians has taken the boy and demanded a thousand pieces of gold for his return. The merchant does not wish to pay. Instead, he has contacted us. He has paid to see the lives of every one of these criminals ended. Leave none alive."

"It will be done, of course, but it seems suspicious. It's certainly costing this merchant far more to hire me, especially against so many, than it would to simply pay the ransom. How many targets are suspected?"

"Between twelve and fifteen," the senior assassin said. "They're untrained buffoons, but they are large and well armed. Speed and stealth are your best options. Encouraging resistance could become messy."

"I understand."

The older man rested a hand on the younger man's shoulder. "Remember to be patient, my young brother. A great deal of assassination is waiting. Waiting can be difficult in youth."

"I will not fail in this," the assassin said.

"Good. I will leave you to prepare. When you're ready, make your way to the mill beside the brook on the western edge of town. A few miles farther upstream, you'll find a wooded hillock with an abandoned house in the center. The boy is being held there. May Thalil hide you in his shadows, brother."

"Thank you, brother." The young assassin turned down a darkened hall and made his way to the small room where he'd been living. Inside, he secured the tools of his arsenal, secreting more blades, barbs, darts, and poisons into the hidden pouches of his red leather armor.

THE SPRING mist carried a heavy odor of wet soil and rotting leaves. Moisture glistened on the young assassin's armor and made his black hair hang in listless clumps beneath his hood, but the heavy fog, tinged with a residual bite of the recent winter, kept most of the villagers inside by their hearths. The assassin still kept to the shadows and off the road. Legends told that the members of his order could materialize from the darkness, and the brethren went to great lengths to keep the stories flourishing. After being trained by the order for as long as he could remember, it took little effort for the assassin to walk in silence and avoid being seen. He even passed within a few feet of a group of twirl-horn deer without the creatures detecting him.

The blades of the windmill spun slowly; the old wood creaked rhythmically. The brook burbled as it tumbled over the rocks in its bed, but there was little other sound. The assassin crouched low and jogged around the side of the old building, staying out of the light of the fuzzy crescent moon. He darted lightly and quickly between the stunted bushes and clumps of dewy bracken so his boots would leave no indent in the mud or wet grass—no trail to follow.

Only a mile or so beyond the town, the forest reclaimed the landscape, the trees growing thicker and the underbrush nearly covering the ground. Little light reached the forest floor through the leaves, and taking care not to rustle the plants or snap a twig, the assassin made his way up the gentle slope until he reached the clearing at the top of the hill. Then he knelt behind a briar bush, watching and waiting.

He had no trouble seeing by the light of the torches the bandits had affixed to the outside of what looked like an old farmhouse—a simple, square, two-level structure that had seen better days. Holes in the thatch exposed crumbling beams, and many of the windows had been boarded over. The porch had collapsed, and the heavy stone chimney listed to the side. The assassin took stock: a single door, guarded by two men in coarse, homespun garments, one with a club, the other holding an ax. There would likely be another entrance at the back, one that led through the root cellar.

As the assassin considered the best way to proceed, he heard the faint hint of footsteps, heavy boots crushing grass and sticking in the mud beneath—a patrol. Though the large man passed less than a foot from where he concealed himself, the assassin knew he wouldn't be seen. He continued to watch, moving quietly through the woods to observe other angles of the building, until he memorized the guards' routine. Two men watched the door, one watched the cellar entrance, and two others walked the perimeter of the property, close to the edge of the woods. He would have to eliminate them in silence, and quickly enough that none of them would find the corpse of a comrade and raise an alarm. The assassin took his time reaching the back door, making absolutely certain he wasn't seen or heard. He waited until one of the men on patrol passed by, speaking a few words to the man by the cellar. He would have about a quarter of an hour before the second patrolman made his rounds, and then maybe as much time until the men at the front of the building missed their associates.

The assassin moved forward until only an inch of darkness separated the toes of his boots from the firelight. He took a tiny dart and a corked vial of greenish-black liquid from a pocket near his waist. After dipping the barb in the poison, he waited for his victim to turn his head. As soon as the man exposed his neck, the assassin threw his dart, and it lodged in the skin of the man's throat. The poison would enter his blood quickly; in seconds he'd be unable to scream, and in minutes his muscles would tense and cramp until he had trouble moving. The toxin would kill him in less than an hour, but the assassin couldn't wait that long.

Leaving the protection of the shadows, the assassin bounded across the grass. His victim saw him at the last second, and the man's paling lips opened and closed, slapping together wetly, like a fish plucked from the stream. The assassin drew a dagger from beneath his left arm and plunged it into the man's throat below his chin, all in a single, smooth motion. Blood oozed from the man's mouth and down his thick neck as the assassin grasped the back of his neck and jerked him toward the woods. Not until they made it a few feet beyond the tree line did the assassin pull out his blade. The blood spurted out in an arc, and he hadn't wanted it staining the grass and giving away his presence. His first target fell facedown in the rotting leaves, and the assassin jabbed at his ribs with his toe. When the man didn't move, the assassin doubled back, winding around the gnarled old trees as fast as he could go without making any sound.

Not more than a few moments after he'd made his first kill, the assassin crept up behind one of the patrolmen. He clapped a palm over the man's mouth and dragged him toward the forest. The man had half a foot and probably seventy pounds on the assassin, and he wriggled and fought for all he was worth, yanking at the assassin's wrist and trying to hit his ribs with his elbow. Though strong, he was clumsy and careless in his terror, and the assassin had been trained to use an opponent's size and strength against him. As soon as the first shadows of the trees fell across them, the assassin wrenched the man's head back and slid his knife across his throat, severing the veins and arteries beneath his skin, the muscles that held his head aloft, and even his windpipe in a single swipe. The resulting crescent of blood splattered the smooth, pale trunk of an arn tree. The assassin knelt to wipe the few specks of blood and the foam from the man's lungs off his glove on a clump of moss.

He reached the second patrolman before the man rounded the corner of the old farmhouse. A night bird called out, and its mate answered. The guard turned toward the sound, and the assassin darted behind a bush. He doubted the man had seen him, but the guard had likely seen movement: a darker blur against the darkness of the woods. With a furrowed brow and squinted eyes, the bearded guard approached the tree line, drawing a shortsword as he took slow, careful steps.

The assassin waited until the guard had passed a few steps beyond where he hid. He kicked the man hard in his lower back, sending him sprawling on his chest and knocking his forehead against a protruding rock. The man scarcely managed a grunt as the breath jarred from his lungs, before the assassin leaped, straddled his shoulders, and drove his dagger deep beneath the base of his skull. The guard's limbs twitched for a moment, and then he went still.

No longer worried about being seen, the assassin sprinted around the side of the building. So far he had done well, but the two men at the door would present a challenge. He had to eliminate both of them before either could scream and alert the dozen or so men he assumed remained inside the house. It wouldn't be easy, considering they stood two feet from each other. The assassin couldn't spare long on planning, though—before long, the men at the door would wonder what had happened to their friends. He considered something ranged: his darts or throwing knives. But then he decided he could be quickest with his blades in his hands.

Heart racing, he crept toward the edge of the wrecked porch and crouched behind the buckling lintel barely supporting the roof. His senses grew even more acute; he swore he could hear the breeze bending the blades of grass, the rattle of it in the dry thatch. Every tiny gesture the two men made caught his attention, and he tried to be patient as his master had instructed. Finally, the moment came to strike. The assassin took a dagger in each hand. Though nothing fancy, the knives were issued to all young agents of his order, and they were sturdy and razor sharp. They felt good, solid, against his palms. They had served his brethren for thousands of years, and they wouldn't fail him.

He jumped from his cover and extended his left arm, catching the guard to his side in the neck below the ear. He twisted that blade as he stabbed the man in front of him, three times in quick succession: first to the throat to keep him from screaming, then twice in the forehead, splitting the bone and dropping his victim to his knees. Turning his attention to the other, he tugged the blade down until his steel hit the man's collarbone. Blood poured out in a sheet, coating his hand, wetting the edge of his hood, and splashing against the side of his face. He closed his eye in time, but in moments the blood began to clot in his eyelashes, and he swiped at it with the back of his forearm. Extracting his dagger from bone took some effort, and the assassin leaned against the warped wooden planks of the house to catch his breath for a few heartbeats.

He was pleased. Clearly, his god had blessed him this night, though he couldn't help but be proud of his own skill. Until now, he had never been called to eliminate more than a single target, and often easy targets, those he could kill while they slept. This mission would gain him honor, status within the order. It would gain him the respect of his brothers and sisters in the order, the only family he'd ever known. He could hope for nothing better. Life and fate had dealt him this position, and he could either excel at it or perish.

INSIDE, THE farmhouse reeked of mold, decay, old ale, and unwashed men. The assassin pulled up the collar of the snug tunic he wore beneath his red leather armor so it covered the lower half of his face. He took care to avoid creaking boards, testing every step before putting his full weight on the rickety old floor as he made his way through the house. Debris and stacks of worthless furs and cloth filled most of the lower level. Some sacks of grain and wooden crates of vegetables occupied what must have been a larder. Rats screeched and scattered at the assassin's approach, though they didn't seem to alert anyone. In a room near the back of the building, he found four men asleep on straw-filled burlap mats, and he cut their throats one by one, leaving them to perish silently as they bled out. He had been trained to kill since he was old enough to hold a dagger, and he felt no guilt at doing so, but unlike some of his brothers and sisters, he took no delight in prolonging pain. This was his lot in life, and he knew no other and accepted it, but he believed in carrying out his work with efficiency. This was no game to be enjoyed.

The assassin wasn't sure if the stairs leading up would hold his weight without splintering, but flickers of light and muffled sounds came from the second floor, so he knew he'd have to chance it. He made his way carefully, staying to the edges of the steps, where fewer feet would have fallen over the years. When he reached the top, he did a quick search of the three darkened rooms before pressing his ear to the door of the one with light spilling from the crack beneath. After listening for a long time, he determined three men waited within—one had a serious limp the assassin could hear as the man moved around. The other sounded mildly drunk, his voice just a little too loud when he spoke. The third spoke little, only grunting now and then at something one of the others said. Then there was a sound in the room he couldn't identify: something shifting, brushing against the wall, maybe squirming on the floor….

He moved beyond the light escaping the room and withdrew his vial of poison again, using it to anoint both his blades, the hooked barbs at the knuckles of his gloves, and the sharp, steel points at the toes and heels of his boots. He pulled the wrappings from his face so he could breathe easier, and since he didn't intend to leave anyone alive who could identify him. Three men. It shouldn't be difficult, but there was no need to take chances. He'd been taught not to become attached to anything, not even his life. Those who failed Thalil didn't deserve life. He was ready to die, if the Dark and Beautiful One willed it, but he didn't want to. He wouldn't mind a few more private lessons in his master's chamber, a few more chances to prove his worth to the others, and so he made a decision. He wouldn't fail, wouldn't die. They would. He moved both his daggers to his left hand and poured the remainder of his poison on three throwing knives. He wedged them between the knuckles of his right hand and widened his stance to kick the door open.

In a few seconds, he took in the relevant details of the room. Three men, armed. One near each corner along the back wall, all wearing rough, simple clothing. The man with the game leg on his left, the drunk on the right. A sword and a mace, respectively. Between them, the leader: a huge man with a knotted beard and a battered breastplate—an open-faced helm with ram's horns. Several teeth missing, the rest rotted and black. Sword in one hand, metal club in the other. And in the center of the room, a young man in a fine linen shirt, long brown hair, fringe in his brown eyes. Skin fair enough to indicate he didn't work outdoors. Gagged. Hands bound behind his back. Fear pouring from his shaking form.

The assassin let training and instinct guide him. He threw his knives, striking the drunk in the left eye, the throat, and the side of the neck. The man howled and dropped to his knees, clawing at the blades, pulling them out and doing more damage than if he'd left them in. He curled on his side, and blood spread in a pool around him. He gurgled and sobbed, not dead, but no longer a threat.

The assassin had underestimated the cripple. Though slow on his feet, the man was quick with his sword, and in a small, contained space, it served him well. He slashed at the assassin's waist, and the assassin barely leaped back in time. Just as he caught his balance, the leader of the thugs swiped at his legs with the club. He managed to dodge and avoid it shattering his kneecaps, but it struck his thigh and tore through his leather armor. With a hiss, the assassin dropped to a foot and a knee, raising his arm just in time to deflect a downward slash from the crippled man's sword with his dagger. Ignoring the leader for a second, he drove the point of the blade in his other hand into the man's belly. The poison lacing the knife would at least slow him down, but the gambit cost the assassin. He'd left his opposite side open to the bandit leader, and the big man took a swing at his shoulder—a swing he'd never dodge in time. He could only hope the injury wouldn't prevent him from completing his mission.

Just before the edge of the leader's sword should have struck the assassin between his neck and shoulder, the man landed hard on his back, his weapons knocked from his hands and skittering across the floor. The captive boy had kicked at his ankles and knocked him down. The assassin pulled his blade from the crippled man, spun on the ball of his foot, and kicked him in the face. The back of the man's head smacked the wall with a hollow thud, and he slid down slowly. Turning, the assassin leaped, straddled the leader, and drove the points of both blades into his eyes, grinding and twisting them until he'd hollowed out the sockets and blood and tissue covered the man's face and his own arms almost to the elbows. Then he stood, panting, to rub at his aching thigh. He didn't think it was broken, but walking would give him hardship and pain. Luckily he didn't have far to go. He was just turning to leave when the boy's gag-muffled cries made him turn back.

An exasperated sigh escaped from between the assassin's teeth. The plea was clear in the boy's eyes. And when his master had said *boy*, he had expected a child—not a young man his age or a few years older. A very comely young man….

The crippled man groaned and moved his head from side to side. The assassin knelt down to cut his throat, then carefully wiped the poison from his blades on the man's shirt. The boy—the young man—flinched at his approach, but the assassin simply cut the ropes around his wrists and the dirty rag between his full, pink lips. Then he turned to leave again.

"Wait."

"I have finished my work here," the assassin said without looking back.

He heard the young's man's steps approach, then stop with a foot of space between them. "That was amazing. There must have been at least twelve of them—"

"Twelve exactly. I anticipated more."

"Goddesses," said the merchant's son. "You killed them all. All by yourself."

The assassin shouldn't have allowed the smile that curled his lips. This young man's praise shouldn't mean anything to him—

"You saved me. Thank you."

He turned slowly and met the other man's sincere brown eyes. "Your thanks are not necessary. Your help was welcome, though."

Light danced in the eyes of the merchant's son. The assassin had learned to read expressions, and he saw hope, gratitude, a plea, and… and something else. Predictably, the young man said, "I would ask a favor of you."

"My favors are not free."

"I-I know. I know what you are, though the goddesses forbid I speak the name of him that you serve. My favor is a small one, and I know where these pigs hide their spoils. They have a chest of coins, at least. Some weapons. Maybe some jewelry. Will that be enough?"

"It depends upon your request," the assassin said. He'd been given no instructions with regard to the boy. He could kill him if he wished, and no one in the order would fault him. He could simply leave and forget about him. He could also help him—if he chose. "Tell me."

"I don't want to go home."

"What?" The assassin took a step back and crossed his arms over his chest. "Do you have any idea how much your father paid for me to kill these men?"

"I'm sure he did, but not because he cares about me. He paid for you because he wants to show everyone what happens to the people who stand against him. It's—it's a pissing contest, you know? When word gets out about what happened here, people will be even more afraid to cross my father. He likes to keep people afraid—even me. He wants to marry me off to some hag with a couple trading ships. He treats me like a whore."

"Many people have worse lots," the assassin noted. "What do you want from me?"

"I want you to make it look like I died here. I just want the chance to start over."

"With nothing?"

"With my freedom," the young man said.

"You'd give up all the wealth and power your father would leave you?"

"Yes." The young man lifted his scraped and bruised chin. "I can make it on my own."

"How?"

"I… think I might be a mage. There's Esperon in my line. Here." He laid his hands on the assassin's thigh, and a blue cloud emanated from his fingers. An ache remained from the wound the assassin had received, but the pulsing, burning pain had gone. His leg barely tingled as he shifted his weight to it.

"What's your name?" The assassin knew it was a mistake before the question passed his lips. Names meant attachment, getting personal, assigning value to another person—things he'd been warned against. Still, he wanted to know.

"Octavian Rosatello—No. I'm leaving that name behind. Octavian Rose. And you?"

"We have no names. My name is whatever my mission dictates. For this assignment, no name was required. It's of no consequence."

Octavian stepped a little closer. "I'd like to know you better."

"You don't need a name for that." The assassin moved in, letting his belly brush against Octavian's, skimming his lips along the stubble emerging on the young man's jaw. "If you want to share some pleasure,

I'm happy to oblige. You're a beautiful man." And strong, independent. Unafraid. The assassin respected that.

Octavian opened his lips and exhaled a damp puff of air against the assassin's cheek. "I'd like that, but not here. This place is disgusting, and it reeks of death. I have no problem with hired soldiers, with men using the skills they have to make a living, but these fools went about it all wrong. They made too many enemies. Powerful enemies—like you. Come on. I'll show you where they kept their treasure like I promised. I'll rub some of this blood on my cloak and leave it behind. Then I know a place we can go to be alone."

OCTAVIAN PICKED the simple lock on the door to the mill and took the assassin's hand to lead him inside. It smelled of wheat chaff and oats, and their boots left trails in the fine dust as they made their way to the center of the room. Walking backward, his gaze locked on the assassin's, Octavian pulled his shirt over his head. It fell to the floor with a small cloud of powder. His nipples stood out dark against his fair, freckled skin, and the assassin caught his waist and bent in to capture one between his lips. Octavian's skin tasted salty and a little stale, and the stink of his armpits reached the assassin's nose. Instead of dampening his ardor, the masculine, human scents incensed him. He gripped the other man at the hips and guided him back toward a stack of grain sacks piled against the wall.

Octavian let himself fall, and an aura of moonlit dust rose around him. He fumbled with the complex buckles of the assassin's armor. "How do I get this off you? Goddesses, I want to feel your skin."

"I'll do it." The assassin picked apart his buckles and shrugged out of the leather shirt. Then he whisked his hooded tunic over his head and tossed it aside. Octavian's skin felt amazing against him, and he ground his erection against the other young man, nipping at his full lips as they both gasped for breath.

The assassin kneaded the muscles of Octavian's hips and thighs through his loose cloth pants, delighting in the feel of the tight sinew beneath supple skin. Then he reached inside, past the waistband, to stroke Octavian's length.

"Your gloves," Octavian said, wet and urgent against the assassin's neck. "Goddesses, touch me with your skin, your hands…."

"Yes." He peeled the leather down his arms and off his fingers and let them drop, forgotten. Octavian's hard flesh was warm, throbbing, beneath his bare fingers, and it felt incredible. He dropped to his knees to pull Octavian's pants past his boots, and then he sucked the other man's erection into his mouth, running his tongue along the underside, just as his master had instructed. His master was a kind man, and so he knew firsthand how wonderful it felt. What he hadn't expected was how amazing Octavian would taste, the prelude to his seed leaking onto the assassin's tongue… the way his belly shuddered and his ribs stretched his skin as he sucked in breath….

Thalil, it almost finished him.

"Stop," Octavian panted, tugging at his hair.

"Why?"

"Because if you don't, I'll be finished. I don't want to be finished. Not yet."

The assassin got to his feet and found his partner's warm, slick lips. "What is it you want?" he asked against them.

"I've never been with anyone," Octavian admitted.

"I know how to do it. I know how to make it not hurt."

"I—yes. Yes, I want that."

"Turn over."

Octavian flipped and rested his chest and belly against the sacks of grain, pushing his backside out and opening his legs to reveal his dark cleft and the wrinkled little opening at the center. The assassin peeled his own pants and thigh-high boots down his legs, past his knees, where the snug leather clung to his calves. The crescents of Octavian's ass practically glowed in the moonlight, and the assassin dug his fingertips into the taut muscle. He eased those mounds apart and grazed Octavian's hole with his pads, feeling the flesh tense in anticipation beneath his touch. By the Cast-Down, that was alluring. The assassin regretted that he had to find his discarded leather shirt to retrieve the vial of oil he carried, but it also gave him time to shed his own boots and trousers.

He fumbled with the cork, then let the thick liquid rain over Octavian's tailbone and wind its way down his cleft. After coating his fingers, the assassin let one trace the tight rim of that hole. It clenched and contracted whenever he touched it. "Relax, Octavian. Don't fight me."

The other man's opening became pliant and soft, allowing the assassin to work one, then two, fingers inside him. He curled those fingers, searching out the inner cluster as his master had when he'd touched him. When he found it, Octavian straightened his spine and cried out.

"Shh, I'll take care of you," the assassin said, just as the older assassin had told him. This time, he was in control; he was responsible for his partner's pleasure. Providing pleasure could be a powerful manipulative tool, and he told himself he relished the chance to practice, nothing more. He massaged the sensitive bundle inside Octavian, feeling the man's opening soften and spread as he did. Soon, he easily slid three of his fingers into Octavian, and he got only pleased moans in reaction.

Octavian rested the side of his face against the grain sacks, his cheeks glowing red even in the gloom of the mill. Lips parted, eyes half-closed, he muttered, "I want you inside me. Please. I'm ready."

The assassin drizzled more oil over his erect cock before lining it up with Octavian's opening. At first, he didn't think he could get inside. He didn't want to force his way past Octavian's resistance, but he remembered how wonderful it had felt to have his master's cock deep inside his body. He remembered the first tingle of electricity up his spine at the moment of penetration. He gripped himself at the base and swiveled his crown around his partner's entrance as he leaned down to kiss Octavian's shoulders. "You'll like it. I swear. You just need to relax."

Octavian nodded, rich brown hair flying in all directions, sweat sparkling across his brow, and the assassin felt his body open. The assassin pressed in slowly, a hair's width at a time, letting Octavian acclimate to being stretched open and filled. They moved together, taking cues from each other, testing their connection, until they felt safe to proceed. Octavian spread his legs a little wider and moaned as the assassin slid into him until he could go no farther, and then he stilled and reveled in Octavian's muscles undulating around him. The contractions around his cock almost finished the assassin, and he dropped his face between Octavian's shoulder blades, breathing in the scent of his skin and trying to ground himself. It had never been like this with his master.

"You smell of blood," Octavian panted out, curling his fingers around the burlap of the grain sacks. "I did not expect you to be so careful with me."

The sensations assailing him made it difficult for the assassin to formulate the appropriate response, and he finally abandoned it. He had nothing to gain by swaying Octavian's emotions, and Octavian felt so good, hot and tight around him, satiny white skin sparkling with sweat beneath the assassin's darker, golden brown skin, the light dusting of soft hair on his narrow ass tickling the assassin's skin where his pubic hair would have begun if he didn't shave it off each day. He raked the hair away from Octavian's neck to nip and lick at the salty skin. "I have no desire to harm you. Why would I? I find you… quite pleasing. Wonderful, even."

"You too. You can start to move. I want you to move…."

Octavian's words trailed off to grunts and rhythmic moans as the assassin began to rock his hips. He dropped his forehead to Octavian's back and let his hands move almost on their own, up and down Octavian's ribs, down the backs of his thighs, over his hitching belly. Octavian pushed back against him, meeting him thrust for thrust, squeezing his inner muscles around the assassin's cock. The assassin clamped his eyes closed and gnawed his lower lip to keep from screaming. He took a handful of Octavian's hair and twisted his head until he could smash their lips together. Their teeth bumped and scraped, lips swelling. The tang of blood filled the assassin's mouth, his own or his partner's, he didn't know or care. Almost against his will, the strokes of his pelvis grew erratic, quick and hard. Their skin smacked together, and their mingled scents filled the assassin's nose. He whimpered into Octavian's open mouth as all his muscles wound tight, then released in a glorious burst. Waves of pleasure shook his body until he feared he'd break apart, and at the edge of his thoughts, he remembered to wedge his hand between Octavian and the rough sacks, take him in his fist, and stroke him.

Octavian threw his head back, smacking the assassin in the mouth as he cried out and wet the assassin's fingers with his seed. He trembled beneath the assassin's hands, and the assassin crossed his arms over Octavian's chest, holding him tight as he fell apart. For a while—he had no idea how long—they clung to each other and shook. Finally, the assassin's quivering thighs could no longer hold him, and he sank to the floor, pulling Octavian down with him. They rolled to face each other and kissed with languorous satisfaction, curling their limbs around each other, oblivious to the dust on the floor.

"I'm glad we did that," Octavian said. "You made a wonderful first for me. I hope you enjoyed it as much."

"I don't even have words," the assassin said, a rare honest declaration. He extracted himself from his partner and reached for his clothing.

Octavian caught his shoulder as he sat up. "Maybe we can do this again sometime."

The assassin shook his head as he found his garments and began to dress. "I doubt that opportunity will present itself. I should go."

"Must you? Can't you stay a few moments more?"

Though he knew he shouldn't, the assassin joined the other young man on the floor of the mill, and soon they were moving together again, connecting lips and bodies. Octavian sat above the assassin, riding him, looking down at him with darkened cheeks and swollen lips as he took what he needed. After, they rested again, both pungent with sweat and spilled seed. Soon, the muted light of dawn began seeping into the mill.

The assassin stood and dressed.

"Will I see you again?" Octavian asked.

"No, I don't think so. Where will you go?"

Octavian folded his hands beneath his head. The assassin battled the urge to stare at the stretched, sated muscles of his lithe, youthful body, though he couldn't help stealing a few glances as he secured his equipment.

"I'll go north. Up river," Octavian said. "Find a band of mercenaries, decent men I can fight beside. You haven't heard the last of me, Crimson Scythe. I have plans. You'll hear my name again. You'll see."

The assassin couldn't resist the desire to crouch down and kiss Octavian one last time. He'd had sex before, but as tutelage. Octavian was the first man who'd ever wanted him, and he planned to remember that feeling of reciprocated desire. There would be other young men and women in his future, he reminded himself. He couldn't delude himself into thinking this one was special. Yet, he wouldn't have minded another day or two with Octavian. They'd worked well together, physically. He had no idea what to say before departing. He settled on, "Shadows of the Dark One surround you."

Octavian looked dreamily toward the morning light filtering in through the slats over the windows and the motes of dust dancing in the beams. "I appreciate that. But I do not need it. I'll hide or reveal myself as I choose."

He would be fine, the assassin knew. Octavian was strong, driven. They could have made quite a pair, though he could never let himself value another person. The assassin finished dressing and then bent for a final kiss. "Octavian, you are sweet. Don't let others know, or they'll see it as weakness. Many will exploit a kind heart if they can. Be wise, and be careful."

"I'll be fine," Octavian said. "And I'll remember you. Will you remember me?"

"I will not have the luxury to dwell on this." He took a few steps toward the door before making a decision and turning back, just as Octavian was pulling up his trousers. The assassin slid one of his daggers from its sheath near his hip. Blood still caked the blade, but he flipped it and held the handle out to Octavian.

The other young man looked confused. "This is for me?"

"Don't read too much into it. If you'll be by yourself on the road, you shouldn't be unarmed. You may have to defend yourself."

"Thank you."

With a single dip of his head, the assassin left the mill as the rising sun painted the land in muted rose and lavender. He made his way off the road, into the forest, and walked in the shelter of the trees until he reached the town. Then he stayed to the shadows the buildings cast, walking with his head down, drawing no attention, until he reached his order's safe house. He struggled to push away the memories of the brown-eyed boy and the strange feelings they dragged behind them, and he almost completely succeeded.

THE MASTER of the house waited on a velvet couch. He rose as the assassin entered the room. "You were successful?"

The assassin inclined his head, ever so slightly. "You doubted I would be?"

"No," the master of the house said, taking the hands of his young protégé. "But I am glad to have you back. You've proved my instincts correct." He leaned in. "You reek of blood, brother. And sex. Sweat, and a man's seed."

The assassin shrugged. "The young man I liberated was grateful. I took advantage of that. I used him as a way to test the skills you've been teaching me."

"Of course." The senior assassin pushed the hood off the hair of the novice and looked into his eyes, probably searching for weak feelings, like longing and attachment. The assassin made quite sure his master saw no such frailty. "I would like to see what you learned."

"I would be happy to show you."

Together, they walked the darkened corridor to the leader's chamber. The younger assassin spun his mentor, then pushed him down over the foot of the bed.

"So eager," the older man said, pushing the younger man off and rising to face him. "You must always remember patience, young brother."

"Patience served me. Urgency served me," the assassin said as he grasped his master's shoulder and guided him back down to sit on the edge of the bed. "Need, lust can be a powerful tool."

"It can." The older man rested back on his elbows. "Just take care you don't allow another to use it against you." He ran a hand down the young assassin's waist and let it rest over the empty sheath that had held the knife he'd given Octavian. "You've lost one of your daggers."

"Yes."

"Well, you cannot be killing for Thalil without a proper blade." The senior assassin got off the bed and went to a stand near the headboard. He slid open a drawer, unfolded a square of black velvet, and removed a beautiful dagger, the length of his forearm, with an ebony hilt and a graceful serpentine blade. He handed it to his protégé just as the young assassin had handed the much simpler weapon to Octavian. "This is probably the finest weapon I have ever possessed. Take it. Use it to spill blood for our god."

The young assassin barely managed to mask his surprise as he took the dagger and watched the firelight glinting off the red-tinted steel. It was a beautiful weapon, far superior to anything he'd held or even seen. "I will use this well."

"I know you will. Consider it a reward for a job well done." The older assassin ran his fingers through the younger's hair and down his cheek. "You're filthy. You should wash. Take off your armor, and I'll run us a bath." He went into an alcove off his chamber and pumped water into a bucket to heat it over the fire.

The assassin picked apart the buckles of his armor and folded the leather carefully before setting it on a nearby chair. He had already taken the pouch of coins and jewelry he'd acquired at the bandits' hideout to his room and hidden it away. He left his undergarments on the floor for the servants to collect and wash. As he ran his hands over his shaved skin, he remembered Octavian's hands on him, the wonder and passion with which the young man had touched him. Checking that his master's back was turned, he indulged in a small smile.

The older assassin began removing his own clothes. "What became of the young man? The merchant's son."

The young assassin schooled his expression. "He set off on his own. I let him go. He had nothing to do with my mission, so I supposed it didn't matter what happened to him."

"True enough. Do you think a privileged young man like him will last long on the road on his own?"

"What do I care what happens to him?"

The assassin's mentor ran his knuckles down his bare arm, raising gooseflesh, and then took his hand to lead him toward the small room where they would bathe. "I wouldn't expect you to care." The older man rippled the surface of the water with his fingertips, testing the temperature before dipping a toe into the steaming liquid. "I merely wonder what you predict will happen to him. Do you think he'll die?"

Lowering himself into the hot water, sighing, and leaning his elbows on the edge of the stone tub, the assassin summoned a memory of Octavian's face—jaw set, eyes determined and burning with ambition. "I don't think he will. There was something about him. I believe he'll make a name for himself. We may hear of him again."

"And what was his name?"

"Why would I want to know that?"

"Of course." The older assassin narrowed his eyes as if he recognized the younger one's lie, and the young assassin waited to see what he would do with an alternate explanation ready on his lips. But his master dunked a cloth in the water and used it to wipe the dried blood from the other's face, making tainted water run down his neck. "You performed just as I expected. Now, remember what you learned from the mission, but forget the rest. You'll do yourself no favors by dwelling on it. I'll likely have another mission for you soon."

"Good. This mission was challenging but otherwise unremarkable. I've put it behind me."

As he washed, the assassin contemplated what his master had said. Would Octavian survive? He would likely never know, and that sat ill with him. His teachers had been right; even the tiny shred of fondness he'd allowed had brought him pain and doubt. He would take the lesson to heart and see it never happened again.

Cairn and Covenant

Chapter One

As ALWAYS, the road stretched out before Octavian Rose looked long, barren, and lonely. The last of the autumn foliage had shriveled to a few curled brown leaves that skittered across the dirt path, and the tall grass alongside it had withered to hollow, washed-out stalks. Octavian hoisted the pack containing all his worldly possessions onto shoulders that didn't feel strong enough to bear it. He checked the dagger he kept on his belt to protect himself and the pouch on his opposite hip that held a handful of copper coins. After a last look back at the quaint farmhouse and barn that had been his home for the past few months, he turned toward the muted gray sky and landscape and started out. The lower the sun sank beneath the mountains to the northwest, the less the contrast between the ground and the heavens. Slowly, all the color bled out of the world, leaving it chilled, numb, and as void of life and energy as Octavian felt as he forced his feet to carry him along the path.

He was dead, at least in the eyes of his father and anyone else who mattered. That spring, he'd left his torn and bloody cloak in the lair of the bandits who had kidnapped him. The memory of the unlikely accomplice he'd found for his ruse coaxed a rare smile to his chapped lips. Whenever he felt like he could no longer be strong, Octavian summoned the memory of the assassin—probably not much older than his eighteen years—who'd killed a dozen men and aided Octavian in feigning his demise. That assassin, who'd refused to tell Octavian his name even after they'd been quite intimate, had been strong, more than capable of taking care of himself against anything the world hurled in his direction, and Octavian aspired to the same.

With renewed determination, Octavian headed north, hoping to encounter a village, a tavern, or a small camp before full darkness fell.

He'd slept along the road before, but it was dangerous, not to mention cold this time of year in northern Selindria. He'd spent the summer helping a family mow their hay and harvest their wheat, and in exchange, they'd given him a share of their meager food stores and a cot in the barn. With winter pounding insistently at their door, the farmers could no longer afford to offer Octavian hospitality, and he didn't expect their generosity or pity, not when he'd never received either from his blood relatives.

The assassin who could have just as easily killed him had granted Octavian a chance to make his own way in the world, to choose his path and live without another's yoke around his neck. Octavian shivered. His belly hurt from too many months of too little food, his muscles ached from too many hours of work for too little coin, and he wanted to collapse in the dry grass by the roadside, but he couldn't. He'd partially earned and partially been given his freedom, and he couldn't squander it, so he forced himself a few hundred yards farther along the rocky path.

Goddesses, he didn't know what he wanted to do with his independence, but he knew it wasn't this: working odd jobs from dawn until dusk for barely enough food to sustain himself. The assassin who had let Octavian go after killing his captors had warned him against displaying weakness, and so Octavian had never asked for charity. He'd earned his keep, but he wanted more. He wanted much more: power, respect, and influence, though not in the way of his Cast-Down savior. He didn't want to live relegated to the shadows, cutting life down from the periphery, unable to walk into the light and claim his just rewards. No, if he played the game, he wanted to win, and more than that, he wanted to hoist his spoils into the air to the cheers of the masses. He wanted greatness, and he wanted recognition. As he trudged along the road, he tried to formulate a plan to achieve his goals. He knew he needed to make a name for himself, a name others would one day speak with reverence.

By the time the crescent moon had risen, frost sparkled on the desiccated grass and rounded stones lining the road. Octavian's breath wreathed his head in a frozen halo, and he rubbed his tingling hands together. Up ahead, a few fires burned a little way from the road, a semicircle of high, jagged rocks partially sheltering whoever warmed themselves beside them. Octavian paused and touched the hilt of his dagger. Campfires could mean many things: traveling merchants, farmers, people visiting friends, or bandits and worse. The small blazes punching holes in the cold and darkness could indicate a group of men who'd slit his throat for the few copper pieces in his pouch, who'd possibly do things that made him wish for death first, so Octavian moved off the road to escape their notice. He might have been raised the son of a wealthy merchant, but life on the road had been a harsh tutor, and he wasn't a fool. Slowly, trying to squelch the crunch of the grass beneath his holey boots, he hid himself behind a copse of stunted, leafless trees to listen to the men seated around those fires.

A quick count revealed six men, and horses snuffled and pawed the ground somewhere beyond the circle of light. Octavian didn't see any wagons or carriages, which meant these men rode. Few people beyond knights and sell-swords rode rather than traveling in coaches or drays. Octavian crouched down and crept a little closer. Being a thief would never bring him the glory he coveted, but hunger had forced his hands to close around the possessions of others before. Growing up, he'd never imagined feeling such desperation, and he'd remember it—being stuck between starvation and dirtying his hands—before he ever judged another man.

Even now, the distant heat of the campfires lured Octavian closer. He trembled, hands losing feeling and nose running, as he observed the men sitting on the ground. They wore mismatched—probably scavenged—bits of plate, chain mail, leather, and furs. An argument seemed to rage between the man in the nicest armor, probably the leader, and a big fellow in a dented breastplate partially obscured by a heavy fur-lined cloak. Plumes of fog, orange in the firelight, sprayed from their mouths as they shouted at each other.

"And I'm telling you, Lyman, reputation is everything in this business! See how many more jobs we can get when word gets around we not only failed in what we were hired to do, but let our patron, the patron paying us to provide safe passage, be captured!"

Lyman, a stout man with an ample belly and a dark beard, pointed a gloved hand at the other man. "We were paid in advance for our work, you goddess-damned fool. We still have the coin, whether the ones who provided it were captured or not."

"You have no honor, you serpent!"

Lyman spat on the ground and wiped his mouth on the back of his arm. "I'm a fucking mercenary, and so are you, Myrddin! You'd do well to remember it."

"It doesn't mean I'm a filthy coward!" the man called Myrddin said. "We need to make this right. It's the only decent thing to do."

Lyman's supporters outnumbered Myrddin's two to one, and the one man sitting behind Myrddin looked even younger and smaller than Octavian. Part of Octavian thought he should cut a quiet path back to the road and put as much distance between himself and an altercation that looked ready to escalate to bloodshed as possible, but more of him sensed a glimmer of an opportunity. If this group of mercenaries split, both sides might be looking to bolster their ranks. Perhaps Octavian could convince whichever side seemed more promising to take him on. Mercenary work paid better than farmwork, and with the tenacious fingers of winter wriggling into the land deeper every day, farmwork would be drying up, and sleeping along the road would no longer be an option. Traveling alone would become more dangerous as men grew hungrier and more desperate.

"What are you suggesting we do?" Lyman got to his feet faster and with more grace than Octavian would've expected from a man his size, and the three men behind him followed suit.

Myrddin neither flinched, stood, nor looked terribly impressed with his leader glowering down at him. When he spoke, he didn't even raise his voice, his tone calm and practical, but defeated. "What I think we should do is track the people who took our patrons and their goods. We should liberate both, and then we should see them safely to their destination, just as they paid us quite well to do."

"Fucking fool. We're in Cracked Tooth territory here. Likely as not, the Teeth are the ones what took 'em. You honestly want to go up against them with a group as small as ours? When we already have the coin for the job?"

"And you honestly want to abandon a family to goddesses know what terrible fate?"

"What do I care, *Tam Myrddin*?" Lyman drawled the other man's name into a mocking snarl. "You'd do well to remember you're not a knight any longer, just a sell-sword like the rest of us. You'd be smart to take the gold we earned and buy yourself a pint of ale, a bed, and a whore to warm it. That's our lot, my fine friend, not your misguided nobility."

Myrddin shook his head. "I'm paid to fight. Paid for my sword. That doesn't mean I'm a swindler, a thief, or a callow-hearted bastard who turns his back on the people he swore to protect. I have my honor, whether or not I have my title."

"Oh, and what are you going to do?"

"What do you think, Lyman? I'm going to do everything in my power to save those people. I want to be able to stand the sight of myself the next time I see it reflected back at me from my washbasin."

"You're on your own, then!" Lyman shouted, spittle flying from his mouth.

Myrddin stood. "I am hardly surprised." He lifted a large sword, slid it into the scabbard on his back, turned in the direction of the horses, and disappeared into the darkness, with the gangly youth scampering behind him. A few moments later, the trotting of a pair of horses sounded on the road and quickly faded into the distance.

Still squatting in the shadows, arms wrapped around his knees, Octavian considered his options. Offering himself to Lyman would be more practical; Lyman had a camp only a few dozen feet away, with fires, bedrolls, and something savory smelling crackling over the flames. Lyman had more men following him, and he planned to move on to another lucrative job while his former comrade, Myrddin, planned to undertake a mission with no chance of recompense and even less hope of success. But some of what Myrddin had said resonated within Octavian. The big mercenary had a point when it came to reputation. Who in the world would ever hire Lyman after word of his cowardly indifference spread? He'd practically swindled those who'd employed him. What would it mean for Octavian to have his name associated with men who couldn't finish a job? Besides, Octavian had no desire to be like his assassin, taking any job for coin. He'd been desperate before, but he was not yet desperate enough to let life force him to that, so he snuck back to the road and started to jog along it. With nowhere else to go, the two mercenaries would be found along this path before long.

After an hour or so of running through the frigid night, his muscles twitching, his chest tight, sweat freezing to his face, Octavian spotted a candle-sized flicker of light about a mile to the east, in a narrow cleft sheltered by ironstone. Taking a deep breath, he readjusted the straps of his pack and raked his sweaty hair back from his forehead. He had to make these men see him as capable, someone they wanted by their sides. He could not let them see the pampered son of a wealthy merchant, a boy who'd been handed everything and waited on in exchange for obedience, approaching their camp. As he walked from the darkness into the light of their fire, he held his hands open and out to his sides.

Both men heard Octavian before they saw him, and before he'd taken three steps into their light, the tip of a sword and a nocked arrow pointed at him. He refused to cower and forced himself to keep walking until Myrddin said, "Stop there, lad. Who in the Shades' are you?"

"My name is Octavian Rose." If he wanted it known, he had to say it, and say it as if it meant something. "I am looking for work."

"Move along, then, son," Myrddin said, lowering his blade a few inches. "Neither of us is looking for a pretty lad to warm our bedrolls tonight."

"You think—what? No! I am not a whore." Later, he would have to isolate the part of him that gave that impression and cut it out. Perhaps his desperation shone through some part of him worn too thin to hold it in. When he had the luxury, he'd find the tear and patch it. "I understand you are about to undertake a dangerous mission, and I thought you could use another blade by your side."

The two men looked at each other. The younger one rolled his eyes, stowed his arrow in the quiver on his back, and went to rub his hands together over the fire, having obviously dismissed Octavian entirely. Myrddin sheathed his sword, and Octavian resented them not seeing him as a threat worthy of holding weapons against, but he didn't let it show.

"Can you use a man to help you rescue your patrons who were taken?" Octavian persisted.

Shoulders slumping and expression softening, Myrddin offered Octavian an indulgent smile. "Aye, a man we might be able to use, but I'm afraid I have less than no time to play nursemaid to a boy with dreams of grandeur. You should get home to your family before you worry your poor mother, lad."

That feeling of desperation, the one he despised controlling him, wrapped around Octavian as he stepped closer to the much larger man. "Look at me. Look at my clothes. My boots. The bones beneath the skin of my face. Look at them, and tell me if I am a man being fed by a loving mother."

Myrddin pursed his lips, then said, "We can offer you something to eat and a seat by the fire." He gestured toward the little blaze with his big hand, and his companion made an exasperated sound and shook his head.

"I can help you," Octavian persisted, struggling to keep the anxiety from tainting his tone. "I am not looking for charity."

"Sit," Myrddin insisted, and Octavian obeyed. He took the canteen the man offered and gulped at the bitter wine within, letting it warm him from his throat all the way to the pit of his empty stomach. He couldn't suppress his sigh of satisfaction any more than he could turn away the strips of dried meat and chunk of hard bread the man offered him, though he resisted his instinct to shove them into his mouth whole and swallow them barely chewed.

After he'd eaten, disgusted at the way his basest needs interfered with his ambitions, Octavian said, "I want to help you on your mission."

The young archer snorted, but Myrddin patted his shoulder to silence him. "Lad, I've no idea how you know what we're planning, but it isn't something we want a novice involved in. Do you know how to use a weapon? Do you even carry one?"

"Aye." In a smooth, swift motion, Octavian reached beneath his thin, tattered cloak, drew his dagger, and presented it, hilt first, to Myrddin.

From a few feet away, Octavian saw the mercenary was probably ten years older than he, maybe more, with long, knotted, blond hair and neatly trimmed whiskers a few shades darker. He had strong, dark brows and pale eyes, though Octavian couldn't discern their color in the flickering light of the dwindling fire. Still, something in his gaze made Octavian want to trust him. Myrddin's eyes were not cold and dead, as his assassin's had been. Again, he thrust his blade toward the other man's waiting hand.

Myrddin reached for the dagger, but at the last moment, he recoiled as if it were on fire. "Sweet goddesses, boy! I—Where in the world did you get that? You—you're not—"

"No, I'm not," Octavian reassured him with a smile. His assassin had done him more than one favor. The dagger the Cast-Down had offered him was distinctive if one knew what to look for, and apparently Myrddin did. Many people doubted the existence of the Order of the Crimson Scythe, the world's most dreaded cult of assassins, but belief or no, everyone feared them.

"Then how?" Myrddin asked. "Goddesses, how do you hold that and still walk in the light of the world?"

"It was a gift," Octavian explained. "The one who offered it to me… I like to think he saw something in me he didn't want destroyed by a petty thief or someone who would accost me on the road. Why, I cannot say."

The young archer grunted and made a few quick gestures with his hands.

Myrddin laughed. "Dirk thinks perhaps it was your… uh, beauty the assassin did not want lost." Clearly, "beauty" wasn't the word the archer had expressed, but Octavian didn't ask for the truth. He probably didn't want to hear it.

"He could have killed me," Octavian protested. "I certainly could not have stopped him."

"No, my lad." Myrddin stirred the coals in the fire with a stick. "No one can stop one of them. Still, it does not mean you can handle yourself in a fight, or that you wouldn't be worse than an annoyance to Dirk and me. We have our hands full as it is. You are not trained to use that blade. If you were, we'd both be dead without having ever heard your breath on the wind. Is there anything else you can offer us?"

Octavian sighed. "Are you wounded anywhere?"

"What?"

"Are you hurt? A bruise? A scratch?"

"Why?"

"Just…." Octavian slipped his dagger back into the scabbard by his hip, frustrated. If he could just convince someone to give him a chance, he'd show what an asset he could be. He knew there was more to him than a small man who'd led an easy life until the past spring. The assassin who had let him live had seen it. But Myrddin still looked at him like he'd sprouted two heads.

Dirk came to his rescue, rolling up his sleeve to reveal an infected cut a few inches above his wrist. Octavian wrinkled his nose at the rotten smell emanating from the wound, but he closed his eyes and rested his fingertips at the edge of the old cut. He felt the life and vitality siphoning from him to the other man, and he grew dizzy. He was vaguely aware of his body curling backward and prepared himself for the impact of the frozen ground against his back and head, but thick arms caught and steadied him. Myrddin's breath warmed his cheek when he spoke.

"Bleeding Shades, you're a mage!"

Hard steel plate pressed against Octavian's cheek, and he leaned against it despite the cold of the metal. "So far, I'm best at healing."

At the edges of Octavian's vision, Dirk the archer gestured wildly.

"Aye," Myrddin said. "I can see it would be useful. So, you want—"

The archer grunted.

"If you say so," Myrddin grumbled. "I hope we're not sorry for taking him on. Personally, I had hoped to avoid the need for a healer's skills. Give me a few big lads who know how to swing a blade over a mage any day."

Octavian wriggled out of Myrddin's grasp and forced himself to sit up straight even though the world still wiggled and spun around him. He didn't want pity; he'd show them he could stand on his own. Though he knew he shouldn't use his magic again so soon, that it would strain him, this was his chance to get himself in with what seemed an honorable and capable couple of men, a chance to do something others might talk about. "I can do more than heal."

Over the summer, alone in the barn where he'd slept, he had been practicing, struggling to understand his gift and make it do his bidding. He'd only been partially successful, but he hoped it would be enough to impress the two mercenaries. Mages, after all, grew rarer with each generation. Noticing a pile of small stones stacked about a dozen feet away, Octavian took aim. No sound or flash of light came from his fingers, but the air rippled with the familiar scent of burnt minerals before the rocks flew apart and scattered in every direction. Octavian willed away the gray glitter pouring in at the edges of his vision. He kept his voice even and strong. "I can knock down at least a few men with that spell."

It was a lie; he'd never tried it against a living thing, but the mercenaries looked impressed. Octavian had to press his advantage. Laying his palm flat against the frigid ground, he closed his eyes to concentrate. A moment later, a tremor ran through the frozen soil, making the gravel strewn over it quiver and bounce. Myrddin swore under his breath, and Octavian opened his eyes in time to see Dirk poke out his lower lip and nod. Octavian pulled his knees to his chest and held them tight, letting his cloak fall around his arms and legs so the others wouldn't see his hands trembling. "So do you think you have a use for me?"

Dirk moved his hands so fast they made Octavian's head spin. In response, Myrddin shook his head.

"What's he saying?" Octavian asked, hoping Myrddin answered before he passed out. Goddesses, he just had to endure until he could pretend to fall asleep of his own free will.

"He doesn't like you," Myrddin said. "He thinks you're soft, inexperienced, and think too much of your magic."

In the world of wealthy merchants and their noble patrons where Octavian had been reared, things weren't said so plainly. The rich and so-called civilized men and women traded snide, subtle insults and backhanded compliments, but no one spoke his mind. In a way, Octavian appreciated not having to decipher the hidden meaning, but the assessment stung—probably because he knew it was true. When he looked over at Dirk, the archer raised his chin and met Octavian's gaze defiantly. Instead of relying on Myrddin to translate, Octavian spoke to Dirk directly. "I thought you said earlier that my skills might be useful."

The archer slashed and stabbed at the air, scowling as he moved his fingers at various angles.

"Dirk says you'd be worth having if the fight goes poorly and we need patching up, but he doesn't think you'd last long enough in battle to draw that cursed knife. Why do you carry that thing, anyway, he wants to know. He says it is bad luck and you should throw it into Estrella Lake or bury it in holy ground."

Octavian skimmed his fingers along the dagger's hilt. "I am fond of it, and it has served me well." He didn't tell them it represented the first stroke of good luck he could remember having, and that it held a deeper, more personal meaning that he'd never share with another living soul.

"Well, Dirk says he doesn't want to take you on just to watch you die, that you'd do better to look for work on a farm, or a shop, or a— Oh, Dirk! There's no need for that! Lad can't help being nice-looking. Doesn't mean he should resort to selling—"

"I suppose I should be on my way." They might not want him, might not see any value to him, but Octavian would be damned if he'd sit idly and let them make him the butt of their crude jokes. One day, when he showed the world what he could do, they would be sorry for turning him away. One day, as soon as someone gave him the chance to prove it. It would not be tonight, though. He'd depleted his energy and left himself vulnerable for nothing.

As Octavian stood, his eyes stinging and his cheeks hot, eager to escape before the mercenaries noticed his childish reaction to their rejection, Myrddin caught his wrist, pulled him back to the ground, and met his gaze. "I have told you what Dirk thinks. I have not said I agree with him. Likely as not I'm an old fool, but the way I see it, a lad who can walk into a mercenary camp as you did has stones, at least. Stones can count for more than skill sometimes."

The big man indicated a bedroll near the fire. "Get some rest. You'll need it. Have some wine too. It might be your last chance. I'm still not sure you won't get yourself killed tomorrow."

"Thank you," Octavian said.

Without meeting his gaze, Myrddin waved at the pile of blankets and furs. "Save it. You can thank me if you survive."

Chapter Two

USING A long stick, Myrddin drew a flowing, vertical line in the dirt between their feet. "The Kanda River," he explained. He pointed to the left side. "Selindria. And Gaeltheon on the right. But here"—he scratched in the dirt with the end of the branch—"along the riverbank on both sides, is land controlled by neither king. Disputed territory, ruled by warlords and mercenary bands. Now, power is always shifting, but some groups have dug their boots in."

He looked up to find Dirk picking his breakfast from between his teeth with a twig. The boy—Octavian Rose—looked serious, his brow furrowed and his lips set in a hard line. He focused on Myrddin's every word, though he surely already knew the history and the lay of the land. The lad was educated; Myrddin could tell from the way he spoke, much more like the son of an aristocrat than a sell-sword or a farmer. Yet he paid attention to Myrddin's account, and from what Myrddin could see in his soft brown eyes, he didn't feign it. Goddesses, Dirk had been right about one thing: the boy was pretty with his high cheekbones, animated eyes, full, expressive lips, smooth skin somewhere between tan and cream, and thick, dark brown hair. Myrddin could picture him escorting a noble lady to a banquet if he'd been cleaned up a bit and inclined to whoring. The rest of what he pictured, what might happen after the feast, he tried to put out of his mind. He would be lucky if the lad survived the day. It would be a foolish mistake to get even remotely attached to him.

Myrddin stabbed at a spot near the top of the line he'd drawn and engraved a circle around the hole in the ground. "This is Crooked Tooth territory we're in. The Teeth aren't the worst of the companies, but they're ruthless. We were hired to escort a merchant caravan through this dangerous area, and I'm ashamed to say we failed. The family, and all the goods they'd been carrying, are likely prisoners of the Teeth. I intend to fulfill the contract we entered with those people, and at least see them to safety."

Octavian nodded, his too long fringe tumbling into his eyes and catching against his eyelashes. He blew out a puff of air to push his hair aside. "Do you have an idea where these Teeth may have taken your merchants and their goods? What were they selling?"

Good questions, Myrddin had to admit. "Well, most of their goods were common: grains, vegetables, and meat from the plains. Dried fish from the south—"

"No one would ambush a caravan for those items," the boy astutely noted. "What else?"

"*Muri-ku,*" Myrddin admitted.

"What?" Octavian asked.

Myrddin shook his head. "It's a foul brew made by the Emiri seafarers who live at the mouth of the river. Fish and slugs and fermented seaweed, from what I understand. A single cup can send a man mad with drink, or facedown on the floor. Still, many of the taverns and brothels here in the disputed territory can sell it to their patrons for exorbitant prices, and they pay accordingly. 'Course, most of the valens and bairns forbid drinking it, but they don't have much say here along the riverbank. Our job was to get the merchants past those few knights guarding the outskirts of the nobles' territory, and then safely through the hostile region. They had a contact just south of the Starlight Bridge. Look, I know the goods are questionable, but they're decent people just trying to make a living."

Octavian met his gaze, and heat rose in Myrddin's cheeks beneath his whiskers. "I am not judging you. I might have, once, but since then I have been hungry, thirsty, and cold. I have wondered where I might find food or shelter, how I would survive another day. Morality becomes relative when you haven't eaten in days. It's easy to judge others while sitting by a fire with a full stomach. I have done things I'm not proud of talking about, and I can understand others doing what they must. Do you know where to look for your patrons?"

Dirk gestured, and Myrddin nodded at him. "The Teeth have about a half a dozen camps in this area. More likely than not, we'll find them at the nearest one, here." He showed Octavian on his crude map. "It's a few hours away. You'll need to ride with one of us."

"Very well," Octavian said. "We should get on the road. Every moment we forsake these merchants might mean their suffering."

The boy checked what passed for his gear, turned on the ball of his foot, and headed toward the horses. Dirk caught Myrddin's attention and signed, *You're falling for a pretty face, old friend. That boy is all talk.*

Dirk could understand Myrddin's speech by the movement of his lips. "You may be right. I'm sure you'll tell me later if it turns out that way, but I see a fire in him. Something special. Rare."

The archer made a rude gesture and a worse assumption.

"The Shades I do! He's little more than a child. I'll grant you he's beautiful, but I would never…. He's an innocent."

In response to Dirk's next gestures, Myrddin said, "I know no such thing. And even if he does, as you so eloquently phrase it, 'want my meat,' I have no intention of providing it. I like a man at least old enough to grow whiskers. Besides, he is not a warrior. I just want him to survive to realize that, and find himself work in a shop or a tavern. No, not a whorehouse. He cannot help what he looks like. Come now, we have work to do. Later, you can hurl your insults at me to your bitter heart's content."

Dirk made a gesture no one could have misinterpreted and mounted his gray mare. Myrddin situated Octavian in front of him, where he could curl himself around the man's smaller body and cover him in his warmth as he guided his animal, and they set out for the Crooked Tooth camp, where they'd likely be outnumbered twenty to one.

AFTER A few hours, Myrddin stopped his mount so the animal could drink from a small stream and dismounted. "I need a piss."

"Goddesses, so do I." Octavian dismounted gracefully and followed Myrddin to a clump of bracken while Dirk wandered in the opposite direction. They stood next to each other, relieving themselves into the bushes. Octavian shook his hands before tucking himself away. Then he bent down and dragged them through some wet grass before patting them dry on his trousers. "Dirk cannot speak?"

"Nor hear," Myrddin said, shaking himself off and ducking his cold-shriveled cock back into his trousers. "But he can shoot a fly off a horse's ass. He's the fastest and most accurate archer I've ever seen."

The lad nodded. "We all have obstacles to overcome."

"And what are yours?" Myrddin asked.

"Isn't it obvious? I'm young, untrained, and no one is willing to take a chance on me. No one is willing to see beyond my appearance."

"Many people have worse lots than being too beautiful." Myrddin shrugged.

"Many people have worse lots. I have heard that before, and I acknowledge the truth of it. But it doesn't mean I haven't struggled. It doesn't mean I should accept a life I do not want. I'm willing to fight for a place. All I want is someone to let me try. Thank you for being that man."

Myrddin thought of the assassin's blade the boy carried. "It seems I'm not the first."

Octavian bowed his head and smiled, his lips barely twitching up at the corners. "That is my memory."

"Very well." Myrddin turned back toward the horses. "Perhaps one day you'll share it with me."

Behind him, Octavian laughed, the forced, fragile sound of something that would take very little pressure to shatter. "I do appreciate what you're doing, helping me as you are. Yet, I don't think I'll ever be inclined to offer you that."

"As you say, young Octavian." They mounted up again and rode a few more hours, reaching a ridge overlooking a shallow valley just as long shadows began to extend from the evergreen trees, striping the forest in bluish shadow and the heavy orange light of sunset. After tying the horses up a mile or so from the ledge, they crept slowly to the edge to look down at the Crooked Tooth camp. Myrddin let Dirk, who could move swiftly and quietly through the underbrush, lead the way.

The mercenaries below had just begun to light their torches and the fires to cook their evening meals. A quick scan from one end of the camp to the other revealed a trio of three-sided log sheds with four tents between them. A shelter for about ten horses stood at the northern end. A carriage and three carts—those had belonged to the merchants—had been crowded into a circle near the makeshift stables. There was no sign of the family or their workers.

Satisfied he'd observed all he could, Myrddin tapped Dirk's elbow, jutted his chin in the direction they'd come from, and snuck back into the woods as quietly as he could. The three men sat down in a circle on the needle-strewn ground, their knees bumping together as they crossed their legs.

"I have an idea," Octavian whispered.

Myrddin closed his eyes and then opened them again slowly. "Look, lad. I appreciate your enthusiasm, but you honestly have no experience in these matters."

"Can it hurt to hear me out?" Octavian asked with a patience far beyond his years.

"No," Myrddin conceded. Dirk rolled his eyes.

The lad found a knotted branch lying among the leaf litter and brittle needles. With the point, he drew an X on the ground. "The main fires are clustered together. That means when it comes time to cook the evening meal, they'll gather at the center of the camp. I say we position Dirk on the ridge, where he'll have a clear shot at all the Teeth as they gather for supper." He moved his stick to the left and then the right. "Two paths lead into the center of the camp from our vantage point. You can take one, and I can take the other. We're looking at probably twelve men, based on the four tents and the ten horses. If Dirk can immobilize half of them before they realize they're attacked, you and I should be able to eliminate the rest. They don't know we're here, and they would never imagine three men would take on twelve. Surprise is our only advantage, but if we use it, I think we can triumph here."

Goddesses damn it, Myrddin couldn't argue. The boy's plan was sound, as good as anything he could have come up with. If he hadn't known better, he'd have thought this Octavian Rose had led men into battle before. He found few flaws in the strategy, but one stood out.

"Dirk cannot hear. How will we signal him to let him know we're in position and that he should start shooting?"

Octavian looked into Dirk's face. "You're not a fool, my friend. There are twelve or so men. Start shooting when most of them are gathered around the fires for their supper. We'll follow your lead." He turned to Myrddin. "When the arrows start flying, we move in and take out the men around the outskirts. If we do this right, I think it can work. We may even find the goddesses on our side and the men unarmed. Unless you have a better idea?"

Myrddin wished he did; he hated following the plan of this greenhorn boy, but it was a solid strategy and one likely to result in success. They took a few moments to hash out the details, and then they secured their gear and moved into position, Myrddin taking the trail down the right side of the knoll and Octavian taking the left-hand path. He hoped he had done the right thing bringing the boy along. No matter how good a plan they'd formulated, dozens of things could still go wrong. He had been fighting long enough to know any battle could be a man's last, especially a man as inexperienced as young Octavian. As he crept through the thick brush, Myrddin tried not to list in his mind the many things that might befall the lad or that could still go amiss.

He should not have been surprised to see the two men a short way from the bottom of the path, but he cursed. With only two ways in or out of the camp, the Teeth would have been fools to leave them unguarded. And a company of fools would not have taken control of such a large territory nor gained such a formidable reputation. Myrddin ducked behind a tree. He should have expected sentries, planned for them. He would have little trouble with two men, but what about Octavian? Myrddin had a strong suspicion the lad had never faced another man in battle. He'd seen young warriors freeze at their first fight, finding actual confrontation very different than they'd imagined it, and if that happened to Octavian, his first fight could be his last. These men would think nothing of skewering the boy and kicking his twitching body into the woods. Again, Myrddin regretted bringing the lad with them. What was it about him that made Myrddin want to believe his words, to see him pleased? He had no time to consider it. With an entire camp and a dozen men between them, he wouldn't reach Octavian in time. He'd have to trust the lad could look after he as well as he had claimed. Worrying over him would distract Myrddin, and he could get himself killed. No matter what he felt in regards to the boy, Myrddin had to put his own life first.

Despite this setback, they needed to keep to the plan. If these guards drew the rest of the company to Myrddin's location, they'd also draw them out of the open, where Dirk could use his bow from the ledge, and Myrddin would find himself facing a dozen men or more on his own. He was a capable warrior and had been for a long time, but he didn't like those odds. He could only hope Octavian would realize the same. If he attracted the attention of the camp, the boy wouldn't live long enough to hit the ground. But he'd run out of time to worry about Octavian. Octavian was just a man he'd known less than a day, a hireling, and Myrddin couldn't lose sight of that. Assigning more value to Octavian than the young man warranted could cost him his life.

Time to concentrate on the task at hand. He had a job to do.

Myrddin quietly drew his sword as he peeked out around the tree trunk concealing him. The two guards leaned against trees, conversing quietly as they passed a canteen. From their posture and the swords in scabbards by their hips, Myrddin didn't think they were expecting trouble. Few in this region would bother with the Teeth, and that would work to Myrddin's advantage. Still, he needed to move quickly.

He snuck up behind the man closest to him, lifted his arm, and clocked one of the guards across the back of the head with the hilt of his sword. With a grunt, the man fell facedown. Just as his comrade turned to investigate the sound, Myrddin thrust the hilt of his blade into the man's chest to knock the wind from him so he couldn't call for help. With his other hand, he drew back and hit the man in the temple and knocked him out. Moving quickly, he tied both men's hands behind their backs, gagged them, and dragged them into the bracken off the path. He removed their swords, then tossed one into the bushes and shoved the other into his belt in case he needed a spare.

Not far from where the trail widened and opened up into the camp, men had begun to gather around the fires, placing meat on spits and filling cauldrons, just as Octavian had predicted. The lack of commotion on the far side of the complex told him Octavian hadn't given them away. Perhaps the boy had lost his nerve and run when he'd seen the guards. At least he hadn't ruined their chances to succeed and get out of here alive. Myrddin moved as close as he dared, keeping himself concealed by the leafless vegetation, and waited.

Dirk's first arrow found purchase in a man's shoulder. He screamed, but the archer got off six more shots—all of them debilitating but none of them fatal—before the Teeth realized they were under attack. Octavian had been right about something else: here, safe in their camp, ready to enjoy a meal, many of the men hadn't bothered to arm themselves. Chaos erupted as men ran to escape the line of fire, the wounded went toward the shelter of the tents, and the rest scrambled for weapons. Myrddin stayed hidden until two men jogged toward the foot of the path, no doubt in search of the archer. Quite cleverly, Dirk had stopped shooting as soon as their enemies had an idea of his position, but Myrddin knew his friend would be looking down, taking the shots he could. They had been fighting together for a long time. For his part, Myrddin had to keep these men away from the uphill path, away from Dirk. As he stood and raised his sword to deflect the downward blow aimed at him, he spared a heartbeat to glance toward the other end of the camp, but beyond men running, shouting, and arming themselves, he saw little through the smoke of the cooking fires.

Myrddin kicked the enemy swordsman in the torso and spun just in time to drive his elbow into the second man's face, breaking his nose with a sickening crunch. The man swiped wildly at Myrddin as he raised a hand to catch the blood gushing from his face. Myrddin leaped backward to avoid the point of his blade. The man his kick had knocked to the ground caught his ankle, knocked him on his ass, and tackled him from the side. As they scuffled, rolling around in the snow and dirt, an arrow sang past Myrddin and pierced the other man's forearm. Using his superior size, Myrddin rolled his enemy beneath him. The man had pulled a dagger from somewhere, and he swiped at Myrddin, nicking the bridge of his nose and summoning an absurd amount of blood but causing little actual damage. With the hand not holding his sword, Myrddin grabbed the man's wrist to keep his small but sharp blade at bay. Then he drove his knee into his enemy's groin and at the same time, his forehead into his nose. He used the man's momentary distraction to hit him in the head with the hilt of his sword, making sure he'd be unconscious for a while before standing.

In spite of his injuries, the other man limped toward Myrddin, an arrow now also protruding from his thigh. Dirk had seen to it he couldn't lift his sword, but he held a small ax in his other hand. He swung for Myrddin's neck, and Myrddin crossed his sword over his chest just in time to parry it. He easily pushed the ax away and kicked the other man in the leg, just above his arrow wound. With a howl, the man dropped to his knees. Myrddin drove his knee up under the enemy's chin and left him sprawled on his back. An arrow sailed past him, narrowly missing his left shoulder, and Myrddin ducked and backed away half-crouched. The arrows came not from the ledge above, but from the back of the camp. Two archers stood near the tents, and between them and Myrddin was little he could use for cover. Still bent in half, he protected his head with his sword arm and ran for the tables set up near the fires. Dirk took out one of the archers, but the other focused all his attention on Myrddin, and Myrddin had a wide swath of open ground to cross.

An arrow struck the side of his calf but pinged off his steel greave. Had that shot been a couple of inches higher, it could have crippled him. Myrddin cursed, but the appearance of a large man with a spiked flail in each hand meant he could no longer focus on the bowman. As steel clashed against steel, Myrddin heaved, moving as fast as he could to deflect the blows aimed at him. The spiked steel balls moved like the blades of a windmill in the big warrior's hands, and they dented and notched Myrddin's sword every time he lifted it to protect himself. He and Dirk both believed in avoiding killing whenever they could, but this whoreson seemed determined to smash his head in, so he drew back, and with a ragged cry, he slashed at the warrior's exposed neck. The man dipped back and raised his mace, catching Myrddin's sword at the edge, the impact reverberating up Myrddin's arm and making his teeth knock together. An arrow passed so close to the back of Myrddin's neck that it ruffled his hair. The mace in the man's other hand came toward Myrddin's head. He dropped into a crouch to avoid it, and an arrow struck his hip. His mail tunic and thick leather trousers stopped it from embedding, but it hurt like a bitch and drew a font of blood. He swung his sword at his enemy's knees, and even though the man jumped back, Myrddin's steel cut deep.

A stream of warm, mineral-scented air rushed past Myrddin, making his teeth feel like they wanted to jump out of his mouth. The force struck the enemy archer, and from the corner of his eye, Myrddin saw him fly into the air and smack against one of their shoddy buildings. Myrddin's cut had sent his adversary to his knees, and Myrddin dispatched him with a backhanded strike. Heart hammering and chest hurting, he scanned the area. Men were lying on the ground, some unconscious, some suffering arrow wounds. Myrddin counted five able-bodied warriors closing in from the outskirts of the camp: three men with swords and two archers. On his own, he didn't stand much chance. If no one had gotten to Dirk, they might get through this together. They had done so before, but nothing was guaranteed in this line of work. Myrddin knew this might be his last battle, but he didn't plan to go down easily, even if he was on his own. The air rippled again, and the archer closest to Myrddin dropped, struck by an invisible force.

A moment later, Octavian came running through the fray, his cursed dagger drawn and reflecting firelight, his skin pale, a bruise on his cheek and a trickle of blood running from the corner of his mouth. He stood shoulder to shoulder with Myrddin and nodded once. Myrddin had no time to contemplate the way his heart soared at the sight of the boy, not only alive and relatively unharmed, but crackling with both magical energy and the lust for battle. A quick glance in the direction Octavian had come from showed the several men he'd left on the ground.

Another arrow whizzed above them, finding purchase in the remaining enemy archer's bicep, and a second struck his opposite arm, effectively preventing him from lifting his bow. The last three members of the Teeth surrounded Myrddin and Octavian. One of the swordsmen hacked down at the boy, but Octavian raised his dagger in an angle in front of his face and deflected it. With his other hand, he directed a burst of magic into the man's belly and sent him sailing backward, the force probably breaking his ribs. As Myrddin struggled against the last two mercenaries, Octavian sprinted a few steps, pounced, and sent the fist still holding his blade into his rival's face. Then he scrambled to his feet and launched himself at one of the men attacking Myrddin, tackling the man to the ground.

Between Dirk's arrows and Myrddin's blade, they subdued the last of the Teeth. Octavian sat straddling the man he'd wrestled down, the edge of his dagger held to the man's throat. Hurting and exhausted, Myrddin staggered over, bent down, and secured the man's hands with a bit of the rope he kept attached to his belt. Then he stood and offered Octavian his hand. "Nicely done," he said with a nod. "You fought well. I thought you'd run away when you encountered those guards along the trail."

Still gripping Myrddin's hand, Octavian raised his chin and looked at Myrddin with eyes lit like bonfires. "I am not a coward. Nor would I leave someone depending on me to die. I see I still have much to prove."

"Not to me." Myrddin ruffled the boy's hair, surprised at the silly smile it earned him. "Come on, then. We still have much to do."

Before long, Dirk bounded into the camp and helped them round up and restrain the other members of the Crooked Tooth company. From what Myrddin could tell, most, if not all, of the men would survive, though some would have a long recovery ahead of them. When they were sure none of their enemies could sneak up on them and stab them in the back, they went in search of their captured patrons. They found them, eight men and two women, inside a locked shed not far from their caravans. The bound merchants flinched when Myrddin opened the door and blinked at the unaccustomed light, but one of them, an older man, recognized him and stumbled forward, holding out his tethered hands. "Goddesses, I remember you! You were with the men we hired to protect us from these monsters! When they defeated you and took our caravans…. We never dared to hope…. Thank you. Thank the goddesses."

"Just doing the job we were paid to do, tam." Myrddin bowed slightly and then turned to Octavian. "Lad, put that damned knife to use."

As Octavian set about freeing the prisoners, Dirk caught Myrddin's elbow and pulled him in the direction of the caravans. The archer opened the carts and flung the lids off a few chests as if checking the goods, but every few moments, he shot a glare at Myrddin over his shoulder. After fighting side by side for several years, Myrddin knew Dirk well and indulged him.

"The fight went well," he tried.

The archer's thin lips twisted up as if he was about to be sick, and Myrddin curled his shoulders forward in defeat. "Look, friend. I've learned to read the movements of your hands, but that does not mean I can read your mind. Don't pout like a spurned maiden, Dirk. It's unbecoming. If you have something to say—"

Fine, the archer gestured, his hands only a few inches from Myrddin's face. *Are you planning to keep that child in our company?*

"I'll go out on a limb and predict you oppose that idea," Myrddin said.

Dirk rolled his eyes theatrically and shook his head.

"I don't understand." Myrddin leaned closer to Dirk and lowered his voice. He didn't want Octavian, who'd freed all the merchants and now crouched down to heal their minor scrapes and bruises even though he was exhausted, to hear. The lad had something to prove, and men with things to prove often died young, in Myrddin's experience. Adding to Octavian's insecurities would only make him more reckless. "He fought very well for a novice. Didn't panic and kept a clear head. He was an asset today. I know you have not liked him from the beginning, but there are only two of us now. Our chances for hiring on with another company are better in larger numbers. And he's a mage. Like it or not, that's an asset too."

He's a spoiled, rich, pretty boy, the archer signed. *He got lucky today. I vote we dump him in the next town. We don't need to play nursemaid to a child. If my opinion still holds weight to you. Or are a pair of lanky legs, big brown eyes, and pink lips worth more than years of friendship?*

"Of course they're not, and you insinuating otherwise is starting to rub me the wrong way. If I didn't know better, I'd think you wanted me for yourself and were just jealous." He puckered his lips at Dirk, winked, and finally earned a silent laugh.

Dirk spat on the ground, shook his head, and mimicked cupping a pair of very large breasts. When he pantomimed kissing and suckling them, Myrddin turned away. For some reason, even with his shock of wild, red hair, long nose, slight overbite, and liberal dusting of freckles, Dirk did well with the ladies. Once, when Myrddin asked him how, he'd held up two of his fingers and licked between them in an expression so filthy Myrddin never wanted to see it again.

Dirk tapped his shoulder to get his attention, and though Myrddin dreaded what he might see, he turned around. He hadn't been expecting his friend's serious expression. *And if it comes down to him or me?*

"How can you even ask me that?" Myrddin grasped Dirk's forearm.

Good, Dirk signed.

"Still, I wish you'd give him a chance. There's something about him. The boy's got stones of solid rock, if nothing else, and determination. I can see something in him…. Goddesses, not that, and get your finger away from my cock. I was going to say potential. Maybe even the potential for greatness."

You are a damned fool.

"All I'm asking is for you to keep an open mind." A glance over his shoulder showed Myrddin a group of people surrounding Octavian, smiling and shaking his hand. Just to make sure he wouldn't be overheard, he switched to the hand gestures only Dirk could understand: *At the first sign of weakness, I won't spare his feelings. I'm a mercenary, not the writer of heroic tales. Not a romantic poet. The very moment he becomes a liability, I'll cut him loose so fast even you wouldn't be able to shoot him in the ass on his way out.*

Good. That seemed to satisfy Dirk, and they set about looting anything useable or saleable from the Tooth camp before packing up. A town lay about a day and a half to the north on horseback, and with any luck, they could reach it without further incident.

Myrddin looked at Octavian—pale, exhausted, ready to fall over but hiding it admirably, and still helping the merchants load their goods onto carts. It all depended on him. He'd either rise up and make something of himself, or he would fail. And if he fell, Myrddin would leave him on the ground, just as he'd promised Dirk. If Octavian couldn't make the cut, then he wasn't worth their lives or their time.

Chapter Three

Octavian Rose's Journal

AFTER SEVERAL weeks fighting together, they still do not accept me. They are cordial, but I can see the doubt behind their eyes, even after my aid at the Crooked Tooth camp, even after my help in the defeat of the Tooth stragglers who later accosted our patrons, and even after my at least adequate performance in the several missions we've accepted since. It's as if they're waiting for an excuse to decide I am not worth the trouble and cast me off. As of yet, I have not given them that excuse, but it frustrates me that I have given them no reason to see me as an asset either.

I am becoming quite adept at healing, as inevitably someone among our growing group suffers at least a small injury during battle. It still tires me to offer my energy, or whatever one might call this power I possess that others do not, to others to mend their flesh, but I am recovering more quickly. I suppose I could find a town to settle in and work as a healer. I could probably make a comfortable amount of coin and lead a peaceful life doing so, but it does not call to me. Something inside me screams for glory, for a position from which I can influence the world, and this has led me to many questions—about myself, about the workings of other men's minds, and about the structure of our society.

Is it arrogance that makes me desire more than a life that would satisfy an ordinary man—a farmer, baker, or merchant? Is it arrogance to consider such men ordinary and not myself? I know, or I have always been taught, that arrogance is a sin against the goddesses. After all, the Thirteen Sisters destroyed the golden age of the world to cast down Emperor Fane, who thought he deserved the peoples' worship more than the goddesses did. I do not want to be an arrogant man, and I do not think I am better or worth more than anyone else. I merely want to achieve all I can in this life, reach the pinnacle, and rise until I can go no further. I do not know where that line will be drawn, but I don't want to stop until I butt up against it. Is that arrogance? Perhaps.

Secondly, I question what a man must possess to command the respect of other men. I thought I had figured this out: capability, dedication, loyalty, and working or fighting hard. I thought if I pulled my weight in the company, such as it is, and didn't complain or ask for special consideration, I would be seen to have value, but I am still seen as a liability, or, at best, as an unknown. I have spent many nights cold in my bedroll along the road, looking up into the firmament and wondering what makes one man great, his name known for generations after his death, while another languishes in obscurity. Good intentions do not seem enough, though I believe staunchly in personal honor. I want nothing that I must trade myself to obtain, but I want greatness, or I want to try for it. I think it is risky. To be great, a man must take a chance. Surely, for every ten men who take a great risk, nine do not live to be remembered. But the tenth….

I am sure destiny favors the brave and ignores the timid. The man who takes impossible chances and comes through them is the man others will follow. I now see two choices: grasp for destiny and succeed or die, or run at the middle of the pack and live an unremarkable and unremembered life.

I know which option appeals to me. It remains to be seen if I will survive to achieve the glory I do not know why I want. Perhaps, many years from now, I'll read over my youthful musings and think myself a fool. Perhaps I will not live long enough to do so.

OCTAVIAN STARED down at the ink drying on the pages of his prized possession: a thick, leather-bound book full of blank pages. The other men in the company, particularly the few new recruits, had spent their share of the profits from their last jobs on wine and ale, whores, or, in the case of Myrddin, better equipment. After the job at the Crooked Tooth camp, Myrddin had given Octavian a sword pilfered from a defeated mercenary, and Octavian had dutifully trained with him every day. Gashes, some scabbed over and some fresh, crisscrossed his hands and wrists where he'd cut himself. Though they stung and itched, they would heal on their own, so he didn't waste his magic. Myrddin had wanted him to keep and carry the sword he'd taken off an enemy, and when Octavian had declined, he'd offered to buy him a blade with his own coin, but Octavian liked his dagger. He could wield it without getting tired as quickly, and he cut himself much less. He supposed he could have used what he'd earned to look for a better weapon—he'd spent some on a hardened leather tunic, bracers, and new boots—but he'd really wanted the journal. The act of writing, of putting his chaotic, confused ideas into words, into some kind of order, soothed him and made him feel a measure of control over his future, even as he conceded both order and control were probably illusions. But perhaps illusions had a purpose sometimes.

After the ink dried, he closed the book and stowed it, along with his inkwell and quill, in his pack. He stretched out on his bedroll in the cheap tavern room they shared—at least the four of them. Dirk had yet to return from the brothel. His bed remained empty. The two newest members of their group, warriors who'd followed them after the attack on the camp and claimed they wanted distance from the Teeth, slept on the floor a few feet away. Myrddin. He lay on his side on the other bed, pretending to sleep, but every few moments, Octavian caught one of his eyes opening a sliver to check on him. He wasn't sure whether to be comforted or annoyed as he pinched the candlewick between his thumb and finger. The little flame hissed out, and he stretched on his back with his arms folded beneath his head, watching the moonlight coming through the dirty window shift across the rafters and chipped plaster ceiling. As he closed his eyes, he decided he'd risk everything on achieving a reputable place in the world. It was either that or resign himself to a life of rooms like this one. He didn't covet luxury, only the power to control his destiny, the path his life would take. Earning that meant taking a chance, and being the one out of ten to survive it. Octavian intended to be the exception that would prove his rule.

WHEN MYRDDIN shook Octavian's shoulder to awaken him, he felt like he'd only been sleeping a few moments, but sharp winter sunlight filled the room, revealing the dust on the furniture and the mold on the walls in merciless clarity. It was likely past the midday meal, and

Octavian's stomach rumbled. He sat up from his blankets, and the older mercenary handed him a small loaf of bread and a few greasy, grayish links of sausage. The room smelled like men's dirty feet and underarms, and the gas they'd released during the night. Crinkling his nose, Octavian caught a whiff of his own odor. On the road in the wintertime, there was nowhere to wash, but it didn't seem to bother any of the others. The two newest members of their group, who had joined only a week or so ago after a conversation in a tavern, a balding, wiry swordsman called Robere Thout, and a big brute of a warrior Octavian thought was called Danno, a man with a southern complexion and gnarled black hair, sat in nothing but their trousers, farting and scratching their balls as they ate their breakfast. Octavian wouldn't judge them, though. He didn't know what they'd been through. Perhaps decorum was the furthest thing from their minds. They might have their reasons. He hadn't known them long enough to understand their individual situations.

Myrddin smiled as he handed Octavian a pitcher of water. His eyes this morning looked a wintry gray to match the snow clouds beyond the windows, but Octavian had seen them with a slate blue cast or even a heathery purple hue. Though he had tried to heal it, Octavian feared the cut across the bridge of Myrddin's nose would result in a thin scar he'd bear all his life.

"Sleep well, lad?" Myrddin asked.

Octavian wished their unofficial leader wouldn't think of him as a child, but the man meant no insult, so Octavian nodded. He had things he wanted to discuss with the commander, ideas about how they could strengthen and improve their company, but he didn't want to voice them in front of the others. Myrddin seemed the only one who believed Octavian had anything to contribute. He'd wait and talk to the older man along the road to their next job. For now, he ate what had been provided, dressed, and armed himself with his dagger and another small knife he kept in his boot.

The four mercenaries left the inn about half an hour later. They followed Myrddin a little way down the street and waited while he knocked on the door of a fancy stone house with red winter berries festooning the lintels and candles burning in the windows as well as the lanterns hanging from the eaves. Myrddin knocked a second time, and a few moments later, a buxom girl in a scanty shift answered. She called something over her shoulder that Octavian couldn't quite hear, but soon Dirk appeared, his hair tousled and his green shirt unlaced and hanging open. He wrapped his arms around the woman's waist and kissed her soundly as he moved past her. Before the archer could leave the porch, two other women, a statuesque brunette and a short, full-figured blonde, came out into the cold in nothing but their dressing gowns to kiss him. The curvaceous little blonde clutched the archer's tunic and tried to pull him back inside as their tongues twisted together. Myrddin raised his fist to his lips and cleared his throat. Octavian had no clue what the three whores whispered into Dirk's red hair, but clearly, they would not be disappointed if he returned to the brothel.

Now complete, the company left the small town on the horses they'd taken from the Crooked Tooth camp. Myrddin chose a few of the best animals and brought them along in case their company acquired more men. A job retaking a ruined fortress from a local warlord awaited them to the north. When they reached their destination, they'd join dozens of other sell-swords and face the warlord's own legions of hirelings. Octavian hadn't been able to discern much about the mission, other than they sought to overtake an area the locals referred to as Rosecairn, and that it would be a difficult undertaking. He knew, as Myrddin did, that it would benefit them if they could bolster their ranks. Therefore, it did not surprise him when the older man agreed to meet with two potential recruits just beyond the boundaries of the village.

"We're the Beasley brothers," the taller of the two said. "Been working as swords for hire going on nine years. I'm Eric, and this is Ted. We're able fighters, and we'd be happy to join you. Your little group is making quite a name for itself in these parts, and, well, we like to throw our lot in with the winning side. We'll fight hard for you, tam. For a fair share of the profits, of course."

Myrddin shook the man's hand. A layer of grime covered his skin and mousy brown hair and had settled into the lines around his eyes and mouth, and his brother, Ted, looked even filthier, with slimy yellowed teeth showing beyond his crooked grin. Octavian had sworn he'd never judge a man on what he had done to survive, but he couldn't understand why some seemed so opposed to hygiene. The Beasley brothers stank like rotting onions and dirty groins when Myrddin motioned them forward to introduce them to the rest of the company.

Dirk scowled, fanned his hand in front of his nose, and would not shake either of their hands. He acknowledged them with barely a nod. Robere and Danno didn't seem to find the stench unusual.

"Octavian Rose." Myrddin said his name the way Octavian had always imagined his father might, had he seen anything in his son to be proud of. It made his belly warm and his body light, but goddesses, these bastards reeked. Up close, where he could see their slightly distorted features—eyes a little too far apart and wide, flattened noses—Octavian had to wonder if their parents had been too closely related to marry under the goddesses' law.

"Rose," the one called Eric said. "And who is this little rose petal? A pretty little lad to warm the men's beds after a hard day's fighting? Or just yours? Is his snug little body fair game or off-limits? Is he your personal seed bin or a pass-around?"

Myrddin colored and drew himself up to his full, impressive height, ready to defend Octavian's honor. But before the words could leave his mouth, Octavian moved in front of him, drew back his fist, and delivered a backhanded blow to Eric's sneering lips. The mercenary stumbled a few steps, landed on his ass, and raised a hand to his bleeding mouth.

"My name is Octavian Rose, and I am a fighter, healer, and mage. The next time you call me a whore, I suggest you draw your sword first, tam. And if you think you're getting anywhere near my bedroll, you should think again. I prefer men who wash."

Eric Beasley nodded once as he swiped the blood from above his lip. Behind Octavian, Dirk made an amused snort, almost a sound of solidarity. It pleased Octavian, though he kept the grin he felt from his face, his features carefully schooled. His risk had finally gained him a few inches of ground. Myrddin, who had moved to stand off to the side of the brothers, beamed at him with wide eyes and a slack mouth. As happened between men like these, the matter had been settled, and so was forgotten. They fell silent as they continued along the rocky, snow-strewn paths. Octavian could only assume they passed into Lockhaven by afternoon.

Dirk scouted ahead on foot, as he often did. The Beasley brothers and Robere and Danno stayed near the middle of the group, huddled close against the wind and drifting snow, passing a flask. The horses plodded through the thickening snow with heads lowered against the cutting wind.

Ice crystals glistened on their whiskers and manes. When Octavian and Myrddin fell a few dozen feet behind the others, Octavian seized the opportunity to speak with their commander. "I wish to thank you."

"Do you now?" Myrddin looked over at him and smiled indulgently, his blond hair whipping across his face and his cheeks nipped red.

"You were going to defend me against the Beasleys."

Myrddin's smile faltered, and he nodded. "You don't deserve to be spoken to that way, Octavian. You're a good lad."

He'd used that word again, the one describing him as a boy, a child. Octavian didn't mention it, but he steeled his resolve to prove to Myrddin he was a capable man. "I appreciate your intentions, but you must realize that protecting me in front of others doesn't raise their estimation of me. I must be allowed to stand up for myself, or the others will continue to see me as weak. They cannot see me as someone in need of protecting, or they'll never see me as someone worthy of respect."

"Son, you claim to thank me and then you aim straight for my bollocks."

Octavian's cheeks warmed with shame, and maybe at the thought of Myrddin's bollocks, which were likely a dusky mauve, like his lips, full and plump and covered in soft golden down—"I didn't mean it that way. I do appreciate what you intended to do for me, but I want you to believe I can take care of myself."

"I believe it," Myrddin said, squinting as if to study Octavian. "You wouldn't have lived this long if you couldn't. You're clever, Octavian, and more ambitious than I've seen in years. But in this line of work, you don't want men around you who won't watch your back. We have to stand up for each other. That's what I'm used to, and that's what I planned to do."

"Would you have done it for Dirk? Or would you have stood aside and waited for that whoreson to pull the arrow out of his filthy arm?"

Myrddin opened his mouth to answer but hesitated before he finally spoke around a fond grin. "His arm? Dirk would have shot his cock off and told him he'd never have use for a whore again."

"I can do the same," Octavian insisted. "I don't need to be taken care of. I don't care much what the rest of these dirty blighters think, but I want you and Dirk to know that."

"I know it," Myrddin said, though he looked somehow sad with his eyebrows tilted up at the centers and his lips canted down. "I'm just…. My instinct is to defend, even if you can do it yourself. But I'll stand down from now on and let you fight your own battles. I know you can handle them."

"Thank you. If you wouldn't mind, I'd like to discuss our future together. If we have a future together?"

"You can fight with us as long as you carry your weight."

Noncommittal, but Octavian accepted it for the time being. "Well, assuming I can, I have to wonder what our plans are to improve our standing."

"I didn't know it needed improving."

"Of course it does." Octavian tugged at the strap of his ridiculously heavy pack, which contained all his worldly possessions as well as the coin he'd earned over the past few weeks. The only way to assure his goods and money wouldn't be stolen was to keep them constantly by his side, even while he slept. "We need some sort of a permanent base. We cannot continue to carry all the gold we earn on our persons. Especially if we continue to expand, take better, more lucrative jobs, and earn more. We need a place to store our wealth and our gear. A home, for lack of a better word."

"And when we left for a job, would we just leave our coin unguarded?"

"Of course not." Octavian had pondered this and written his ideas in his journal. "If we established a company, we could rotate which men went on missions. Provided we surround ourselves with trustworthy and honorable warriors, we could depend upon those left behind to keep watch over our things, as we would do the same for them when their turn came to go off fighting. Not only would it offer us security for our possessions, it would give us, and the rest of the men, a chance to rest and recuperate between jobs. Healthy, rested men fight better than hurt and exhausted ones."

Myrddin chuckled. "Very grand dreams you have, lad. That would require an awful lot of men."

"But what men wouldn't want to enter into such an arrangement? Have trusted friends watching their households while they worked? It would afford them the chance to marry and start families, and that in turn would inspire loyalty and dedication to our company. After all, no decent man will turn against those who help protect his wife and children, not for any amount of gold. Of course"—Octavian wrinkled his nose as he jutted his chin toward the Beasleys and Robere, who he also mistrusted—"we would have to be selective about which men we chose to include."

"Grand dreams." Myrddin shook his head. "I take it you do not approve of the inclusion of the honorable Eric and Ted Beasley."

"No." Octavian saw no reason to coat his words with honey, not anymore. "Fighting for profit is one thing, but being cruel, taking advantage of those you view as weaker, is another."

"Oh, I don't know if they were being cruel. They were just establishing their place in the order of the group, like dogs, I'm sorry to say. They viewed you as weaker, as you so keenly observed, someone to push around, but you showed them your teeth. I doubt they'll bother you again."

"I am not worried about them," Octavian said. "I don't want to be presumptuous or question your wisdom, your superior experience, but I think we can do better than the Beasley brothers. My goal, and yours if you'll stand with me, should be to establish a company of elite fighters, men of honor, and build ourselves a defensible base. Not a camp, but a place we can leave without worry. A home that will inspire men to defend it."

"Those are all lofty ideas," Myrddin said cautiously. "I hope you manage all of it. I hope the others of the world don't disappoint you. Octavian...."

"What?" They'd reined their mounts to a stop and turned in their saddles to face each other.

"I just hope you can keep your honor and still gain the power you seek so desperately. I have found, in this world, a man must often trade one for the other."

Octavian looked away from the older man's barely cloaked regrets, to the peaks of the mountains standing white against the darkening sky. Crag after crag, each one paler and more ethereal than the last, marched in a jagged line until they disappeared beyond the dome of the world. Looking at them, Octavian felt small and insignificant against their great age and majesty, but they made him want to carve his place into the bones of the world, inscribe his name in it even if he had to use his bare hands. "I will trade nothing. I *will* accomplish my dreams, but I will remain Octavian. I will be great, but I'll still be me. I'll show you, Myrddin. I can't wait to show you."

ONE PHRASE echoed in Myrddin's mind as they made camp for the night beneath the leeside of a rocky outcrop: *I prefer men who wash.* Octavian hadn't thought twice about announcing his preference for men. As he pitched his simple tent and laid out his blankets beneath it, Myrddin wondered if the lad knew what that entailed—if it was something he had experienced or just a passing whim. Goddesses, had he even known what he was saying? Did he mean it?

It didn't matter. Octavian was too young for him, and despite the lad's wishes, someone he wanted to protect. He wanted to protect the faith in men and the world Octavian held but too many others had lost. He never wanted to look at Octavian and see a man who'd do anything to succeed, who'd lost hope in accomplishing his dreams without sacrificing his personal honor, who saw no other alternative. He didn't want to see in Octavian what he had become.

Still, when Octavian approached him and said, "The night is cold. We could bunk up together," Myrddin hadn't hesitated. Octavian laid his bedroll beside Myrddin's, and after they'd had a cheerless dinner of cold meat and stale bread with the others, they settled in. Plenty of the other men had doubled up for warmth; they would even wrap their arms around each other to keep the bone-chilling cold at bay, so Myrddin shouldn't feel the apprehension he did lying next to the young man. But he could smell the polish Octavian used on his leather armor and the koria-scented soap he washed with, above the sweet, rich fragrance of his skin. He felt like a virgin boy lying there, wondering if he dared drape an arm across Octavian's ribs, wondering if he might get away with grazing his back if he pretended to be asleep, his stomach twisted up and his heart fluttering. He wanted so badly to touch Octavian's deep brown hair that the thought of how to accomplish it consumed him.

Octavian shivered beneath the thin wool blanket he carried with him. He needed better gear, but Myrddin could never persuade him to part with much of his coin, though he couldn't imagine why the young man hoarded it so. Myrddin laid a hand on Octavian's shoulder to still his trembling, but it persisted. "Cold, lad?"

"The cold is coming up from the ground. It hurts my bones and makes my muscles tense. It's difficult to sleep with my teeth banging together, but I'll manage. The others are fine, and so am I. I'll get used to it."

"Come here." Myrddin rolled his eyes in the darkness, opened his arms and, with one hand splayed over Octavian's belly, drew his back against his chest. The lad resisted for only a moment before settling in. "Freezing when you could avoid it is no show of bravery or fortitude." Myrddin arranged his furs and blankets over them as Octavian wiggled to find a comfortable position, his shoulder blades moving against Myrddin's chest while his ass grazed Myrddin's groin. When he'd made himself comfortable, he nestled his face against Myrddin's bicep, muttered his gratitude, and sighed, closing his slender arms over Myrddin's to seal them closer together. Myrddin let his nose sink into Octavian's hair, and he drank deep of his scent and the sensation of the silky strands against his skin and whiskers. The sweet smell of Octavian's hair and skin, the faint fragrance of cheap wine on his breath, affected Myrddin like no man had in recent memory. He suppressed a groan as he tried to angle his body so Octavian wouldn't notice how it responded to him. But what might Octavian do if he felt Myrddin's erection against the base of his spine? Myrddin almost dared finding out, but he didn't want to drive the chilled and tired man from his bed. Octavian needed and deserved a good night of rest, not to be molested by an old lecher.

"This is better," Octavian murmured, now warm and clearly drowsy. It pleased Myrddin more than it should have that the boy found safety and comfort in his arms. He wanted to keep them around Octavian's smaller body, keep him sheltered and secure, for as long as he could. Goddesses, he wanted to do much more with the beautiful young man, but Octavian had already fallen asleep. His breathing was deep and even—satisfied and unworried. It delighted Myrddin to have made him feel so… protected. Whoever had been entrusted with that duty before Myrddin had failed, and he would not do the same— whether Octavian wanted it or not.

Tired as he was after riding all day, Myrddin could hardly bear to give up his chance to feel Octavian's chest rising and falling slowly beneath his arms. Octavian went limp in his embrace in a way a more jaded man never would, trusting Myrddin would take no advantage while he was vulnerable. Myrddin would do what he could to preserve Octavian's trust in others and faith in the goodness of man, but with the lad's aspirations, he couldn't imagine he wouldn't eventually sacrifice his ideals to meet his goals. Most men did. Few men possessed strength enough to resist, and it turned them hard and bitter.

But this lad—this man—was special; Myrddin knew it. Strong but soft. He moved his hand up to touch the bump at the center of Octavian's throat, and then the corner of his jaw and the soft tab of his earlobe. Octavian made an unconscious sound, almost a purr, and nestled his face against Myrddin's arm. Then he clutched Myrddin's arm to his chest and held it tight, like a boy might grasp a favorite toy while sleeping. So bloody young—not just in body but in his lofty principles. Such feathery hair in contrast to the taut muscle pressed up against Myrddin's belly. Something burned in this Octavian Rose, something Myrddin had rarely seen but would draw men to his banner like moths to a flame: an impossible characteristic to define, but just as impossible to resist. Myrddin felt it blazing around him, drawing him in, yet he didn't possess the common sense to run from the fire. He would have to be very careful not to move the few hairs beyond the pleasant warmth to the place where that white heat would blister and blacken him.

Sometime after he'd finally overcome his frustration and doubts and fallen asleep, Myrddin woke with a start. He'd rolled to his back, and Octavian had draped himself across Myrddin's chest and nuzzled his face into the crook of Myrddin's neck. Warm breath coming from between his parted lips moistened Myrddin's skin, and Octavian's erection pressed against his waist. It would take so little to shift him over and align their cocks, rub them together until they both found satisfaction. But a scream sundered the night beyond their shelter, and Myrddin had no time to consider it. He shook Octavian awake, and the young man bolted up just as a sword ripped through the canvas flap of their tent.

The fabric fell away to reveal firelight, frigid air, and the silhouettes of three men holding weapons. Instantly alert, Myrddin groped for the sword he'd left beside his bedroll and found it just in time to deflect the ax one of the attackers brought down toward his head. Though the blanket hampered his movement, he managed to kick the man in the groin, and when he doubled over, Myrddin arced his blade down to slash him across the belly. He avoided killing when he could—he was no assassin—but when it came to his life or his enemy's, he didn't hesitate. His blade penetrated whatever the man wore for armor, and blood and innards spilled out in steaming, stinking coils across his blankets. With his free hand, Myrddin shoved the dying man backward so he wouldn't collapse on him and trap him.

The other two men converged on Octavian. Octavian raised his arms and crossed them in front of his face in an instinctive gesture, but his worn wool tunic would do little to stop steel. Myrddin swung at the man closest to him, hit his leg just above the knee, and practically chopped it in half. Hot blood splattered his face. The limb buckled, and when the man went down, pitching forward, Myrddin drove the point of his blade into his back and gave it a savage twist to make sure he wouldn't rise again.

The other attacker swung a spiked mace toward Octavian's head. The force of the blow would have shattered the thin arm the lad had raised to protect himself, but instead, the weapon bounced off a translucent blue dome around Octavian's head. Reacting quickly, Octavian took advantage of his enemy's surprise and hesitation, aiming a bolt of magical energy at his chest and sending him sprawling on his back. Without hesitation, Octavian picked up that cursed dagger, leaped, and stabbed the man through the throat.

Beyond the tatters of their collapsing tent, men hollered and ran in a flickering parade of light and shadow. Myrddin grasped Octavian's elbow, hauled him to his feet, and pulled him through the ruined entrance to the tent. Outside, the rest of their company fought their adversaries. From somewhere Myrddin couldn't see, Dirk's arrows dropped man after man. The Beasley brothers, side by side, held their own against four enemies. Danno faced two warriors, and at least half a dozen more approached from beyond the light of the campfires, ready to overwhelm them. Their horses' breath fogged the air off to the left as the animals whinnied and pulled against their tethers. Myrddin shoved Octavian behind him and held his sword in both hands, ready to meet the attack he knew would come.

"Stay beside me," Myrddin said to Octavian. "No debate. We stand a better chance of surviving this if we face it together."

Octavian nodded and raised his dagger as two men sprinted toward them. Before the pair made it within range of Myrddin's sword, Octavian threw his blade and struck one of them in the gut, a lucky blow that found purchase between the man's breastplate and cuirass.

The enemy dropped to his knees, arms wrapping around his stomach and steam rising from his wound. Just as Myrddin raised his weapon to meet the adversary rushing him with a large ax, Octavian sprinted forward and kicked the kneeling enemy hard beneath the chin. His head flew back, and a cloud of snow rose around him as he fell.

Myrddin's enemy made a loud, guttural sound at the loss of his comrade and bared his teeth as he doubled his efforts, hacking down at Myrddin's head, swinging at his belly, and chopping at his legs with so much speed Myrddin barely managed to deflect the savage blows. "You don't steal from the Crooked Teeth without paying, you bastard!" he cried. "You sorry sons of whores are going to regret fucking with us!"

The edge of the ax scraped along the side of Myrddin's sword, and when it reached the point, the man pulled back and swung, hitting Myrddin in the side of the arm and cutting through to the bone. Myrddin screamed at the pain as his blood flowed in a sheet over his hand. The wound prevented him from hoisting his two-handed sword, leaving him defenseless. In an effort to save himself from the ax falling fast toward his head, he dropped to a crouch and kicked at his enemy's ankles. The man bounced to avoid his attack, and Myrddin scuttled backward, his useless sword carving a furrow in the snow as the axman raised his weapon to finish him. Myrddin watched the man's face, his eyes, waiting to dodge until the last moment, hoping to throw his adversary off-balance, but holding little hope he'd survive the next strike. Without his armor, he had no way to deflect the strike he knew would be coming.

The man raised the ax over his head, holding it in both hands, ready to put all his strength into what would probably be a deadly strike. Just as he began to arch the weapon downward, his eyes went wide, his mouth fell open, and his tongue lolled out from between his lips. He dropped the ax to clutch at his throat as he made awful, gurgling noises and spittle flew from his mouth. A red ribbon bisected his neck, widening into a deep gash that poured blood until he collapsed, facedown, in the fouled snow. When the larger man fell, Octavian stood behind him, pale, covered in blood, blood dripping from his goddess-damned dagger. Octavian kicked the axman's body aside and offered Myrddin a hand to haul him to his feet.

His gaze darted to Myrddin's bleeding arm, and Octavian stowed his blade in his belt and closed a hand over Myrddin's wound. As the throbbing pain in Myrddin's arm numbed, Octavian grew whiter and whiter, his lips turning bluish gray and his eyes fluttering.

"Stop," Myrddin grunted past the intoxicating sensation of Octavian's essence flowing into him, mending his torn flesh and renewing his energy. Maybe the magic was to blame, but Myrddin felt larger, stronger, and faster. Indestructible. But the better he felt—better than he had since he'd been an idealistic eighteen-year-old—the worse Octavian looked. "There's still fighting to do, lad. Don't waste your energy on me."

"Strategic move," Octavian panted through lips as white as his waxen face. "Need your sword." He canted his head to the left, toward another pair of men running in their direction.

An arrow struck one of the men in the temple, killing him instantly, and with Octavian's magic singing in his veins, lighting his flesh on fire, Myrddin had little trouble with the other, cutting him down before he even heaved for breath. Goddesses, his sword felt lighter than a twig as he swung it, vanquishing the man he faced before sprinting to assist Danno and practically cutting the man he struggled against in half at the waist.

With a triumphant laugh, Myrddin watched the Beasley brothers overwhelm the men they faced as Dirk emerged from the shadows beyond the campfires. Turning, scanning for enemies and finding none, Myrddin saw Octavian on his knees clutching his head in both hands. Myrddin sprinted in his direction, but skidded to a stop before reaching him. Octavian didn't want his assistance—he'd made that plain. All Myrddin wanted to do was pull the young man into his arms and hold him, shield him from all this ugliness, but Octavian didn't want that, and so Myrddin held back as Octavian staggered to his feet, tripped over them when he tried to take a step, and landed back on the ground. Goddesses, it hurt not to help him, even offer him a hand up, especially after Octavian had saved his life. He had fought with honor and valor; no one could deny that now. Finally he steadied himself and walked slowly into the circle of men gathered around the fires, his chin held high, belying the pallor of his skin and the dark crescents below his eyes. When he turned to face them, the flames outlined him in glowing orange.

"Does anyone need healing?" Octavian asked. Ted Beasley limped up to him, blood oozing from between the fingers he pressed to his thigh, and the two men sat down in the snow. A warmth that had nothing to do with magic or victory spread through Myrddin's chest as

Octavian laid his glowing hands over the man's wound, while the other Beasley brother looked down on him with grudging acceptance. One way or another, this Octavian, this bloody young bastard, would fight his way into their ranks, and for some reason, that made Myrddin happy.

Chapter
Four

OCTAVIAN STRUGGLED to still the trembling of his legs as he stood at the center of their company. After the fight and the healing he'd done, his limbs felt like jelly, and all he wanted to do was curl in a ball and sleep for days, but he couldn't let the others see his weakness. They still saw him as a liability, and collapsing after a battle would prove the frailty they wanted so badly to find in him. He wouldn't do it, even if nothing but willpower kept him on his feet. "We need to go after the Crooked Tooth company. Eliminate them."

Predictably, Eric Beasley shouted, "You're bleeding mad!"

Gesturing toward the still body covered in a scrap of torn canvas—Octavian had been unable to heal the deep gash across Robere's torso and he'd died slowly and in pain—he said, "Don't you even want to avenge your comrade?"

Ted Beasley scowled as he jutted his chin toward the corpse. "What in the Shades' do I care about 'im?"

Octavian clenched his fists in an effort to keep his shock and affront from streaming out of his mouth in a string of obscenities. He bit the inside of his cheek until he tasted blood; he hadn't been overly fond of Robere either, but he couldn't dismiss the man's life as worthless. After shutting his eyes for a moment and taking a deep breath, he met Ted Beasley's gaze. "And would you be so indifferent if I had been killed tonight?"

The mercenary barked out what might have been a laugh. "I'd care even less if it'd been you, boy."

Well, at least he knew where he stood. "The lives of your companions aside, we must deal with this threat. If we let this attack go unpunished, we'll be in danger any time we do work in this territory.

We'll have to watch our backs even passing through here. We should eliminate the threat so we'll be safe. Besides, can you imagine the benefit to our reputations if it's known that we not only would not stand for intimidation from the Teeth, but were the ones to destroy them? It would mean more lucrative jobs, as well as fewer men bothering with us. It might even mean we could get some quality recruits to join our company."

As Octavian had expected, the subtle insult went over the brothers' heads. He couldn't quite shake off the dialogue of the parlors of the wealthy, where what went unsaid often meant more, but it would not serve him among men like these. "To be plain, if we do nothing, we'll be seen as cowards at the mercy of the Teeth. If we move against them and succeed, we'll earn both glory and gold in the long run.

"It will be a risk, and it will take courage," Octavian persisted, looking into the faces of the five men crouched around the sputtering fire. The Beasleys rolled their eyes and shook their heads. Danno stared dumbly as if struggling to understand the debate. Dirk had apparently found something in urgent need of his attention on his glove, and Myrddin gazed at Octavian with something Octavian could only interpret as pity. He was not a child struggling to demonstrate a new skill, and being viewed as one incensed him. Myrddin looked like he was waiting sadly for Octavian to fall and skin his knee. Surely Myrddin, out of them all, would appreciate the validity of his words. Why wouldn't the older soldier add his voice to Octavian's in favor of going after their enemies? Then Octavian realized—he'd asked, demanded, even, that Myrddin not offer his assistance. The man was only complying with his wishes, and Octavian was on his own.

Since logical strategy and honor clearly would not sway these men, Octavian abandoned all attempts at diplomacy. He'd speak their language, give them one final chance, and if they wouldn't stand with him, then he'd find worthier allies. "Fine. Sit here on your asses, cowering, waiting for the rest of the Crooked Tooth company to finish the job. Surely you can see that they'll be even thirstier for vengeance after this last failed attempt. We're now a greater threat to them than we were before, and any company worth a damn will want to eliminate such a threat. Tiptoe through this territory like meek servants trying to go unnoticed, or send these men a message that we're not the kind of men to trifle with. It's a simple choice: hunter or prey. Do you want to be at the top of the heap, or begging scraps at the bottom? I know which I choose. For me, there's no choice at all. I won't be intimidated or pushed around. If you are the kind of men to accept that treatment, I don't want you beside me."

Without waiting for a response, Octavian turned in the direction of his ruined tent. He hadn't gone more than five paces before Eric Beasley cleared his throat. Octavian didn't glance over his shoulder again until the other man spoke.

"Supposing we'd like to have the Teeth off our backs… just what are you proposing? That the six of us go after the dozens of men the Teeth got? That'd be killing ourselves."

Octavian turned slowly on the ball of his foot. He still felt weak, and the illusion of strength and fortitude he wove for the others drained him, but he had to keep it up. Lifting his chin and lowering his brows, he took three slow, deliberate steps toward them. "I am not a fool, and I have no wish to meet the goddesses just yet. I do not speak without having considered my words. I know our small group cannot defeat the Teeth on our own. Tell me: Who is the second-strongest company in this region?"

Myrddin scratched his whiskers. "That would be the Bitter Tide. They operate a little farther north than the Teeth, but much of the territory overlaps."

Octavian walked over to Myrddin and flopped down on the frosty ground beside him. Goddesses, it felt good to sit down, better than he'd ever imagined it could to take the weight off his feet and legs. Just beyond the light of their fire, the bodies of their enemies littered the ground, dark against the snow, already beginning to disappear beneath the drift as the wind whipped through the camp. Octavian bunched his shoulders up in a vain attempt to shield his ears and face from the frigid air as he turned toward Myrddin. "Tell me about this company."

All of them moved closer to the fire until they sat almost shoulder to shoulder against the increasing cold, leaning in until their drooped heads and rounded shoulders formed a dome over the flames. It did little to shield Octavian from the savage northern wind. For a moment, Octavian recalled how he'd felt sleeping next to Myrddin in their tent: safe, protected, warm for the first damned time since early autumn, content. He couldn't remember the last time he'd fallen asleep so fast, without lying awake for hours and parsing and ordering his thoughts, trying to shove them into neat, labeled boxes until they made some sort of sense, trying to keep the lids on those boxes shut so his doubts wouldn't spill out and litter his careful plans and aspirations with meaningless debris. There, lying close to the other man, absorbing the heat coming from his body and feeling his soft breath in his hair, Octavian's mind had been oddly quiet. Later, when he had the luxury, he'd need to try to determine the cause of that serenity, since it was likely false. Now, he had to concentrate on his plan to bring down the Crooked Tooth company. If he could achieve that victory, he'd climb several rungs up the ladder toward whatever goal waited at the top.

Octavian scooted a little closer to Myrddin as the other mercenary spoke and poked at the embers of the fire with a stick. A font of sparks spiraled up into the dark sky. "Don't know what I can tell you about the Tide, lad. They're a fair-sized group made up mostly of men who sailed together until the Emiri seafarers made raiding along the southern coast more trouble than it was worth. They still have some ships, but now they keep to the northern parts of the river."

Octavian tucked his numbing fingers into his armpits. "Are they honorable men?"

Myrddin chuckled. "They're mercenaries. Same as we are."

Octavian's sigh of frustration came in a thick, white curl. "Yes, of course. But not all mercenaries are cut from the same cloth. Are the men of the Bitter Tide the sort to take coin to escort a wealthy patron or join a just battle, or are they men without honor?"

"You're a damned fool, boy, and you need to get back on your mother's teat if you think mercenaries have honor. We do the work we're paid to do. We don't ask questions, and we don't judge. If you have a chance in the Shades' of making it in this line of work, that's the first thing you need to learn. We don't have the luxury of deciding which jobs offend our delicate sensibilities." Ted Beasley spat into the fire.

Octavian had no intention of explaining to this cur that he had a line he would not cross for any amount of gold. If he attained riches and glory, he'd do it without sacrificing the things that made him Octavian. He'd succeed as himself or not at all, but since the opinions of the Beasley brothers mattered little to him, he didn't waste his energy trying to convince them. It would likely be a futile attempt, anyway. He turned to Myrddin and held his gaze as the dwindling firelight carved deep furrows from the lines on the man's face, making him look older than he did in daylight. "Let me be plain. Are they the kind of men who would kill a farmer and rape his wife and children without asking questions? Or are they the kind of men who would turn from such an idea in horror?"

"If they're the second sort, they're fools," Ted Beasley said.

Ignoring him, Octavian concentrated on Myrddin's pale eyes. He'd noticed the other man knit his brows and wince when he'd described his vile scenario, and it gave water to the small seed of hope within him that not all men would do anything for coin. He'd known he saw something decent in Myrddin the night he'd chosen to follow him over his former associate. It pleased Octavian that his instincts had been right as he urged the other man to answer.

Myrddin scraped his upper teeth along his lower lip. "The Tide… I would say they are not cruel. They're hardly His Majesty's knights, but villagers don't hide their wives and daughters when the men come into town, not like they do when they see the Teeth coming. As for what jobs they would take… I don't think they'd take the one you described, not unless the coin was too good to resist. The Teeth, on the other hand, would likely do it for free."

"There is honor among mercenaries," Octavian said softly, more to reassure himself. "Myrddin, please. Tell me everything you know about the leader of the Bitter Tide. Tell me any detail you remember about him, down to the smallest."

OCTAVIAN ROSE'S Journal

My hands are still trembling as I write tonight, and ink is speckling my page as it drizzles from my quill. We have salvaged all we could after the ambush from the Crooked Teeth, and I am in a cobbled-together tent along with Myrddin and Dirk. We have managed to construct something to keep the elements at bay, but I am cold. I am so tired of being cold. The others are asleep, and though every fiber in my body cries out to surrender to unconsciousness, I am restless. I cannot find any peace until I figure out my current conundrum: how to sway the leader of the Bitter Tide mercenaries to my banner.

Before I took up my pen and inkwell, I lay awake, going over and over the details I learned from Myrddin in my mind. I can only hope listing them on this page will allow me some new insight into their significance. I have learned Julien Cassis, a former pirate raider, abandoned the southern shores of our kingdom when competition from the Emiri became too great. By all accounts, the man despises the seafaring race. Would mutual hatred for the Emiri people give me the bond I need to earn this man's assistance? But I have never laid eyes on an Emiri, and I do not hate them. Would feigning such disdain for a people I know nothing about diminish me, make me less Octavian? Or would it simply be a means to an end, a harmless ruse? I cannot help but to think the former rather than the latter. Pretended hatred—hatred of any kind—seems to me like a slow-acting poison, and it is not something I'm eager to take into myself.

Myrddin told me of the sea captain's long, dark hair and love of jewelry. That speaks of vanity, a vice from which I am not immune. Others see my beauty and assume frailty, and yet I would not have it gone. I would never say so beyond these pages, but I enjoy being admired. I enjoy the smiles of those who find me pleasing. Though I am young, I know this beauty will fade, and I wish to enjoy it while it lasts. Perhaps I have this in common with Captain Julien. I would prefer to appeal to his appreciation of beauty than to his abhorrence of an entire race of people. I wonder if he appreciates the beauty of men. Myrddin surely does, but I cannot allow that to distract me now, as much as I might like to lose myself in such contemplation. Truth be told, if I had the privacy of my own quarters, I might like to imagine it in all its vivid glory.

Captain Julien is loyal to the men who served with him at sea. He wants to see them taken care of, and this I can respect. He is not like the Beasley brothers, but akin to Myrddin and Dirk, who view each other as family, along with the men who fight beside them. Perhaps my strategy should be to appeal to the advantage to his men—how eliminating the Teeth will benefit his followers.

In summary, I shall be dealing with a man who resents his livelihood being stolen, one who can appreciate aesthetic appeal, and one who values those who fight beneath his banner. Clearly, Captain Julien is a self-made man, a man who has forged his path outside the confines of societal expectation, and we have this in common. I think I have figured out how to deal with him, and now I can rest, but still my mind spins like the blades of a windmill in a gale....

I still have so many doubts, and no confidant beyond these pages. Surely even the greatest and bravest of men entertain insecurities, wonder if their decisions are for the best. I am young and untested, and I know I have much to learn, but I have nowhere I can turn for advice. I would never say so aloud, not when the others seek so desperately for a chink in my armor, but I cannot help but wish for someone I could trust… someone I could be weak and wavering in front of without fear of being exploited. This act, the hiding of any imperfection under layers of feigned strength and stoicism, is more tiring than the fighting and marching. But I cannot help but fear any show of vulnerability will be an excuse for these men to drive me from their company, and so I must carry on pretending to be something more—and less—than a man.

Why did being within Myrddin's arms grant me peace? Why, even now, do I crave so desperately to be wrapped within his strong limbs? Goddesses, perhaps I just want to be warm, accepted, and valued in the way I always desired from my father. I must not let that coldhearted bastard influence my decisions, yet I cannot help the longing I feel to lie against Myrddin. He is good and honorable, and he deserves better than to be a substitute for the love I never received from my family. Still, the night is cold and the wind is vicious, and might my warmth be so unwelcome? It is only practicality, is it not? Perhaps I shall try to lie next to him, in nothing more than the hope that I can get some sleep before I face the master of the Bitter Tide on the morrow. I will need every advantage I can get, for if he refuses me, all is lost, and I, and the rest of the men who fight beside me, can do nothing but wait for the Crooked Teeth to exact their vengeance. And I doubt, and I pray to the goddesses I shall speak the right words.

I just want to satisfy my basic needs and spend a night without shivering until my muscles cramp. That's all. It's a strategic decision, to go where I can rest best before facing Captain Julien. I will need my wits about me upon the morrow, and so I'll lie down next to Myrddin, wrap the blankets around our bodies, and hope he won't turn me away.

Chapter Five

RATHER THAN turning him away, Myrddin had wrapped his thick, solid arms around Octavian's waist when he'd slinked beneath his blankets, clutching him close as he buried his face into the crook of Octavian's neck and wetted Octavian's skin with his deep breaths. The warmth rising from Myrddin enveloped Octavian, made him feel safe and comforted until he fell asleep with his nose burrowed into the man's unruly blond curls.

Sleeping there, sheltered in those strong arms and wrapped in the sweet, earthy scent of the man, made it hard for Octavian to rise when the stark winter sunlight penetrated the walls of their makeshift shelter. He blinked at the stinging radiance and nestled his face against Myrddin's chest, pulling the blanket past his brows to shut out the light. Goddesses, he could lie forever like this, his muscles limp as bowed blades of grass and his mind quiet as the frozen landscape when the wind paused. Why this contentment? It was false. He had a job to do, and a plan to succeed in it. Rubbing a hand down his face, massaging his eyes with his thumb and finger, Octavian rolled to his back, bunching the blankets around his neck to stave off the cold. Beside him, Myrddin murmured and scratched his balls. Before waking, he reached for Octavian, closing his hands behind Octavian's back and pulling Octavian's throat to his lips.

"Stay. Just a few more moments."

A few moments more warmth, free from the threat of the Teeth, the daunting task ahead, and all the fears and doubts flapping around his mind like bats in an old temple proved too much to resist. Octavian released the tension from his neck and let his forehead lean against Myrddin's. He couldn't remember the last time his back and shoulders had felt so blessedly free from aches and cramps. It would have been so easy to return to slumber and sleep the day away. "Only a few."

"Mmm." Myrddin wriggled closer, pressing their bellies flush and rubbing his whiskers against Octavian's cheek. "Warm. Smell so good." The man was clearly still ensnared in some dream, Octavian's body a substitute for the memory or fantasy playing out in his sleeping mind. Octavian wasn't bothered. For once he was comfortable, and he hardly resented the other man's confusion. Still, he couldn't help wonder who had put the shy smile on Myrddin's face and the pinched pink color across his cheekbones and the bridge of his nose. He could imagine how that flushed skin would feel beneath his lips.

"Sweet and soft. Octavian…."

Goddesses. Octavian bolted up, threw the coverings aside, and reached for his boots. After pulling them on and wrapping his cloak around his shoulders, he slapped the torn square of canvas serving as their door and stepped out into the sharp light and cutting cold of the morning. Huffing out a thick cloud, he rubbed his arms. What was going on in his head? First, he'd been jealous of whoever he'd imagined Myrddin dreaming of, and then, when Myrddin uttered his name, he just wanted to run, could no longer bear the man's skin touching his. Was that the reason Myrddin had been his advocate? In the hopes of securing himself a traveling bed warmer? Surely he'd been more genteel about his intentions than the Beasley brothers, but did it matter?

It didn't, Octavian decided. To the Shades' with all of them. He wouldn't honor Myrddin's cruel deception by letting it hurt him. He had plans, and nothing else mattered. He didn't care if the rest of them saw him as nothing more than something pretty to fondle. They'd learn otherwise soon enough. Reaching beneath his cloak, Octavian ran his fingertips along the hilt of his dagger. No matter how cold the weather got, the metal always seemed warm against his skin. Not for the first time, he wished his assassin had taken him along. But wishes were as foolish and useless as dreams, and that assassin hadn't cared any more for him than Myrddin and the others—but at least he'd been honest about his intentions.

He would not pity himself; he'd try harder. He'd prevail on his own if no one stood at his back. At least he wouldn't be foolish enough to misplace his trust again. Without speaking a word to anyone, Octavian practiced the words he would say to the Bitter Tide leader in his mind as he ate the beans and bacon Dirk cooked. Then they broke camp, packed up, and rode southeast until they almost reached the river's edge.

The Bitter Tide stronghold consisted of a few dozen buildings huddled around a deep, narrow cove. All consisted of planks and shingles warped and washed pale by the constant rain and mist coming off the river. Small and square, the huts melded almost seamlessly against the bleached bank, the pale rushes, and the stunted, twisting trees growing among them. Snow blanketed the mossy roofs and twisting lanes serving as streets, save where it had been ground into mud by the feet of men and horses. Nothing broke the monotony of dirty white and leached-out brown. The river in the distance reflected the mottled gray sky. Beyond the drape of ice around the riverbank, about half a dozen ships, grayish tan to match the buildings, bobbed on the lazy waves. Everything smelled waterlogged: mold and wet soil. Aside from the thin streaks of smoke rising from the crooked chimneys, the settlement stood so still Octavian wondered if it had been abandoned by living souls.

Their party reined their horses to a stop at the edge of the knoll overlooking the village. Octavian swung his leg over his mount's haunches and landed lightly in the frozen grass. A moment later, Myrddin dismounted and joined him, looking out over the cluster of muted hovels. He patted Octavian's shoulder, and Octavian swallowed down his flinch and shudder as he remembered how badly he'd misjudged this man. He reminded himself he had no one to blame for that mistake but himself.

"Shall we, then?" Myrddin asked, raising his brows into his hairline.

Octavian no longer trusted him; he'd been naïve to do so in the first place. Now, he didn't know if Myrddin's presence would help or hinder his goals. He couldn't say for certain which Myrddin intended, or what his true motives might be. "This was my idea. I'll go myself."

"What, alone? There are dozens of men down there."

Octavian took long, quick steps toward the path leading into the settlement. He couldn't look at Myrddin when he knew what Myrddin had wanted from him all along, so he hurried toward the trail. Nothing in the Bitter Tide camp could be worse than looking at the older mercenary who he'd thought believed in him. When Myrddin grasped his elbow, Octavian wrenched his arm away and spun to face him. "What?"

"You shouldn't go by yourself." Myrddin reached his big hand toward Octavian's shoulder, but Octavian twisted his waist to avoid the contact.

"No one else has my interests at heart."

Myrddin reached for him again, and Octavian swatted his hand away. Taking a step back, eyes wide with probably pretended hurt, Myrddin said, "I do. I thought you knew that."

Though Octavian wanted to smack that false-innocent look from the mercenary's face, yell at him and accuse him, he schooled his features into indifference. "Please, do not touch me."

"Octavian, you could be in danger. Let me come with you."

"No," Octavian said through teeth clenched so tight he worried they'd crack. "I do not want you. I would rather go alone."

"I—Very well." Myrddin took a few steps backward and rested his hand on his horse's neck. Without looking back, Octavian picked his way down the path that was in itself a defense to the settlement. Between the steep slope of the narrow trail, the slippery rime on the ground, and the sharp rocks he had to navigate around carefully, it took him nearly an hour to reach the bottom of the hill and the edge of the camp. Aside from some water birds calling out as they glided in lazy circles above the river, the camp stood silent.

Last night in his tent, Octavian had felt confident, sure he'd figured out the answer to his conundrum, sure he'd succeed. Now, standing in this forsaken place with only the lonely cries of the birds to remind him anything living existed but him, he was afraid. But he had to persevere; it was either that or wait for the Crooked Teeth to kill him while he slept. It was either that or continue to languish in obscurity among men who only grudgingly tolerated his presence. Octavian continued cautiously past the two narrow buildings standing sentry on either side of the path, even though he had no idea where to seek Julien Cassis. The creak of a bow being drawn, loud in the hush over the camp, followed the distinct swish and snick of a pair of swords being pulled from their scabbards. Octavian pushed his shoulders back and straightened his spine as a trio of men came around the corner of the building on the left, the points of two swords and an arrow aimed directly at him.

Octavian pushed his cloak open to show the men his empty hands. Before they could ask his business, he said, in as clear and confident a voice as he could muster, "My name is Octavian Rose. I have come to speak with your leader, Captain Julien Cassis."

One of the swordsmen, a small, wiry man in dark leather trousers and a matching doublet, with a red scarf holding his black hair out of his sharp, brown eyes, asked, "What business do you have with the captain?"

"That is between him and me," Octavian said. "Will you tell me where I can find him?"

The man holding the other sword, a portly, bald fellow with a gnarled brown beard, sneered, revealing a few crooked, rotting teeth. "We could do that, or I can put my sword through your belly, toss your carcass in the river, and go back to gettin' drunk. Give me one reason why I should waste my time, or the captain's, on you."

"I have a proposal." Octavian refused to shrink away from the man's cruel glare or horrible breath, refused to look anywhere but directly at his close-set, bloodshot eyes. "I know of a way for all of us to make a great deal of money, and I think your leader may be interested."

The archer, who wore a hooded shirt that obscured most of his face, lowered his bow a few inches but didn't release the tension on the string. "You don't seem terribly impressive, friend."

"Looks can be deceiving." The blue glow Octavian summoned from his fingers burned bright against the oppressive gray of the overcast winter sky. "I ask only for the opportunity to speak with your captain. If he does not like what I have to say, he can decide what to do with me. If he does not like the sound of my plan, I'll leave and not trouble you further. After all, even my magic cannot hope to threaten your entire camp. What can be the harm of taking me to talk with him?"

"The boy has a fair point," the man in the red scarf said. "Jobs have been scarce since this goddess-damned cold set in. Jule might be keen on a chance to make some coin."

"Aye, or it might burn his ass that we bothered him with this instead of doing our damned job and guarding the entrance." The bearded man spat on the ground.

"I don't know," the archer said, lowering his weapon and replacing his arrow in the quiver at his back. He had a low, smooth voice, like aged wine, pleasing on the surface but complex in its subtle undertones, and the swath of skin visible beneath his hood looked clear, smooth, and golden. One corner of his shapely lips quirked up as he continued. "Jule might like this one."

The bearded man sheathed his sword at his hip and poked a chubby finger at the archer. "Well, if it turns out he gets his pants in a bunch at bein' disturbed by this nonsense, I'll be quick to tell him it was your idea, Sylvain."

"You do that." The archer smiled, but Octavian couldn't see if it reached his eyes. "And while you're at it, go back to guarding the entrance. I think I can handle escorting this man to Jule on my own, and goddesses forbid we leave the road unattended, what with everyone so eager to get into this camp."

He turned on his heel without waiting for their responses, and Octavian hurried to catch up. When they'd gone a short distance from the others, Octavian said, "Thank you."

Sylvain kept his gaze on the river in the distance as he shrugged. "It is no skin off my back. Truth told, I'm glad for an excuse to get away from those two. I think Jule only stations them at the entrance so he doesn't have to endure the stench."

Octavian chuckled along with him. "I guess I cannot blame him for that. I notice you don't speak like the others, not like a common sell-sword."

"Oh, Octavian Rose, there's nothing common about me."

"You speak like a noble, or at least a wealthy merchant," Octavian persisted.

"And so do you," Sylvain replied.

Octavian felt comfortable around the archer, as if he were having a conversation at a banquet at his father's manor, trying to read between the lines and find the treasure buried beneath layers and layers of pretty, polite words that conveyed so little. He had always been good at banter, at dealing both compliments and insults within the strict lines of so-called civilized society. To him, it had been the closest thing in life to a game, and he enjoyed it.

"Well, that's because there's nothing common about me either," he told Sylvain.

"Only a simpleton would assume otherwise," the archer said.

Octavian wanted to know more about the other man—where he had come from and what had led him here, but he would have to tread carefully. "Shall I take that to mean polite conversation is scarce here?"

Sylvain kept walking without glancing in Octavian's direction. "Scarce, but not nonexistent. You'll see that if Jule agrees to speak with you. Still, it is not unwelcome. Of course, pleasant things never are." He turned toward Octavian, and their gazes caught for a moment, though Octavian could see little more than the glitter of Sylvain's eyes in the shadows cast by his hood. "Ah. Here we are. If you'd like, I can wait outside while you talk to the captain and escort you back through the camp when you're finished."

"I would appreciate that." Octavian extended his hand, and Sylvain took it in a confident but not overwhelming grasp. "As long as I won't inconvenience you."

The archer, still clutching his hand, chuckled and said, "Hardly. A few more moments with… your pleasant conversation will be anything but a hardship."

"Then I shall look forward to it."

"As shall I." Sylvain crossed his arms and leaned a shoulder against a lintel of the porch. "I'll be waiting."

Octavian went up the stairs and knocked on the door of what looked for all the world like a simple cottage, like the home of a merchant or artisan, right down to the wreathes of winter berries hanging in front of the windows on either side of the threshold, the coarse rug in front of the door, and the cords of firewood stacked neatly in an iron box.

When his knock went unanswered, Octavian rapped on the door again.

"Oh, very well," said a deep, gravelly voice from inside. "I'd rather have you come inside than pound on my door all day."

This was it. Octavian took a breath deep into his chest and held it there as he twisted the blackened iron doorknob and stepped into the home. Shelves of books lined the walls of the sitting room he entered, and a small fire banished the cold and gloom. Furnishings—chairs, couches, and tables—cluttered the limited space, and books, dishes, scrolls, and wine bottles littered them. Bearskin rugs covered the plank floors, and the scent of something savory cooking wafted in from another room. It was nothing like Octavian had expected. Granted, some swords and axes hung from the walls, probably trophies, but it felt much more like a home than an armory. He couldn't afford to let that throw him off his game.

"My name is Octavian Rose, tam. I would speak with you." The lifeless eyes of a twirl-horn buck's head mounted above the hearth stared down. The resident of this house had spread a pair of pants to dry across the animal's antlers. A sapphire necklace encircled the poor beast's throat, the gems sparkling in the firelight. Octavian waited for a response, and when many moments passed without one, he curled his fingers and cleared his throat into his fist.

"Forgive my manners," said the man who rounded the corner holding a wooden spoon. "My name is Julien Cassis. I was just making a stew."

The man, like his home, defied everything Octavian had anticipated. He wore his simple white shirt untucked atop a pair of snug gray trousers, and his black hair with the streak of silver at his left temple pulled back into a knot at the crown of his skull. Though an old scar, healed to a silvery pink line, cut across his right eye from the outer edge of his brow to the corner of his nose, his expression promised hospitality. He indicated one of the upholstered benches, and Octavian carefully pushed the open books, charts, and what looked like recipes aside to make a place to sit down.

"It's been a while since I've had a guest. What can I do for you, Tam Octavian?" The lanky sea captain with the sun-kissed skin and ebony hair situated himself on a bench facing Octavian. Despite the lines the harsh sea light had carved in his skin and the severe angles of his face, he was a very appealing man, and clearly one who knew it. He bent to lean his elbows on his knees, his dark brown eyes locked on Octavian's. "I assume you have a good reason for interrupting my leisurely cooking."

"I do. I have a proposal for you."

"Go on, boy."

"I am no boy," Octavian said, "and I think you and your men should take this territory away from the Crooked Tooth company."

Julien laughed. "Is that what we should do?"

Realizing how arrogant he sounded, Octavian shifted his gaze to his boots as warmth rose in his cheeks and up his ears. "I realize I must sound pretentious to you, such a young and inexperienced man telling you how to conduct your business. I swear, that is not my intention. But why not? Would it not benefit your group to control this territory, to be rid of the Teeth, to take all the jobs they would receive?"

"Sure it would. You make it sound like such an easy task, young Octavian. I have to wonder what makes you think you can accomplish what has eluded our entire group these past few years."

"With only a few men, I have not only raided a Crooked Tooth camp, but survived an ambush. The Teeth are weak right now from the blows we have struck. It is time to act, to take them out once and for all."

"And what do you get out of this?" Julien asked.

"I get the security of traveling through this region unmolested. I get to know blackguards will not attack me in my camp. You, on the other hand, get control of this entire region. I stake no claim upon it, and I'll hand it over willingly in exchange for nothing more than safe passage when I come this way."

"Very generous of you, lad," Julien said. "By the confidence of your words, it barely sounds like you need our help. Why include the Bitter Tide if you're so assured you can be rid of the Teeth?"

Octavian locked his gaze with the captain's. "I may be young, but I am not a fool. My group cannot overcome the Teeth on its own. We don't have the numbers. I come to you because you are a man of honor, a man who, I believe, wants to protect everything he and his men have fought and bled to build. You and the men who follow you have suffered and strived to carve a place for yourselves, and I have no doubt you want to defend the home you have made. I want to help. I do not pretend my motives are altruistic. I would like to travel through this territory without the threat of the Teeth over my shoulder. I think we can aid each other. With everything you have built, I would assume this small risk would be worth taking to strengthen and sustain it."

"Small risk?" Julien asked, leaning in. "The Teeth are formidable. What do you propose?"

He was interested, receptive. At least he hadn't driven Octavian away, or worse. That was a good start, but Octavian still had to sway this man to trust in his plan. "Do you have a map of this area?"

"Aye." Captain Julien fetched a scroll and unfurled it across the table between them.

Octavian leaned over and pointed. "The Teeth have five main camps—here, here, here, and here. This one, we destroyed and looted.

Goddesses willing, the other four will be lightly guarded, since many of the Teeth will be out looking for me and my associates. With the element of surprise, we can take these camps."

"Goddesses willing." Julien shook his head, making the gold rings in his earlobes rattle. "Forgive me if I don't have much faith in the fickle bitches."

"Even so," Octavian persisted, "an opportunity like this is not going to present itself again anytime soon. The Teeth are away from their camps, looking for us, leaving them easy targets. If we split our forces into four groups, attack the camps simultaneously… we can pick off the stragglers along the road without much trouble afterwards."

"And what of the men in those camps?" the captain asked. "Are they to be slaughtered?"

Octavian smiled and shook his head. "Absorbed. By your company. I'll wager few of them will refuse. After all, they'll be doing the same work, just for a leader who controls a larger territory. To them, that will mean more jobs and more coin. They'll side with the victor, and they'll be at least as loyal to you as they were to the Teeth. What can the Teeth offer them that you cannot? Why would they refuse? You can double your force as well as the land you control."

"You don't think there's a possibility any of these men are loyal to their leader?"

"You have more experience in these matters than I do," Octavian said. "What do you think? It seems to me that it takes a very extraordinary leader, an extraordinary man, to make other men willing to die for his cause. Do you think the leader of the Teeth is that sort of man?"

"You… are much more clever than you look," Julien said slowly. "You understand men's natures in a way many twice your age never will."

"So you agree this plan could work?" Cautiously, Octavian let himself hope he might finally succeed, might finally set something significant in motion.

"And you ask for nothing in return?"

"Nothing but safe passage," Octavian said. "Maybe a friend, should I ever find myself in a position to need one and with the means to reciprocate the favor."

"Friends can be valuable." Captain Julien scratched the coarse black hair of his sideburns. "At least some friends."

"I will be a valuable ally to you one day."

"So you say, young Octavian. So you say. But this is a hefty risk you propose."

"Aye, it's a gamble. But when is there ever glory without a gamble?"

Julien looked up through his black fringe and met Octavian's gaze with narrowed eyes. He stared without blinking, lips scowling down, a deep crease between his brows, until Octavian feared he'd overstepped. In a few arrogant words, he'd estranged a potential ally, a man who even seemed to respect him, or at least had started to. His palms grew clammy and his heart raced and faltered, but he didn't blink or shy away from the captain's sharp glare. Appearing weak would only make things worse. After what felt like hours, Julien grinned wide and reached across the table to clap Octavian on the shoulder. "Aye, lad. Truer words were never said. But tell me this. With the information you've offered, what stops me and the rest of the Tide from taking the Tooth camps without your help?"

Octavian shrugged to veil his disappointment. He wanted a fair portion of the victory, wanted his name associated with the defeat of the Crooked Tooth company. Still—"I will benefit the same either way. The people who wish to kill me will be gone, and I will be safe. If you would rather attempt it without me, and the plan I've formulated, and the men who fight with me, who have faced the Teeth before, well, I suppose you'd be doing me a favor."

"Then perhaps I should thank you for your advice and send you on your way." The captain stood and waved his hand toward the door.

Growing desperate, Octavian got to his feet and wiped his sweaty hands down the sides of his trousers. "I think I—me and the men traveling with me—could benefit you."

Julien smiled and shook his head. "Octavian, you seem like a good lad, and a smart one. Actually, I kind of like you. But I did not get where I am by offering charity or taking in wayward boys. It may sound cold, and perhaps it is, but the fact is, you have nothing to offer me but the promise of some vague favor in the distant future. That isn't enough reward for me to take a risk on you."

"But you have nothing to lose either." Octavian tried to keep the pleading out of his tone. If Julien refused him, he'd not only lose the chance to make his name conquering the Teeth, he'd lose whatever scrap of respect the others held for him. The next time he proposed a plan, they wouldn't even consider it. He'd never live this failure down. He couldn't give up. "We aren't asking for territory, or even any more of the profits than we can loot and carry away. You'll have a few more capable fighters at your back, and if we die, you've lost nothing. If we live, you've lost nothing, and possibly gained something in the future."

Again, Captain Julien stared at him, and it felt to Octavian like his dark, sun-squinted eyes cut right to his core and pried the lid off the box where he hid his doubts and confusion. Octavian felt him sorting through the contents of that locked chest as if deciding how they weighed against the facets of Octavian he found promising, deciding which side of Octavian he should gamble on. Finally the captain blew out a sigh that ruffled his lips. He went to a sideboard along the wall, opened a door, pulled out a brown glass bottle, and dusted it off on his sleeve. After setting it on the table, he fetched two tin cups and poured a few splashes of brick red liquid into each glass. Pushing one toward Octavian, he said, "Sit down, lad—"

"Octavian."

"What?"

"Octavian. Captain, I walked into this camp alone, not sure if I would ever walk out again. Isn't that enough to earn me the right to be addressed, if not as a warrior, at least as a man?"

Julien took a deep swallow from his wine, and when he looked up, Octavian couldn't mistake the admiration on his face. "Aye, that it does, Octavian. The rest you still have to prove to me, however. If I find out you've… exaggerated your claims, or if you disappoint me, I'll be a very unhappy man."

Octavian fought to keep his expression serious when he wanted to grin and punch the air. He sat carefully on the edge of the bench facing the other man and picked up his cup. "Yes, Captain. I know you won't be disappointed."

"See that I'm not." Julien smoothed the map on the table between them. "Now, show me exactly what you propose."

Chapter Six

THE WATERY sun, little more than a yellowish smear against the gray sky, rose to its zenith as Myrddin and the others sat on the bank overlooking the Bitter Tide camp. By the time it began sliding into the west behind them, tinting the cloud cover with rose and gold and dragging the scant heat away with it, Danno and the Beasley brothers had grown restless. They paced and mumbled behind Myrddin, passing a wineskin while Dirk prowled back and forth at the edge of the cliff.

"Oh, I've had enough." Ted Beasley kicked a rock the size of an apple, sending it sailing only a few inches from Myrddin's left cheek. "It's been hours. Either your boy's dead down there, or the raiders have him bent over a barrel, taking turns."

Though he rarely lost his temper, something—either his worry over Octavian, the confusion over what had changed just as they'd started to become friends, or just the goddess-damned cold and damp sinking into his bones and making them ache like a bitch—made Myrddin snap. Gnashing his teeth, he hopped to his feet, turned, and drew his sword in a single motion, aiming the point at the other mercenary's throat. "Shut your foul mouth or I'll shut it for you. You didn't have the bleeding bollocks to go down there on your own."

"Because I'm not an idiot boy who belongs in his nursery sniffing his nanny's underpants. What's it to you, anyway? Why so bloody defensive? His ain't the only tight little ass along this riverbank. But I'm sure you know that firsthand."

His pulse thudding between his temples and his fists shaking with rage, Myrddin threw his sword into a tuft of bleached grass and raised his fists. "I'm tired of listening to you. Let's settle this like honorable men."

Ted spat on the ground. The last light of the setting sun glinted off steel as he drew a small dagger from inside his sleeve. "I don't know who the fuck you think you are, honorable tam, but I know what I am. I'm a mercenary, and I ain't ashamed of it." Eric Beasley moved to stand behind his brother's shoulder, his hand on the hilt of his blade.

The three men squared off, and just as they prepared to advance on each other, an arrow whizzed through the air and lodged in the thick, folded cuff of Ted's leather boot. Had it hit a hair to the left, it would have pierced his knee and done irreparable damage. Myrddin knew it was no accident. To his right, Dirk stood with another arrow nocked, his stance wide and his sharp gaze locked on the Beasleys. Without releasing his hold on his bow, he made a few quick motions with his fingers.

"And what's your dumb friend have to say?" Ted asked with a sneer.

Dirk's next arrow clipped off a chunk of Ted's greasy hair before skimming along the edge of Eric's gorget, opening a thin gash but inflicting no real injury. Eric looked more surprised than hurt as he lifted his fingers to the minor wound and scowled at the blood on his glove.

By the time Myrddin glanced from the Beasleys to Dirk, Dirk had already drawn a pair of arrows from his quiver and held them ready to fire. Myrddin arched his brows at the brothers. "Do you simple sons of whores need me to translate that for you?"

The Beasleys lifted their hands. Ted's dagger pinged off a slab of stone as it fell. Danno continued standing with his mouth hanging open and great gusts of fog puffing out, as he had during the entire exchange.

"Turn around and leave, if that's what you want," Myrddin said.

Dirk signed, *Good riddance.*

"Leave?" Eric snarled. "We signed on with the understanding there'd be some profit in it, and now, when it finally seems there will, you want us to leave?"

"So, you suddenly believe in Octavian's plan?" Myrddin asked.

"I couldn't give a rat's ass about that little shit stain," Eric said. "I'm here for the loot the Teeth are hoarding. I was promised a share of it, and I mean to have it."

Dirk made a few quick gestures, and Myrddin nodded. "He says there are no promises in this life, and this situation is no exception. We never guaranteed you or your brother anything beyond an even share of anything we earn doing what jobs we find. You have been paid for your swords, and fairly. But if you don't have the best interests of our group at heart, we can put an end to that arrangement. As Dirk says, one must grow accustomed to disappointment, for life is full of it."

"Don't be a dunce," Ted said. "All of us are better off together, at least until we take care of the Teeth. Strength in numbers and all that."

Myrddin bent to retrieve his sword, brushed the dead leaves and frozen mud off the blade, and replaced it on his back, his momentary flare of rage burned out. Though filthy and crude, the Beasleys could hold their own in a fight, and Ted spoke the truth. Maybe once Myrddin would have chosen idealism over survival, but that had been years ago, in another lifetime. "A fair point, I concede. But all of us means all of us. Octavian is one of us. If you want to continue working together, you'll stop dismissing and insulting him. Say what you want about me, but I won't have it."

Ted shook his head and chuckled. "Friend, you're too good a soldier to fall for a pretty face."

"What I think or do is nobody's affair but my own," Myrddin said. "If you want to be a part of this group, you'll show common decency to the men who fight beside you. All of them." To Myrddin slight surprise, Dirk nodded and lowered his bow.

"Right," Eric said, his face contorted as if the word caused him physical pain. "We'll do it your way, for now."

"Don't change the fact that it's been over half a day," Ted said. "Likely as not, those pirates ran him through and tossed him in the river. Can't see much point in waiting here longer. It'll be cold as the Shades' soon, and there's a little trading village to the north. We can find a tavern, warm beds, wenches and ale, if not work."

"Octavian isn't coming back?" Danno sounded like a child who couldn't comprehend the death of a puppy.

"I don't know." Myrddin looked down at the squat gray buildings huddled between the rocks. A heavy mist was rolling in from the river, cold as the grave and reeking of wormy damp. One by one, torches and lanterns appeared, burning only pitiful pinpricks in the blanket of fog. Damn it, he shouldn't have let Octavian go down there alone, no matter how much his insistence might have hurt the boy's pride. Wounded pride mended easier than wounded flesh. Myrddin found a perch on the edge of a stone and tried to discern movement in the shadows and vapor below, but the world seemed frozen, as still as a painting, with only the occasional, fleeting shift in the cords of mist. Awful images of Octavian beaten and bloody—or worse—flashed across his mind. Squeezing his eyes shut only made them more vivid, more gruesome. "Maybe we should go after him."

"Wait just a minute," Ted said. The sound of his voice made Myrddin want to squeeze the breath out of his throat. "I ain't risking my skin down there. I said from the beginning this was a stupid idea."

"Nobody asked you to go," Myrddin said, standing and brushing the snow from his backside. His ass was numb, and it added to his irritation. "Bleeding Shades."

Dirk caught his elbow and pulled him aside. *What's going on with you?* he signed. *You're acting like this is your first battle. Why so restless?*

Worried, Myrddin signed.

He made his choice, Dirk noted. *You offered to go with him. It isn't like you to get so emotional, to act without thinking things through. I don't like the effect this boy is having on you. If he comes back, and if we get rid of the threat of the Teeth, you need to send him on his way. He's no good for us—for you.*

"You're right," Myrddin admitted. Myrddin couldn't help wanting to protect Octavian, and Octavian didn't want protecting. For some reason, he no longer wanted much of anything from Myrddin, and it shouldn't matter…. Goddesses, he hadn't acted this way since he'd been younger than Octavian. "He's a distraction. He'd… we'd all probably be better off if he found a place with another company. Maybe if he's satisfactory in this battle, the Tide might take him. They're not the worst lot."

No. That would be a good compromise. If he comes back.

"I can always count on you to lift my mood, old friend." Myrddin feigned a smile until he could turn away and resume gazing into the camp as if he could will Octavian to materialize from the gloom.

"It's fucking cold," Ted complained. "And I'm out of wine. Can we at least light a fire?"

"There's no need for that." Octavian's voice, strong and cheerful, brought a grin to Myrddin's face that earned him a disapproving look from Dirk. "I have convinced Captain Julien Cassis to aid us against the Crooked Tooth company. We've spent the day hashing out a plan, and it's a good one. Jule, the captain, has invited all of us to spend the night in the Tide's camp. They're preparing the evening meal now, and they have beds for us and stables for our horses. Follow me. Jule showed me a path that isn't as steep, so it will be easier for the animals to make it down."

When all of them just stood staring, clearly shocked at Octavian's success, Myrddin laughed, genuinely amused. Goddesses, he had done it, and Myrddin was so proud his heart swelled. He'd gone down there alone and come back victorious. What would the Beasley brothers say about him now?

"What are you waiting for?" Octavian hopped from foot to foot, his excitement cracking his carefully schooled veneer, the one he thought made him look strong and capable. "Did you not hear me say the Tide are onboard? I think Jule is actually excited about the prospect. They're planning quite a feast. Come on!"

He pivoted on the ball of his foot and jogged toward a path off to the right, one carefully hidden between banks of stone. The others gathered up the horses and led them after him, into the heart of the Bitter Tide camp.

AFTER TAKING care of their mounts and stowing their belongings in the vacant cottage the Tide provided close to the docks, Myrddin, Dirk, Octavian, Danno, and the Beasleys ascended the slippery narrow path to the center of the settlement. Simple benches made from fat trees cleaved in half surrounded a bonfire. Dozens of men, flickering black silhouettes against the flames behind them, sat around drinking ale from the many barrels or taking food from the long tables set at the edge of the firelight. Though Myrddin felt anxious and acute, the way he always did around strangers, men he wasn't sure he could trust, Octavian strode confidently into the center of the clearing. Trailing behind, Myrddin watched him approach a tall, lanky man with a hood shadowing his face. The two of them clasped hands and stepped close. Myrddin couldn't see the newcomer's expression, but Octavian smiled genuinely, his eyes scrunched and sparkling. The two of them exchanged a few words before Octavian waved his hand to motion the rest of them forward.

As flushed and grinning as a boy who'd spent his first afternoon with a sweetheart, Octavian said, "Please, my friends, may I introduce you to Sylvain Damasca? If it wasn't for this man, I would have never passed through the front gate. Sylvain, this is Myrddin and Dirk, who graciously accepted me into their company. And this is Danno, a fine fighter and loyal. The Beasley brothers, Ted and Eric."

There was something catlike in this Sylvain's smirk as he regarded Myrddin and the others—a hint of mischief barely held in check. Since he didn't extend his hand, neither did Myrddin. Instead, he muttered a few obligatory words.

"What sort of man greets guests with a hood covering his face?" Ted asked. "Hiding something, tam?"

"Nothing that isn't mine to hide," Sylvain said in a smooth, slightly amused tone. "But if you'd like to look at me, I'll indulge you. I can hardly blame you, after all."

He swept the hood off his hair and let the dark cloth wrinkle around his neck and shoulders. Thick waves of dark hair spilled around a golden brown face with an aquiline nose and strong, pointed chin. The man had smooth skin and broad, shapely lips, but his eyes were truly arresting: almond-shaped, framed in long black lashes, and green enough that their color looked bright even in the heavy shadows, adding to his almost feline quality. From Octavian's soft gasp, Myrddin guessed this was the lad's first good look at his benefactor and that Octavian liked what he saw. Sylvain darted his eyes in Octavian's direction and then back so quickly Myrddin would have missed it had he blinked. He couldn't miss the man's wide smile or the flash of his straight, white teeth as he raised his chin a little higher and said, "Now, by the kind hospitality of our good captain, all of you are guests of the Bitter Tide this night. Let me offer you some refreshment."

As Sylvain turned, he brushed his fingertips almost imperceptibly down the back of Octavian's arm and elbow. Octavian, still smiling, fell into step beside him. Myrddin decided he didn't quite trust Sylvain and that he'd keep a close eye on him until he discerned what the man found so bloody entertaining all the time. He found the way Sylvain always seemed to be smiling at some joke only he understood disconcerting. His perpetual grin masked any true motivation his face might have shown, and Myrddin wondered if that might be the point.

At the tables, they filled their plates with roast venison, fish, root vegetables, bread, and cheese, and their cups with wine or ale—with the exception of Octavian, whom Sylvain took aside and said, "If your palate is as sophisticated as the rest of you, this swill will scorch your tongue. We can't have that. Come sit with me. I have a bottle of fierrine from a fine, old winery not far from here. I'd be happy to share it in exchange for your company."

Without hesitation, Octavian nodded and thanked him. The two of them found seats on the side of the clearing opposite the tables while Myrddin and Dirk took the first bench they found. Myrddin made sure he had a good view of Octavian and his new friend as they sat close, eating and passing Sylvain's bottle. Dirk nudged Myrddin in the ribs. *Jealous?*

Thankful for the silent language they shared, Myrddin signed, *Concerned. Poor lad doesn't seem to think that scoundrel may have ulterior motives. I'm afraid he may be too young to realize what the blackguard probably has in mind.*

Maybe he has the same in mind, Dirk noted. *Octavian is a healthy young man. Maybe he wants to do what all healthy young men enjoy. Why does that bother you?*

It doesn't, of course. Not if he knows what he's getting into.

Dirk rolled his eyes. *You're a sorry excuse for a liar, and I have never known you to be jealous. I say, let the pretty boy have him. I'll be glad to see him go. He makes you act like a petulant maiden, and honestly it's making me sick.*

Prickling, Myrddin bit his words out between his clenched teeth. "Go bugger yourself, Dirk. Do I judge you when you waste all the gold you earn on pockmarked whores who probably don't pleasure you half as much as you pleasure them? They should be paying you. Yet I say nothing, I…."

Myrddin trailed off as the appearance of Captain Julien Cassis caught his attention. The tales he'd heard of the good-looking raider hadn't been much exaggerated. The men around the fire cheered and clapped for their leader as he leaned down and said something close to Sylvain's left ear. Sylvain nodded and jutted his chin in Myrddin and Dirk's direction. The captain patted Octavian on the shoulder before approaching another group of men. Six or seven of them huddled around their leader before solemnly checking their weapons and disappearing into the shadows beyond the firelight. Gooseflesh rose on Myrddin's arms as he wondered if they could take the Bitter Tide at their word, or if they were being manipulated.

When Julien Cassis approached their bench, Myrddin set his food and drink on the table and stood to clasp the other man's hand. It would do him no favors to deny common courtesy to a man who had clearly earned it. "Captain, an honor to make your acquaintance. I have heard many mentions of your valor over the years."

Julien squinted as he held Myrddin's gaze. He seemed to decide Myrddin's words were sincere enough not to warrant a retort, and he smiled. "And I assume you are Myrddin and Dirk. Young Octavian speaks very highly of you."

Myrddin released the captain's hand and the two of them sat down. "The lad is young," Myrddin said, sparing a glance at Octavian and Sylvain. "He does not know any better than to see the good in all men."

Julien canted his head and knit his slender black brows. "Excuse me, but are we referring to the same young man? The Octavian Rose I met today is impressively astute, hardly naïve. If he has granted you trust and respect, you should be honored."

Had he? Myrddin had thought so once, but now he couldn't be sure. And if he was the profound judge of human nature Julien considered him, what did that say about Myrddin? "I only mean that he is young and full of lofty ideals, eager to see the good in the world. I'm sure he spoke well of all the men in our little group."

The captain's gaze moved slowly to the Beasley brothers as he said, "No, he didn't."

Since he could think of no response, Myrddin picked up his plate and tore a chunk of meat off with his teeth. After chewing it and swallowing, he said, "Octavian is delighted to have secured your aid. I can only hope what you say about his instincts is correct. I would hate to see him disappointed, and I won't see him harmed."

"Say what you mean," Julien hissed. "If I wanted hints and innuendo, I would talk to Sylvain. Do you have a problem with me or my people?"

Myrddin shook his head. "I mean no offense, but I have lived this long by mistrusting every man—especially every mercenary—until he proves otherwise. Surely you understand and have done the same. And

I have to wonder where you sent that group of men you spoke with a few moments ago. The ones who slipped off into the shadows."

"Ah." Julien offered him a lopsided smile and a wink. "Yes, that would look dubious to me as well. I sent those men to some of the inns, brothels, and taverns the Teeth are known to frequent. They'll casually plant rumors of your company being seen in the woods to the southwest and hopefully lure more of their companions away from the camps we plan to attack tomorrow night."

"A clever plan," Myrddin admitted.

"Young Octavian's," the captain said, looking across the snowy clearing with admiration. "He's rather special."

"Yes." Though he knew he shouldn't, that it would sound petty and was none of his concern, Myrddin couldn't resist asking, "And what about your Sylvain? He seems an interesting fellow."

Julien chuckled while watching the two young men fondly. "Interesting is putting it mildly. Sylvain is… Sylvain." He didn't seem inclined to offer more, and Myrddin worried pushing would make him appear desperate. He returned to his dinner, finding the hot, hearty fare welcome. A few moments passed before Julien patted him on the knee. "Enjoy the feast and diversions. Tomorrow, we'll solidify our plan and raid the Tooth camps when darkness falls. If we are all sharp, the next time we meet like this, it will be to celebrate our victory."

Myrddin and Dirk ate their fill. Most of the Bitter Tide men, though clearly hardened fighters, became friendly after a few mugs of ale. Some women of the type who normally populated such camps plied their trade at the edges of the light. When the feast concluded, the men gathered to wager a few coins on fist-fighting contests. At Dirk's insistence, Myrddin stripped off his armor and tried his luck. Though he left the match with a split lip and a bloody nose, he defeated the dark-skinned raider he faced and earned himself a few pieces of copper and a little more esteem in the eyes of the Tide. Ted Beasley didn't fare as well, and left his match with a swollen eye and a mouthful of dirty snow. As Myrddin held the cool rim of his cup against his torn mouth and nursed his ale, Octavian and Sylvain ignored the fights, ignored everything outside each other, talking as if they'd been friends for years. When the boxing lulled and the current champion, a wiry man with a long braid down his back and a patch over one eye, stood unchallenged, Sylvain nodded to Octavian and nudged him toward the center of the group.

Myrddin almost put a stop to it, and would have stood to intercept Octavian and talk some sense into him if Dirk had not stretched his arm across Myrddin's chest. Dirk was right, of course. Octavian had as much right to test his skill as anyone, and it was only a game. He didn't face any worse than some bumps and bruises, but Myrddin didn't want to see him suffer even that, or the humiliation of a quick loss. But maybe it was a lesson he needed to learn.

Sylvain handed Octavian the bottle they'd been passing, and Octavian tipped the bottom up to drain it. Then he handed it back, shrugged out of his ratty cloak, unlaced his doublet, and pulled his shirt over his head. Sylvain took his clothes and held them on his lap, but he refused to touch Octavian's dagger, and Octavian stowed it under the bench. Either the wine had warmed him or Octavian feared ruining his only shirt, but he stood bared to the waist, his skin smooth and white against the darkness, the definition of his muscles accentuated by the hard light against his youthful body, his hair and eyes contrasting sharply. Goddesses, he was beautiful. The shy way he grinned and looked over his shoulder at Sylvain for reassurance made Myrddin drain his goblet. He was such a dichotomy, this Octavian: young and uncertain, but wise; confident, even rash, but still full of doubt; full of hope, but cynical; timid, but determined to seem strong. His silken, unmarred skin above sinew hardened by toil and deprivation echoed his duality. One thing was certain—he was not a child, and Myrddin would never be able to think of him as anything but a man from this point on. A damned alluring man, one who sent tremors up Myrddin's spine even from several feet away. It had been a long time since Myrddin had felt so drawn to another man.

Subdued cheers went up from the men gathered as Octavian stepped onto the patch of mud churned up by the other fighters. He lifted his arms above his head, revealing the dark strips of hair of his underarms, and Sylvain pressed his fingers between his lips and whistled.

Going to bet on him? Dirk signed.

Myrddin shook his head, unable to tear his attention away from Octavian as he faced off with his opponent. Both men raised their fists, and he chewed his lower lip as he recalled his lessons with Octavian. How much had he learned? Enough to save himself from embarrassment?

The pirate with the braid feinted with his left hand but failed to distract Octavian, who blocked his right-handed blow with his forearm and even landed a jab to the man's ribs with his left. The hit knocked Octavian's adversary back, but he recovered quickly and kicked out at Octavian's shins. Octavian leaped up and back, avoiding his foot, and both men backed a few steps away before closing in on each other again. Octavian swung, but the other man dodged. The raider's next swing connected, splitting the skin over Octavian's eyebrow and making him stumble back as blood spilled into his eye. As the pirate pressed his advantage and struck with his other hand, Octavian dropped into a crouch to avoid his fist. Before rising, Octavian drove the heels of his hands into his opponent's stomach, landing three quick blows before the man doubled over, winded. Octavian swiped the blood out of his eye with the back of his hand and flicked it onto the ground.

Though an opportunistic man would have finished his enemy, Octavian stepped back and allowed the man to recover. A few of those watching hollered and clapped, and more coins changed hands as the odds shifted. If nothing else, Octavian hadn't embarrassed himself. Far from it. He raised his fists to protect his face as the raider jabbed at him with a series of punches. Conserving his energy as Myrddin had instructed, Octavian blocked and dodged, landing a hit here and there, while the other man wore himself out. Sweat poured from the man with the braid, and he heaved for breath as he whaled his fists wildly at Octavian, who avoided him with careful sidesteps, dips, and bends. The cords of muscle on his chest, arms, and belly bunched and stretched as he moved gracefully to avoid the pirate's blows. Probably out of sheer luck, the pirate managed to strike Octavian's ribs with the back of his hand, but as exhausted as he was, there was little force behind it. Wincing, Octavian kicked a roundhouse to the side and hit the other man in the hip, sending him skidding through the dirty snow. Surprisingly the man pushed himself up and staggered to his feet. Octavian held his hands up to indicate the fight was over; he had clearly won and didn't want to cause his opponent any more injury.

Some of the men watching applauded, while others—those who had lost coin on the match—groaned, but all agreed it had been a satisfying fight. Frozen breath and steam rose from Octavian as he turned to leave the arena, blood from the cut on his forehead leaving a speckled trail on the filthy snow. Thinking the matter was concluded, the lad never noticed the pirate picking up a round stone, skulking up behind him, and raising his fist. Myrddin ran, but before he could reach

Octavian, the other man struck him in the back of the skull. Octavian fell facedown, and the disgraced pirate raised the stone to finish the job. Before he could land a second blow, an arrow pierced his wrist. The rock fell to the ground. Myrddin paid little attention to Sylvain, who stood with his next arrow trained on his comrade, as he rushed to kneel next to Octavian. When he inspected the wound, he found a small cut on Octavian's scalp, some swelling around it, and a trickle of blood matting Octavian's hair. Carefully, mindful of the bumps and bruises on Octavian's torso, Myrddin turned him over and lifted his head and shoulders into his lap.

Octavian pinched his features against his pain. "Shades. I guess he didn't like me winning. Did you… ah. Did you bet on me? At least make a couple coppers?"

"Goddesses, you were wonderful," Myrddin said, as proud as if he'd won the fight himself.

"You… you didn't bet on me." That seemed to hurt him more than the rest of it put together. Octavian's eyelids fluttered and fell shut. His head drooped over Myrddin's arm.

At the edges of his vision, the more honorable members of the Tide dragged their disgraced companion out of the ring. Dirk, Danno, Julien, and Sylvain encircled Myrddin and Octavian.

"I can't express enough regret that a man under my banner would act so shamefully," Julien said. "He no longer has a place in the Bitter Tide."

Sylvain crouched down and laid his hand across Octavian's forehead. As much as Myrddin didn't want Sylvain touching Octavian, now was not the time to protest. "Will he be all right?"

"I don't know," Myrddin said. He never liked it when a man passed out; he couldn't know how the raider's blow had rattled Octavian's head. "Do you have a healer who can take a look at him?"

"Aye, I'll send him," Julien said.

Myrddin's blood boiled as he looked at Octavian's pale face and bluish lips. "Fucking Shades. I thought this was friendly competition."

"That man will pay for what he's done," Julien said. "I assure you I'll see to it. You see to your friend. Take him to his bed. Wait for the healer. I hate to state the obvious, but we have a small window of time to act against the Teeth. We cannot give them time to recover the damage your group did or bolster their ranks. If your Octavian isn't ready to fight tomorrow, we'll have to leave him behind. I know he will be disappointed if it comes to that, but I won't risk my people or this endeavor by waiting."

Nodding, Myrddin lifted Octavian's smaller body into his arms and held it tight against his chest. Bleeding Shades. Goddesses, he knew he'd spent many quiet moments imagining Octavian in his arms, but it had never been under these circumstances. As he made his way carefully along the icy path to the building they'd been offered, he could not have cared less about the Teeth, the Tide, Captain Julien, Sylvain, or any of the others. He just wanted Octavian to be all right, to not be reduced to a simpleton by the head wound he had suffered. He wanted to speak with him and repair whatever damage he'd inadvertently done to their growing friendship, and he wanted to spend cold nights along the road with Octavian sheltered in his arms, even if nothing ever happened between them. Goddesses, he didn't want to live in a world where a brilliant spirit like Octavian's could be stamped out by a bitter man who'd lost a silly fistfight and a rock, but only time would tell. For now, he could do nothing but put Octavian into bed, wait for the healer to arrive, and stay beside him until he either woke or didn't.

Chapter
Seven

OCTAVIAN WOKE to a feeling like someone driving a steel spike into his left eye socket. The pain pierced through his head to the back of his skull. Groaning, he lifted his hand to press it against the ache, but the throbbing agony only intensified until even his teeth vibrated. Tears leaked from the corners of his eyes as he drew his knees to his chest and curled into a ball. He had never hurt like this. Part of him worried he'd be sick all over whatever bed he found himself in, while the rest just wanted respite, or even a distraction, from the torture.

The supports beneath the thin, straw-filled mat he lay upon creaked as someone next to him shifted. The smell of the river in the distance reminded Octavian that he'd spent the night in the Bitter Tide camp, and slowly the events of the previous evening returned to him. He didn't recall getting into bed, though. The last thing he remembered was Myrddin crouching down and pulling him into his arms. He remembered looking up at Myrddin's blue eyes and concerned expression and knowing he'd be safe, that Myrddin would take care of him if he couldn't take care of himself. Even now, he felt safe knowing it was Myrddin lying next to him, because no matter how much Myrddin might want to, he would never take advantage of Octavian. He just wasn't that kind of man.

Most of the anger Octavian had felt had left him. He'd overreacted; he knew that. So what if Myrddin found him pleasing to look at? In retrospect, he didn't even know why he'd been so incensed, except that it had hurt to realize Myrddin was more interested in his beauty than his skill. Out of them all, he'd thought Myrddin recognized his potential. But it didn't matter. Soon enough, everyone would see what he could do. He would keep fighting until all of them saw it.

Octavian rolled to his back cautiously and waited for the renewed throbbing in his head to subside enough for him to focus on the planks and plaster ceiling above him. From the weak, grayish light seeping in from between the slats of the shutters, he assumed the sun hadn't fully risen yet. Along with the pain in his head, tender spots covered his ribs and belly, and his shoulder sockets felt stretched. Going back to sleep, giving his body as much time to recuperate as possible before the coming battle would probably be the best course of action, but he didn't think he'd get any more rest until he found something to drink. His mouth and throat felt as dry and gritty as if he'd been swallowing sand. With an effort, he pushed himself up on his elbows and closed his eyes until the darkened room stopped spinning around him.

The bed squeaked again, and a gentle hand stroked over the side of Octavian's hair. He leaned into the touch, taking comfort from it, as Myrddin asked, "How are you feeling? How's your head?"

"It hurts. Is there water?"

Myrddin grunted and handed Octavian a clay pitcher. The tepid water inside tasted sweeter than Sylvain's fine wine had the night before, and Octavian drank until he worried his belly would protest being filled so quickly. He handed it back to Myrddin and lowered his head carefully back onto the pillow. Nearby, someone—probably Dirk—snored softly. Myrddin, looking down on him, seemed fuzzy and bluish in the gloom, but his look of concern was unmistakable. "I wish to tell you something," Octavian said.

"Go on, then." Myrddin kept his voice soft, almost a whisper, probably to avoid waking anyone else who slept in the small cabin.

"Thank you for looking after me when I was hurt."

"I'd do the same for any man who fought beside me. You bested that bastard fairly, and what he did was reprehensible."

"Still…." The pain in his head made it hard for Octavian to choose the words to express himself, which he usually did quite well. Maybe now he would just have to say it simply, as the others did, without prettying it up. "The last thing I remember is you looking down at me, and because it was you, I knew I would be safe. It's been a long time since I felt that way, if I ever felt that way, and I want you to know I appreciate it."

"I… thought you were cross with me, Octavian, though I must admit I had no idea what I had done to offend you." Cautiously, as if worried Octavian might recoil, Myrddin stroked his knuckles down Octavian's temple, over the apple of his cheek, and around his chin. Octavian pressed his face against Myrddin's touch and draped his fingers over the back of Myrddin's hand. The poor man had been half-asleep and probably not aware of saying anything. He almost certainly didn't remember his half-conscious utterings. "I had thought we were becoming friends, and then out of nowhere, it seemed you could not stand the sight of me."

"I should apologize for that. I… I did not realize you appreciated me… appreciated me as a man."

Myrddin rubbed small circles over Octavian's throat with his fingertips, his touch soothing and invigorating at the same time. "I take it such appreciation is not welcome."

On a whim, driven by sheer desire and abandoning strategy, Octavian knitted his fingers into Myrddin's and lifted his hand to his lips to kiss the back. Myrddin gasped and squeezed his hand. "Your appreciation is not unwelcome. I just want to be valued for my contributions to the team, and not just for my beauty."

Myrddin rolled to his side, and Octavian turned to face him. There still wasn't much light, but Octavian could see the other man better. He lightly traced his nails along Myrddin's gold whiskers from his ear to his chin.

Myrddin smiled and moved a little closer to Octavian. Their bellies brushed together, and he wrapped an arm around Octavian's waist as he traced his lips across Octavian's forehead. "And why can't it be both? Why can't I find you both capable and incredibly beautiful… desirable? You are an amazing young man. You fought like a dream last night. I was so worried about you. I didn't want to lose you, and I… I have wanted to kiss you for some time. Maybe from the first time I saw you. May I kiss you, Octavian?"

His skin tingling, his belly tight, and a delicious tension across the base of his body, Octavian nodded and slid his fingers into Myrddin's hair to pull their faces together. When their lips touched, bursts of sensation erupted down Octavian's arms and legs, and gooseflesh sprung from his skin. Groaning, he curled against Myrddin and wrapped a leg over his hips. A gust of surprised breath filled his mouth, and Octavian parted his lips to draw more of it in. He thrust his hand beneath Myrddin's shirt and dug his fingers into the long, hard muscles of his back as Myrddin pushed his tongue, gently but insistently, between Octavian's teeth. Holding tight to Myrddin's taut, wonderful body, Octavian curled his tongue out to meet it. Myrddin took control of their kiss, and Octavian deferred to his experience, opening his lips wide for Myrddin to explore and just reveling in the sensation, the sweet taste of the other man and the dizzying fragrance of his skin and hair. Myrddin filled his perception, commandeered his every sense, until his pain, along with everything else but the two of them connecting, bled away.

When Myrddin pulled away to catch his breath, Octavian licked his lips for another taste of him. It had been much too long since he'd enjoyed another man, and Myrddin was nice-looking, and Octavian trusted him. From the movement of his tongue, hands, and hips, Octavian thought Myrddin knew how to pleasure another man. He could do far worse. "Are you interested in anything more than kissing?"

Myrddin pulled Octavian tight against him. When he spoke, his lips and breath warmed and moistened Octavian's neck, sending tremors down Octavian's body and making him tremble. "We're not alone. Dirk, Danno, and the goddess-damned Beasleys are here. But you… you want more?"

He wanted it so much he thought it would tear him apart. "Yes. Goddesses, yes. I want to touch you…." He wanted to wrap his hand, his lips, around the thick cock he felt pressing against his belly, rub his own cock against it, feel skin and soft hair catching against sweaty skin while he drank in the other man's desire.

"How?" Myrddin panted against his skin, pressing his fingers hard against the back of Octavian's neck. "How do you want me to touch you?"

Octavian dragged his lips over the coarse hair on Myrddin's neck and nipped at his earlobe before whispering into his ear. "I would put my mouth on you everywhere." He reached beneath Myrddin's shirt to graze the hard nub of his nipple. "Kiss you." He did, until both of them had to pull back to drink in air. "Open my legs for you, let you inside me. Would you—"

"Goddesses." Myrddin rutted against Octavian's belly, and Octavian cupped his asscheek to pull him closer as he returned his thrusts, his cock sliding nicely against the furrow in Myrddin's stomach muscles. "I'd give my right arm to be inside you. Octavian, I would never hurt you. I'd make you feel so good. Have you done that before?"

"Once." The sweet memory of his assassin mingled with the sweeter sensation of Myrddin rubbing against him, breathing hot and hard into his hair, hard and solid and warm next to him.

"Did you like it?" Myrddin pushed his shirt up and pulled their trousers down so their skin could connect. "Did you like a cock in your tight little body?" Octavian's leaking erection slid against Myrddin's belly as Myrddin's velvety length rubbed against his skin.

"Yes." Octavian's balls drew up, and his anus clenched. "Oh goddesses, yes."

Myrddin closed his big fist around both their cocks and pressed them together. "Come for me."

"Yes."

He stroked, hard, short, jerky movements, while Octavian threw his head back and rocked his hips up into Myrddin's hand. "Octavian…."

"Give me your mouth."

Myrddin pressed their faces together, and Octavian sucked his lower lip between his teeth as he pushed his throbbing dick against Myrddin's cock and into the tight tunnel of his hand. Blue and violet sparks that had nothing to do with his head wound fired behind Octavian's eyes. He bit into the flesh of Myrddin's mouth as his entire body wound tighter and tighter. "Yes. Yes, yes, yes."

Myrddin's whiskers scraped his skin, making his face feel warm and sensitive as Myrddin twisted his fist over the heads of their cocks. "Come for me, Octavian," he whispered, a harsh breath against Octavian's ear. "Do it now."

"Yes!" All the tension that had been building in him released in a torrent. He wanted to scream, but Myrddin caught his mouth and swallowed his cries, holding him close so he didn't break into pieces, grounding him against the certainty of his broad, strong body. "Goddesses, yes." He twitched and thrust until he drained himself and fell limp against Myrddin, the other man's seed coating his belly, the scent of it making his mouth water. Octavian pulled his fingers through a glob of Myrddin's come and brought his fingers to his mouth. He closed his eyes as he savored the bitter, salty flavor and flopped onto his back. "What does this mean? Will we do this again?"

Myrddin kissed him, his lips and then the tip of his nose and his eyelids. "It means whatever you want it to mean. I'd like to do this again. I enjoyed it. It doesn't have to mean more than that—two men having a nice time. But I'd like to do more, give you more. It certainly doesn't mean you aren't free, though. I stake no claim on you."

"All right, good." Sated now, Octavian was exhausted. He curled against Myrddin and smiled against the soft hair on his chest when Myrddin wrapped him protectively in his arms. "I like sleeping this way. Being warm."

Myrddin stroked the back of his hair. "So do I. That archer, Sylvain. He fancies you."

"I know." Octavian nestled down against Myrddin's chest and bunched the blankets against his shoulders. "Pretty, isn't he?"

"Aye." Myrddin kissed his hairline. "You like him?"

"Maybe. Not like you. I can trust you. You're beautiful in your way, maybe more beautiful, more… I don't know." Octavian's words melded with his thoughts as sleep dragged him down. He couldn't remember the last time he'd been so warm, relaxed, and replete. Safe. Myrddin wound his arms around him and burrowed his nose into the top of Octavian's hair, and Octavian's worries mixed with his dreams. In a few hours, he would face the Crooked Teeth. Now, he needed to rest, enjoy the feeling of a lover next to him, in case he died and never got to experience it again. In this life he had chosen, the possibility that any night might be his last loomed constantly overhead.

THE DAY passed too quickly for Myrddin's liking as his men and the men of the Bitter Tide shored up their plans for their raids on the Crooked Tooth camps. By afternoon, maps had been consulted, and after many arguments, parties had been formed and plots finalized. Just before the sun set, the men shared a quick dinner before preparing their arms and horses. Myrddin and Dirk would be accompanying Captain Julien on the attack on the main camp. The captain tasked Sylvain, who he seemed to trust, with the ambush on the encampment they deemed the second most critical, and Octavian would be going with him. As the captain continued to divvy up his fighters, Myrddin tried to devise an argument to keep Octavian with him that wouldn't sound like the boy needed his protection, or that wouldn't make him sound jealous of the attention Sylvain paid Octavian—and that Octavian returned. The two of them had hardly left each other's sides as they planned out their leg of the assault, and only the secret smiles Octavian sent Myrddin kept him from descending into a foul mood. He couldn't help recalling the coarse, eager declarations Octavian had made in his bed. Goddesses, he wanted to give the young man everything he wanted. He thought of the way Octavian's cheeks had reddened and his lips had fallen open when he came and tried to imagine his expression when Myrddin breached his tight ass for the first time.

Too soon, the time came to set out. As the men in their company loaded their gear onto their mounts, Myrddin went to where Sylvain sat on a bench. "Goddesses go with you tonight, Sylvain."

"I appreciate the sentiment, but I do not need them." Again, that smile that looked like he had his eyes trained on some unsuspecting prey curled lips that bards wrote ballads about. He didn't reciprocate Myrddin's wish for good fortune, but returned his attention to the black feathers affixed to the ends of his arrows, smoothing them sharp between his thumb and finger.

"You're very confident." Myrddin sat down beside Sylvain.

"I'm very good." He looked over and caught Myrddin's gaze, his green eyes glittering from the shadow his hood cast. "At many things. Perhaps you'll survive long enough to learn that firsthand."

"Me?"

Sylvain chuckled. "You're an appealing man, and I enjoy frequent diversions. And variety."

Myrddin blew a breath out between his teeth. "Do you take nothing seriously?"

"I take everything seriously. That doesn't mean I don't look for beauty and pleasure where I can find it. What's the point of life, if not to experience it to the fullest?"

"I suppose. Listen, friend. I came to wish you good fortune, and to ask you to look out for Octavian."

"Octavian hardly seems to need a chaperone," Sylvain noted.

"He's young, that's all. He hasn't seen as many battles as you and I have."

"And he's important to you, yes?" Sylvain arched one slender brow as he abandoned his arrows to regard Myrddin.

"I consider him a friend."

"And yet you don't trust in his abilities." Sylvain stowed his arrow in the quiver at his back.

"It is not that. I just don't like to imagine him fighting with no one who cares what happens to him by his side. Forget it. You are clearly not capable of understanding." Myrddin stood to leave before he said or did something he would regret, but Sylvain caught his arm and held his elbow as he stood to face him.

"Just because I like to have a good time does not mean I don't value the men who fight alongside me. Nothing will happen to your young friend if it's within my power to prevent it. I would like to know Octavian better, and we can have more fun together if he's breathing. So calm yourself."

"I… thank you. If all goes well, we'll see each other again." Myrddin clasped the archer's hand.

"Much more of each other, I should hope," Sylvain said as Myrddin turned to walk away.

From the saddle of his horse, Myrddin watched Octavian ride out of the camp with his party. The cold had nipped his cheeks as red as they'd burned when he'd come in Myrddin's hand the night before, and his long, dark hair whipped around his face. He smiled, showing white teeth between ruddy lips, clearly eager for the hunt and lusting for battle and glory, his eyes shining to rival the gold of the failing sun reflecting off the water. Myrddin remembered riding into battle with that feeling of righteousness, the certainty that he'd prevail because he fought for the right side, the burning need to carve a place for himself in an indifferent world. How quickly all those illusions had fallen away, been ripped from his grasp by the reality of man's avarice and just dumb luck. He dreaded seeing the same happen to Octavian, seeing that light of justice in his eyes smothered, but he didn't know how he could prevent it. He watched Octavian and the others gallop up the hill until they disappeared, and then he grasped the reins of his mount and followed Captain Julien over the crest of the cliffs and into the orange light of the western sunset.

They rode for probably two hours, until the cold grew so severe ice crystals lodged in Myrddin's whiskers and he had to wrap a length of wool around his face to keep his skin from chapping and the frigid air from stabbing into his chest. Finally, Julien held up a hand to halt them and reined his animal to a stop with the other. Myrddin, Dirk, and the twenty-five or so men with them circled their horses.

"There's only one road in and out of this particular camp," Julien said. "It will be guarded. Dirk, and anyone who can remove those guards without alerting the rest of the Teeth to our presence, should continue on foot. Our plan from there is to station enough men at the end of the road to prevent their escape, and then lure the rest onto the narrowest part of the trail where we can surround them. We're hoping most of these men will surrender and be persuaded to throw their lot in with the Tide, but know this: their leader, a man called Pearce Vargate, will die before capitulating. You will know him by his mask—a skull with crooked teeth. The quicker we can be rid of him, the better. Show this man no mercy, as he will show you none. Now, see to the guards."

Dirk and three other men dismounted and crept into the shadows. Snow clouds, thick and oppressive, nearly obscured the white sliver of a moon rising above them, and the night was especially dark—good for this sort of mission. Myrddin and the others waited a quarter of an hour more, and the lack of commotion from the camp indicated Dirk and his party had been successful in eliminating the guards. The captain sent another half-dozen men to secure the road leading out of the camp, so the Teeth couldn't flee once they'd coaxed them onto the road.

Myrddin, Julien, and a few of the other fifteen or so men remaining went to put the next stage of their plan into motion. After leaving their horses tied where they wouldn't be noticed but they could get to them easily if they had to retreat, they strung a series of ropes between the center of the camp and the small sentry building at the southernmost point of the road. While the rest of the men drew swords, axes, and bows and went to crouch in the bracken at the edges of the narrow dirt trail, Myrddin and Julien took some glass bottles filled with flammable oil and tossed them at the small shed. With a wink and a smile, the captain struck his flint and lit the end of a rag shoved into the last of the bottles. Fire arced through the night air as he tossed it, and the building went up like a bonfire, shooting sparks into the sky as the two of them ran for the cover of the shadows beyond the firelight, waiting with their weapons ready.

Before long, the fire drew the Teeth to investigate. As the men, thirty or so by Myrddin's quick count, came up the path, several of them tripped over the ropes they'd strung across the road, giving the Tide archers ample opportunity to incapacitate them with shots to the arms and legs. Myrddin thanked the goddesses their recent attacks on Teeth, combined with Octavian's plan to draw them out, had reduced their number. Jule had estimated this camp boasted a rotation of between fifty and sixty warriors, and facing the entire garrison would have led to doom. Already, the traps they'd set had disabled a fraction of the enemy. Of course, after a few men went down, the Teeth discovered the snare and cut the ropes, but the Tide had fewer men to face. Just as Octavian had planned, nearly every man in the camp gathered on the road in front of the burning building, and as anticipated, the men they'd stationed farther down the road rushed out to flank them. Myrddin and Julien, along with the men who'd been hiding in the bushes, ran to surround their enemies. More of the Teeth than they'd predicted turned to fight, and soon a battle raged on the narrow stretch of road.

Julien and the Tide hadn't expected the archers the Teeth had stationed on rooftops throughout their camp, and the arrows raining down on them claimed several of their men. Dirk knew his job, and hopefully the Tide archers did too, and they'd locate and eliminate the enemy bowmen. Myrddin had only one target in his sights: Pearce Vargate. The notorious leader of the Crooked Tooth company appeared near the back of the throng. When Julien had described the man's mask, Myrddin had imagined a skull shaped from steel to form a protective covering, not the actual human skull the giant of a man wore held across his forehead by a gnarled leather strap, its twisted teeth stretching between his brows and over his nose. Swinging his sword in wide arcs, Myrddin fought through the Teeth until he reached Vargate. Killing this man would be like cutting the head off a beast: it would leave the body of the Teeth without direction, open to being absorbed into the Bitter Tide. As Myrddin ran toward the huge man, he noticed nothing but matted fur covered his body between his breastplate and cuirass, leaving the sides of his waist vulnerable. Myrddin braced his sword against his right side, gripped the hilt with both hands, and charged.

The point of his blade penetrated Vargate's vulnerable area, sinking deep into the soft flesh and drawing forth a geyser of blood. The enormous man roared and drew back a hand covered in iron plate and spikes over the knuckles. Myrddin twisted and thrust with his blade, dragging it to the left to tear through his enemy's guts, while he braced himself for the coming blow he had no way to block. Spiked gauntlets struck him in the mouth, ripping his hands from his sword as the blow sent him flying backward. Blood poured into his mouth, and the breath jarred from his chest as his back smacked the ground. He hurried to drag himself away from the feet of the men struggling around him, toward the side of the road. A quick glance showed his side prevailing, with most of the Teeth out of action and the few that remained outnumbered. Dirk seemed to have taken care of the archers, but Vargate, his teeth stained red and his innards pouring out beneath his bearskin tunic, rushed at Myrddin, roaring and shouldering his own men as well as his enemies out of his way. One hand tried to hold the gash Myrddin had opened across his belly shut, but the other swung a mace the size of a man's skull in wild circles around his head.

When he reached Myrddin, Vargate brought the steel ball down in a blow that would have shattered Myrddin's head, had he not rolled out of range at the last moment. Instead, the weapon threw clods of mud up and lodged in the frozen ground. Myrddin struggled to his feet as Vargate growled and tugged against the handle of his weapon to free it. Unarmed, Myrddin could only use his fists, but he whaled against the side of the man's head for all he was worth. He drove his knee into Vargate's ribs, near the wound he'd previously inflicted. He had no idea how the man stayed on his feet with his insides pouring out and his face black, split, and swollen from Myrddin's fists. He just knew he had to kill the son of a bitch, put an end to this, make it so the people he cared about would be safe traveling through this area. Through the haze of battle lust and blood pounding in his head, Myrddin's thoughts flitted to Octavian. If he wanted to see him again, he'd have to survive, fight for it, and he would.

It had been too many years since he had fought for anything besides a handful of coins.

With a ragged cry, Myrddin aimed his fist at Vargate's temple. The blow connected, and the skull the mercenary leader wore shattered and flew from his forehead as spittle shot from his mouth. Vargate roared, the last rage of a dying beast, a sound of desperation and vengeance. Myrddin balled his fist to aim for the man's throat. As he raised his hand, an arrow cut through the smoke, pierced his shoulder just below his pauldron, and sent him staggering back, his right arm useless.

Even dying, his life's blood and innards pooling on the ground, Pearce Vargate showed his stained and misaligned teeth in a cruel grin. The man obviously knew his life was reaching its end, and he planned to die as he'd lived: leaving pain, blood, mangled flesh, and death in his wake. He lifted his mace, and Myrddin had no way to block the blow that would crush his skull. He shielded his face with his left arm, for all the good it would do, screwed his eyes shut, and hoped the pain would not last long. He hoped Dirk would find a woman and father half a dozen children, and that Octavian would find whatever he wanted in life.

Something between a grunt and a gurgle, followed by a spray of warm wet against his face, made Myrddin open his eyes. Julien stood behind Pearce Vargate, blood dripping from a small dagger he held in his left hand. A gash widened across the huge mercenary's throat as the last of his blood poured in a sheet down his chest and puddled on the ground. He fell facedown, and the captain kicked him to the side before offering Myrddin a hand up and an appreciative smile. Once Myrddin could stand on his own, Julien walked a few feet away, knelt down, and retrieved something from the blood and churned-up soil. He pressed what was left of the skull Vargate had worn—a shard of the forehead, part of the nose, a cheekbone, and a few teeth—into Myrddin's hand. "You should have this. You brought him down. Bloody beast he was, too. Well done."

Feeling sick, his head spinning and his body throbbing, Myrddin could only nod. He didn't want the gruesome trophy. Maybe he'd give it to Octavian. It had been Octavian's plan, after all. Bleeding Shades, he would puzzle through it all later. Now, he just wanted to lean against the trunk of the closest tree he could stumble to and close his eyes for a moment.

Julien, a long, slender sword in one hand and his dagger in the other, moved to the center of the throng. "Pearce Vargate is dead." He spat on the ground. "The Crooked Tooth company is no more. However, the Bitter Tide are always looking for loyal and able men. If you wish to join us, you'll be given the same pay for the same work you did for the Teeth. All we ask in return is dedication and a quick hand with a blade. This is our territory now. You can be an ally or you can be our enemy. You have already seen what happens to the enemies of the Bitter Tide." He sheathed his weapons and turned on his heel, strolling slowly up the path toward where they'd tied the horses. Most of the men who were able followed him.

Dirk patted Myrddin on the arm signing, *Mad bastard*, with a shake of his head and a roll of his eyes.

Myrddin clutched the fragment of skull to his chest with one hand while he threw his injured arm over Dirk's shoulders so Dirk could help him back to his horse. He swallowed down a shout at the pain in his shoulder. The wound hurt like the Shades, but it wasn't fatal.

"Bleeding Shades," Myrddin mumbled, the world growing fuzzy, turning to a blurry tangle of blacks and grays he stumbled through. "Old friend, we did it. We did, didn't we?"

Maybe, Dirk signed with his free hand. *Let's not count our gold until we get back to camp and see if the others fared as well. If they died trying to take the other camps, this victory might ring hollow.*

Octavian couldn't be dead, Myrddin thought as he let Dirk guide, and sometimes drag, him up the trail to his horse. All of this had been his idea. Octavian wouldn't accept anything less than the outcome he'd envisioned—absolute victory or nothing at all. Dirk helped Myrddin into the saddle, and he leaned forward to rest his face against his horse's mane. The animal would follow the others, and he couldn't keep his eyes open any longer. They'd won, but the thrill of victory, the desire for a few pints of ale and a man to celebrate, didn't rise in him as it normally did. He could barely feel fortunate they'd succeeded when they'd set out with a slim chance at best. He was just aching and exhausted. At least they were safe, and now he needed to rest. Just for a moment.

Chapter Eight

"THERE YOU are." Octavian smoothed the yellow fringe away from Myrddin's eyes. Myrddin blinked up at him, clearly confused. Since they were alone in their small cottage by the river, Octavian leaned in to press a kiss to Myrddin's forehead. "You've been sleeping. Bastard rattled your skull worse than it seemed. I've been healing you, or trying to. How do you feel?"

"Octavian?"

"Yes, I'm here. How does your head feel?"

Myrddin lifted the arm that had taken the arrow and winced before letting it fall to the bed. With his other hand, he touched his bruised forehead, then the scabbed-over gashes on his right cheek. The wounds looked angry, harsh and purple in the light of the oil lamp in the room, but Octavian knew they hadn't festered, and that was the important thing. He'd worked hard to make sure the scars they left would be faint, if they scarred at all. With the amount of energy he'd expended mending Myrddin's ripped and broken body, it surprised him Myrddin didn't have the skin of a man half his age. Still, he was proud of what he'd been able to accomplish with his magic, and what he had learned from the Bitter Tide healer. Slowly, so he didn't scrape it against any of Myrddin's injuries, he pulled the coarse blanket down to inspect the arrow wound. A greenish halo, sickly yellow at the center, surrounded the puckered gash Octavian had sewn up with black thread after the healer had removed the arrow. The color of the bruises meant they were on the mend, the healer had told him, and much faster than they'd be without Octavian's arcane assistance. The important thing, the man who'd looked no different from any of the mercenary raiders—hardly the bearded sage Octavian envisioned—said was to patch the torn muscles so Myrddin wouldn't have difficulty moving that arm. Octavian had focused his efforts on that, and it had left him stretched and brittle, like steel hammered too thin at the edges. He felt like he'd stumbled, only half awake, through the past two days.

"Hurts like the Shades," Myrddin said, and Octavian handed him water. "But I've been wounded in battle before, and I know it should be worse. You did this?"

"I tried." The pitcher of water had felt as heavy as a boulder, and Octavian let his hand fall into his lap, hoping Myrddin wouldn't see it trembling. "I'm still learning, but I think a competent healer will be of value to our company."

"*Our* company?" Myrddin's eyes still looked cloudy and unfocused. "Are we a formal company now? Me and you?"

Smiling, Octavian traced his fingertip over Myrddin's tawny eyebrow and then circled his prominent cheekbone, where the sun and the cold had brushed a strip of red over his tanned skin. "I think we should continue on together. Look what we've accomplished. We make valuable allies… and I'd like to." Octavian's face grew warm, and he realized he'd said too much. He turned away and looked down at the floor, not tearing his gaze from the rough, dusty planks until Myrddin pinched his chin between his thumb and finger and guided his face upward until they faced each other.

"I'd like to as well."

Octavian grinned and stroked the back of Myrddin's hand. "It was really something, what we managed. Not that we did it alone, but the idea was mine, and you… I know you were the one who brought down Pearce Vargate. Everyone is saying you deserve the credit for the defeat of the Crooked Tooth company. Everyone is saying you're a hero, or at least a hero among mercenaries."

That made Myrddin chuckle cautiously as if he feared it would hurt to laugh. "Well, I'll take the compliments I can find. I know I'm not a prince or a champion in an old story."

The tales the others had told when they'd returned to camp still made Octavian's chest swell with pride, and he wished he'd been there to see the fight that was reaching legendary proportions as the story spread among the Bitter Tide. Just thinking about it invigorated him, made him imagine all they might accomplish. Without considering, he blurted, "You are! You are to—to the men who fought with you. You probably saved many lives by keeping the skirmish short. Jule told me that once the men saw Vargate dead, most of them gave up without a struggle. It was your victory that won the day, Myrddin."

"And what about you? How did your campaign with Sylvain go?"

"Sylvain is very clever," Octavian said, though he couldn't help thinking their exploits paled in comparison to Myrddin's, even though they'd been successful. Despite Myrddin's eyelids fluttering, even to the point where it seemed he'd fallen back to sleep for a few moments, Octavian recounted every detail of the battle he'd taken part in. "My contribution wasn't particularly glorious, but we worked well as a team. I suppose I still have time to heap some glory on my name, though. I'm just starting out."

When Myrddin exhaled, he sounded exhausted, ground down. "Octavian, believe me, I understand a young man's thirst for recognition, but in this line of work, gaining the reputation for being a consistent, reliable soldier is the best you can do. Most men would rather fight beside a man they can depend upon to do his share than one who risks himself, and everyone else, for adoration."

Octavian didn't want to run at the middle of the pack; he wanted to lead it. He had little battlefield experience, but from what he had read, the men remembered by history weren't the reliable soldiers, but the risktakers. Still, he would never endanger his comrades for personal gain, and in truth, he hadn't decided where the line should be drawn. He'd keep these matters to himself until he could speak with conviction. Besides, Myrddin looked tired. Octavian shouldn't strain him with his ill-defined concerns. "Are you hungry? You must be. I can bring something. Or would you like to try to have dinner in the camp? The men would be enthusiastic."

"I… think I would like that," Myrddin said. "I feel stiff lying in this bed like an old maid. I'd like to stretch my legs and breathe some fresh, cold air. Can I trouble you to help me?"

"Help you?" Octavian looked up into Myrddin's guileless blue eyes. "I'll always help. Be there for you." He cleared his throat. "That's what it means for men to be brothers-in-arms, is it not? To know when you stumble, there will always be a hand extended, waiting to help you back to your feet. That no matter what you face, you'll have someone to face it beside you."

"That's very poetic."

Octavian rubbed his forehead. "I'm sorry. I only meant that there's a bond between warriors, men who face death standing next to each other."

"I know." Myrddin smiled at him and touched the center of his lower lip with his thumb. "You expressed it well. There's nothing wrong with saying beautiful things. This sad old world can always use more beauty. Now, extend that hand, lad. Help me get my trousers on so I don't have to face my adoring supporters with the little fellow on display."

OCTAVIAN ROSE'S Journal

Myrddin is sleeping next to me, his arm stretched over my lap as I write by the light of a single candle, as not to keep him awake. He is still healing, and still weak, no matter how he pretends for the others or makes jokes to distract them. I know. For two days, I have funneled all the strength and energy I could spare into him, hoping only to make him strong and whole again. It surprises me that I seek no accolades for my sacrifice; I know myself, and I know I seek glory, and even that, in a deep, fetid place, I resent that Myrddin, and not me, got to slay Pearce Vargate. To realize this is to look into a mirror and see hideousness and greed reflected back, but I would rather face it than stare into an illusion. I will look upon Octavian, scarred, scabbed, rotting, but genuine, before I will fool myself with a gossamer veil.

I would not admit this if anyone asked, but I do not know what to do next. Two paths lay before me, though within a few steps both become obscured with the jagged shadows cast by fate and the future. Both culminate in the crest of a hill, and I cannot see what lies beyond the slope, let alone farther down the road. Captain Julien, Jule—I think of him that way now—has asked, and practically implored me to join the Bitter Tide. Apparently my skills at judging character and devising strategy impressed him, and he has made no secret of his desire to include me. I am flattered. The Tide is a reputable company, and joining it, working my way up through the ranks, would be a responsible decision. I know I could learn a great deal from these seasoned fighters, and that I could earn a fair share of gold. Part of me does not understand why I am reluctant. The other part, though, craves more—craves to stand at the head of the army, to command it, even though I am not yet worthy. I know this. I must still make a name for myself.

Jule would happily include Myrddin, Dirk, and Danno in his group. I could care less about the Beasley brothers, and might even advise the captain against taking them on. I wonder if Myrddin values me enough to go where I go. It is a scary thought, almost a weight upon me, to imagine my decisions affect us both. It worries me to think we are wound so tightly together so soon, no matter how much the idea gives me comfort and even hope for happiness. These are my pages, and no one else will see them, so I'll permit myself an indulgence. After all, I have no one to confide in beyond this parchment and ink. Myrddin is a beautiful man—brave, strong, capable, yet kind and just. I am more captivated by him than I should allow myself. My thoughts wander often to his eyes, the shape of his lips, the feeling of his body pressed against me. Sylvain is more beautiful, but somehow less desirable to me. He represents an enjoyable time, but Myrddin represents more. I cannot say why.

But the important decision I must make is whether to join the Bitter Tide company, and thus secure for myself a lucrative, sound, if unremarkable future, or to continue on to Rosecairn, alone, or with whatever men will accompany me. The decision to feign my death and make my way without the wealth and power of my family was a rash one, prompted by, among other things, my lust for the assassin who freed me. But I do not regret it. I am free. I cannot waste it. I must make the name Octavian Rose mean something. I have only this one lifetime in which to do it, but at least I am young, and have time.

Talk around the supper fires of the Bitter Tide has taught me much about what awaits me if I venture forth to Rosecairn. Several noble houses, merchants, temples, and concerned citizens of means are offering a substantial purse to anyone who can rid the area of the vicious warlord Brealan Lavock and his men. Thus far, no one—not the knights of Gaeltheon nor the slew of mercenaries drawn there by the gold—has been able to accomplish it. Is it the worst sort of arrogance on my part to imagine I might succeed where so many men, more experienced, better trained, and better equipped than I am have failed? But if I could…. If I could, no one would be able to deny my merit. I would have the means to start a company of my own. I would have the Rosecairn, which is by all accounts a desirable and defensible location. But from what I have overheard, it would mean defeating a hundred men or more, some fanatically loyal to their leader, but most toiling in servitude, terrified to leave the group or earn Lavock's displeasure. I have even heard Lavock occasionally chooses a few of his warriors at random, ties them to posts in the center of the camp, stabs them through the bellies, and leaves them to die slowly and in agony, just to maintain the control he holds over the others. What chance do I have against that kind of cruelty? It is not something I can even comprehend.

So I must choose whether to take the responsible route and join the Bitter Tide, learn what I can, and work my way up through the ranks, or risk everything, quite possibly my life included, for a slim chance at glory. Again I find myself sorely needing a confidant, someone I could trust to truly advise me and not consider only his own interests. If I were to ask for counsel from Jule on this matter, I know he would think me a fool for even considering going to Rosecairn, but he would do it out of his desire to put my skills to use for the Tide. Myrddin is a puzzle to me. He seems to want to see me succeed, even while he wants to coddle me. At first, I thought this inclination to keep me from danger stemmed from a lack of confidence in me and my abilities, but I sense it may be something more, some need of his own he fulfills by what he certainly considers protecting me. And I do not think it is me; I suspect Myrddin has a deep-seated urge to protect something, and I am convenient. After all, don't all men fulfill their own needs first, to root out whatever tenacious worm wiggles into their spirit, using any tool at their disposal? Perhaps they do not even know they are doing it, like picking at an itchy scab while sleeping, sating the itch at the cost of blood and damage.

I sigh and shake my head over the words I have just written. I am still too quick to judge other men. I do not know anything of Myrddin's past, and I do not feel a few stolen kisses and fumblings in the dark give me the right to question him. He was clear that they meant nothing, and I am glad not to have another complication. Still, the hour is late and I look forward to burrowing beneath the blankets and sharing his warmth.

How can I know another man when I cannot find the spiny worm working so fervently into my own mind? When I do not know the source of the itch that torments me until I tear my flesh open to alleviate it? And does knowing men's hearts matter? Will it help me achieve my goals? I do not know, and I can consider it no longer. The hour is late; even the revelry in the center of the camp has faded, and I must try to sleep.

OCTAVIAN WAITED for his ink to dry before carefully stowing his journal, quill, and ink bottle in his satchel and pushing it under the bed. Trying not to disturb Myrddin, who still needed his rest, Octavian nestled down and turned on his side, nuzzling his face into the blond hair falling across Myrddin's neck and releasing a sigh of contentment. The fire burning low in the hearth banished the worst of the chill, and beneath the bedclothes, when he curled his body close against Myrddin's, it was wonderfully toasty. As he let his head sink into the feather pillow, Octavian felt sure he'd be asleep before long, but it didn't last, as those insects began to crawl and writhe through his mind, chewing, tunneling deeper until he could no longer ignore them. If he refused the offer to join the Tide, he wouldn't get another. Still, though they called themselves warriors for hire, the Tide weren't above raiding ships that came up the river, and Octavian didn't—couldn't—condone profiting from terrorizing innocent merchants. He wanted to build a legacy he could look back on without regret, wanted to be able to say he had made it and remained true to his beliefs. He could do that as part of the Tide, probably. But he would have to make concessions.

Octavian's right arm, jammed between Myrddin's body and his own, started to go numb and tingle. Mindful of the arm Myrddin had draped over his waist, Octavian twisted and flopped on his back. Myrddin groaned as the mattress shifted. Octavian settled and tried to lie still, tried to sleep, but knowing one needed slumber and had less and less time to enjoy it was the surest way to keep rest at bay. His mind kept returning to the decision he faced. He banished it by trying to think of something else, but the worms returned by the dozens, coiling through his thoughts, refusing to be ignored. His lower back hurt, strange since he occupied the most comfortable bed he'd had since the bandits had abducted him from his father's estate. When he flopped over with his back to Myrddin, the other man made a sound of obvious pain. Octavian tossed and turned for a while longer, his restless movements causing his bedmate discomfort, before he slipped from beneath the covers to stand on the cool, smooth wood of the plank floor.

Knowing he would find no rest and loath to keep irritating Myrddin, Octavian pulled his boots on and threw his cloak over his shoulders. Perhaps some fresh air and a walk would tire him out enough to get at least a few hours of sleep. Padding softly across the floor, careful not to wake Dirk, Danno, or the Beasleys, Octavian cursed himself for abandoning warmth and comfort, but he couldn't stay in the little hut any longer. He needed to move. He opened and closed the door as quietly as he could and started up the hill toward the center of the camp.

Mist as thick as wool, and just as dense and oily, lay over the clearing between the buildings. It soaked through Octavian's garments and clung to his skin like the greasy salve the healer had told him to spread over Myrddin's wounds. He didn't know how anything so cold could remain vapor. Shivering, he pushed his shoulders around his ears and made his way toward the faint glow of the fires. Everyone else had abandoned drinking and fighting contests in favor of their warm beds, and aside from the shrill whistle of the wind and the lulling lap of the river's tides, the night was quiet. Octavian went to the brightest of the fires, knelt to pick up a stick, and stabbed at the embers. Swirls of sparks rose into the thick white fog, and he watched them spiral and spin until the heavy moisture in the air drowned them out. He poked at the coals again, but little heat remained, and it wouldn't be long before the embers succumbed to the crushing mist.

"Trouble sleeping?"

Octavian snapped the twig and tossed it into the fire before turning. Sylvain stood a few feet behind him, his arms crossed beneath a thick cloak lined in dark fur. His hair curled in the heavy air, falling in dark, shiny ringlets around his shoulders, glimmering droplets beading the strands.

"And how come you're not in bed?" Octavian asked.

Sylvain stepped closer until he could smooth a damp strand of Octavian's hair out of his face and pin it behind his ear. "Me? I don't spend much time in my bed. At least not alone. But you didn't answer my question."

"I found myself craving a walk."

"Restless? Why?" Sylvain swept his hand in the direction of a bench, and Octavian followed him and sat down. The archer reached beneath his cloak for a skin of wine, which he offered to Octavian.

It was hardly the fierrine they had shared before the battle with the Teeth, but it wasn't bad, and it warmed his belly and eased some of the tension from his shoulders, so Octavian drank deeply. "How do you like being a part of the Bitter Tide?"

"Why do you ask?" Sylvain took the canteen and sipped daintily.

"I'm sure you know Jule has offered me a place here."

"Of course," Sylvain said, passing the skin. "He'd be a fool to let you slip through his fingers. I take it you are reluctant?"

"I'm flattered to be offered the opportunity." Octavian hadn't quite figured Sylvain out yet, so he didn't divulge his doubts and reservations. Still, it felt good to talk to someone, whether the concern was feigned or not. "I know I could learn a great deal here, and I respect the captain and the company."

Sylvain slid closer, pressing the length of his thigh to Octavian's leg and cupping Octavian's knee. The warmth was welcome, and his hand sent a thrill through Octavian's body, but he would not be manipulated. "Your cloak is pathetic," Sylvain said, opening his own and draping it over Octavian so it covered them both. "Have you really not earned enough to afford something better? You would earn enough for five cloaks, lined with fox fur, after a month working for the Bitter Tide."

Octavian sighed and didn't pull away when Sylvain wrapped an arm around his shoulders and pulled him close. "I know. And I wouldn't have to compromise my principles, at least not much. In a way, this is what I have dreamed of: being included among a group of men who respect me and see I have something to contribute."

"It seems you've made up your mind. What's the problem?"

Octavian didn't resist Sylvain's urging to lean against him. It felt nice just not being alone. "I wonder if I could accomplish something at Rosecairn. I know I'm young and inexperienced, but I cannot help but see an opportunity there. Goddesses, if I could succeed… I am inclined to try, in spite of the grievous risk. Am I a fool?"

Sylvain chuckled and turned on the bench so he faced Octavian, his eyes seeming to catch and reflect all the available light. "Not in my estimation. Actually, you're a man after my own disposition. For what it's worth, I would be inclined to try if for no other reason than it would be a challenge, and an entertaining one. I would try simply to see if I had it in me to succeed. Here, with the Tide, this is safe for the most part. An easy living. There's no fun in that, nothing to get your blood singing."

"Yet you're here."

Sylvain closed his eyes slowly before looking up at Octavian through his lashes. "For now."

"Why?"

"In all honesty, I'm here because you are here." Sylvain slid his hand up Octavian's leg, grazed his crotch, and moved up his waist until he could grasp the small of Octavian's back and guide them closer together. Their legs bumped and jumbled awkwardly until Sylvain used his free hand to hook Octavian's leg over his knee. He pressed his other thigh between Octavian's splayed legs, and Octavian's heart pounded so hard it hurt his ribs. "From the day you walked into this camp, on your own, facing a likely death, I have thought about you often. You're brave, cunning, and goddess-damned beautiful, Octavian."

When Sylvain moved his face close, Octavian could formulate no response. He arched his chest against Sylvain as he let his lips go slack and receptive for the other man to explore. Sylvain took full advantage, sliding the tip of his tongue over Octavian's lips and the edges of his teeth before pressing inside his mouth. Octavian opened to let him in and curled his tongue out to crest against Sylvain's like a wave breaking over the shore. Sylvain grasped Octavian's hips and pulled him into his lap so Octavian straddled him on the bench as he continued to drive his tongue into Octavian's mouth. He kneaded Octavian's ass, pressing his fingertips into the muscle. He nipped and suckled across Octavian's lower lip before thrusting his tongue past Octavian's teeth and lapping at the roof of Octavian's mouth until Octavian forgot everything but the taste of him. When Octavian rocked forward, desperate for more contact, his hard cock poked against Sylvain's taut belly. Sylvain's erection pushed insistently into Octavian's inner thigh.

Grabbing handfuls of Octavian's hair, Sylvain pulled him back and looked into his face with his shining green eyes. "I wanted you from the moment I laid eyes on you. I want you, Octavian. My home is only a stone's throw from here. Will you go?"

Goddesses, he wanted to, but he hesitated. He didn't know why, but he broke free of Sylvain's embrace and stumbled to his feet, rubbing arms that felt much colder without Sylvain and his cloak surrounding them. His dick tented his pants, and he hurried to throw his cloak over the bulge Sylvain had already seen and felt. "I—"

"What? Are you spoken for? If you belong to Tam Myrddin, I suppose I should respect that. If I must."

"Belong?" Octavian prickled, reminded of how his father had tried to use him to further his trading goals, attempting to trade him off to whatever family offered him the sweetest pot. It was the reason he'd left a life of wealth and leisure and now stood freezing in his ratty cloak. "I belong to only one man, and that's Octavian Rose. No one has claim or control over me, and no one ever will."

Sylvain didn't apologize as Octavian thought he might. Instead, he reached his hand out, and Octavian took it. "Good. We're very much alike. Come to my house. Let me make you feel like you have gone to the goddesses' paradise. I swear I can do it. But don't believe me. Make me prove it to you, sweet Octavian. Let me show you."

"And nothing else?"

"Nothing else. I don't want an iron manacle round my ankle any more than you do."

"All right." Octavian let Sylvain lead him to a house—square, simple, and similar to the others—and through the door to the front room. A fire burned in the inglenook, a healthy blaze that made Octavian wonder if Sylvain had been sitting in front of it and watching him through the window. It didn't matter, and Octavian took little time to survey Sylvain's belongings, though he did notice the décor seemed sparse, borrowed more than owned. No small possessions or errant items cluttered the mantle or shelves. It was as if Sylvain didn't want to put down roots and Octavian could appreciate that. He was only here for a quick bout of pleasure, after all.

The two of them stood a few feet apart, half of them lit by the fire, the other halves in darkness. "Take off your shirt," Sylvain said. Octavian balked. "Please. Will you take it off? Let me finally look at you?"

"If you will." Octavian let his cloak fall in a pool around his feet and then grasped the hem of his shirt. He waited until Sylvain shed his cloak and tugged his own shirt over his head before stripping his garment off. Sylvain was smooth, deep olive skin over compact, slender muscle, with little hair to conceal it. He was long and lithe where Myrddin's muscles bulged, sturdy and thick. He had a boneless, almost liquid grace when he moved. From the jut of his chin and the angle of his shoulders, Sylvain knew how pleasing he was to look at. So did Octavian. Months of fighting or toil combined with too little food had stripped every ounce of fat from his body, and his muscles popped in the harsh light. He was proud of the body he'd earned through hardship and deprivation, and Sylvain's soft gasp said what he saw surprised him.

"I knew you'd be strong, and beautiful, but goddesses...." Sylvain ghosted his palms up Octavian's waist and over his chest, catching Octavian's nipples between his fingertips before he brushed them toward Octavian's collarbones and neck.

A soft heat sizzled over Octavian's skin in the wake of Sylvain's hands. His eyelids fluttered and his head lolled back as he pushed against Sylvain's touch before he realized he was doing it. His heart floundered, beating so fast the rush of blood into his skull made him a little dizzy. With shaking hands, Octavian took hold of Sylvain's waist, just above the cut *V* of muscle angling into his trousers. Goddesses, his skin was impossibly soft. Even the trail of hair that caught Octavian's fingertips when he brought his hands around felt like fluffy down. "Soft," he whispered, barely aware of uttering it aloud.

"Not everywhere." Sylvain gently guided Octavian's hand a few inches lower. Earlier, by the fire, Octavian hadn't realized how large he was. Now with his fingers barely closing around Sylvain's girth, with the flared ledge of his corona defined even through his trousers, Octavian knew Sylvain had the thickest cock he'd encountered in his limited experience, if not the longest. The thought of running his fingers, his tongue over its veins and ridges, the vision of it pressed against his own erection, slipping over his belly, prying his flesh apart to enter him… Impossibly, his heart beat faster and his cheeks prickled with heat. His apprehension and the splash of fear ratcheted his arousal higher. A few beads of sweat tickled down his spine, and a wet patch grew beneath his trouser lacings.

Sylvain ran his hands up the sides of Octavian's heated neck and around to the back of his head, where he grasped Octavian's hair and inclined Octavian's head back so he could look into his eyes. "Are you nervous?"

"A little." Octavian continued to stroke and explore Sylvain through his trousers. Goddesses, he couldn't wait to get a look at that cock, get his hands on it without the cloth between their skins. "Mostly excited."

Sylvain rubbed his fingertips against Octavian's scalp in soothing circles as he pecked, light as a thief, across Octavian's lower lip, then his upper lip. His breath crashed warm against Octavian's chin when he spoke. "I'm not boasting when I tell you you're in very, *very* good hands. I'm no selfish lover either. By the time I'm finished with you, you won't have a drop of seed left in you to spill. Besides, what's the worst that can happen? Even if it turns out we're not great together, we'll still have some sort of fun."

"I don't think that's going to happen," Octavian panted against his lips, feeling more confident. "I think we'll be just fine together."

"So do I." Sylvain chuckled wetly against Octavian's mouth before joining their lips together again. This time, they met with more fire in a bruising kiss, their teeth scraping as they bit and sucked at each other's lips and pressed their tongues deep into each other's mouths. Sylvain skimmed his nails lightly down Octavian's back, the playful scratches pleasant and cool against Octavian's heated flesh. Then he pushed his hands into Octavian's trousers and cupped the crescents of his ass. Octavian continued to stroke him lightly, running the heel of his hand back and forth over Sylvain's length as he traversed the bumps and cords of subtle muscle along his waist with his other hand. Mostly, he just struggled to keep his buckling knees from betraying him as he weathered the little lightning storms of pleasure and sensation Sylvain's fingers and mouth conjured over his body. Goddesses, the man seemed to have four sets of hands. They were everywhere: gliding over the edges of Octavian's shoulder blades, down the knobs of his spine, kneading the taut muscle of his lower back and hips, then his ass, the sensitive, rarely touched skin of his inner thighs, the seam at the center of his tightly knotted sac….

Octavian thought he could come a dozen times just from Sylvain's reverent exploration of his body, but he didn't want to be a passive party in this. He doubted he had a fraction of Sylvain's experience, and while he might not give as good as he got, he intended to give something. Emboldened, desperate to get his hands on that thick cock waiting like buried treasure, he fumbled with Sylvain's trouser lacings until he spread them apart enough to peel the cloth down Sylvain's hips and free his erection and his heavy sac. He groaned at the musky masculine scent he'd unleashed, and his mouth watered and he leaked a few more drops into his pants. With one hand, Octavian cradled Sylvain's sac. It felt full and heavy against his palm, apple-sized, but not drooping, instead knotting tight against the sparse, silky hair framing it and that wonderful cock.

"I want to know what it tastes like," Octavian said in a harsh whisper. Without waiting for a response, he dropped to his knees and clawed at Sylvain's trousers until he pulled them a little farther down his legs. He burrowed his nose into the patch of hair at Sylvain's inner thigh and drew the earthy, aroused scent into his nose and throat, holding it there until he released it in a hard exhale that fluttered

Sylvain's curls. He pressed Sylvain's cock against his belly and examined the underside, with its thick blue veins and strong central muscle, with his fingertips, then his tongue. Sylvain tasted of salt, spice, leather, with a slight bitterness, like underripe fruit. Octavian moaned softly with satisfaction, and Sylvain rested his hands on Octavian's shoulders, not holding him in place or urging him forward, just touching, and it was nice—sweet, almost, and it stripped the last of Octavian's nerves away.

Slowly, he dragged his tongue up Sylvain's length until he reached the head. Then he pulled back a few inches to get a better look at it. He'd been with men before—two—but had never really had the chance to appreciate a cock in a brightly lit room. Most of Sylvain's hood stretched away from his wine-dark cock head, and Octavian carefully thumbed it back the rest of the way before tracing the heart-shaped mound with his pinky. Sylvain stroked his hair indulgently, but the bead of clearish white liquid pooling in his slit belied his arousal. Octavian darted his tongue out and caught the little pearl on the tip. The taste burst in his mouth like the juice of a grape at the first bite, and his mouth watered until it hurt. Spreading his lips wide, he worked Sylvain's corona into his mouth, worried at first it wouldn't fit. He drew in an inch, then another, but he could go no further, so he just enjoyed the hot weight, the stretch of his lips, the flavor, as he rubbed his tongue against the deep groove on the bottom of Sylvain's crown. When he looked up and met Sylvain's gaze, Sylvain's cock twitched in his mouth.

"Octavian, I must have done something virtuous without realizing it, because you are a gift from the goddesses." Sylvain pushed the sweaty fringe off Octavian's forehead and regarded him with a mixture of hazy-eyed satisfaction and wonder. "We should move to the bed, before just the sight of your pretty lips wrapped around me finishes me off. Then I swear to all the sisters and the Cast-Down at once, you can feast on me until you've sucked the meat from my bones."

Reluctantly, Octavian slid his mouth off Sylvain and wiggled his chin to work out the cramp in his jaw. Sylvain offered him a hand up and they kissed again, the archer clearly greedy for the taste of himself on Octavian's lips and tongue. Achingly hard and almost disoriented with lust, Octavian ground his erection on Sylvain's thigh as Sylvain kissed down his neck. He held tight to Sylvain's hips so he wouldn't fall over.

Teeth grazed his collarbone and scraped along his neck before sinking into the skin near the center of his throat. Octavian straightened his arms at the minor twinge and pushed Sylvain back. "Do not mark me."

Sylvain stretched his neck toward Octavian's flesh, pulling like a dog against a leash to taste him. But one could hardly leash an alley cat, and Sylvain, in typical feline fashion, gave up his struggle and stepped back, looking almost uninterested. "Why not?"

Octavian couldn't read him, could glean nothing from the squint of his eyes but mischief. "Because I'm not yours."

Sylvain's eyes widened for a fleeting moment before he grinned broadly, showing teeth, and seized Octavian's waist with more aggression than he'd shown so far. He licked up Octavian's neck and nipped his earlobe. "For tonight you are."

Sylvain backed Octavian up until his knees bumped the bed in the corner of the single-room home. With a light nudge to his chest, Sylvain pushed Octavian onto his back, and he landed lightly in a thick layer of furs. With his almost predatory smile still in place, Sylvain tugged Octavian's boots off and tossed them away, followed by Octavian's loose and threadbare trousers. After adding the rest of his own clothes to the pile on the floor, Sylvain left Octavian lying there, confused, naked, and feeling vulnerable, while he went to the hearth a few feet away and retrieved a copper kettle. When he returned, he poured the steaming water into a ceramic basin on his night table, and then added cooler water from a pitcher. He added a few drops of something lavender scented and swirled his fingers over the surface of the liquid.

"Here now. Lie down on the pillow." Sylvain dipped a cloth and wrung it out as Octavian did as he asked. Then he perched on the edge of the mattress and wiped the heated, slightly scratchy cloth across Octavian's chest, taking extra care to circle his nipples before moving it down his belly. He dipped it in the water again before rubbing it around Octavian's balls and up his length, easing his hood back to clean his corona.

At first it felt strange, too intimate, to be cleaned that way, but against the fire in his cheeks, Octavian dismissed his embarrassment. He was picky about cleanliness himself, and mercenary work could be dirty in more ways than one. By doing this for him, Sylvain was saying what they were about to share didn't have to be dirty; it didn't have to be something rushed in the darkness. It could be something to prepare for with anticipation, like dressing for a banquet, something to look forward to instead of some filthy secret. Octavian closed his eyes and enjoyed the attention coupled with the heat wrapping around his cock. But when Sylvain urged his legs apart, guided his heels to his hips, and spread his cheeks to wipe his cleft, Octavian gasped and flinched away. His eyes flew open.

Sylvain pulled back, looking a little disappointed. "Off-limits, then?"

"I—" It was just too strange, even if it made sense.

"Tell me." Sylvain leaned in to kiss his forehead and kept kissing around the perimeter of his face as he spoke. "You must tell your lovers how to please you. Any man who doesn't want that isn't worth your time. Tell me. I want very much to please you."

"I…." Goddesses, why had it been so much easier to say it to Myrddin? After a quick mutual rub-off, he'd just blurted it out, wanton as a whore. Octavian took a deep breath. "I… like being touched there. Very… very much."

Sylvain made a sound between a purr and a growl as he kissed Octavian deeply, hooking a hand beneath Octavian's knee, guiding it alongside his chest, and curling his spine to expose his opening. As he wiped back and forth, circling Octavian's rim and pressing the tip of a cloth-covered finger against his hole, Octavian's cock swelled and filled until it felt hard enough to cut glass. "Goddesses, this is so… decadent."

"Is it?" Sylvain's breath cooled Octavian's kiss-swollen lips as he pressed a little farther into him to wipe a circle around the very edge of his insides. "To me, it's just practical. If I'm going to put my tongue inside you, I'd rather you be clean." He suckled the skin along Octavian's jawbone as he did a very thorough job of it.

His words, or maybe his touch, made Octavian's muscles tighten around the slight intrusion. "It is, though. Doing this, putting so much care into getting ready, it feels almost like a… ritual. Something beautiful. I don't know what I'm trying to say, only that I've never been so aroused. Exposing myself to you like this, without hiding in the dark like a thief, like we're doing something illicit… I can't express myself." He wanted more, wanted to be filled, peeled apart and taken properly, long and hard.

"Whatever made you think what we're doing isn't beautiful?" Too soon, Sylvain pulled away, leaving him empty and wanting. He stood, dunked the rag, and carefully washed his own cock, balls, and ass. Watching his hands moving over his flesh, leaving it wet and glistening in the strong firelight, was almost as good as feeling his touch on Octavian's own skin. "Now, tell me what will make you happy, and I'll tell you what I desire. Then we can please each other. Do you want to play with my cock some more?" He dropped the cloth in the basin and stroked himself languidly, moving his foreskin to and fro and spreading his fresh precome over his big, sculpted bell-head. "You seemed to enjoy that. If you like, we can lay opposite each other and lick, suck, and play till morning. Longer. No one in the Tide camp demands we rise with the sun. We can work up an appetite until the midday meal, if you want."

"No." Octavian touched his wrinkled opening, still damp from Sylvain's ministrations, still twitching and acute. Hungry. "I think I have a better use for that pretty cock. If you'd like it, I'd like to feel you inside. If—" That inky smear of worry returned to taint Octavian's warm arousal, winding like an icy serpent into his belly. "If you'll fit. You're thicker than I've had before. I could barely get my mouth around it."

Octavian had expected anything but the look of concern on the other man's face. Sylvain sat next to him and touched the center of his lips with his thumb. "My game is pleasure, giving it and receiving it. Pain has no place in this for me. Not even a little." He leaned down to kiss Octavian. "I'll fit, and I'll make sure you love every moment of it. It'll be easiest if you turn over and raise up on your knees and elbow. Easiest for you, and easiest for me to kiss that wonderful hole. Roll over. Good. Spread your legs a little more. Arch your back. Ah, that's lovely."

Octavian felt a little exposed and vulnerable with himself on display to Sylvain. It was thrilling in a way, and he had nothing to be ashamed of. He'd honed his body taut and pliant as a sapling, and Sylvain seemed to enjoy it, judging by the appreciative sounds he made as he massaged and caressed the backs of Octavian's thighs and his ass, digging his fingers pleasantly into the muscle. Their bodies would bring each other pleasure; letting Sylvain explore his opening was no different from the way he'd explored Sylvain's cock earlier. What was wrong with being fascinated by each other? Sylvain took full advantage of what Octavian offered, lapping at his opening and circling it with his tongue for delightful, agonizing moments before pressing past the muscle to lick Octavian's insides. He thrust his tongue in and out until Octavian grew so wet he hardly needed the spicy-scented oil Sylvain drizzled between his cheeks. Something in the tincture heated when Sylvain rubbed his fingers around the edge of Octavian's hole, making it more sensitive, making it throb and ache to be filled. With a fingertip, Sylvain pushed a little of the tingly mixture into Octavian, making him moan.

"You like that?" Sylvain asked, delving a little deeper.

"I—"

Sylvain kissed across his shoulders as he pushed another finger in, setting Octavian's body alight like a bonfire. "Don't be ashamed. Tell me if you like it."

Goddesses, with his ass clenching, trying to pull Sylvain's fingers deeper, he didn't know if he could speak. "I feel like my guts are on fire. In a pleasant way, though it sounds, ugh… contradictory. What is that stuff?"

"Just some oil I picked up at a whorehouse in Elvara." Sylvain jabbed in until Octavian felt his knuckles curl and press against his taint. He found the sweet spot inside Octavian, and Octavian buried his cry at the intensity of it in the pillow. "To increase sensitivity. Enhance pleasure. Is it working?"

"More."

With a chuckle and a nip to Octavian's asscheek, Sylvain pushed another finger in, then another, until only his thumb remained to push against the point of Octavian's tailbone. He pulled his hand back, swiveled it horizontal, and sank it into Octavian's wanting flesh.

"Good, goddesses, yes. Yes," Octavian muttered, pushing back against him, feeling the last of Sylvain's knuckles breach his body. He squeezed his muscles tight around them, and a tingle shot like an arrow up his spine at the added sensation.

"No pain?"

"Exactly the opposite."

Sylvain's lips tickled and teased up his waist until they reached his ear. "If that's not hurting, you can take my cock. Ready for it?"

"Goddesses, so ready."

"Mmm, you're wonderful." Sylvain withdrew his fingers as he gave Octavian's ass a playful smack with his other hand. Though he scowled at his partner over his shoulder, Octavian opened his legs a little wider, and Sylvain aligned himself and pushed inside. He glided smoothly against Octavian's slicked flesh until he buried himself and their skins met. "Still no pain?"

"Only the pain of wanting," Octavian muttered, turning his heated face to the side and resting it over his crossed forearms. He tried to push back, but Sylvain held his hips firmly.

"That's no pain. That's just the hunger that makes a feast so much more satisfying when you can finally sit down to eat. The longer you wait, the better the flavor. It only gets better as you get hungrier."

"I'm hungry enough," Octavian mewled, surprised at the desperation in his tone.

"What are you hungry for?"

"Hard," Octavian panted. "Deep. Lose yourself in me."

"Goddesses help me, I may have already done." Sylvain snapped Octavian's hips back hard against him, and Octavian squealed, more from surprise than discomfort. Gradually, Sylvain began to pull out, and then when he'd withdrawn almost completely, he speared inside with another quick, sharp thrust that made Octavian cry out. He set a torturous rhythm, dragging himself back slowly before each quick jab. The slow out, quick in, soon reduced Octavian to a whimpering mess on the pillow. The intervals between Sylvain's cock against the sensitive places inside him went on long enough to drive him mad, and the quick, fleeting press against them wasn't nearly enough. His lips moved; he might have been pleading, but he doubted Sylvain would fish a comprehensible word from his gibberish, and he didn't care.

One thing Sylvain had said proved true: the waiting, the mouthwatering scents of the feast made everything more delicious when they finally tucked in. Sylvain wrapped his arms around Octavian's waist and curled over him, lapping and nipping at his back and shoulders as his thrusts grew shallow, quick, and needy. Octavian pushed back against him until his legs turned to custard and the base of his body cramped and knotted so tight it felt like his muscles would tear. He could do nothing but try to stay on his knees as the tension built until he could no longer contain it.

"I—Sylvain—I'm—"

"Bleeding Shades, my furs!" Sylvain reached beneath Octavian to try to push them out of the way, but he was too late. Octavian's release felt like liquid fire tearing through him and out of him, maybe because of the potion Sylvain had worked into him, maybe because of the waiting. Bracing himself on his elbows, he clutched handfuls of the bearskin as he fell apart, shaking, moaning rhythmically, and seeing stars fall behind his eyelids. He didn't know how long he lost himself to his pleasure before he realized Sylvain had stopped moving to hold him together through his rapture.

Panting so hard spit flecked his lips, Octavian said, in a trembling voice, "Sorry. About your furs. Think… I soaked them."

Sylvain bowed his back and rocked against Octavian again, setting a gentle rhythm that was almost too much for Octavian in his acute, sensitive state. He swore he could feel each of Sylvain's hairs brushing his opening. "Octavian, I don't care. I'd give a dozen skins, two dozen, to see you come like that again."

He hit Octavian's honey spot again, and impossibly, a few more drops of seed shot onto the dark fur. "Don't have to give… anything. I should give you skins for making me come like that. Or a wagonload of gold. Emeralds, to match your eyes."

"My little poet." Sylvain's strokes grew more erratic, more desperate, and he raked his nails down the sides of Octavian's ribs.

"Sylvain…. Sylvain, I want to please you, make you feel as good as I do, but I cannot take much more. It's too much. Too much feeling."

"Do you need me to stop?"

"No, just finish soon, and hold on to me, because I feel like I'm going to shatter."

"Aye, Octavian. Gladly." He wound Octavian tightly in his arms and wrapped his soft lips around the rope of muscle between Octavian's neck and shoulder, pulling up the skin with his mouth but not biting—not marking. With a few more thrusts, Sylvain was grunting, openmouthed and wet, against the side of Octavian's neck as the heat of his seed filled Octavian.

After Sylvain came, they both collapsed, muscles twitching, gasping for air as if they'd been held under water. Octavian flopped on his belly and Sylvain sprawled across his back. Gradually, Sylvain's cock softened and slipped out of Octavian. Octavian wriggled, and Sylvain answered with a curious purr.

"Chamber pot?"

Sylvain led him to the far end of the house, near the small stone pantry, and each of them took a turn seeing to their needs.

Then they returned to the bed and lay facing each other in the dying light of the hearth fire.

Octavian explored Sylvain's face, tracing his eyebrows, the contours of his cheeks, the curve of his chin, and the reddened, swollen mounds of his lips with his finger. "That was lovely."

Instead of kissing him, Sylvain pressed his forehead against Octavian's temple and closed his hand around his bicep. "We can do it again anytime you like. You need only ask."

Octavian blew a breath into his fringe, pushing it out of his eyes. "For now, you mean. You'll grow tired of me eventually."

"It's true I'm easily bored. But you, I think you've got years. I still have much to discover about you and how to please you. Speaking of, what do you want to do now? I could sleep for a spell, but I don't want to be a bad host."

"No, sleep sounds wonderful. I really am sorry about your furs."

"Worth it, Octavian." Sylvain settled in and arranged the mostly warm and dry furs over them. "I'll clean it. Or I'll kill another."

Though it was warm in Sylvain's bed, Sylvain didn't hold Octavian in the protective, cherishing way Myrddin did, and Octavian knew asking for it would seem desperate. So, like Sylvain, he curled on his side, and the two of them pressed their backs together. Octavian tried to close his eyes, but the scabs at the edges of his mind, his undecided course of action, itched enough to irritate him and keep him awake. He couldn't help scratching at those doubts, and in no time, they bled. He squirmed a little before rolling to his back and folding his arms beneath his head, resigned to stare at Sylvain's ceiling until he weighed every consequence of every path before him.

Sylvain snorted, turned over, and put a hand across Octavian's belly. "Calm yourself. If you want to go to the Rosecairn, I'll go with you."

"You will?"

"Aye, but don't see it for more than it is. Truth be told, I'm growing complacent here. I could use a new challenge, and this one is the mother lode. Riches and excitement, that's what I'm after. So I'm with you. Now, for the love of the goddesses, go to sleep and stop floundering around."

His mind made up, Octavian pressed his back against Sylvain's chest and fell asleep within moments.

Chapter Nine

AFTER SLEEPING until well into the afternoon, judging by the tangy yellow light pouring through Sylvain's front windows, Octavian rose a little guiltily, washed as best as he could with the basin and kettle, dressed, and prepared to set his course of action in motion. He didn't see Sylvain meandering around the center of the camp, but he spotted Myrddin, Dirk, and Danno on a bench and approached them, not sure if they'd guessed where he had been or how they'd react if they had. No matter. He'd know soon enough. He walked up to them and stopped a few feet away, tenser than he wanted. He tried to smile and not let his nerves show.

Dirk looked up from the arrowhead he was sharpening and gave Octavian a terse nod. Myrddin slowly lifted his head and offered a tight smile, which Octavian attempted to return. Danno, bless him, rose to his feet and clapped Octavian on the shoulder, almost knocking him over, before shouting, "Good morning, Octavian!"

"Good morning, Danno." Octavian regained his balance and smoothed his rumpled shirt. "How are you?"

"Danno is good. How is Octavian?"

"Octavian is very good."

Dirk made a few truncated gestures, and Myrddin snorted.

"What?" Octavian scowled at them. "What does he say? If you have something to say—"

Myrddin raised a hand. "Calm yourself, lad. Dirk only says you likely have reason to feel good this morning, though I might observe, morning is long since past and gone. Don't be so quick to take offense. Dirk only taunts you because he likes you—"

The archer quickly shook his head and frowned at Octavian.

"—at least a little more than he did before."

"Myrddin, how are you feeling? Do you need me to heal you?"

Myrddin chuckled. "I appreciate what you've done for me, but I'll be fine now. I've had worse, and I'd be willing to wager you're too tired out for magic."

"Bleeding Shades." Octavian kicked a charred chunk of wood toward the fire. "You're like children. It's as if I'm the first man to spend a night with another person. Can it truly amuse you that much? All right, yes. I spent the night with Sylvain. Is it so miraculous?"

"It was for me." Octavian didn't turn toward Sylvain's voice, but he appreciated the allegiance. The others might tease him—probably because he reacted to it so predictably, he realized—but they wouldn't taunt Sylvain. "Octavian, if we're going, we should not waste time. I'd like to say farewell to Jule, and then we should be off."

"Off where?" Myrddin sounded alarmed, and Octavian barely thought before resting a hand on his shoulder. Their gazes caught.

"I'm going to Rosecairn. The purse being offered is too much for me to resist. I'd like to try for it, and Sylvain is coming with me. Will you? Will you come with me?"

"Of course." Myrddin stood and grasped Octavian's forearm in his fist while Dirk lowered his face into his palm and shook his head. "Is that not what we planned? To go along together?"

"Aye." Octavian nodded, wanting so much to be wrapped in Myrddin's strong arms, even if it came with a scolding about being reckless and arrogant. "But our chance of success is slim, as I'm sure you know. I—You could stay here, become a part of the Bitter Tide, and earn an assured and low-risk living. Myrddin… don't come with me out of pity."

Myrddin jerked his hand back. "You think too highly of yourself, you little bastard. I'm a mercenary, same as you, and I go where the gold is. What makes you think I wasn't already planning to make my way to Rosecairn, that I needed your invitation?"

"Myrddin, what in the Shades'…."

"Get your things together, Octavian. Say your good-byes, and meet us at the gate that leads up the hill." Myrddin turned and stomped away. Sylvain caught Octavian's shoulder when he started after him and shook his head.

"Leave off me." Octavian shrugged free of Sylvain's grasp and hurried after Myrddin, catching up to him at the foot of the wooden stairs leading down the embankment to the river. He grabbed Myrddin's wrist so hard the larger man skidded to a halt on the soggy, slimy boards of the dock. Reluctantly he faced Octavian, and Octavian met his gaze. "What in the Shades'? Why are you cross with me? Is it because I spent the night in Sylvain's house?"

"Of course not." Myrddin's toe etched furrows in the frozen algae on the wood.

"Then what? I don't want to offend you. I need you. Bleeding Shades, I thought we agreed to not stake claims on each other. I thought it did not matter to you, and if you spoke false words to me, I can hardly be blamed for believing them!"

Myrddin drew in a deep breath and let it out, dampening like a doused lantern. "You're right, lad, and I have no say in how you spend your evenings. I just wish you'd shared your plans with me, maybe asked my counsel. But that's arrogance. After your recent victories, it's clear you don't need my advice, or me."

"Yes, I do!" Octavian grasped Myrddin's biceps, sinking his fingers in as far as he could past the leather and mail. "I only had the courage to make this decision because I assumed we'd do this together. Succeed or fail, together. Sylvain is an asset. You cannot deny that. Myrddin, this is a rare opportunity, for all of us, but we must work as a team. Goddesses, it's probably a show of weakness to say this aloud, but I would feel much more confident if you were beside me. I don't know that I can do this without you. I don't know if I want to."

Myrddin's expression softened as he moved closer, until his chest and belly grazed Octavian's, and he petted Octavian's damp hair as he said, "I said I would stand by you, and I will."

"Then why are you cross?"

Myrddin's blue eyes looked like they'd melt with the sadness they held. "I just want you to be safe. You'd be safer here than at Rosecairn, but that's not what you want. I don't want to hold you back, but I don't want to see you hurt. It can be difficult to reconcile the two. Please, try to understand."

Octavian fell against Myrddin, into his arms; he couldn't resist. "I understand. I just want you to see me as worthy, able to take care of myself. I... I need you, but not to protect me. Does that make sense?

Goddesses, it's my spirit and heart that need you, not my body, at least not to keep it from injury. It does enjoy other things you offer."

Myrddin held Octavian tight, so tight the gray mist off the river seemed to obscure the rest of the world. "It also enjoys what Sylvain offers."

"It does. I do. Is that a problem?"

"No." Myrddin kissed the top of his head. "You're not a wife, and I don't need to ensure your offspring are mine. That's a part, a large part, of the reason I chose this life. To step beyond the rules men and women must obey. I overreacted. I hope you enjoyed Sylvain, but I also hope you'll give me another chance. There's no reason you can't enjoy us both. I would never prevent you. But you are becoming special to me."

"You're special to me too," Octavian said. "And if Sylvain becomes special, it doesn't take away from that. Friendship, lust, whatever we name it, is an infinite pool, an ocean. I feel so much inside, I feel it overflowing, to the point where I can give to him without taking from you. There's not a limit to my affections. Giving to one does not take from another. And, Myrddin, you should try him. He's… a very giving lover, generous. Just damned good. And I know he fancies you."

Myrddin rested his forehead against Octavian's. "I'm sorry for behaving like a horse's ass. In my defense, you stir up the possessiveness in me, for what man wouldn't want to call you his? But I understand, Octavian. I could just as easily claim the wind or the sea. I can hold you like I can hold a gale in my fist. Doesn't mean I don't want to."

"And I'm called a poet." Octavian pecked his lips, and their gazes locked as they smiled at each other. "Come with me to Rosecairn if you want to fight with me, to overthrow this vicious warlord. Come for no other reason. Come for gold and glory. I can promise you victory, for I will see that done, but I can promise nothing else. I'm not ready to be tied down."

JUST BEFORE sunset, their party, comprised of Octavian, Myrddin, Dirk, Danno, Sylvain, the Beasleys, and seven other Bitter Tide members who wanted to try their hand at the purse, rode northeast for the Starlight Bridge that spanned the Kanda River between Lockhaven and northern Gaeltheon. In the dead of night, when all of them were practically frozen solid to their saddles, they reached a small river town and secured a large attic room in the only public house. Their suite had four narrow beds against the walls. Sylvain took one, Dirk another, and Myrddin the third. It surprised Octavian when they allotted him the fourth bed. He declined it, choosing instead to nestle close to Myrddin even if the full quarters prevented anything else. The others spread their bedrolls on the floor. As he fell asleep, Octavian decided they should be happy to have warmth and shelter.

Most of the men rose with the sun and shuffled out of the room, now stagnant with their stale breath and nighttime gases. Octavian didn't really care if they returned or not. He'd be glad to see the last of the Beasleys—and their stench. He combed his fingers through his knotted hair, thinking it could use a trim. Then he rose and washed as best as he could. Goddesses, what he wouldn't give for a proper soak in a tub, submerged in bubbles, dunking his face beneath the fragrant water and rubbing perfumed ointments on his skin afterward. He'd given up that life, but that didn't mean he had to give up being a civilized man whose odor didn't offend everyone he passed. Octavian scrubbed at his underarms with the inn's bristly cloth, and then he combed his hair and dressed. The light outside the inn where they'd slept was teary, streaks of sun dripping through the heavy gray clouds, collecting in sad little puddles of gold among the downtrodden mud.

Octavian looked up and down the street. The faded shingles above the shops swayed and creaked in the paltry wind, but there weren't many people walking the main thoroughfare, probably because of the cold. "I need to shop for better gear. I'm tired of freezing my ass off."

"I'm heading to the tavern," Myrddin said. "Get something hot to eat."

"A brilliant idea if ever I heard one," Sylvain said from beneath his hood. "Would you be terribly opposed to some companionship?"

Myrddin grunted in what could have been the affirmative, and the two of them started toward the building bearing the sign with an overflowing cup and a wedge of cheese on it. Octavian tried to staunch his disappointment that they wouldn't be accompanying him; he was hardly a pampered maiden who needed ladies-in-waiting to choose gloves to match a gown. Squinting at the watered-down light reflecting off the snow, he surveyed the shops in the vicinity. One displayed a banner bearing a sword and shield, which, along with the wads of black smoke rising from behind the building, marked it as a smithy. Myrddin wanted Octavian to buy a sword, to carry anything but the dagger he'd been given by his Cast-Down assassin, but Octavian remained reluctant. He'd learned the feeling of that dagger in his hands, its weight and the way it moved. It was a quick, sharp, and deadly weapon he could wield without exhausting himself or slicing himself to ribbons, as he still tended to do when he practiced with Myrddin. Maybe he should talk to Sylvain about learning to use a bow. But he'd always found exceptional archery an innate talent—like magic—and he doubted he possessed it. It required far too much patience. What he needed today was warmer clothing, better armor, and perhaps a pair of boots that he couldn't feel the gravel through the soles of. He'd bought his current pair secondhand, and they were already badly worn. He couldn't tell which of the shops might have the items he needed.

Dirk knocked Octavian in the shoulder with his own and jutted his chin at a small stone building a little way up the street. He raised his ginger brows before turning to walk toward it. Octavian, surprised the archer who made such a show of disliking him wanted to take him shopping, called out his thanks before remembering Dirk couldn't hear him.

A little brass bell above the door jangled when they entered the shop. Aside from the sunlight sneaking through the slats in the shutters and the fire that kept the single room as hot and damp as a southern summer, it was dark. It smelled of musty cloth, old leather, horses, and oddly, cabbage. Octavian touched Dirk's elbow and shot him a confused look, but Dirk ignored him in favor of a rack of leather garments set against the wall. Octavian joined his perusal and soon found the outfits and armor ranged from newly tanned and still stiff to barely held together at the seams. The scraps of parchment declaring the prices quickly told Octavian the newest articles were well beyond his grasp, so he tried to look for the best tunic he could afford. The shop proprietor, a tall man with a potbelly, bald head, and gray beard, watched them without offering assistance or a greeting.

After a while, Octavian settled on a black leather tunic reinforced with blunted steel studs. Though worn in places, the leather was thick, and the metal would help protect him. Best of all, he could afford it. When he caught Dirk's gaze, Octavian held the tunic in front of him and raised his brows. The approval he expected never came. Instead,

Dirk moved his hands too quickly for Octavian to follow, at least until he fluttered his fingers as he moved them away from his forehead. Octavian had been on the receiving end of that gesture enough to know it well: idiot.

"What's wrong with this?" he asked.

Dirk took the tunic from his hands with a roll of his eyes, replacing it on the rack before signing, very slowly, as if to a child, *It is all appearance.*

"Well, then, what would you get?" Octavian wondered if Dirk had accompanied him just to belittle him and make him miserable. Everyone knew there was little love between them.

Dirk held up his palm to indicate Octavian should wait. After passing through the clothes on the rack carefully, he draped a few items over Octavian's arm. One by one, Octavian held them up to inspect them. The first was a long tunic of sturdy brown leather with three-quarter-length sleeves. Tan fur dotted with umber lined it and folded over at the hems. It had been patched with swatches of other leathers at the elbows and seat, but it looked warm. The leather trousers almost matched, but were more cobbled together at the knees, and still better than Octavian's coarse cloth pants that did nothing to keep the chill wind from his skin. Last of all was a hooded suede cloak lined in matted dark fur—probably bear, maybe harrow-wolf. Octavian could find no argument with what Dirk had chosen. As he looked up to nod his approval, Dirk thrust a pair of heavy gloves into his arms. Then he went to a table near the hearth and chose for Octavian a well used but serviceable chain-mail vest that would fit nicely over the tunic and a set of simple steel pauldrons and bracers. Knowing Dirk had chosen better than he could have on his own, Octavian took his items to the shopkeeper.

"I'd like to trade this tunic I'm wearing toward them," he told the man. "It's fairly new and hasn't seen much battle. It should fetch a fair price."

As he unlaced it, the burly shopkeeper took a tally of the garments on the counter. "You've chosen some nice pieces. Five gold with your trade."

Octavian reached for his coin purse. It was more than he'd intended to spend, but after their raid on the Crooked Tooth camps, he could afford it, and he needed to stay warm and stay protected, especially when they reached Rosecairn. Just as he was about to hand the man his payment, Dirk grabbed his wrist, shook his head, and held up two fingers.

"Two?" the shopkeeper roared. "Your quiet friend is out of his mind. Four gold, three silver pieces, or a trade of equal value. You looking to get rid of that dagger?"

Octavian clutched the hilt possessively. "No. Four gold and five silvers seems a fair bargain."

Again, Dirk stopped his hand and held three fingers up to the proprietor.

"No, I can't do three," the man said. "Four gold is my final offer."

Dirk made an offensive gesture to the shopkeeper and grabbed Octavian's elbow to tug him out of the shop, leaving the items Octavian really wanted—and was more than willing to pay four gold pieces to own—behind on the counter. Just as Octavian yanked free of Dirk's grasp, the store owner came around the counter to intercept them before they reached the door. "Three gold," the portly man said. "And that tunic you're wearing. Deal of a lifetime, lad."

Dirk rolled his eyes and pointed to Octavian's feet, where his toes poked through his worn boots.

The man shook his head. "And I'll throw in something better than what you've got on your feet. Not that that's saying much." He went back behind his counter and picked up a scraped and sagging pair of boots. They were rough and a little smelly, but as the shopkeeper had astutely pointed out, they exceeded what Octavian had. And, goddesses, he was throwing them in for free to prevent Octavian and Dirk from taking their business elsewhere.

Octavian happily handed off the three gold coins and changed into his new garments before leaving the shop. Outside, the wind didn't feel so much like a knife piercing his flesh. Surprisingly, his new attire kept him comfortable in the northern cold. He turned to Dirk and waited until Dirk focused his attention on his lips. "Thank you. You did me a great favor. I admit, I didn't know about bargaining with shopkeepers."

Rich boy, Dirk signed.

Octavian knew he was right. Before, as the son of a wealthy merchant, he'd never worried over the prices of goods. He'd never tried to talk out a deal. If he'd wanted something, he bought it. Now, he wondered how many savvy shopkeepers had benefited from his lack of concern. It was different with coin he had worked for, bled for, than with gold he'd been given to squander. Dirk had helped him, saved him from being taken advantage of. "Why?"

What? Dirk signed.

Why did you help me? Octavian struggled to perform the complex hand gestures perfectly. *I know you do not like me. Why help me?*

Myrddin is my brother.

What…. Octavian squinted in frustration, trying to recall the gestures he needed to express himself. *What is that to do with me?*

Dirk signed more quickly, but Octavian managed to follow most of what he said. *I wanted him to leave you behind. But that's not going to happen. So I help you to help him. If I'm saddled with you, you might as well have decent armor. I don't look forward to dealing with Myrddin when you die.*

I am not going to die. Octavian stabbed the words into the air with his hands and fingers. *I don't care what you think. I'm not dying. Not yet. I'm not done.*

Oh, sure, Dirk answered. *My only concern is Myrddin. You hurt him or fuck him up, and I'll kill you myself.*

Fine. Octavian slashed the word between them. *But know this. I offered him nothing but occasional pleasure, and he agreed. I made it clear I have no more to give. He agreed. So if he has spoken false to me, he has hurt himself. I won't bear the blame for that. But I do not think Myrddin is a lovesick maid. He understands our arrangement. He benefits from it the same as me. This is between us. Goddesses, Dirk. Your loyalty to your friend is admirable. I aspire to earn it for myself one day. But we warm each other's beds, nothing more.*

Dirk nodded. *Hurt him, I'll kill you.*

Octavian hung his head. "Your point is taken. Shall we have a look at some of these other shops?"

Dirk nodded, and they spent the next few hours perusing the goods on offer along the main street of the town Octavian didn't know by name.

After spending half an hour sorting through piles of blankets, Octavian sensed what he could only identify as magic. The hair on the back of his neck stood up, and his teeth wiggled and ached in his mouth, the throbbing spreading up the base of his skull until his whole head thrummed. Something seemed to hook, catch, and sink into his mind, and the line attached pulled him to an alley between the fabric store and the buildings near it. Following the unexplainable draw, the tug at the back of his head, Octavian wandered down a garbage-strewn alley cast in perpetual shadow by the buildings surrounding it. When he saw nothing but an old woman covered in rags huddled near the shoddy fence at the end of the passage, he almost turned back. But the magic he felt was strong, drawing him on like the moon drew the tide. Almost before he knew where his feet had taken him, he knelt before the woman with skin like a well-folded map and angry red gums devoid of teeth.

She smiled at Octavian and patted his hand. "Ah, so you're the one I sensed. I felt your magic."

"You're a mage?" Though incredulous and perplexed as to why someone who possessed the gift would live as a vagrant, he couldn't deny the power radiating from the old woman in her stinking furs.

She opened her toothless mouth wide, tossed her head back, and cackled. "Better one than you, I'd be willing to bet. Look at your eyes. You're all used up. You're not using your power the right way."

"I'm not?" Octavian silently thanked Dirk again for his clothing choices as he sat in the rimy gravel. The leather and fur protected him from the worst of the cold and sharp edges. "I must admit, I have never been taught. If you'd be willing to share what you know, I can pay you for it."

Octavian waved Dirk off when he appeared at the mouth of the alleyway, and Dirk shook his head as he turned away. Octavian returned his attention to the woman, fishing in his pouch to offer her a piece of silver. She widened and then narrowed her eyes as she took it. "I can tell you this much, boy. You're likely the same as all young mages, using your own energy to fuel your spells."

"And is that wrong?" he asked.

"Does it leave you tired, nauseous sometimes?"

He nodded.

"That's because you're turning the energy your body needs to function into power, trading one for the other. Look around you. The world's full of two things: solid forms and energy. Men and women manipulate solid forms with energy—think of a blacksmith. He changes the shape of the metal with the strength of his muscles, trading his vigor for the item he wants to produce. It's the same with seamstresses, farmers, and cooks. They trade the energy of their bodies to influence things. Mages can do that too, but mages alone can turn energy into energy—or solid forms into energy."

Octavian leaned closer, fascinated. "How?"

"Magic can be fueled by three things: your own energy, as you've been straining yourself to do, other worldly energy, or by tapping into the magic already out there. First way's fine for little things, like healing small wounds, lighting a fire, but judging by your clothes, you make your living fighting. You probably already know that's no good in a battle. Gets used up too quick. Now, you've got to be careful with the second way. Nothing worse in the world than a mage who steals energy without realizing it. Better to wear your own body out than suck the life out of the people and things around you to fuel your enchantment. It's a vile way to work spells."

"I had no idea such a thing was even possible," Octavian admitted.

"Sure," the woman said. "Some healers work that way, drawing the life and strength from a healthy person and directing it into a wounded one. Some of them know what they're doing and can take only a little, but it's a bad path to go down. That power is too easy to reach for, too available. Lots of mages, once they get a taste, can't stop themselves from drinking deeper and deeper, and it poisons them. Still, give it a try just so you know how." She pointed a finger like a gnarled twig toward an evergreen tree growing on the opposite side of the fence. "It's turned the soil, sunlight, and rain to the energy it needs to live. Take a little. Pull it inside and hold it in your belly."

Octavian let his gaze relax and his mind empty of worry. At first, he heard the sounds of the town: merchants hawking their wares, people talking, dogs barking, sheep bleating, and chickens pecking in the gravel. He smelled wet straw, hearth fires, and meat cooking, felt the wind in his hair and the cold nipping at the edges of his ears and the tip of his nose. Inside, at the pit of his belly, he felt the energy he usually drew upon to use magic. He tried to ignore it, casting around for another source. He felt nothing for so long he'd started to think it was an exercise in futility when a fissure opened in his perception. It felt like standing at the eye of a lightning storm. Power crackled and swirled around him, overwhelming his senses with its sheer magnitude. If he really tried, he could separate the energy coming from the ground beneath him and the air moving around him. They weren't really colors—they were nothing he could see—but they felt like colors, or flavors, maybe, or some combination of the two. The stunted tree felt like pale ochre, juniper, and loam with a peppery sensation sprinkled on top. Even though he knew he couldn't use his hand to pull the power toward him, reaching out his arm helped him focus his intention, and soon he had a store of magical energy spinning inside him.

His tutor made a disapproving sound, something between a gurgle and a grunt. "And that's why you have to be careful doing that."

Octavian let his eyes focus on the physical world, reluctantly letting go of the smears and ribbons of color that weren't true color. Blinking, he looked at the tree. Most of the blue-green needles had faded to brown, and many had curled and shed to the ground. The tree's bark had peeled and split. Octavian had literally sucked the life out of it. He doubted it would recover. Suddenly he felt sick and ashamed.

The old woman patted his arm. "Just an old tree, boy. Probably be chopped down for firewood before the winter's through anyhow, so no harm done. But you can imagine if it had been a man. You're a fast learner. Drained it dry. Might as well do something with it. Make me a butterfly."

"How?" Power surged through Octavian's blood, making his skin tingle with something like fire and frost at once. If he didn't do something with it soon, it would spill from his pores and take whatever form it chose.

"Will it. Picture it in as much detail as you can."

Octavian struggled to remember the last butterfly he'd seen. Surely he had seen them, in the gardens on his family's estate in the summer, but he'd never thought to observe one closely. He envisioned what he could: a slender wand of a body, gossamer wings with lacy edges. When he opened his hand, some purplish blue, amorphous blobs floundered into the sooty gray air before sparking out. They seemed a paltry reward for all the energy he had stolen.

The old woman ground her lips together. "Not bad for a first try. What you have to realize as a mage is that you're a vessel. You fill up with energy, you use that energy, shaping it to your will, and you release it. Some mages instinctively draw on the energy of the life around them, but luckily you aren't one of those. It's a greedy and nasty way of getting power. Your inclination is to sacrifice yourself, which is almost as bad."

"You mentioned a third way." Octavian gave his teacher another piece of copper for good measure.

She nodded as she hid it somewhere among her filthy rags. "Magic into magic. Great mages do it without thinking. I'm afraid you're not a great mage, but you may make a fair one. You'll have to try to find the threads of magic to draw on. They lay like a net over the world, but they're always moving. If you can sense magic being used, you can find them."

"Where do they come from?" Octavian asked.

The old woman laughed. "Where do you think you are, boy? The university in Espero? How should I know? I just know there's magic all over, and any mage who wants to practice will find it and use it. Some say there's less and less available, but if you don't want to level the mountains, you should be fine."

"But never great?" Octavian said softly, ashamed at the need for approval in his voice.

"Be glad you're a mage at all. There aren't many of us left these days. The greatness of a mage is part hard work, part how much magic you can channel. You, from what I can tell, are like a nice swift stream, almost a river. Just not the Kanda River. Your magic will serve you, but you'll need to practice. Now, I've earned me piece of silver, and I'm tired. Be off."

Octavian still had questions, mainly why this wise and skilled woman lived as a beggar, but he had been raised in a world where personal queries weren't so blunt. "Perhaps you'd rather instruct young mages than spend your time here."

"Perhaps I'd rather put my foot to your backside. I said I'm done with your company. Be off."

Confused, Octavian handed her another coin and left the alley. It was getting toward time for the midday meal, and having skipped breakfast, he was hungry. He made his way toward the small town's tavern, following his nose to where he knew he'd find Myrddin, Sylvain, and Dirk.

THE TAVERN wasn't the finest Myrddin had visited, but their bacon, beans, and eggs arrived on clean plates, and while the little place smelled of stale ale, at least it spared them the reek of urine and vomit. This early in the day, Myrddin and Sylvain were alone except for the wench cooking and tending the bar. They had seats by the fire and hearty, if plain food. As for conversation, Myrddin could think of little to say to the archer, and Sylvain kept looking up from his breakfast, catching Myrddin's gaze, smirking, and looking away.

"Excuse me, but do I have something on my face?" Myrddin said when he grew tired of the game.

"Would you like to?" Sylvain asked in a low purr.

Myrddin slammed his knife down on the table. "Are we twelve years old?"

Sylvain narrowed his eyes. "A simple 'no, thank you' would have sufficed. I'm just wondering how we'll pass the time while Octavian and Dirk are out at the market. Is Dirk fond of shopping?"

"He's not frivolous, but he prides himself on finding a good bargain," Myrddin said. "Personally, I hate the time it takes to dig through racks and shelves and then haggle with shopkeepers. It irritates Dirk to no end that I'd rather sacrifice a few coppers than waste my time. Luckily, I rarely need much."

"Your armor seems of a very good quality," Sylvain noted.

"It is." Myrddin hadn't figured Sylvain out, and he wasn't about to share his life's story with him, no matter how artfully he fished for information and batted his sumptuous lashes. "What about you? You strike me as a man who enjoys fine things, nice clothing. Your leathers look like they cost a fair amount."

Sylvain canted his head and dragged the tip of his knife through the yolk of his egg, swirling it into intricate patterns before looking up. "I suppose you could say I recognize some things are worth what they cost."

"You manage to say much without saying anything at all."

"One of my many talents." Sylvain smiled. He had a nice smile, bright and open, when he wasn't trying to manipulate. "But we should try to be friends. We'll be fighting together and spending a great deal of time together. That will be more pleasant if we can get on. So ask me what you want, and I'll answer with words that mean something."

Though Myrddin feared another game on some level, he couldn't deny the truth of Sylvain's words, and he had no reason to hold animosity for the man—at least no good reason. "I have to wonder why you're here. You had good standing with the Bitter Tide, and as comfortable a living as a sell-sword is likely to find. Captain Julien clearly valued you. Why give all that up? Forgive me, but you don't strike me as the type to risk your livelihood and future just to lay with Octavian Rose."

Sylvain opened his mouth to speak but must have thought better of it. After taking a sip of the wine he'd insisted the poor barmaid scare up, he said, "No, I would not. The truth is, I put myself ahead of most men, and I value my own prosperity highly. I have a restless spirit, though. Things with the Tide were secure and comfortable, as you observed. I was growing tired of it even before that brave boy walked into our camp like he owned it. Now, do me the courtesy of an honest response. Why are you going to Rosecairn? You could have stayed on with the Tide, and you could surely find other work. Are *you* going because of Octavian?"

Myrddin moved the limp peas on his plate around with his knife. Sylvain would likely see through it if he lied. "Yes."

"Do you love him?"

That was a harder question to answer. "What does that mean? I love Dirk—he's like my brother, a man I know will walk through fire for me, one I would gladly die to see safe. He's been by my side for years. I have only known Octavian a few moons. He's driven, and he's clever and brave… many things I admire. I'd miss him if I lost him, but I don't know if that's love. I'll help to keep him safe if I can, at least until he learns he's mortal. After all, I would not be sitting here today if wiser men had not done the same for me when I was a foolish youth ready to take on the world."

"In the knighthood, you mean? Why did you leave it?"

"For reasons of my own."

Sylvain lifted his goblet. "Then I would wager those reasons were valid. I appreciate you speaking with me. I hope you understand that my pursuit of Octavian was never meant as a slight against you."

"I just don't want to see him hurt."

"Why in the goddesses' names would I do anything to hurt him? I'm not that sort of man. My lovers leave my bed smiling. I would be happy to show you why."

"Perhaps another time." Myrddin found Sylvain's advances obnoxious, but almost endearing. He was a man, after all, and it felt good to be desired by a younger, more beautiful man. But he had no intention of letting Sylvain steer the conversation away from Octavian. "I know you would not harm him. Not his body. But if you don't tread carefully, you may hurt his heart. Don't make him think you care about him if you don't."

"I do care about him. I just don't want to put him in a white dress and lock him in a tower. He knows this. If anything, he was more worried than me about forming attachments. He's young, and he's learning what it means to be a man with another man. He's enjoying the discovery, and why not? I wonder if you know him at all. You should talk with him, learn what he's really like. You have an idea of him, I think, and it does not match the reality. He's not as fragile—inside or out—as you imagine."

"I think you do not know him as well as you profess," Myrddin said, trying to quell his anger at Sylvain's honesty. Some of what Sylvain said rang truer than Myrddin wished. Yet—"He wants so badly to prove himself. To be of value to someone. He needs someone to think he is important."

"Being valuable on the battlefield has nothing to do with pleasure in the bedchamber," Sylvain said. "I remember many men who thought I could not fight because I prefer cock. Most of them are dead now."

Myrddin just shook his head and forced himself to eat the last of his peas. They tasted disgusting, and he was no longer hungry, but he had learned to eat when food was available. "But Octavian may not make that distinction. To him, being valued is being valued. He's young, and I worry over him."

"You should speak with him. Learning what he's truly like will assuage your worry, I think. I know he looks up to you."

"Only because he has had no one else."

"Nonsense, Myrddin. He does it with good reason. You are capable, and you have honor. You're also quite desirable. I can certainly understand his fascination with you as a man."

"I just never want to see him turn hard or bitter." Goddesses, maybe it was just Sylvain, a man who would view his words as nothing but the opportunity for a joke or a way to direct the conversation back to himself, but it felt good for Myrddin to voice his concern. "I don't ever want to see him sell himself and his ideals to scrape out a place in this cruel world. I think I'll see it sooner than later, though. Men do what they must to get by."

"He's different," Sylvain said, then laughed. "Truly, a rose among thorns."

"Roses are delicate."

"They are. But sometimes they can bloom out of ironstone."

Before Myrddin could respond, the tavern door opened and Dirk joined them at their table by the fire. At first, he worried when he didn't see Octavian with Dirk, but then he remembered Sylvain's words and realized Octavian could probably handle buying new boots without a chaperone. He'd been on his own for months before he'd found his way to their camp. The tavern wench came to the table, and Dirk pointed to Myrddin's plate as an order. It didn't matter. Dirk would gladly eat whatever she put in front of him. Being between breakfast and the midday meal, he ended up with sausage, cheese, beans, and bread, which he happily tucked into as if he hadn't eaten in days. The way Dirk ate, Myrddin couldn't fathom how he stayed so wiry.

For an hour or so, they talked about Rosecairn and what they would do with their portions of the gold if they succeeded. Sylvain bought another bottle of wine and they shared it while they contemplated what awaited them in Gaeltheon. Then Octavian joined them, looking resplendent in the new gear he'd procured. The deep brown of his leathers accentuated the rich color of his hair and eyes and contrasted with his creamy skin, and the steel girding his body reminded Myrddin he was every bit the warrior he now looked. It turned Myrddin's thoughts to the feeling of the hard muscle and soft skin beneath all that leather, mail, and fur. Something else about him seemed different as well, though Myrddin couldn't put his finger on it. Octavian had a glow to his skin, and, it seemed, a greater wisdom and age in his eyes. He seemed more confident and assured as he took his place at the table.

"Is there any stew?" Octavian asked the barmaid. She nodded. "Good. A big bowl, please. Bread and cheese. Lots. Thank you. I cannot remember the last time I was so hungry."

I see your toothless lady friend wore you out, Dirk signed with a warmer smile than Myrddin ever imagined him directing at Octavian.

After giving Dirk the single finger salute, Octavian signed, *That she did. A very knowledgeable lady.*

"You were with a woman?" Myrddin asked, the skin of his forearms itching at the thought. Sylvain was one thing—men, especially warriors, understood pleasure without strings—but a woman, even a whore, would try to get her claws into Octavian and claim him for herself. To certain kinds of women, men like Octavian were trophies, security. Purses.

"A very old one," Octavian answered with a smile and a wink at Myrddin. "And a mage. She offered me some very valuable lessons about using my gift. Well, actually I paid for them. But I think if I practice, I can be much more useful to you in the future."

With Dirk and Sylvain looking on, Myrddin couldn't tell Octavian he found him useful just as he was. It would humiliate them both. "Your new gear should serve you well," Myrddin said instead.

"I'd have been robbed if not for Dirk. It seems I still have much to learn."

"Acknowledging that is great wisdom," Sylvain said. "And I must say, you look ravishing."

Octavian pinked, and Dirk signed, *They have rooms for rent upstairs. Use one if you're going to continue. I'm trying to eat.*

Sylvain looked from Octavian to Myrddin. "I'm not sure I caught all of that, but it didn't seem complimentary."

Myrddin cleared his throat. "We should talk about Brealan Lavock and the Rosecairn, formulate what strategy we can."

"I have some ideas," Octavian said, ignoring the food the barmaid set in front of him as he explained his plans, using the cutlery and plates as a crude map. They passed the rest of the afternoon in conversation, and then they returned to the inn for what might be their last good night's sleep in some time, if ever.

Myrddin held Octavian to him throughout the night. He might not love Octavian, but he savored his warmth, his scent, and the knowledge that for now, in Myrddin's arms, he was safe and cherished. Goddesses, he hoped Octavian had felt valued as he'd fallen asleep to Myrddin sprinkling kisses over his forehead and into his hair. He would not be able to protect Octavian when they reached Rosecairn, but tonight he could, and he treasured it.

Chapter
Ten

ON THE last day of Fayelle's Moon, with a sliver of a moon fighting through the fog, they crossed the Starlight Bridge, spanning the Kanda River between Selindria and Gaeltheon. Though the knights of Lockhaven protected the bridge and kept the passing safe, they landed in hostile territory almost the moment they put their feet on the opposite bank of the river. After half a day's journey inland, merchant stalls and traveling vendors disappeared. They passed through what Octavian assumed had once been farmland, though it was desolate and abandoned now. No inns or taverns operated in the area, so they were relegated to camping. Luckily, they'd filled up on gear—including sturdy tents—in the last town they'd visited. Now and then they found an abandoned cottage to take shelter in for the night, though Octavian never slept well within the overgrown, and sometimes burned and shattered, stones of the walls. He lay awake thinking of a family being driven out or destroyed by the warlord Lavock, and with every forgotten homestead they visited, his resolve to end the man and his reign of terror strengthened.

Doing that alone would be a worthwhile legacy to leave behind.

Some nights, Octavian shared a bedroll with Sylvain. Other times he lay beside Myrddin, but with twelve men and two tents, nothing beyond holding each other was possible. The cold was so intense, so brutal, that all of them nestled close in the night just to avoid freezing to death. Thankfully Octavian usually shared a tent with Myrddin, Dirk, Sylvain, and a few of the men from the Bitter Tide, who at least made an attempt to keep their bodies clean—unlike the Beasley brothers. Octavian gagged to imagine the stench in the other tent, and he felt sorry for Danno, who would tolerate the stink in dumb silence before suggesting they wash.

Sylvain smelled of buttery leather, clean skin, wine, and the campfire. He slept with his arm curled in Octavian's lap, on his side, with his forehead pressed to Octavian's hip. The closer they drew to Rosecairn, the more restless Octavian became. After probably half an hour of listening to the other men in the tent snore, he'd known he'd find no rest and had sat up to write by the light of the single lantern hanging from the tent's supports, his book resting atop his bent knees.

Octavian Rose's Journal

I want to write about magic, but magic is too big, too encompassing for me to distill into words. Loyalty is almost as abstract, as difficult to define. What is the nature of loyalty? What makes a man willing to die for another man, a cause, or a country? I can think of nothing and no one I would sacrifice myself for to see that they continued. Yet continuity must be the key to loyalty. To be willing to die, a man must trust that what he's dying for will continue beyond him, whether it's a country, a family, or a group of friends. To be willing to die, he must know that his blood will water fields that will continue to produce, to feed his line after he is gone. This is a difficult concept for me, as a man who has never had family except in the most literal sense.

But I think this, and I am young and likely wrong, but at this point, this is the best I can do. Loyalty means fighting for something that will endure beyond the brief span of a man's lifetime—the sense of being part of something larger and more profound that one's self. Men will fight for a home for the same reasons they'll fight for an empire: to ensure a place for their progeny to live in safety after they're gone, to ensure their line will continue. Loyalty, patriotism, is man's way to immortality. While the body may die and rot in the ground, the cause—the empire, the home—will live on. I wonder what that means for me, a man who will never have natural children. I suppose it means I can build a home, a place where other men can have families and put down roots—a place they will die defending so their offspring can live on. Goddesses, am I worthy, or able to build something like that at the Rosecairn? I don't know, but I plan to try. I wonder what the others whose opinions I value—Myrddin and Sylvain—would think if they knew my true plans. I wonder if they'll stand with me when I make my intentions clear. I would like to say it does not matter, but I would feel less, diminished, without them, and Myrddin especially. Myrddin does not flatter me, and I appreciate that. The weaknesses he sees in me inspire me to be better.

Which makes me wonder about loyalty and reciprocity. At what point is a man obligated to give his life to save the man who has saved him? Is obligation, debt, ever a valid reason to sacrifice oneself? I cannot see myself dying out of obligation, but love… that feeling that someone else living and walking in the light is more profound than living yourself…. Goddesses, maybe I can understand just wanting someone else to be whole and happy so much that I would cease to be to ensure it…. Maybe I can acknowledge the possibility of that sort of love, even if I have never experienced it. I don't think I have, but I am unsure. Yet again I long for a confidant who would offer an opinion. These pages seem drier and colder each time I look at them, and they do not offer me the answers I seek as I spread my ink across them. It feels base, animalistic, to verbalize this, but spreading my fluids across Myrddin or Sylvain would do better to calm my mind than all this contemplation. What I truly want, but am unlikely to find anytime soon, if ever, is a person who could see my cracks—my doubts, fears, insecurities, arrogance, selfishness—and not turn from me in disgust. Maybe even someone who would appreciate my flaws and not mind listening to my concerns: a friend, I suppose. Young as I am, I do not mistake what Myrddin and Sylvain offer as friendship. I haven't offered any more than either of them, and I'm not sure I should.

I will not venture into the blurred territory of which man has more merit than the other. For now I'll enjoy them both. There is no reason to choose; it's not a proposal of marriage, just… skin, lips, hands, cocks…. Goddesses, I wish this tent was not so crowded. But it is, and I should try to sleep. The Rosecairn awaits, and I mean it to be mine. Nothing else is important.

ROSECAIRN LAY a few days' ride east on the shore of Estrella Lake, sheltered on both sides by the steep northern mountains, with streams and tributaries running along the western edge of the huge area the warlord and his men had boxed in with crude fences of sharpened logs and stacked rocks. With only one—very well guarded—road leading into the camp and no way to flank or attack from any other angle, Octavian wasn't surprised the dozens of men below had failed to take Rosecairn.

For hours, Octavian had been pacing along the edge of the steppe where they'd stopped to rest, looking into the sheltered camp only a few miles away now, and the dozens of campfires surrounding it. Now more than ever, he needed a confidant, someone to hear his ideas and point out flaws he might be missing. But as far as any of the others knew, he planned to dispatch the warlord and hand him and the Rosecairn over to the knights and aristocrats of Gaeltheon in exchange for the reward. If he told them about his true ambitions—to claim the entire territory known as Rosecairn for himself and the good men who would defend it, to make it a home and a base of operations for the company he planned to form—they might abandon him. Less than a dozen men shouldn't matter, but they mattered to Octavian. He didn't want to tell them, but having them in whatever capacity he had them made him feel less alone.

The setting sun washed the snowy mountains and sharp, gray rock in rubicund light, pulling odd shadows from the crags and turning the frost pinkish lavender. Octavian kicked a loose rock with his toe and watched it bounce down the mountainside, stirring up clouds of powder where it hit. He swore under his breath, trying desperately not to let the others see his frustration. If they noticed his hesitancy and confusion, they might not trust his plan. But he had no bloody plan, no goddess-damned idea how to penetrate that camp and take it when probably a hundred men with more experience and better weapons had failed to do it for moons. Anyone trying to breach that single gate on that narrow road would fall quickly to the archers likely stationed in the tall towers on either side of the trail. What had all those men, sitting around their pinprick fires below him, not attempted? What had they missed? What was he missing?

Octavian had paced furrows in the frozen ground to rival a plowed field. He swore again and dropped his face into his chilled leather glove. He couldn't look into that valley anymore. What if he couldn't do this? What if he had led these men here for nothing? A dull throb behind his eyes moved into the rest of his head, the ache spreading down the back of his neck and across his shoulders as his feet continued moving of their own volition, his body unable to be still while his mind ran in circles that took him nowhere at all. Like the strands of magic the old woman had mentioned, the solution to this problem felt just out of reach, circling his head like birds over the river, close, but eluding his grasp.

A hand closing around his shoulder paused Octavian's pacing. He dropped his hand from his face. Myrddin looked at him, concerned, the lines deep around his eyes and mouth.

"What is it?" Octavian asked.

Myrddin moved his hand down Octavian's arm until he could grasp his wrist and guide him toward a copse of stunted trees. "Octavian, I would speak with you. Come here, where the others won't overhear us." When they reached the trees, Myrddin released Octavian, leaned against a gnarled trunk, and crossed his arms over his chest. "You're troubled."

Octavian had to do something with his hands, so he dragged them through his wind-knotted hair. "Yes, how very astute of you."

"There's no cause to be nasty, lad."

Octavian turned his face to the sky. He wanted to scream against the orange-rimmed snow clouds, but his frustration came out as a growl. After taking a few deep breaths to compose himself, he turned toward Myrddin. "You're right, and I'm sorry. I'm perplexed, but it's not your fault."

"Perplexed how?"

"There's no way into that camp," Octavian said, spinning on the ball of his feet to look at the sky again. "Even if we could convince all the men camped outside it to follow us, we'd never make it past the gate. The warlord knows this—that is why he suffers them to wait on his threshold at all. I just… I cannot conceive of any way to take this fortress. There's no way around that single entrance. I-I don't know what to do."

Octavian flinched away at first when Myrddin came up behind him, wrapped his arms around Octavian's waist, and rested his whiskered chin on Octavian's shoulder. But Myrddin's touch calmed him a little, and he leaned his back against the other man's chest as both of them looked toward the fires dotting the darkening valley. "Octavian, it does not fall to you alone."

"If you have a suggestion, I'm listening."

"Would you listen if I suggested we left this cursed place and went to seek other work?"

Myrddin's breath warmed Octavian's cheek, and he rested his head against Myrddin's shoulder, letting some of the tension bleed out of his neck. "This is just such an opportunity. Do you really want to let it slip through your fingers?"

Myrddin squeezed him, holding on to Octavian like he was some sort of rare treasure. "Lad, I gave up seeking great fortune and glory for my name long ago. Perhaps I'm just too old. All I want at this time in my life is to feed myself and see a few more days. But I remember being your age, and so I understand. It's a substantial purse, after all. With what you'll earn if you turn the warlord and his territory over, you'll be able to spend a year without lifting your sword—or that cursed dagger I wish you'd throw into a pit. I hate you wielding that thing. It's bad luck."

"I don't think I believe in luck." Octavian turned in Myrddin's arms and took Myrddin's face in his gloved hands, staring at him hard, trying to determine whether to share his plans with this man, looking for some visible trace of… of loyalty, he supposed. But the shadows had lengthened, casting Myrddin's face in darkness until Octavian could discern little but the firelit outline of his cheek and jaw. "I—Myrddin, can I trust you?"

"If you cannot, me saying otherwise will do little good. I'm here, am I not?"

Octavian nodded. "I'm going to tell you something I don't want the others to know, not even Sylvain, because I don't think you'll betray me. I hope I'm not wrong. I don't plan to turn Rosecairn over, Myrddin. I want it for myself. It's defensible—almost impregnable—and there's fresh water and access to the lake and river. I want it. I want to make it a place where good men can make a home, one they'll fight to defend. Do you remember the plans I told you of when we first met? Of having my own company, a company of honorable warriors, and a place where they could put down roots? Rosecairn could be that place. In our hands, the ravaged farms we passed could return and flourish. That's food, and food at a reasonable price if we're liked by the locals and we keep them safe. This place… it's everything I ever dreamed of for us."

"Us?"

Octavian's cheeks tingled. "I only mean you'd have a place if you wanted one. You're the sort of man I want—practical but honorable. I won't surround myself with thugs like the Beasleys. You… you know how I feel. Don't you, Myrddin?"

"Your feelings are changeable and difficult to track, young Octavian."

Octavian sighed and braced himself, because he didn't know how his words would be received. "I'd have you by my side. You're the closest thing I've ever had to a real friend. Or am I seeing something that isn't there?"

Myrddin kissed the part of his hair. "No. I'd like us to be friends, and I'll stand with you. I'll give you what aid I can, but your plans are beyond anything I ever aspired to, at least before I met you."

His words made Octavian feel better, and they rallied his confidence. "I'm glad. But that still leaves me with the problem of how to get into that camp."

"Lad, there's no way in. None that I can see, not unless you can put wings on men, which I'll wager even a mage like you can't do. It's a bleeding shame. From everything I've heard, most of the men in that camp might come over to our side if they knew you weren't planning on handing Rosecairn over to the knights. Lavock keeps them like slaves and kills them for fun. I doubt many of those men would stay if they weren't afraid of being killed if they tried to leave."

Octavian contemplated Myrddin's words as the stars came out above them, almost the mirror image of the many small fires in the valley below. Suddenly, as if lightning had struck his mind and lit it up like dawn, he knew exactly what to do. He backed away from Myrddin and bounced on the balls of his feet. He was so excited he couldn't resist kissing the confused man, pressing their lips together hard. "I have it. Oh, goddesses. You figured it out, Myrddin. Bless you." He kissed him again, deeper, pushing his tongue between Myrddin's lips.

"Slow down, friend." Myrddin chuckled against Octavian's mouth.

"Don't want to." Pecking along Myrddin's jaw, tasting his sweat and skin, Octavian just wanted to push him to the ground. He didn't care about the snow or sharp icy rocks. He knew what he needed to do now, and he felt light, free. He would take Rosecairn. With the worry of it removed, he tingled with anticipation and a premature thrill of victory. "I want—Goddesses, is there someplace we can go?"

Myrddin wound his big hands around Octavian's biceps and held him at arm's length. "Tell me what's going on in that head of yours."

Octavian grinned so wide his cheeks hurt. He wanted to jump up and down. "We can't fight our way from the outside in, so we'll fight our way from the inside out."

"How?"

"Don't you see? If the men inside that camp truly want free of their warlord, they can be persuaded to help us, especially those who guard the gates. If we can unite this force, and then unite the force within, we can strike at that prick Lavock from both sides. He'll never know what hit him."

Myrddin looked dubious. "The only problem is, we can't get inside. Even if we could sway those men to our banner, we have no way to reach them. No way to get through that gate."

"I do. I've already figured that part out. Of course, before I proceed, we'll have to convince the men camped outside the gates to fight as a single force when I can get them inside. But then—I know what to do! We can do this!"

"Slow down." Myrddin smoothed the fringe off Octavian's forehead. "What makes you think you can get through that gate?"

Octavian kissed him. "Another idea I owe to you. Don't you remember what you thought I was up to when I first approached you and Dirk? That's the ruse I'll employ. If I go alone, unarmed, just a whore looking for work, I won't be turned away. For once my youth and small size will be an advantage."

"No. I don't like that idea."

Octavian broke away from him and started pacing again, this time with excitement instead of frustration. "It's the only way. Of course we must first convince the men down there to go along with our plan. How hard can it be? They've obviously been down there months without coming up with a better idea themselves. And it's no risk to them— only to me. We can talk them into it. Then, when I get inside and convince the warriors to open the gate and stand with us, I'll give some sort of signal. You can lead the forces on this side. I'll have no one else. There's still a great deal to work through, though. I need my book. I need to record my ideas so I can weigh their merits, draw maps. I'll know more when I get a chance to speak with the men who have been here longer than we have. Come on. I need to write this down before I forget."

He turned and started back toward the horses and his things, filled with hope, his blood singing with the promise of glorious adventure and next step in the fulfillment of his goals.

"Octavian."

He turned around to find Myrddin pale, shoulders curled forward in defeat and gaze on his boots. "This is a terrible idea."

That stung. Octavian thought it a brilliant plan, one the warlord would never expect, one that could work, damn it. "Do you have a better one?"

"No, but…."

"Then come on! I don't want to wait to do this. I want to see what Dirk and Sylvain think. They may have ideas to contribute. But, Myrddin, you won't tell them what I plan to do when I take Rosecairn, will you?"

"No. I said I wouldn't, and I keep my oaths. I wish you'd hear me out, though. You're going to get yourself killed."

With a bad taste in his mouth, Octavian turned to face Myrddin, who appeared as a black silhouette against the snow gray sky, the weak moon and starlight glimmering off the edges of his armor. "No, I won't. I just want you to believe in me. Have some faith in me. Why can't you do that? Am I so lacking?"

Myrddin shook his head. "Not you. You're brilliant and full of fire. It's the rest of the world I doubt. Things seldom work out as idealistic men think they should. This is too great a risk. You're placing too much faith in others. Octavian, those fires that blaze the brightest also burn out the quickest."

"No. I can do this. I will do it. Help me or don't. It would mean a great deal to have you by my side, but if you cannot trust in my plan, I understand you doing what is best for yourself." Without waiting for Myrddin's response, Octavian turned and jogged back toward the fires the others had lit to prepare their dinner. He had to get his book and his quill, puzzle through the finer points of his strategy, nail everything down until he figured it out exactly. He'd find no respite until he did.

Chapter Eleven

THE CAMP in front of the gates to Rosecairn had grown to the size of a village, though it reminded Myrddin more of a rabbit warren with its confusing paths and dark passages. Every group of mercenaries who'd come in search of the treasure formed a separate, insular patch in the confused mess. Many of them were hostile to outsiders, mistrustful, though Octavian approached the leader of each group with his head held high and the maps and plans he'd drawn in his journal at the ready. He would let no one accompany him but Myrddin and Sylvain, and after three nights, they managed to sway most of the sell-swords to their banner. After all, none of them had any better plans, and Octavian's passion and absolute assurance they'd succeed drew the others like moths to a flame. Adding to that Myrddin's military knowledge, the legitimacy he added by saying the right terms, and the fact that Sylvain was—to the Shades' with him—damned charming and persuasive, they soon had most of the larger companies and probably half of the smaller ones on their side. Then again, if Octavian failed or died in his attempt to infiltrate Rosecairn, they had little to lose. If he died in there, he'd die alone, implicating no one and leaving the rest of them free to wait for another inspiration or simply leave.

None of them stood to lose a thing if Octavian perished horribly beyond those gates, and Myrddin held no illusions. These men were mercenaries; they cared about the gold they stood to win, nothing more.

Tonight, a group of the men who supported Octavian's plan gathered around him near the southern edge of the camp. "When I convince the men to open the gate and allow us passage, I'll make my way to the highest point within—the top of the cairn. Then I'll signal the rest of you to advance with a spray of blue sparks. I don't know how long we'll be able to keep the gates open, so you have to be ready to move at any time. Keep people on watch round the clock. All of you know what areas of the camp you'll concentrate on. Obviously I'll have to leave the maps and plans we drew up together behind, so you can each continue to plan how best to take your part of the camp. I've outlined the area we need to secure based on the information available to us, and we have selected the best possible men for each mission. If I do my part, you should encounter little resistance, though you will meet some. Still, we have enough skilled men, and we have developed a sound strategy. If all of you stay to your roles, we can win the Rosecairn. After each of you defeat the areas you're assigned to, you'll make your way toward the warlord's camp. The best information I have been able to gather through gossip tells us it's located at the northwestern corner of the area. There, we'll surround his home and take him down. I'll meet you there if I still live, and we'll see this thing to its end and make ourselves a fortune. It has been too long in coming."

Most of the men cheered, while a few grumbled about placing their fortunes in the lap of an inexperienced boy dressed as a whore. A scarce few sheathed their weapons and left, electing to take no part in Octavian's gambit. Still, he had an impressive force following him. Myrddin wanted to be happy for him and what he'd accomplished, but his sadness and dread swallowed his pride. He hated this idea.

The gathering broke up, men going off to drink and enjoy themselves before Octavian attempted entering the gates tomorrow evening. Octavian stood at the head of the group until it dispersed, and then he went off, head drooping and looking so painfully alone against the towering whitecaps in the distance that Myrddin hurried to catch up with him. He met him at the farthest corner of the camp, where they'd pitched their two shabby tents on a muddy patch next to a jutting outcrop of rock. Octavian stopped in front of them and hugged himself, so Myrddin stopped several feet back, wondering if he should intrude or if Octavian would rather be alone. He already figured out Octavian didn't want anyone seeing him display weakness or doubt, and he wondered if he should spare him forcing it all down, give him the time to break apart in private.

As if reading his thoughts, Octavian said, "Don't linger there. I don't want to be alone. I would appreciate your company, if you're not occupied."

"Of course not." After scanning the shadows to make sure they were alone and unseen, Myrddin wrapped his arms around Octavian and burrowed his nose into his soft hair. He felt small and slight in Myrddin's arms—his bones too thin and fragile for him to walk into that cruel camp without even a dagger to protect himself. But saying so would offend Octavian, so Myrddin asked, "Are you all right?"

"I… no." He tensed against Myrddin, his anxiety rising from him like the morning fog from the snow. "Everyone is depending on me. If I fail, all is lost. It's a heavy burden to bear and… and, Myrddin, I'm afraid. After all the stories I've heard of this monster, I know what kind of death I'll be facing if I don't succeed, or if I'm discovered or betrayed."

Myrddin pulled him closer. He didn't want Octavian to be afraid, didn't want him to worry, and surely didn't want him in danger with no one to watch his back. He also knew, could picture, probably in more grisly detail than Octavian, what those men might do to him. "You can still say no. It's just a job, Octavian. There will be other jobs. There's no sense in losing your life for this one. You may not want to hear this, but I do not want to lose you."

"Why?"

Why. How to answer that, Myrddin wondered, when he couldn't figure it out himself. Octavian shouldn't matter so much to him. No decent young man deserved the nightmarish torture he could face, but…. "Because I care about you, and I think you're a remarkable young man. It would be a sad waste for you to die here when the world is better with you in it. You should die well into old age, surrounded by people who love you, not as a young man with so much left unfinished."

It surprised Myrddin when Octavian laid his head on Myrddin's shoulder and consented to be held—practically begged to be held. His lips tickled Myrddin's throat when he spoke. "I would rather die young, doing something meaningful, than old at the end of a meaningless life."

Myrddin wrapped him in his arms as if he could prevent death from snatching him away, and he never wanted to release him. Part of him wished Octavian had been born with a milder spirit, while the rest knew he wouldn't be so fascinated, so enthralled with the young man if his passion didn't burn so brightly. Dumbly, he muttered, "I do not want you to die. It would… pain me greatly."

Octavian angled his face so his lips moved against Myrddin's. "Give me a reason to live… to come back."

Myrddin tangled his fingers in Octavian's rich dark hair and inclined his head back. Goddesses, that fire in his eyes would destroy Myrddin, but like the moth, he couldn't stay away. It drew him beyond his ability to resist. He didn't know what compelled him toward it, but he wanted to drown in it, let it consume him. He pressed his lips to Octavian's, and Octavian's mouth opened to his tongue. They kissed in the shadow of the central fires, clutching at each other's armor and grinding their groins together as their breath came out in thick clouds.

"We should—" Myrddin rubbed the tip of his nose against Octavian's, unable to relinquish contact. "Someone might see."

"I want to feel your body," Octavian panted, "your skin against my skin. Will you come inside the tent with me?"

As if Myrddin would even consider refusing. "I'm completely infatuated with you, Octavian. I want you more than my next breath."

"Then what are we waiting for?" With their bodies still pressed closed, Octavian tugged Myrddin through the tent's flap. He sprawled on his back, and Myrddin covered Octavian with his body, careful to prop his weight on his elbows so he wouldn't squash Octavian or press his hard plate into him. Octavian's erection pressed against Myrddin's, firm and wonderful even through the layers of leather, fur, and chain mail separating them. He stretched his neck to reach Myrddin's lips, and then he nipped at them, tugged them into his mouth, and ran his warm tongue along their edges. His innocent enthusiasm and honest need, combined with the muted sounds of satisfaction and desire he made almost finished Myrddin in his trousers. He'd been with his fair share of men over the years, but he couldn't remember the last time he'd felt so needed by someone.

Octavian rocked his hips up as he pulled his mouth away and let his head fall against the bedroll. His sigh came out in a warm cloud against Myrddin's neck and chin. As he spoke, he raked through and toyed with Myrddin's whiskers with his fingers. "I don't want this to be something we do in the dark, our clothes pushed aside just enough to manage it. I don't want this to be just a hurry to come. Nothing dirty and desperate like that. I want more than that."

"Tell me." In that moment, Myrddin would have done anything Octavian asked, anything to make him happy, because hearing the desire cracking his voice made him feel like the most important man in the world, the most desirable. The luckiest bastard to walk in the light.

All he wanted was to make Octavian shred apart with pleasure, make him feel as wanted, maybe show him he didn't have to dive into the arms of death to be of value to someone. "Tell me what you want, and I'll do it. Anything."

"Are you sure it's all right?" The lust-hazed, distracted tone left his voice. "What if the others come back?"

Myrddin chuckled against the sweet skin of his throat and nipped his skin. "They'll be drinking. Probably for a good many hours. Sylvain is likely prowling the camp in search of his next conquest, and Dirk…. Dirk will know better. We've been friends a long time."

Octavian relaxed beneath him and lolled his head to the side to offer Myrddin better access to his neck. Myrddin's kisses summoned little moans of pleasure until Octavian panted and squirmed. He clawed at the straps holding Myrddin's breastplate, but clearly didn't understand how it all fit together. "Myrddin, I want light. I want to be able to see your eyes while you look down on me, the sweat on your skin. Your lips red and wet and swollen from my kisses. Your expression when you come inside me."

Myrddin's balls knotted against him so hard it almost hurt. He buried his face against Octavian's chest and growled, clutching at the edges of Octavian's heavy cloak and cleaving it open to fall on either side of him. A few thrusts of his hips, a few more of those wanton words coming from those lips, and he'd spill in his trousers. Aroused as he was, he almost wanted to grab Octavian's waist and rut against him until he satisfied himself.

"Myrddin, the lantern?"

"Goddesses, I like hearing you say my name." Myrddin sat up on his heels and found the small lamp and the flint beside it. The flame illuminated Octavian lying in front of him, his arms folded beneath his head, waist twisted, one hip thrust up toward his ribs, and his legs splayed open. Myrddin took a moment to admire his long legs in those tight leather trousers, and then he reached for Octavian's hand and pulled him up to sit. They faced each other, and as Myrddin traced the contours of Octavian's face, Octavian's eyelids fluttered shut and his lips fell open. Myrddin pulled the chain-mail vest over Octavian's head and let it fall with a rattle before starting on the laces of his tunic. "Do you know how beautiful you are?"

"Tell me."

Myrddin brushed the tunic off Octavian's shoulders and pulled his old woolen shirt away. His nipples hardened in the cold, dark against his firelit skin. Myrddin ran his thumb over one, and Octavian shuddered. "I don't think I've ever wanted a man the way I want you. I've never met anyone like you. You're beautiful, and fierce, and clever, and you make me crazy. Make me behave like a besotted lad… I…. Just hearing your voice could undo me."

Octavian parted his languid eyelids, and the single flame reflected off his dark eyes. "That would be a shame. I would much rather have you undo yourself buried deep inside me."

Myrddin almost couldn't hold back. He felt moisture below his belly button and tremors shaking his body. "You have a vile tongue, you know that? I should put you over my knee and teach you some manners."

"My words are not vile." Octavian straightened and narrowed his eyes. "I was asking you for pleasure. I have no desire to be hurt or humiliated, and if that's what you want—"

"No, goddesses." Myrddin reached for him and pulled him close, kissing him lightly, showing him his adoration, before saying, "Only a joke. A very poor joke. I hope you know I'm not a man who enjoys the pain or degradation of others. I hope you know that."

"I do." Octavian cradled the back of Myrddin's head to pull him in for a deeper kiss. Their teeth scraped together as he spoke. "I know you're a good, honorable man. That's why I followed you all those moons ago. You're the kind of man I want to be. I just… the idea of others abusing me for their entertainment isn't one I want in my head right now."

"I wish you wouldn't go. Octavian, it isn't worth it."

"I have to go. Those men are depending on me. They'll never respect me if I tuck my tail between my legs and run. I told them I could do this, and against all reason, they believed in me. Why can't you?" Octavian scooted back a few inches. "Are you really just beside me for… to fuck me?"

Myrddin's head and cock both hung in defeat. He could be such a fool sometimes, and now he'd ruined their night together, the only one they might ever get. "Goddesses, what's wrong with me?"

"Myrddin?"

"I just don't want you to die! Can't you understand that? I don't want you raped and tortured for days before they finally kill you! You take that as a lack of confidence, but I mean it as concern, because I care about you. I—"

"Goddesses." Octavian crawled into Myrddin's lap and straddled his hips, holding his face in both hands. "You really do."

Myrddin ran his fingertips through the swatch of dark hair between Octavian's chest muscles. It was softer than he'd imagined and framed his lean muscles beautifully. "Yes, Octavian, I do. For one so brilliant, so clever with strategy, you can be simple as a mule when it comes to seeing a man's intentions. I don't think you lack skill, or courage, but the odds you're going against—"

"Stop talking. Stop talking about this. Take off your armor. I don't know how." It didn't stop him from fumbling with the straps and grunting with frustration as he battled against the metal plate.

"All right." Octavian wanted him, not talk of the future, and Myrddin would oblige him. It was what he needed, what they both needed: to frolic together, just be men and ignore the storm clouds gathering over them. Myrddin needed to stop thinking and just do what felt right. He wasn't sure Octavian ever stopped thinking, but he could damned well try to make him. "You'll have to get off me, lad."

Octavian made a pouty sound as he slid off Myrddin's thighs. His gaze never left Myrddin as Octavian pulled off his boots and began working the leather cord loose from the grommets at the front of his trousers. The way his expression smoldered, Myrddin almost expected to burn his fingers when he touched Octavian's skin. But as he watched Octavian peel the leather down his legs, as his perfect cock sprung free and slapped his belly, the tip poking from the hood and already glistening with his excitement, Myrddin didn't care. He'd touch him if his fingers blistered and blackened.

Myrddin made short work of getting out of his worn breastplate, pauldrons, bracers and greaves. Space in the tent was tight, so he piled his armor between his bedroll and the wall of the tent. He put his chain-mail tunic, the padded shirt he wore underneath, and his leather trousers and boots carefully on top.

"I like the way you move," Octavian said. "I like your muscles and how they lengthen and bunch, and how that makes your skin catch the light. And the gold hair on your belly." With his thumb and finger, Octavian slid his hood back to expose his dusky pink head. When he ran his pinky along the groove on the underside and chewed his lower lip, Myrddin forgot to breathe.

"Tell me what you want." It took all Myrddin's concentration to form the words as Octavian spread out below him, touching himself, his pose relaxed and welcoming, his skin like ivory satin lined with mauve.

In a smooth motion, Octavian sat up and tucked his feet beneath him. He reached out for Myrddin, and Myrddin sat down facing him, their knees brushing together. Octavian put his palms on Myrddin's thighs and moved them slowly to his hips, leaving a trail of heat in the wake of his touch. "I want to see you up close, have a chance to look without being afraid of being caught looking, touch without feeling like I have to steal it." He moved his hands lightly over Myrddin's ribs and up his chest, where he squeezed the mounds of muscle.

"I've never been accused of being a beautiful man," Myrddin muttered, his skin tingling and turning to gooseflesh beneath Octavian's hands. This was probably as new for him as it was Octavian. Until now, his idea of making love had been to find a willing partner and somewhere hidden and dark, and then slam into whatever opening was offered before tucking himself away. Often, no words were exchanged. This slow exploration, this drowning in the flames dancing in Octavian's eyes, exchanging slow, wet kisses while they took time learning the contours of each other's bodies—it felt like the first time he'd really connected with a man beyond a few moments of grunting and a rush to release.

"I think you're beautiful." Octavian skimmed his nails up Myrddin's neck and held his cheeks in his hands as he had before they'd undressed. "You're probably the finest man I've met in my life. That's why I don't want to waste this." He ran his tongue over Myrddin's Adam's apple and chin before circling his lips, sliding it along the seam until Myrddin opened his mouth. They kissed slowly at first, testing and discovering with their tongues as they had with their hands, but it soon turned hard and desperate: tongues bumping and twisting, lips tugging at lips, teeth denting sensitive flesh. They kissed with a foot of space still between them until Myrddin felt dizzy with lack of air and had to pull away. Myrddin grasped Octavian's shoulders and eased him down to his back. Octavian's eyes widened for a moment before he let his body sag into the blankets and furs. He reached for Myrddin, and finally, they lay chest to chest, their skin damp and sticking together, the hair on their chests catching as they shifted to fit together. In no time, they clicked into place like a key in a lock, perfectly, as if made for no other purpose.

Myrddin took his time kissing and nibbling down Octavian's body, exploring the muscles of his belly with his lips and enjoying Octavian's gasps and groans, the way he twitched and twisted when Myrddin found a ticklish or sensitive spot. He flicked each of Octavian's dark rose nipples with his tongue, then circled the left one and sucked it into his mouth. Octavian held his hair, clearly enjoying Myrddin's attention, but he didn't seem especially receptive there. Some men weren't, but there was one thing all men liked.

Myrddin pushed Octavian's legs a little farther apart and rubbed his face and nose against the dark hair between his legs, inhaling his scent as he cradled Octavian's balls in his hand. With Octavian this excited, his balls huddled close to his body, and Myrddin could fit his whole sac in his fist. "Pretty cock," he mumbled. He ran his tongue over the pink length, tracing the veins on the underside, and then licked over the crown and slit. Octavian's taste made his mouth water, and he sucked greedily on his tip as he kneaded the firm back of Octavian's thigh with his free hand.

"Wait!"

Myrddin let Octavian slip out of his mouth, but he kept rubbing his cock against his chin and cheek, smearing his whiskers with Octavian's precome, as he asked, "What's wrong?"

"It's too much, Myrddin. It feels too good."

He chuckled, making sure Octavian felt the vibration by pressing his cock against his throat. "It's supposed to feel good, lad. I want to make you feel good. Octavian, has anyone ever done this for you before?"

"Yes."

"Sylvain?"

"No."

Myrddin didn't question him. Octavian kept to himself about his experiences prior to joining them, as was his right. All that mattered was this moment. "Well, then you should know your job is just to lie back and trust me to see to your pleasure. I won't disappoint you."

"I know… I just, I don't want to embarrass myself. Your mouth feels so good. Seeing your lips on me… I won't last."

Myrddin swiped his tongue around the ledge of Octavian's cock head and made his erection jump. He moved his unoccupied hand up to the *V* of muscle angling over Octavian's hips. Goddesses, that was a delicious spot. Myrddin could have spent hours lavishing affection on Octavian's belly. His skin was flawless now; it would bear a network of scars one day if he stayed in this occupation. Myrddin had plenty of his own, but they didn't stop Octavian from wanting him. The young man fought the urge to lift his hips and thrust his cock against Myrddin's face and mouth, though he obviously wanted to. Eyes clamped shut, he tossed his head from side to side and curled his toes around the furs beneath them.

"You're young, Octavian. So young. Just let go. I want that, want to taste you." Myrddin slid his mouth down Octavian's shaft, and when it slipped into his throat, Octavian cried out. His whole body clenched beneath Myrddin. He dug his fingers into Myrddin's scalp. He lifted off the bedclothes before realizing what he'd done and muttering an apology. "Don't be sorry. Fuck my mouth."

"Are you… are you sure?"

"Sure as the goddesses made us. Take my mouth. Please. I want it." He slid down Octavian's erection and sucked until his cheeks caved. Tentatively at first, with shallow, jerky movements, Octavian curled his pelvis and pushed his cock into Myrddin's throat. Myrddin groaned his approval, and soon Octavian pumped into his mouth with deep rhythmic thrusts.

"That feels unbelievable. Are you sure it's all right?"

Unwilling to lift his mouth off Octavian, Myrddin made what he hoped was a sound of assent.

"Oh, goddesses, oh, all right…." Octavian knit his fingers into Myrddin's hair and let go, lifting his hips off the bedroll with short, quick, erratic thrusts. "Goddesses, that's… oh fuck. Myrddin… you… you're so wonderful." Myrddin wrapped an arm around Octavian's lower back and urged him on. In moments, his seed erupted over Myrddin's tongue, and he threw a forearm over his eyes as he cried out and mumbled nonsense, his entire body convulsing so violently his belly smacked Myrddin's forehead. Myrddin held on, determined to accompany Octavian in his ecstasy, to hold him together as he fell apart. If nothing else, he wanted Octavian to see he was someone to trust when he was most vulnerable. He burrowed his fingers into Octavian's waist, in that beautiful place just above his hipbones, as Octavian shot spurt after spurt of bitter, salty come across the roof of Myrddin's mouth and down his throat. Myrddin swallowed eagerly, wanting something of Octavian inside him, as Octavian softened in his mouth. Myrddin sucked and laved his cock until he'd cleaned away and swallowed every drop of his seed. "Stop… please. It's too much."

Myrddin released him and left his cock hanging wet and limp between his legs. He kissed his way back up Octavian's torso until he could catch his lips. He'd never grow tired of that soft, full mouth against his or the enthusiasm with which Octavian devoured his lips and tongue. The way Octavian kissed him and ground against him, one would never know he'd satisfied himself so fully only moments ago. Myrddin hadn't, and he remained hard, painfully so, his cock leaking across Octavian's belly, but he wouldn't relinquish this wonderful sensation of their kissing, Octavian's warm skin beneath him. Holding him this way felt more intimate than coupling.

"Myrddin, can I see your cock?" Octavian said in a warm rush against his ear.

He was quickly warming to Octavian's inquisitive and open nature in bed, and he chuckled. "You've seen it before."

Octavian pecked and nipped along Myrddin's neck, leaving his skin slick and heated. He bit lightly into Myrddin's earlobe and then said, "I touched it. I liked touching it. But it was dark, and we had to be so quick and quiet. I'd like a look at it now so I can take the time to appreciate it. Not shy, are you?"

"No, it just isn't something a lover has asked of me before."

Octavian chuckled and nibbled around the shell of Myrddin's ear while he stroked the muscles of his back with his other hand. "Then I get to be the first." He smiled; Myrddin felt him smiling with every fiber of his body, and he smiled in return. "I rather like that idea. Turn us over?"

"Your wish is my command." Myrddin crossed his arms over Octavian's back and rolled them. Octavian straddled him and curled over him, kissing him until Myrddin thought he'd sucked out his sanity. Then he sat up and slid down Myrddin's body; Myrddin parted his legs to accommodate him.

The gasp of astonishment Octavian made as he ran his fingers over Myrddin's balls and shaft sent a shiver up Myrddin's spine. He toyed with Myrddin's foreskin, pulling it over his crown and off, making little sounds of appreciation as he looked on. It took all Myrddin's will and patience to lay complacent as Octavian explored. He wanted more and was quickly reaching an edge he couldn't keep from tumbling over, but it felt incredible to be so revered, almost worshipped. Octavian leaned in rubbed his cheek up Myrddin's length, leaving slippery strands of Myrddin's fluids on his cheek. He held Myrddin's cock at the base and rubbed the tip in circles against his lips.

"Pleased with it?" Myrddin choked out between jagged breaths.

"It's perfect." Octavian pulled at the skin of Myrddin's sac with his lips before moving his tongue along the underside of his dick. "Just the right size. Sylvain's is a monster."

"Lad, no man wants to hear himself compared to a bigger man by a lover." Myrddin didn't feel the jealousy he expected, though. How could he, with Octavian kissing up and down his length and moaning with delight? Octavian didn't acknowledge his words.

"I like your gold hair." He ruffled it with his chin and cheek. "I like the way you smell. I like how you curve." He ran his thumb over the gentle bend at the center of Myrddin's erection. "I can imagine how you'll feel inside me. You'll find just the right place."

"I will certainly try." It surprised Myrddin he managed to speak at all with his whole body on fire, tense and tingling, wound so tight he felt like he'd blow apart. "Love, I cannot take much more. If you keep touching me like you are, I'm going to disappoint you. I'm not as young as you, and I won't recover as quickly."

Octavian straightened and met Myrddin's gaze, licking the remnants of Myrddin's seed from his lips with relish. "I'm ready. Do you have anything to make it easier for me?"

"Aye." Goddesses, it was really going to happen. Everything Myrddin had dreamed of and fantasized about since he'd laid his eyes on Octavian Rose was about to happen, and it was so much better than he'd ever envisioned. Luckily he could reach his discarded trousers without getting up. He found them, and in their pocket, the small vial of oil he'd had little cause to use, except to pleasure himself on the rare occasion he had the privacy to do so. He pressed it into Octavian's hand.

Octavian pulled out the stopper and drizzled the liquid over his hands. His gaze never wavered from Myrddin's as he reached behind himself, though his eyes rolled back and his lids fluttered as he prepared.

Myrddin had never seen nor imagined anything so alluring. Part of him wished he could see Octavian pushing his fingers into himself, but he'd hate to lose the view of his face and the way it reddened and pinched with pleasure. He bit into his lip and tried to concentrate on the twinge to keep from spilling. "Goddesses, you…. Please. Please hurry."

"I'm ready." With his oiled hand, Octavian grasped Myrddin's cock at the base. He guided the head up and down his crevice, pausing at his opening, pushing a little farther with each pass. As he circled his hole with the tip of Myrddin's dick, adding Myrddin's fluids to the oil, his cheeks darkened until they looked almost bruised, his nipples stood out, his mouth fell open, and his erection bobbed up and down with his movements. Finally, he dropped down, and Myrddin's cock sank a few inches into the warm pressure of his body. "Goddesses!"

Resisting his instinct to thrust up into Octavian, Myrddin petted his chest. "Take your time. Don't hurt yourself. I don't want that. I want…. Goddesses, you feel good. I want you to feel only pleasure."

"I'm very pleased," Octavian said as he sank down a little farther. "You've been very good to me. Now it's my turn to be good to you."

He took his time to adjust to Myrddin inside his body. His pretty pink cock swelled and dripped with every inch he took, until finally, he sat atop Myrddin, joined flesh to flesh. He smiled. His muscles clenched and rippled around Myrddin. "Do I feel as good to you as you do to me?"

"Octavian. I can't… you can't expect me to be eloquent right now. You feel like paradise."

"You're beautiful. Bronze and gold. I—" Octavian fell forward to kiss him, and he tasted like heaven: wine, swollen lips, and the bitter tang of Myrddin's seed. As their tongues twisted and dueled, Octavian swiveled his hips, driving Myrddin in and out of him. He kept the strokes shallow at first, but before long his body opened and accepted Myrddin's, and he rode Myrddin hard, with complete abandon.

Myrddin had often been used to satisfy another's needs, but lying beneath Octavian, trying to hold on to his waist as he bounced up and down, felt so much different. With every ounce of his will, he held his release back, because watching Octavian move, watching his eyes roll back and his lips go slack, all because of Myrddin, was almost better than letting go.

"Do you like me inside you?" Myrddin panted. He couldn't help thrusting up to meet Octavian; his resistance had nearly reached its end.

"Bleeding Shades, yes. Yes! Give me all you have. Give it to me now!"

Myrddin gripped Octavian by his hipbones and pulled him down hard. Octavian put a hand beside Myrddin's head to brace himself, and they pushed against and into each other for all they were worth, skin smacking against skin, both of them moaning inarticulately through open mouths as they drowned in each other's eyes. Octavian came first, spurting thick ribbons of come over Myrddin's belly and chest. The rhythmic squeezing of his muscles around Myrddin's cock finished Myrddin. "Kiss me," he managed to mutter before his seed erupted from him and into Octavian. They knit their lips together as Myrddin tensed and then broke apart in glorious release. As the world shattered around him, he held tight to Octavian's hips, held Octavian's lips between his teeth, let Octavian anchor him so he wouldn't be burned away with the power of something he'd never felt before.

Moments later—Myrddin didn't know how long he'd spent within Octavian's inferno—Octavian collapsed beside him, his ribs stretching his skin as he gasped for air. Myrddin scrubbed a hand over his face, smearing sweat into his hair, as he caught his breath. His sweaty body felt cold almost as soon as they separated, and he rolled to face Octavian. "Can I hold you?"

"Please." Octavian nestled against him and pressed a leg between Myrddin's thighs. Goddesses, they fit together so well, like two pieces of a puzzle, their bodies a single being. "Cold, Myrddin…."

Myrddin pulled the blankets and furs over them and held Octavian close. Octavian relaxed against him, and before long he snored against Myrddin's chest with his arm draped over Myrddin's shoulder. Myrddin hated to rouse him, but they had to dress, and sleepily, Octavian pulled his trousers and shirt on before settling back in.

"One day, I'll find a way for us to lay naked together all night," Myrddin said softly into his hair.

"I'd like that," Octavian mumbled. Shortly he fell back asleep.

Eventually the others returned to the tent, stumbling drunkenly into their places before falling into oblivion. Each noise awakened Octavian, and he squirmed and muttered until Myrddin soothed him back to sleep by petting his hair and kissing his face. A few times, in the darkness, he kissed Myrddin and rocked against him, clutching at Myrddin's hips to draw him close. Though he wanted more, Myrddin smoothed Octavian's fringe and peppered his forehead with light pecks, sheltering him in his arms until he fell back asleep. Tomorrow, Octavian would have to stand on his own, but tonight, Myrddin could keep him protected and cherished within his arms. He prayed to the goddesses it wouldn't be the last time he held Octavian like this, but Octavian burned so brightly to prove his worth, and Myrddin knew he wouldn't be diverted from his course. He would have better luck trying to contain the sun within his arms.

Chapter Twelve

THE DAY, and the time for Octavian to attempt his infiltration of the fortress of Rosecairn, dragged on in an endless wash of gray and sporadic bouts of snow, yet in some ways time moved too quickly. The most important moment of his life approached, and he couldn't decide if it came to slowly or too fast. Finally the sun set, turning the mountains to an irregular black line between the flushed gold of the sky and snow. Octavian went into the tent to make his final preparations. It seemed he was of two minds about everything today, because part of him wished he'd found Myrddin inside, while part of him was glad he hadn't. Myrddin had made it clear he didn't want Octavian to take this risk, and seeing the hope and fear warring in his eyes might have made it difficult to take those steps to the gate. On the other hand, it was precisely the way Myrddin looked at him, whatever he saw in Octavian that inspired him, that made Octavian desperate to succeed. No one had ever looked at him with so much expectation, seen him as so much more than the men around him. He wanted to be the man Myrddin imagined when he looked at him.

But it would have been a small comfort to get a kind word of farewell and a kiss for luck.

The time to be a child and covet words of approval had passed, though. Octavian knew he was doing the right thing—the only thing he could do. He stripped out of his armor and clothes, folded them, and left them piled in the corner. On top, he set his dagger in its leather scabbard. He already felt naked without its protection, without the symbol of freedom and the reminder not to squander it that the dagger has always been for him. But he would never be permitted to pass through the gates carrying it, and Myrddin had promised to keep it safe for him. Wit and luck would be his only weapons. He had to believe they'd be enough.

Octavian dipped a cloth in the pail of water and twisted it to wring out the excess. He held it between his hands for a few moments, but it remained cold enough to steal his breath when he swiped it over his face, armpits, and groin. He cleaned his teeth and combed his hair. Over the past few evenings, Octavian had traded for and cobbled together the things he needed to perpetrate his ruse: a tight gray pair of leggings that clung to him and showed off his ass, thighs, and crotch; a billowy white shirt with bell sleeves and scalloped edges that might have been meant for a woman; shiny red boots that folded just below his knees, and a red velvet vest held together by a gaudy brooch of copper and inexpensive stones. He wanted to appear a successful prostitute, but not one too wealthy to resort to risking his safety in the camp. Sylvain, who seemed to know more than was proper about such things, said his disguise would be perfect. He threw his fur-lined cloak on over top, because even whores had to keep warm. Finally, nothing remained but to leave the tent and take those steps. Octavian's stomach lurched, and he hurried to lean over the chamber pot, glad he hadn't been able to eat more than a bowl of broth and a crust of bread.

He took the pot out to empty and returned to the tent to rinse the sick taste from his mouth. A skin of wine hung from one of the supports. It wouldn't do to attempt this drunk, but maybe just a few swallows for courage, to stop the trembling of his hands....

The wine helped, bolstering his confidence enough to leave the tent. A little way up the road, Sylvain met him at a makeshift tavern the others had constructed by leaning some boards across barrels beneath an oilcloth tarpaulin. He rose from where he sat playing a card game with three other men. His teeth flashed in the torchlight when he smiled at Octavian, and his eyes glinted from beneath his hood. "Onward to glory, then?"

"That's my intention." Octavian forced a laugh. "If I could do this, me out of everyone, well, that would be something."

"If anyone can do it, it's you."

"Do you really believe that?" Octavian asked.

"I stand to gain nothing by lying or flattery." Sylvain leaned in and lowered his voice. "I've already coaxed you to my bed, and it's been my experience you'll come back of your own accord. But yes, I believe you can succeed."

"Why?"

"I'm a good judge of character. You're as sharp as an arrowhead, brave with just the right amount of recklessness. I can't think of another man in this camp who'd have the bollocks to try. They'd be too crippled by their fear."

"Sylvain, I—" Octavian swallowed his panic. "I wish we could be alone for a moment."

Sylvain looked dismissively over his shoulder at the other men, but even he didn't dare show Octavian affection in front of others. "I'll make it up to you when you get back."

"I'll hold you to that." Just as he'd worried it might, the desire to fall trembling into Sylvain's arms, to sob on his shoulder and admit he was scared enough to puke his insides out, grew with every moment they stood regarding each other. He had to turn around and leave or his resolve would crumble. "Tell Myrddin and Dirk I said farewell, won't you? And if I… if I don't come back, tell Myrddin I'm sorry. Tell Dirk I'm sorry I robbed him of the privilege of telling me he'd been right all along. And you. I'm glad we met."

Sylvain squeezed his shoulder, then quickly brushed his cheek with the back of his hand. "Octavian…."

"I should go before it gets any darker." Before Sylvain could argue, Octavian turned and jogged through the camp. He kept darting his gaze from side to side at the groups of men he passed, those gathered around fires or beneath torchlight, huddled together against the encroaching night. He thought he might see Myrddin, meet his eyes one last time. But he reached the edge of the light, of the camp, without catching a glimpse of him.

And there the road stretched out before him, long, barren, and lonely. It already felt colder, with a sharper edge to the wind, but Octavian knew he probably imagined that the stars seemed farther away than ever, and Octavian felt small beneath them. By going over his plan in his mind, silently repeating the words he intended to say, he managed to force his feet to lift and touch down, lift and touch down, until he stood before the massive gate with its two watchtowers. As soon as he stepped into the light cast by the torches, he threw his cloak back and held his empty hands out to his sides. He hoped the men on guard wouldn't see how hard they shook.

"Who goes there?" someone yelled down. Octavian tried to answer but the lump in his throat blocked the well-practiced words. "Answer, or we shoot you down!"

"I am a peddler." Octavian's voice rang out strong and clear, maybe too clear for a prostitute. "I would speak with the gatekeeper. Please, I pose no threat to you. I beg you to let me inside. You can just as easily kill me there."

For agonizing moments, nothing but the wind skittering over the snow broke the silence. With a tiny motion, Octavian looked over his shoulder, trying to gauge the distance he'd have to run to be out of range of their arrows, to be out of the light. If he closed his cloak over the white shirt that made such a bright target....

A low groan rent the night, and the heavy wooden gates that took three men on each side to drag open carved deep gashes in the snow and frozen ground. Octavian stumbled back a few steps as a big man in heavy plate appeared, backlit by the fires from within, his breath coming out in orange clouds. "Approach."

Octavian held his chin high and did as he was told.

"Now, tell me why you're here and why I shouldn't run you through."

"Please, tam. I am only looking for work. Lads down in the camp are running low on coin, as well as anything they might trade for my services, so I thought I'd try my luck here. I thought maybe all of you could use some entertainment after being shut up in here all this time. I'm a very good entertainer."

"What, you want me to let you in here after you've spent the past moon down there fucking our enemies?"

"It's nothing personal." Octavian grinned and batted his lashes, though he didn't know if the guard would be able to see. "I'm only trying to make a living with the skills the goddesses gave me. Besides, I've done you a favor. Those men will be leaving with much less gold than they came with."

The man narrowed his eyes. "And where is all this gold?"

"I may be a whore," Octavian told him, stepping a little closer, "but I'm not a simpleton. That gold is safely hidden for me to retrieve when I move on from here. Now, will you let me see if I can bring some happiness to men who could surely use it?"

"Move your cloak aside." Octavian did, and the man quickly but thoroughly ran his hands over him. Since he didn't linger over Octavian's legs or ass, Octavian assumed he had no interest in his supposed services. Satisfied, the man nodded toward the crack in the massive gate. "The camp's a dangerous place. Steer clear of Lavock. You'll do well to keep out of his notice. You're just the kind of innocent little thing he likes to cut to pieces over the course of a couple nights. And that's if he's in a generous mood." The disdain in the man's voice was as clear as the compassion in his tone when he spoke again. "Look, my name's Karl. I watch the gate nights. I been a sell-sword most of my life, but that don't mean I like to see anyone suffer. If you need to get out of here fast, come find me."

"Thank you. That's very generous. Is there something I can do to repay you?"

Karl chuckled and patted Octavian's shoulder. "Only if you have a sister, lad."

"Thank you."

"Watch your back… what's your name?"

The truth couldn't hurt his plans. "Octavian."

"Octavian. Be careful where you sleep. If you sleep. Be careful what men you offer your services to. Many of them are decent enough, but some of them are sick and cruel, and the only pleasure they'll take from you is by watching you suffer."

"Thank you, Karl." Octavian wondered if Karl would stand with him when he took Rosecairn. He hoped so; he seemed like a good man. But Octavian was getting way ahead of himself.

The gate groaned closed behind him. As soon as Octavian escaped the light, he pulled his hood over his head and drew his cloak shut in front of him. The whore's clothes had served their purpose, but since he didn't really plan to sell himself, he preferred to go as unnoticed as he possibly could. As he slowed his pace, he tried to get a lay of the land, sketch a rough map in his mind. Like the camp at the opposite end of the road, it was chaotic: tents, lean-tos, and shoddy buildings grouped in no particular order, with muddy, overlapping trails between them. It had the same air of impermanence as the gathering of mercenaries, and it was less tidy. Garbage, empty bottles, and even animal carcasses lined the paths or sat in stinking heaps. Octavian kept his head down as he passed a man singing drunkenly as he pissed on the side of a tent, and he crossed to the other side of the road to avoid a trio of portly, shirtless men tormenting a mangy dog on a chain.

As he made his way toward the center of the camp and the cairn itself, Octavian realized something was very wrong. In a place like this, by all accounts well supplied and relatively safe from threat, men should be gathered together, playing games, drinking, singing, or preparing food. Full darkness had only fallen an hour ago; the moon had barely crested the mountain peaks. Something drove these men inside, kept them quiet when they should be merry. Octavian knew it was fear—a fear profound enough to keep lifelong warriors and mercenaries of the most vicious reputations cowering in the shadows like rabbits. At first that thought terrified Octavian, for if these men, renowned for their savagery, had to hide, how could he hope for victory? But then it also spoke to their dissatisfaction. Why would they want to live this way? Why wield their swords and risk their lives if they couldn't reap the rewards? He could offer them more, and excitement replaced his worry.

But he had to find these men first, convince them to listen to him. He could hardly go from tent to tent, especially when he did not know what sort of reception he'd receive. After hours of circling around, avoiding the brightly lit northwestern section, where Lavock lived, Octavian sat down on a wooden crate to rest. He'd ventured close enough to the warlord's abode to observe four men hanging from their wrists while others beat and stabbed them, and with the gates closed this long, he knew the victims were Lavock's own men. He shuddered to imagine what would befall him, an outsider, so he stayed away as Karl had advised. Dawn would come soon, and he'd do well to hide himself through the daylight hours so he didn't have to explain his presence. It frustrated him to have accomplished nothing, and he'd have to devise another strategy. Would these men gather to eat? He rubbed his hands together against the numbing cold. No soft bedroll or warm bedmate awaited him, nor would they until he succeeded here.

There'd be no food either, and he hadn't eaten the previous day. That was proving a grievous oversight. He'd also hoped to find a weapon—even an iron poker—but weapons were expensive, a warrior's most prized possession, and they didn't leave them laying around. He'd need water, but at least he could suck on the filthy snow to keep himself alive.

The shuffle of feet and the low hum of voices compelled Octavian to crouch behind the crate. He laid his elbows across it and let his hood cover his face, so he'd hopefully appear as a discarded scrap of cloth and nothing more.

"And if you're the next one he chooses to string up to entertain himself, what then?" one of the men said.

"I'm not disputing that," another said. "But trying to get away from here, that's certain death."

Another man in the group of probably eight, judging by the sounds of their footsteps, said, "I can't take much more of this. I've lost too many men I considered friends—not to battle, but to the man who is supposed to be our leader. What kind of a man tortures his own for sport? He's lost his mind. There's no future here, not for any of us."

"But we cannot get away! We'd be shot down before we made it to the gate!"

"There's no more reason to stay. Lavock keeps every last piece of copper this so-called company earns. He doesn't even care if the rest of us eat. I joined this group to fight and make money, not to be a slave, and not to watch over my shoulder for daggers in the dark from men I should be able to trust!"

"And what are you proposing?"

"Karl is sympathetic to our plight."

Their voices began to fade, and Octavian rose to follow them, keeping to the shadows and far enough away not to be detected. These men were the best chance he'd found, and he wanted to hear the rest of their conversation.

"Karl is a good man," one of them said. "He doesn't want to see anyone hurt, and he'll spare us if he can, but not at the risk of his own neck. Can you blame him? We all know what happens if Lavock even thinks you looked at him wrong. If it was just death, that would be one thing, but…."

"We must formulate a plan. We have to get ourselves free of this madman."

"Again, I ask you how?"

"We have to come up with something, or he'll pick us off one by one."

"Well, I'm listening."

The group of men had reached a rough shelter on the outskirts of the camp, little more than a three-sided shed with a scrap of canvas over the entrance. From the shadows against the cloth, Octavian estimated another half-dozen men waited inside. One by one, the men slipped behind the curtain. Octavian waited until they'd all gone inside, and then he knelt at the edge of the structure, listening.

"We should take the gate. There are enough of us!"

"That's bleeding mad! We can't be sure who we can trust."

"Do you think there's a single man here, save those sick bastards, Lavock's favorites and little pets, who want to go on like this? We're not being paid, we're barely eating, and we're all in danger of becoming his next plaything. Should we just wait to die?"

"We've said these same bleeding words again and again. What good is repeating them doing us? None! Even if we could get out of here, which we can't, we'd be cut down by all those waiting down the road."

Now or never, Octavian thought. The opportunity was ripe for the plucking, and he'd reach out his hand even if it might be bitten. He stood, brushed the dirt from his knees, and slapped the canvas aside to enter the small building. Ignoring the dozen plus swords and daggers pointed at him, he said, "Honorable tams, I can help you. I have the solution that has eluded you."

"Who in the Bleeding Shades' are you?" one man shouted.

"My name is Octavian Rose."

"And give us one damned reason why we shouldn't kill you, Octavian Rose."

"Because you would be killing your only chance to free yourselves of Brealan Lavock."

"Oh really? So much more clever than all of us, are you? We should run you through."

Octavian held up his hands. "Hear me out. You can always kill me afterward if you don't like what I say." He opened his cloak. "I carry no weapon. Even if I did, I doubt I could stand against such superior numbers."

"Right," said a man with a grizzled red beard and a patch over one eye. "Give the pretty lad his moment to talk. We can kill him after."

"You will not want to do that," Octavian said, "because I have the answer to your problems. I can free you from Lavock. I have a formidable force assembled outside your gates, and all I need is a way to get them into the camp. Then with your help, we can overthrow the warlord. He'll have little chance against our combined might."

"And then you can hand us all over to the fine knights and lords, so they can kill us in place of Lavock," said the man with the beard.

"Why would we want to help you and your mates earn the reward on our heads?" another asked.

"The reward is only for the head of Lavock," Octavian said, "and that's the only head we intend to turn over."

"That and the Rosecairn," said a dark, oily man in a leather skullcap. "The best damn fortress in Gaeltheon. That leaves us what built it up with nothing. Fuck that." He spat on the ground.

"That's just the thing," Octavian said. "My plan is to rid this place of Lavock, turn his corpse over, and keep Rosecairn. Keep it for all of us, the men who will fight to defend it. What do we need with a leader? This place can be a fortress for us between our mercenary jobs. We'll split the purse and keep the land. That I can promise you. I have no intention of relinquishing this place. Any honorable warrior will be welcome. I don't think many of those down the road are planning to stay, but those of you who will can help me make something great of this place, make it what it—and you—deserve."

"And why should we listen to you?" said the man with the red beard. "You're a child. What makes you think you can do what we can't?"

"I can't deny I am young," Octavian said. "And I have to admit, the only reason I have a chance at accomplishing this is because I have found myself in a fortuitous position. I'm here at the right time, with the right idea. It's a simple one, and it can succeed. I'll share it with you if you're interested, or I'll leave. Or you can kill me, and with me, any chance you have of crawling out from beneath this madman's boot. Tell me which it will be. I do not wish to waste my time, especially if it's short."

For a few moments, the men grumbled and conversed behind their hands, but it didn't take them long to reach an agreement. "Speak, then," said a lanky man in leathers similar to Sylvain's. "If we like what we hear, maybe you'll walk out of here."

"May I sit down?" Octavian asked. A man indicated a bench, and he sat on the edge, looking at the faces of the warriors gathered around him, gauging their expressions and their eyes, hoping to show them the sincerity and conviction behind his own. "There is no way into Rosecairn. Your gate is impenetrable."

"Then how come you're here?"

Octavian opened his cloak. "I disguised myself as a prostitute and begged your gatekeeper for a chance to ply my trade. I am here because I came alone and unarmed. I took that risk because I know we have a chance to be victorious."

"What would you have us do?" asked an older man with white whiskers and a scar across his forehead.

"I need only for you to organize the men who would stand against Lavock. The army I have assembled beyond your gate is capable of taking Rosecairn and throwing him down, but I need a way to get them through those gates. If we can get those gates open, and if you will fight beside me, we can have this place for ourselves."

The man with the red beard grunted. "It's… not a bad plan. And if we can get Karl on board, we can get the gates open."

Octavian felt giddy with excitement and the anticipation of victory. Goddesses, it was really going to happen. He really had a chance….

"But how can we trust you not to turn the cairn over to the knights?"

"Let me try," Octavian said. "If you cannot believe my words you can believe this: a hundred men can hold Rosecairn against a thousand."

"True," said a man sitting in a darkened corner. "Once Lavock is gone, this place is ours."

"So tell me again why we need you," Red-Beard said. "We open the gate, and we fight alongside your force to defeat the bastard. What exactly do you bring to the table, beyond dressing in whore's clothes and saying fancy words?"

Octavian waited for their laughter to taper off. "I know I am not much to look at—" A catcall interrupted him, and he couldn't help a small smile. "I mean to say, I know I do not look like a warrior to you, but I am. With the help of the Bitter Tide, I decimated the Crooked Tooth company to the south of here. The plan, the only viable plan, to depose the cruel warlord Brealan Lavock, was mine. The men down there follow me, and only at my signal will they enter this camp."

Red-Beard scrubbed at his round nose. "Any of us can signal those men that the gates are open."

"No, you can't." Octavian sent a stream of blue sparks up from his fingers, to the audible shock of those assembled. "But do not follow me because I am a mage. Follow me because I'm a man with a viable plan, a man who can rid you of this scourge, a man who would see honorable warriors prosper and the wicked brought down."

"And what do you get?" asked the man in leather.

Octavian didn't hesitate. "A place to belong, men I can be proud to call my brothers-in-arms, and work I'm not ashamed to do. The chance to build something and make a name for myself. That's all. Now, if you like, I can go outside while you decide whether you'll stand beside me."

"There's… there's no need for that," said Red-Beard. The men around him nodded and grunted their assent. "You're offering the best chance we've had in moons. If I was a religious man, I might say the goddesses sent you. I'll talk to Karl myself—we're old friends. He'll be behind us, and he'll see those gates open. Now, what else do you need us to do?"

"Can you spare anything to drink?"

A metal cup containing the bitterest ale Octavian had ever tasted slid in front of him, and he was thirsty enough to down over half of it. He felt even more confident afterward. "Get word to the men who will sympathize, those who want free of Lavock's yoke. Be careful. He could have eyes and ears hidden anywhere. Let them know to be ready, as my men have careful plans to take each area of the camp. The northwestern area will be our greatest challenge, and the more allies we have, the better. Talk to Karl. Set a time when he will open the gates. As soon as they part, I'll make my way to the top of the cairn and give the signal. My people are watching for it and will be ready. In the meantime, I must stay hidden. No one can know for what purpose I'm really here, and if anyone could get me a weapon, I would feel much better."

Red-Beard stood and slapped Octavian on the back. "Go on, then, lads. Talk to your friends, but only your friends. Get them ready. I'll handle Karl, and I'll keep our little rosebud secreted away. For the love of the goddesses, use sense, and be careful who you talk to. This is the first real chance we've had in moons. Now, boy—"

"Octavian."

"Octavian. What's your weapon of choice? Sword and shield? Or a bow? You look like a bowman."

"Dagger. One for each hand, ideally."

"A man who likes to kill close up and intimate. You might yet be all right. I'll get you your knives, Octavian. What else do you need?"

"I'd like to know your name."

"Quinn." They clasped hands.

"Well met, Quinn. We're going to do great things together."

"So you say, young Octavian. I hope I'm not a fool to believe you. Come now. It might take us a few days to get word to our would-be allies, and we can't have you found out until we're ready. You look like you could use a decent meal and a few hours of sleep. I have a place here. I'll see that you're safe while you rest."

"Will you?"

"You'll have to trust me as all of us are trusting you."

"Yes, you're right." Octavian followed him through the bluish pink morning light, knowing if Quinn betrayed him, he'd end up on Lavock's torture rack. "I will." He prayed to the goddesses he wasn't making a fatal mistake.

Chapter Thirteen

"Three days," Myrddin murmured as another sun dissolved in orange scraps behind the western mountains. "Three days, and no signal, no word. Do you think—?"

Dead, Dirk signed.

"No," Myrddin said, staring at the darkened mountains. "We would have known."

Known what? Dirk responded. *That they used a whore and then killed him? You knew this was a possibility. It was a stupid plan from the beginning, and Octavian is a stupid, reckless bastard with too much to prove. I warned you not to get attached to him, but you never learned to listen to me.*

Myrddin was in no mood for Dirk's superiority or sarcasm. *Shut up,* he signed. *Why do you claim to be my friend and then poke at my open wounds with such enjoyment?*

I tried to spare you this pain, Dirk said. *Everyone but you saw it coming. I knew I'd be stuck with patching your wounds when the pretty little boy died, but I didn't think it would be this soon.*

Just stop tormenting me, Myrddin signed. *Go find yourself a pudgy whore like you usually do.*

No whores, pudgy or otherwise, here, Dirk replied. *Nothing here but cock, and I'm not that desperate.*

Find a drink, then.

Fuck you, Myrddin, if you cannot stand hearing the truth. We never should have come here. Dirk turned on his heel and strode down the path toward a fire and some men gathered around a table.

"All right?" Sylvain slunk from the shadows and draped an arm across Myrddin's shoulders.

Myrddin couldn't find the contact or comfort unwelcome, even though he and Sylvain had only started growing closer on the journey to Rosecairn. Myrddin hadn't quite figured Sylvain out yet, but he trusted Sylvain enough to unburden himself. He shook his head. "Three days."

"You must trust him."

"I do, but it's been so long."

"He needs time to rally the forces on the other side of that gate," Sylvain said. "Neither of us can deny he has a silver tongue. He'll sway them to our side."

"If he is not dead," Myrddin said. "If they did not strike him down before he had a chance to speak."

"How much longer should we wait?"

"I'll wait until I know there's no chance," Myrddin said, staring at the gate at the end of the long road. "I'll wait."

"I'll wait with you," Sylvain said. "We can do nothing for him now but send him our hope and good thoughts."

"Not our prayers?"

"Prayers have done little in my experience," Sylvain said as he pulled Myrddin's back against his chest and wrapped his arms around Myrddin's waist. "Trust him."

"I'll try," Myrddin said.

"I hate to give you more cause to worry," Sylvain said as he burrowed his face into Myrddin's hair, "but have you seen our friends the Beasley brothers around the camp today?"

They'd been the last thing on Myrddin's mind, but thinking back, he realized Sylvain was right. "What could they be up to?"

"Betraying Octavian?" Sylvain dragged his lips over Myrddin's jaw.

"Stop that. Someone will see. More importantly, if what you say is true, what can we do?"

"Do you think our Octavian is more clever than the Beasleys?"

"Of course."

"Then we must have confidence in that. We can do nothing more until the gates open. But I for one will remember this when I see the Beasleys again."

KARL HAD heard what Quinn and the others proposed, and he longed for a way to free the men he fought beside from Lavock. This Octavian

Rose, the boy who'd snuck past him disguised as a whore, had a solid plan, a plan Karl would willingly risk his position and life for. Tomorrow night, when the half-moon reached the pinnacle of the sky, he would open the gates. Octavian would be ready to signal the attack, and the men of Rosecairn would be ready to aid him.

So when the two grubby brothers approached the gate with the intent to betray Octavian to the warlord, Karl pretended interest. He led the two of them into the watchtower, and then he brought the hilt of his sword down across the backs of their heads and left their limp bodies on the floor. He returned to his post and waited for the signal from Quinn. As he stood watch, looking out over the fires at the end of the road, he thought about the kind of courage it must have taken for that slight boy to walk into the most dangerous mercenary camp in Gaeltheon without even a kitchen knife to defend himself. Karl wondered if he could find that kind of fortitude in himself, and he decided he'd find out tomorrow night when he opened the gate. He hoped he'd survive the battle. It would be good to get back to honest work and honest money, and the honest spending of it on ale and women. Goddesses, women. It had been far too long since he'd enjoyed that simple comfort. But with Lavock in power, a woman wasn't safe within twenty miles of the cairn.

The night passed by mostly without incident. Once, half a dozen soldiers with a battering ram had made an attempt to breach the gate, but Karl and his guards had driven them off with a few flaming arrows. The illusion of an attempt made sense—probably Octavian's idea— because if all efforts ended suddenly, it might arouse suspicion. Brealan Lavock might be a sick fuck content to spend his time surrounded by the blood and screams of those who could no longer fight back, but he was no fool, and he missed nothing.

As the first light of dawn broke over the mountains, Karl knew he had to make a decision regarding his captives. If he hated one thing above all others, it was a turncoat, especially a turncoat who would throw a supposed friend to the wolves for gold. Well, he had to take care of the brothers. If he left them able to speak, they'd speak, and the men who watched the gate during the day would listen, and those men might take the brothers before Lavock and ruin the only chance Karl and his friends had. What Lavock would do if he got his hands on Octavian would make his previous atrocities look mild. Karl sighed. He should probably just run them through and toss their bodies over the gate.

He turned from the battlement where he'd been standing and entered the watchtower with his sword in his hand. When he reached the room where he'd left the brothers unconscious, the wooden frame of the door had been splintered, and of course, the small cell behind it stood empty. Karl swore. The bastards had escaped. He should have killed them when he'd had the chance, and now he could only pray they wouldn't spoil everything. They only had to make it through one more day. The men were ready to fight, and as soon as darkness fell, Karl would open the gates, even if that meant killing the one man on his rotation loyal to Lavock.

Still, much could happen in the course of a day.

NOT LONG after first light, Octavian startled awake. Once again, he'd fallen asleep huddled in the corner of Quinn's hovel, his head and shoulder leaning against the wall and a tattered blanket covering him. His teeth hadn't stopped chattering in days, and he felt the cold in his bones even while unconscious. Soon it would all be over. Just one more day, and either he would hold Rosecairn or he would be dead.

Octavian took the metal cup of water and plate of sausage and beans Quinn handed him, and he ate although food was the furthest thing from his mind. "I'll be glad to see this ended."

Quinn made a grunt of assent as he poked at his hearth fire.

"I suppose I can do nothing but continue concealing myself here until the time comes for Karl to take his watch and open the gate. Goddesses, I am restless, though."

"It's only one more day."

"Too much, and then again, too little."

"What are you on about?" Quinn growled.

"Nothing." Octavian wished he had his book to write in. Perhaps if he could get his words down in ink, he could ponder through the maelstrom of doubts and emotions pulling him in every direction. Perhaps if he could force the chaos into the neat boxes of words, he could understand what he felt in the hours before he'd find victory or death. Either way, it would be a better way to pass the time than staring at Quinn's smoke-stained walls.

An hour went by, and then another. Octavian sharpened the crude daggers the others had scared up for him. Quinn didn't believe in sparing water to wash or clean one's teeth, so Octavian made do by raking his fingers through his hair. They shared hard bread, cheese, and more greasy sausage for their midday meal, along with more bitter ale. Despite the taste, Octavian drank more than he should have.

A knock at the door, or the scrap of wood that served as one, distracted Octavian from staring at the ceiling. Quinn went to the entrance, and the wiry man in the skullcap entered, panting. "We're found out. Lavock and his lackeys are searching the camp for the whore Octavian Rose."

Octavian bolted up and placed his daggers in his belt. "How in the fucking Shades' did this happen?" Quinn said.

"I don't know. Someone betrayed us. I don't know who. What does it matter? They're going to find him. And if they find us offering him help—"

Octavian pushed his way in front of Quinn. "They know about me, fine. What else?" He shook the other man's shoulders. "What else? Do they know of our plan to open the gate and take the camp? Goddesses, speak!"

"I-I don't think they know that part," the man said. "All I heard is that they're looking for you, a whore who's spying for our enemies. Lavock wants you found and brought to him. If that happens, fall on your own blade. Don't let him take you alive."

"No one is taking me." Everything had been going so smoothly, and maybe he should have had the wisdom to mistrust that. No matter, they weren't taking this away from him, not without blood and fire. He turned to Quinn. "They have forced our hand. We cannot wait. Go and find Karl. We need that gate open now. We can't wait for nightfall. Can you do it? Do you have enough men?"

"I think so," Quinn said, picking up his sword. "They've left us no choice. But what about you?"

"I must make my way to the cairn and give the signal," Octavian said.

"You'll never make it," said the man in the cap. "They're searching every building for you."

"I *will* make it," Octavian said. "Just see it isn't for nothing." He clasped Quinn's arms. "I will see you when this is over, when the Rosecairn is ours." He left the hut and jogged around it, daggers in hand, making for the center of the camp and the legendary ruin from which it drew its name.

After rounding a group of tents, he encountered three men. They drew weapons, and Octavian widened his stance and prepared to face them, his breath puffing out in clouds as wide flakes of snow began to fall. "Let me pass."

"Why?"

"I am Octavian Rose, on my way to the cairn to give the signal. If you would be free of Brealan Lavock, don't stand in my way. Get to the gate, where your friends will welcome your aid." He waited to see if they'd challenge him, but they just looked at one another briefly before sprinting in the direction of the entrance.

Octavian's luck ran out when he met two large men in black leathers, both of them wielding spiked flails that looked like they could take him apart with a single blow. He identified them as Lavock's pets by their cruel smiles, the hunger in their expressions for causing pain. He didn't waste his words. He lunged, driving his right dagger into the closest man's shoulder, twisting the blade on the way out and effectively preventing him from raising his mace. The other man swung for his head, and Octavian sunk into a crouch, striking out with his left hand as he dropped but landing only a superficial gash across his thigh. The man staggered back, and Octavian jumped to his feet just in time to raise his arm and catch the open-handed blow aimed at his face. Abandoning pride, he kicked the first enemy in the groin and stabbed him in the back—between his gorget and his breastplate—as he doubled over.

Kicking him out of the way and leaving him to bleed out, Octavian turned to the other man. The cut he'd inflicted hindered his enemy little, and the man swung his flail. Octavian jumped backward, but the spikes on the weapon tore through his simple clothing and the flesh beneath. Pain seared his belly, and blood stained his shirt. He ignored it and swiped with his dagger. This was taking too long. If Karl and Quinn had opened the gate, he had to signal his men, because he didn't know how long they could keep the gate open. He swung again, nicking the man's neck, but doing no real damage. Octavian's enemy lifted his flail over his head and brought it down in a strike that would cripple if not kill Octavian if it connected. Octavian tucked and rolled to the side, and snow and dirt erupted as the mace hit the ground. Finding himself behind his enemy, he swung with his daggers and sliced through the tendons at the backs of his knees. With an agonized cry, his adversary fell facedown, and Octavian knew he would not be able to stand.

He couldn't spare the time to contemplate taking life and whether that sacrifice was worth his victory. Though panting from the skirmish, he forced himself to run, and he kept running until he tasted blood in his throat and his thighs trembled. The next man who stood in his way got a slash across the face that split his nose and lip in two. Another enemy got a stab to the belly. Finally, he had the cairn in his sights. He'd expected a small pile of stones, like the tombs of the savages predating the goddesses that dotted the countryside, but this sepulcher rivaled a castle. Built from smooth stones the size of grain sacks, it rose into the gray sky, covered in gnarled vines as thick as Octavian's wrist and coated with snow and rime. Ten men stood guarding it.

Octavian couldn't defeat ten men; he'd barely fought his way past two. But he had to reach the top of that cairn and give the signal. Karl and Quinn would have the gate open by now, or they were dead and all was lost. He had one task, and he considered his options. Could he use his magic to drain the life from those men as he had from the evergreen tree? Did he dare set his feet on that dark path? No. No, he'd sworn he would succeed without sacrificing the ideals he held sacred. He would come through this and remain Octavian, or he wouldn't come through at all. But he had to find a way to the pinnacle of that cairn.

He could still use magic. In his acute state, he found it humming all around him, and he latched onto a vein and pulled its essence into him. Then he aimed his fingers at the group of men and let it go in a glorious release. Soldiers lifted off their feet and flew to the side of the burst. Octavian ran. He'd done little but knocked them to the side, winded a few and maybe knocked some out. If the gate was open, he had to signal his force. He could not wait, could not become embroiled in lengthy combat. He ran hard through the opening he'd made, leaped, and grasped the ice-slicked stone of the cairn. Pushing his fingers and toes between the grooves in the stones and grasping what vines he could reach, he began to climb, forcing his broken and exhausted body higher, gaining every inch he could before his foes recovered. He clawed his way up as the snow fell harder, coating the top of his head and his shoulders, and his blood froze his clothing to his chest and stomach.

He climbed though his muscles ripped with pain. Arrows sailed past him and pinged off the stone, and he could do nothing but hope and try to move faster. He had only a dozen feet or so to go before he reached the top of the cairn when a hand closed around his ankle and tried to pull him down. Octavian kicked, but his enemy held firm, gaining ground and taking hold of Octavian's belt. Octavian turned, clutching a vine with one hand while he balled the other into a fist and drove it into the man's face. His nose snapped under Octavian's first blow, and blood poured over his lips. Octavian drew back and struck again, and again, splitting the man's lips and blackening his eyes. The bastard wasn't stealing his victory or the freedom of the men of Rosecairn. Octavian hit him repeatedly, reducing his face to a mangled soup of blood and flesh, before the man let go and somersaulted down the stones of the structure.

With his knuckles split open, his nails torn off, and his chest burning, Octavian found the climbing harder, but the summit was so close. He pressed on, ignoring the arrow that ripped across his calf and took a chunk of flesh with it. Blood ran down his leg and filled his boot, and the pain made it hard to move his right leg. But he had come so far, and he would not fail. Not now. He repeated it as he ascended a hard-won inch at a time, his hands barely containing the strength to grip the rocks and vines. *Not now. Not now. Not now….*

From the top of the cairn, Octavian could see the whole camp. The gates stood open with a dozen or more men defending them, but eight or ten attacking his allies as they fought to keep the gates ajar. He had to do his part. Getting to his feet at the apex of the cairn, which was barely wide enough for him to stand, he raised his arm to the sky. He found the magic without effort and transformed it into an eruption of sparks that rivaled the stars and lit up the gray sky with brilliant blue. His men wouldn't miss the signal, and the gates stood open. Octavian staggered and sat down, hugging his knees to his chest. No matter what the old woman had said, magic tired him out, and it *hurt.* Luckily for him, anyone who stood against them abandoned the cairn in favor of the gate—either to keep it open or shut it— where his people had already started to ride through. Octavian smiled, imagining Myrddin leading them and Sylvain grinning beneath his hood, his bowstring taut, as he took a few moments to regain his strength.

The mercenary force entered Rosecairn like a storm, battering down what resistance it met, striking down the men on the ground from the backs of their horses. The men of the cairn who'd allied themselves with Octavian joined the surge and strengthened it, and the combined army ripped through the camp like a flood, washing aside all who stood in their way. From his perch, Octavian watched them advance through the camp until only the northwestern corner resisted: the sanctuary of the warlord

Brealan Lavock. Time for Octavian to rejoin the battle. This wouldn't be decided without his hand. He slipped and stumbled his way down the cairn until he reached the ground, and then he drew his blades and ran, catching up with the others just outside the wooden fence shielding the warlord's compound. Amidst a shower of arrows, the vast force sought to tear the barricade down. Men kicked at the posts and hacked at it with their swords. Horses reared against the thick logs and struck them with their hooves, and men with axes swung at the wood and tore chunks of it away. Eventually the logs shattered and the men vaulted over them, pushed the fence out of their way, or guided their mounts to jump the debris. Octavian shouldered his way to the front of the throng as the warlord's men—more than they'd anticipated—rushed out to meet them.

The two forces clashed with cries and the clang of steel so loud Octavian thought it would split his head. A man rushed toward him, and Octavian raised his blade to meet his enemy's sword. They traded blows back and forth until Octavian subdued the man with a boot to the shin and an elbow to his temple. He didn't know how badly he'd injured the man or whether he would live or die as he fell beneath the boots of those struggling around them, and he didn't have time to worry about it, because another enemy soon took his place. By the time Octavian fought his way past him, he could taste his lungs in his mouth and his entire body quivered with exertion. He didn't think he had the strength to take another step, let alone lift his weapons, but another warrior faced him, and if he didn't defend himself, he would die and it would all be for nothing.

With a ragged shout, Octavian drove the heel of his hand into the nose of the man in front of him, bending the guard on his helmet and summoning a spectacular font of blood. He swung his fist to knock the man out of his path and gained a few more steps. His next adversary hit him in the face, splitting his lip and slicing his chin before Octavian subdued him with a few quick jabs to the chest. When the enemy fell, Octavian spat blood on the ground and held his knees for a few precious seconds. His chest was on fire, and he didn't think he'd ever get enough air into his lungs. He stumbled to a clear patch to survey the battle, but with the snow falling heavier, he could make little sense of the bodies struggling clumsily. He couldn't tell if his side was winning or losing. He just saw blood, so much blood, running in rivers through the mud and frost, so thick men slipped in it. Bodies lay on the ground, and men trampled them into the foul muck. Octavian searched for a friendly face, anyone he knew, but everything was a swirl of white, red, and gray. Then a man lifted an ax and swung at him, and he had to fight again.

Octavian didn't know how long he fought or how he managed to keep his body moving, but miraculously, his side managed to clear a swath. Almost as soon as they did, a fresh group of warriors emerged from the inner circle of the compound. Despite the advantage of numbers, Octavian's side was struggling against Lavock's elite warriors. The corpses of men and horses littered the ground, and still men in black leather and good, steel armor seemed to materialize out of the ether to face them. Goddesses, they might actually face defeat. The fresh fighters were pushing them back, and men on Octavian's side were falling. With every passing moment, they lost ground, lost precious inches they'd fought so hard to gain. No. No, not now. Not when they had come so far.

Lavock's men got to a series of huge crossbows mounted along the walls of the rounded courtyard they'd fought their way into after they'd shattered the barricades. Bolts the size of spears—four of them—fired into the throng, and at least one hit its mark and skewered a man through the chest, right through his breastplate. Octavian looked on in horror. This could end the battle for him and his allies. Luckily the devastating weapons seemed slow to load, as it took two big men to draw them back and another to load the bolts. Octavian cast around wildly, blood spraying from his face as he searched for Sylvain, Dirk, or anyone who could take down the men manning those crossbows. He shouted for them, calling, "Archers!" and pointing with his dagger. In the encroaching darkness, he saw the arcs of arrows, but none of them met their targets, which meant they hadn't been fired by Dirk or Sylvain. Octavian couldn't wait. He couldn't depend on others to win him this battle, this prize. Though it would further drain his already exhausted body, he could think of only one thing to do.

He let himself become a vessel, let the magic collect inside him until it boiled over, and then he raised his arm and took aim for the nearest crossbow. Just as the men manning it prepared to loose the bolt, Octavian released the magic. It tore through his body and down his arm like boiling oil, and he screamed at the sensation of his bones and muscles dissolving in the white heat of the power. When the energy connected, it sent the three men flying, splintered the weapon, and tore a jagged piece from the thick wood and stone wall. Octavian focused on the next trio of warriors. He tried to restrain himself, because he'd like to keep those crossbows, but he was still new to this, and he sent the weapon bouncing along the wall and the men over the back of it.

"This is *mine!*" Octavian shouted through his shredded throat. "Mine!" He drove his dagger through the throat of the enemy in front of him and kicked the corpse out of his way. His attack had drawn attention to the threat on the battlements, and soon his archers took care of the rest of the men. Octavian shouted to the warriors on the ground, instructing them to tear down the ladders and block the stairs leading up to the wall. He didn't know if the enemies had steps on the other side, but hopefully Dirk and Sylvain and the cairn archers would keep the crossbows out of use. Lavock must be a suspicious bastard to hide his inner sanctum behind not two, but three sets of sturdy walls. That just left the tenacious force facing them on the ground.

A few dozen feet away, the warlord Lavock stood in nothing but leather trousers, bracers, and a wolf pelt slung over his massive shoulders, cutting down every man who came near him with the jagged, rusty axes he held in each hand. He wore a leather thong decorated with small bones over his clean-shaven pate, and a trio of deep, ugly purple scars ran down the right side of his face. More scars, thick and raised, crisscrossed over every visible inch of his skin, many layers thick in some places. He cleaved a man's head off and kicked it into the throng as Octavian watched, licking his lips. "Mine," Octavian said under his breath. "You're mine."

Octavian kicked, punched, and slashed his way through the battle until he stood only a few feet from Lavock. Their gazes met. Octavian grasped his daggers, and the warlord ran his tongue along his crooked, yellow teeth.

Octavian cried out and leaped. The dagger he'd planned to sink into the warlord's exposed chest was deflected with the flick of his ax, and Octavian was thrown and landed hard on his back. As he fought for his wind, the huge man stood over him and lifted his weapon to finish the job. At the last moment, Octavian rolled to the side and avoided the blow. Lavock's ax caught in the frozen ground, and as Octavian rose, he kicked the man in the face and sent him sprawling on his side. He dove for Lavock and drove a dagger toward his throat, but the bastard deflected and swatted Octavian off him. Octavian raised his arms to shield his face as he tumbled through the snow. Just in time, he crossed his blades over his face. Lavock's ax pinged off his steel, and Octavian kicked him in the groin. The warlord staggered back, and Octavian got to his knees and stabbed him in the thigh. Lavock growled and swung, slicing Octavian over his hipbone, cutting through fur, cloth, and flesh. Octavian cursed at the pain and swiped his knife toward the warlord's face, opening a deep gash across his brow and destroying his left eye.

"You little son of a whore!" Lavock bellowed, dropping one ax to cradle his ruined face. "You're less than nothing, and I am Brealan Lavock. I am the master of Rosecairn. I'm going to peel the skin from your body an inch at a time! You useless little slattern. I'll make you pay!"

"I'm right here, you arrogant prick." Octavian licked the blood from his lips, and he forgot how exhausted he'd been. Something—glory, victory, or the desire to prove his worth—compelled him.

Growling, spittle flying from his mouth, Lavock backhanded Octavian with the bloody hand he'd been using to cover his eye. Octavian couldn't block the blow in time, and pain erupted across his cheek. He was lifted off his feet, and his back and head struck the wall. He landed on his ass, and by the time he drove the dizziness from his head and managed to focus his vision, Lavock had grasped his throat and hoisted him off the ground. Octavian kicked and swiped at him, twisting to try to free himself, but the man just laughed. "I'm going to play with you for a moon. The Cast-Down would turn away from what I'm going to do to you. You'll be begging for death, but I won't let you have it. Not until the Shades' Abode looks like a paradise."

Gray fuzz leaked in at the periphery of Octavian's vision, and the sounds of the battle grew muted and warped. With the last of his strength, Octavian stabbed up with his dagger and drove it clean through Lavock's forearm. He twisted his blade and yanked it free as Lavock dropped him and he fell to his knees. Lavock kicked at him, but Octavian dodged to the side and took the blow in his shoulder, instead of his face, as intended. It still made him smack his head on the wall again, and gave Lavock the opportunity to chop down at him with his ax. Octavian twisted, and the rusted edge of the cleaver caught his shoulder, opening a cut his leathers probably would have spared him. Octavian, dizzy and desperate, drove the point of his knife toward the man's groin with all the strength he could muster. Myrddin had told him speed was his greatest asset as they'd practiced together, and his blow connected before Lavock could block. The warlord howled with rage and agony and launched himself at Octavian, crushing Octavian against the ground and covering him with his bulk. "I'm going to pound your pretty face to mush with my bare hands!"

Octavian raised his knee, and it connected with the hilt of his dagger, driving it farther into Lavock's body. With a broken cry, the warlord rolled off him and staggered to his feet. He pulled the knife out, and blood poured down the insides of his thighs. He staggered and reached for the wall for support.

Octavian stood shakily and drove his remaining dagger into the left side of Lavock's ribs. Without his sight, the warlord couldn't block. Blood spattered Lavock's lips, and he tripped over his feet. Octavian hit him as hard as he could at the right side of his face, and he crumpled in the snow, blood pooling around his head. Octavian braced himself against the wall and brought his heel down against the warlord's temple, stomping his head until he'd almost flattened it. Then he dropped to his knees in the ruddy snow and steadied his dagger in a hand shaking so hard it could barely hold it. He grasped the back of Lavock's head and hacked at his neck. Six times. Eight before he reached the spine. He kept sawing with his dagger until he liberated the warlord's head from his body, and then he grasped it by the leather thong and stood.

He didn't know if his voice would resound over the din of the battle, but Octavian stepped atop a pile of debris and shouted, "I am Octavian Rose! I have slain Brealan Lavock. It is over. Goddesses, it is over."

The men fighting lowered their weapons. They looked up at Octavian, coated in blood and holding the warlord's head. "We've won!"

Octavian huffed white clouds as tears spilled down his face. He raised Lavock's head again, and the men cheered. It was heavy, though, and he'd never imagined his muscles could endure the torture they'd been through on this day. He didn't know a man's body was capable of such exertion. Still, he lifted the head again, and the men cheered like thunder. Then he descended, taking each step carefully so he wouldn't fall. They couldn't see him fall. As if through a red, smeared haze, he saw Myrddin and Sylvain gathered with some other men he thought he recognized, and he forced his battered body to remain upright and walked with his chin lifted until he could throw his arm across Myrddin's shoulder and pant into his hair: "I don't have anything more. Get me out of here." He trusted Myrddin, who looked much better than he did, to take care of him now, and he let his friend carry most of his weight, though he held tight to Lavock's head.

Chapter Fourteen

ALMOST AS soon as Octavian lifted the warlord's severed head, Sylvain saw the Beasley brothers pushing their way through the crowd. Their side had lost, their gambit had failed, and now they planned to run. Sylvain smirked as he skirted the gathering and met the Beasleys just as they emerged from the throng, the point of his arrow inches from their dumbfounded faces.

"Going somewhere, my fine friends? Why would you want to leave before our lovely Octavian celebrates his victory? It was a brilliant victory, was it not? You might call it… unexpected."

"I might call it horseshit!" Ted Beasley snarled as he and his brother backed away. "That cock-loving little pervert just got lucky."

Sylvain arched a brow. He hoped the Beasleys could see it in the thickening darkness. It was a devastating gesture. "Lucky? Again? Like at the ambush? Or at the Crooked Tooth camp? Or the *other* Crooked Tooth camp? My, my. Octavian must be the *luckiest* young man to ever walk in the light. It's as if the goddesses themselves are standing in a circle around him with their hands joined to protect him. But I ask you this: If he's such a terrible deviant, why would the holy sisters focus so much of their divine attention on his well-being?"

"What the fuck are you on about, you piece of shit unnatural whoreson?" Eric Beasley muttered. Sylvain could have sworn his eyes crossed as he tried to puzzle through what, to his unwashed ears, probably sounded like Esperon.

"It hardly matters what I think. It's up to Octavian what becomes of you now."

Ted spat on the ground. "Hoping he'll suck your cock for your efforts?"

Sylvain grinned, showing teeth. "I don't have to hope. And the next one of you who says anything disparaging about me or Octavian is going to get an arrow through the tongue and thus never trouble this world with his prattle again. Come on now." He tilted his head toward where Octavian stood at the center of a ring of cheering warriors.

"You can go to the Shades', where your kind belongs!" Ted drew his sword and lunged for Sylvain, but Sylvain calmly uncurled his fingers from his bowstring and sent an arrow through his wrist, and then another through the meat of his shoulder. As Ted's weapon clattered to the ground, Sylvain turned on the ball of his foot and nocked two more arrows. The first pierced Eric's thigh, and the second penetrated the top of his boot and secured his foot to the soil. Sylvain swung his bow into Eric's smug face and knocked out one of his few remaining teeth before he stowed it on his back and grasped the man's elbow.

"Here, let me help you." Sylvain grabbed his elbow and yanked him forward. Eric howled as the arrow in his foot pulled free of the ground. He pitched Eric forward and kicked him in the ass when he landed on his hands and knees. Then he grabbed Ted by the ear like a nursemaid would a charge as he kicked his sword out of his reach. "This is growing tiresome. Come on."

Near the back of the group, Sylvain caught the eyes of some of their allies: the man with the red beard and eye patch and the big fellow who'd opened the gate. With a jerk of his chin, he motioned them forward. "I've apprehended the scum who betrayed us and told Lavock of our plans. When it seemed their treachery would not be beneficial, they tried to run. Personally, I think it would be amusing for them to face Octavian and the rest of the men they tried to keep under this monster's thumb for their own profit. Do you agree?"

"Oh, aye," said the gatekeeper. "I remember these two."

"Good. Thank you. Will you do me a service and keep an eye on them while I see to my friend? Be careful—they're slippery, and not just because of the layer of grease that covers them."

"Don't worry, friend," the gatekeeper said. "They won't get the drop on me a second time."

"Then I leave them in your capable hands." Sylvain made his way back around the crowd in time to see Octavian staggering down from the pile of stone and broken logs he stood upon. He was badly wounded, white as the sky and shaking like a leaf in the wind, but goddesses, the fire in his eyes as he looked out from beneath a mask of blood—that fire could have leveled the camp.

Octavian's ankles crossed, he stumbled, and only just caught himself before falling to his knees. Myrddin, looking stricken, stepped in his direction, but Sylvain laid a hand over his arm. "No."

"He's hurt. He's lost a lot of blood, and—"

"And these men need to see him walk away from this battle under his own power," Sylvain interrupted. "To deny him that is to take this victory from him, and he has fought too hard to lose it. Let him come to us. He will."

Octavian came—to Myrddin. It made sense; Myrddin was his protector while Sylvain was a friend to get into mischief with. When he wanted fun and adventure, Octavian would seek Sylvain, but hurt, confused, and in need of comfort, he went to Myrddin's arms. Sylvain accepted that as he followed them to the opposite side of the wall. Either Lavock or someone in his company had known the history of warfare, because they had constructed a killing field between their outer wall and their inner with that courtyard. Enemies who made it through would be trapped and at the mercy of those crossbows, trapped and waiting to be shot down. Of course, they hadn't anticipated Octavian, and Sylvain had done his part as well. Myrddin's friend Dirk wasn't a *bad* archer either. Sylvain looked over his shoulder at the wiry man with the wild red hair. He smiled, and Dirk responded with an obscene gesture.

Beyond the second wall stood a series of shoddy buildings no grander than any others in the camp. The warlord had chained some of their doors shut and surrounded others with spikes. They stood in a circle, surrounded by the wall. Myrddin led Octavian to the fire at the center and helped him sit on a bench. Sylvain sat on his other side. He was still bleeding from his belly, his hip, his shoulder, and his poor blackened and swollen face. It pained Sylvain to see those perfect lips split and oozing, and despite what he'd said to Myrddin, he worried about Octavian. He touched Myrddin's shoulder across Octavian's back. "We must get him cleaned up, get some food and wine into him, and get him someplace warm."

"People need healing," Octavian mumbled, his chin against his chest. "I saw men bleeding, lying on the ground...."

"You must heal yourself first." Myrddin sounded almost frantic.

"There are others hurt worse," Octavian protested.

"Beg your pardon," said a gangly man in a leather cap, "but something has to be done with those what fought against us. We have them surrounded for now and, er, subdued, but they're having none of it. They'll rebel before long."

"It must be your decision," Myrddin told Octavian.

Octavian lifted his head and blinked hard a few times, some of the banked fire returning to his eyes. "Take me to them."

Sylvain and Myrddin supported him as he limped back to the courtyard, but as soon as they came in sight of the others, Octavian broke free and walked on his own. He slammed Lavock's head down on a waist-high pile of wreckage and faced them. The men cheered and backed away from the thirty or so men bound between them.

"Kill them!" someone shouted. Others roared their agreement.

"Say the word and I'll cut their throats," the gatekeeper called out. "Them and these filthy traitors." He indicated the Beasleys, bound and kneeling at his feet. Sylvain winked at Ted and made sure he didn't miss it. Ted growled and thrashed, earning himself a smack to the back of the head from the gatekeeper.

Octavian looked blank for several moments, firelight reflecting off his wide eyes. The men began to grumble, and he lifted his hand. They quieted, and he said, "No. We will not kill them bound and on their knees. They were worthy adversaries, even if their cause was not our own. Killing in battle is honorable and glorious, but killing a man who cannot defend himself is a cowardly act. We have shown we are not cowards, and we will continue to show it. We are neither murders nor executioners. We are warriors. Take these men to the gate. Let them leave. If they ever show their faces at Rosecairn again, I will not defend them."

"And what of the Beasleys?" Sylvain asked. "They betrayed you to Lavock for their own benefit, and ran as soon as you proved the better man."

"Take them to the gates," Octavian said, clearly trying to fight the exhaustion dragging his words toward slurring. "Just get them out of my sight. They're not worth my time or consideration. I have more important matters to attend to."

"You filthy little whoreson!" Ted bellowed. "Cock-sucking whelp! Think you're worthy of dismissing us?"

Octavian pushed his shoulders back and met Ted's gaze. "Yes. You claimed to be my allies, and you turned against me. You would have condemned all of these men to a terrible fate for a handful of coins. I won't have men like you here, not anymore. I'm dismissing you. You should be thankful that's all I'm doing."

"We were promised gold for this job!" Ted continued. "We followed you into these goddess-forsaken mountains because we were told we'd be paid. We'll leave as soon as we get our share of the purse."

Myrddin's mouth dropped open, and he pointed at Ted. "Are you out of your mind? You expect us to pay you for fighting against us?"

"Look around you." Octavian swept his hand over the mire of snow and mud in the courtyard. "Look at the men lying on the ground, men you swore you'd fight beside. Less of them would be lying there if you had not given away our plan. Rosecairn men and those from the camp down the road died because Lavock knew to expect them—they died because of you."

"We should string them up!" someone yelled, to the vocal support of many others.

"Avenge our friends."

Octavian's voice carried above the din. "We cannot run this camp as Lavock did. There will be no torture or killing of other warriors. Take them to the gate. I swear to split the reward for Lavock's head with every man who fought beside me and split it evenly. I killed him, but I could not have done it alone, and I'll share the gold fairly, because I believe I fought beside honorable men. Please don't prove me wrong now."

His words stunned Sylvain. The murky and unspoken code of sell-swords said, by rights, Octavian had taken the head and was therefore entitled to the entirety of the price on it. None of these seasoned mercenaries would likely dispute that claim, especially since Octavian had done them a service. But his generosity and loyalty served the purpose he'd likely intended, and the men silently gazed up at him with clear surprise and respect. He swayed where he stood, though, and if they didn't get him warm and fed, he would collapse. Sylvain had seen more experienced warriors grow sick and cold with horror and strain of battle, and Octavian had lost blood on top of it.

Just as he prepared to turn, Ted Beasley got to his feet, howled like a wounded animal, and broke through the crowd. "You're nothing but an unnatural piece of filth! You think me and my brother want your pity? Think you can stand in judgment of us?"

Octavian drew his dagger. "Just stop there."

Even though Sylvain couldn't imagine even Ted was thick enough to charge Octavian while unarmed and bound, with arrows sticking out of his body, he pulled an arrow from his quiver and smoothed the feather between his finger and thumb. Beside him, Myrddin readied his hand on the hilt of his sword.

"I should have put an end to you a long time ago!" Even though Octavian held out his blade in warning, Ted Beasley, mad with rage or maybe deranged or just stupid, ran toward him, shoulders low. Octavian easily stepped out of his way and left him to pitch off-balance. He righted himself and butted into Octavian with his head. Octavian pushed him away, and when he made a third attempt, he impaled himself on the dagger Octavian held even though Octavian tried to dodge him. When he threw all his bulk toward Octavian, he fell on the dagger and it lodged deep in his belly.

Octavian freed his knife and looked with horror and disbelief at the fresh blood on his hands, bright and scarlet in contrast to the dried, rusty gore covering the rest of him. Ted fell facedown and a pool spread around him. His brother screamed and thrashed, but a man had taken each of his elbows to hold him in place. From the crowd, he choked, sobbed, and hurled threats of vengeance at Octavian and everyone who stood with him.

"Ass," Octavian said with a sadness Sylvain couldn't comprehend. "He didn't have to die."

"I'll kill you for this, Octavian Rose!" Eric screamed. "If it takes me the rest of my life, I'll hunt you down and kill you! I won't forget this. Not ever!"

"Give him his brother's body," Octavian said. "Then, by the goddesses, I beg you to take him out of my sight."

Myrddin stepped to just behind Octavian's shoulder and pressed a hand to his back where the others couldn't see. "You heard him! Take them to the gate. Then see to your fallen friends and your enemies, those of you who are well enough. If we leave these corpses here to rot, disease will tear through this camp. We must tend to the wounded and bury the dead." Though he curled his lips, he picked up Octavian's prize and let the head dangle from the band around the forehead.

"I can heal," Octavian said, though so quietly only those closest to him heard it. Sylvain thanked the goddesses for that.

"Tomorrow," Myrddin told him as he guided him away. "After you've rested."

"But by then—"

"Tomorrow, Octavian." Sylvain smirked at the way Myrddin's patient but commanding tone silenced Octavian the way a father's might.

They made their way back around the wall, and a group of men followed them. Sylvain paid them little attention; at this point, no one could think less of Octavian for tending to his injuries. As Myrddin helped him to a bench, Sylvain turned to one of the Rosecairn warriors. "Is there a place we can take him to patch him up? Somewhere he might sleep comfortably?"

One of them pointed to a hut with a square of leather tacked over the door. Smoke curled from the crumbling chimney, and orange light flickered behind the single window. "That's… that was Lavock's place. There's a fire and a bed. I'll have someone bring water."

"Thank you." Sylvain patted his shoulder. "And if you can spare any food, we'd be in your debt. Oh, and if you could, would you encourage these men to move on to their own places for the night? You saw that battle. Octavian needs rest, and he needs quiet. The sooner he recovers and can deliver that head to the nobles offering the reward, the sooner we can all claim our shares."

As he knew they would, those words got a quick response from the young man. "I'll see what I can do."

He moved among the clusters of men, and a few of them went off, hopefully for food and water, but the rest seemed reluctant to break up. Sylvain rolled his eyes. Normally he'd be first in line for a night of drinking and celebration—possibly the chance to make a new friend or three—but that kind or racket would make Octavian miserable. But since he could hardly stop the men, many of whom had already produced flasks and skins, he would do the best he could. He went to the bench and put his hand on Myrddin's thigh. "There's a fire and a bed—"

"What's that sound?" Octavian cut him off and lifted his head and looked from side to side.

"I don't—" Myrddin started, but Octavian shushed him as he rose from the bench. Myrddin hurried to take his elbow in case he succumbed to his injuries or exhaustion, and Sylvain exchanged a worried look with Dirk.

Octavian screwed his eyes shut and canted his head as if doing so would aid his hearing. Sylvain caught himself doing the same, squinting as he tried to parse the words of the men around him from the sounds beyond the wall to discern what had Octavian so interested. Then he heard it: soft sobbing muffled by walls and distance. Along with the others, he followed Octavian to a small, windowless shed near the back of the complex. A heavy chain and padlock held the double doors shut, and Octavian broke free of Myrddin's grasp and knelt in front of it to prod at it with a shard of steel.

After a few moments, Octavian cursed. "What in the Shades'? I used to pick the lock on the door to the mill my father owned all the time. I used to go there to be alone. It was easy. I can't seem to get this, though."

Sylvain crouched down behind him and took the pick from his hands. "You're trembling, my flower," he whispered into Octavian's ear. "And this lock is complex. Let me."

Sylvain coaxed and toyed with the tumblers until they yielded to him, and then he opened it and threw off the chain. Octavian pushed the doors open, and they entered a dank room foul with human waste and unwashed bodies. A group of about a dozen women, wearing nothing but sheer chemises or shifts despite the cold, huddled against the back wall. Their dirty faces bore the marks of weeks or moons of tears, and Sylvain's skin tightened. Ropes constricted the women's wrists and bound them to each other.

"Bleeding Shades," Octavian breathed as he reached out his hand. The woman closest to him flinched and tried to cover her head with the range the ropes allowed her.

Behind them, some of the men hooted and clapped. A few of them started undoing their trousers, and Sylvain's bile rose at the comments he heard from them as the women wept and pressed as close to one another as they could. If no one else would stop what the others had planned, he would.

Octavian turned on the others, his dagger drawn. "What is wrong with you? Do none of you have sisters or wives? Goddesses, you all have mothers! What if one of these unfortunate victims was your mother? What would you do to the man who would violate her honor?"

"Tam," one of the men said. "Tam Octavian, you're new to all this but, but, begging your pardon, the women always go to the victors. They're part of our spoils. The men will expect it."

Octavian stood straight and solid as if he'd never been injured. With a backhanded blow, he sent the man sprawling on the ground. "No one's life is a spoil of battle. These are people, scared and hurt. They have been through more suffering than anyone should have to endure. No man or woman is prey to another, not while I can stop it. Do you want to challenge me? Any of you? Because you'll have to go through me to get to these women. Do you want to try?"

The man shook his head.

"Do you want to try to torment innocents in front of me?" Octavian shrieked.

"N-no, tam."

Octavian grasped the man by the breastplate, hauled him to his feet, and hit him again. Blood trickled from the man's nose and lips. "Take advantage of me, who isn't starved and bound, if you want to violate someone. Or are you such a worthless coward you can only exploit those who are weakened with hunger and abuse? Try it on me, pig!"

Sylvain hurried to calm Octavian. "They have seen your point, my treasure. Let him go."

Octavian shook his head and rubbed his eyes with his thumb and finger. "They haven't. They don't stand down because what they want to do is wrong, only because I can stop them. I don't want men like these at Rosecairn. I want men who know the difference between justice and exploitation. Take them to the gate with the others."

"A good decision," Sylvain said, kneading the steel-hard knots of Octavian's shoulders. "They are not worth your time." He nodded to some men nearby, and they seized the arms of the offenders and dragged them away. "You need to come into the hut and let us tend to your wounds. Rest."

As if he couldn't hear him, Octavian pulled away and faced the knot of crying, embracing women. Sylvain couldn't bear to imagine what they had been through, and so he understood when they shrunk away from Octavian, who'd drawn his dagger. He stepped toward them, but his hand shook so hard he dropped his blade, and when he crouched to pick it up, he couldn't seem to find the strength in his fingers. He left the weapon on the ground and stood. "I will personally see each and every one of you gets home unharmed, but I… I can't do it tonight. Someone should…. Dirk?" He seemed to realize Dirk couldn't hear him, and turned and gestured.

Dirk clapped Octavian on the shoulder and knelt to retrieve the dagger Octavian had dropped. He cut the ropes holding the women's hands, and soon the man with the red beard joined him, speaking softly to reassure the captives, promising they would get home, promising to find them food and warmer clothes in the meantime.

"Dirk will guard them through the night," Sylvain said to Octavian. "You know he will."

Octavian nodded with a clear effort. "We must check the rest of these buildings. There could be others inside who need our aid."

"It can wait until the morning," Myrddin said, even as he grasped Octavian's waist to help him walk, because by now he couldn't set one foot in front of the other on his own, and he'd abandoned the pretense.

"Could those women have waited? No. We check these buildings before we worry about my scratches. Help me or don't, but I have to make sure no one else is held prisoner here. I'm not letting a single person suffer another night."

Sylvain met Myrddin's gaze, and they exchanged a nod. Sylvain had little trouble picking the locks on the doors. Inside the first building, they found a grisly scene. Sylvain retched, and Myrddin vomited on the floor at the sight of the bodies strapped to poles, skin stripped away, muscle and sinew glistening red. Corpses lay on tables, their limbs chained down, flesh carved out in furrows, organs exposed. Horrible implements Sylvain couldn't fathom the purposes of hung on the walls or lay scattered on the bloodstained tables. The stench was unbelievable. Piles of tortured bodies and severed heads and limbs lay in the corner, while a body, little more than a wet, red skeleton, hung from the rafters. The warlord's torture room.

"Get Octavian out of here," Sylvain hissed. "He's in no state to see this."

Myrddin hurried to comply, but Octavian said, "Some of these were his own men. I'm glad I killed him. I've never been more proud of anything in my life. I should see it—they all should."

"If that's what you want," Myrddin said cautiously.

"Then I-I want it torn down and burned," Octavian said.

"Good choice." Sylvain shuddered and drew his suede cloak tighter around him. He too wanted this horror burned to the ground, obliterated.

Maybe then he could purge it from his memory. If he had known he would see this, the blood clotted black over the stretched sinew, the teeth exposed in an eternal scream of agony, the clouded orbs of the eyes, the wisps of colorless hair protruding from the desiccated scalps—If he had known, he might not have come here even for Octavian Rose.

Outside the building, Sylvain emptied his stomach. His gut's contents steamed against the frozen ground. Would he ever banish the images of those bodies from his mind? Would he ever be able to sleep without imagining the pain those people had endured? He spat a mouthful of bile on the ground. Octavian, still caked in blood, touched the back of his head and said, "Sorry. I know it's awful, but because of us, this won't happen again. I wish I could have spared you—"

Sylvain mopped his lips with his sleeve. "You should have been spared. I'm used to this sort of thing… see it every other day."

"Of course." Octavian helped him up, and they went to the next building as Myrddin left to begin heating water in the warlord's hut so they could all wash. It wasn't locked, and contained sacks of grain and flour, barrels of ale, and meat hanging from the ceiling. The following shed held blankets and worn saddles, but the third….

"Sylvain, goddesses," Octavian gasped as he lifted the lid from a wooden crate and found it filled with gold coins. He scooped up a handful and let the coins fall, tinkling softly, as he looked over his shoulder and met Sylvain's gaze. "There's a fortune here."

They opened the other chests and crates the small building held and found more coins, along with jewelry, gemstones, golden goblets, and fine weapons. Sylvain whistled through his teeth. "Goddesses, my flower. You can buy yourself a castle, maybe even a title!"

"It makes sense," Octavian mused as he turned a dagger encrusted with emeralds and sapphires over in his hands. "The bastard has been terrorizing this area for years, and lately he's taken to keeping all the spoils for himself. It was one of the reasons I was able to convince the men to follow me. They haven't been paid in moons."

"You're already sharing your reward with them," Sylvain said as he draped a string of pearls as fat as arn nuts over his fingers. "You are not obligated to split this up as well. Listen to me now. We should tell no one what we've found."

"But those men are entitled to part of this," Octavian said. "They earned it."

"Part, perhaps." Sylvain dropped the pearl necklace into a pocket of his cloak. "But if they become aware of this amount of gold, do you honestly think they won't turn against each other, and you, to fight over it? Many of these men seem decent, and they supported you, but make no mistake—they're sell-swords, not knights. Acquiring wealth is their loftiest goal, and fighting and killing for coin is at the core of who they are. Besides, you can give this to those men, and they'll squander it on whores and drinking, or you can keep most of it for yourself and use it wisely, perhaps to supply the camp or improve it. You, unlike them, have the wisdom to invest it in this place. You should keep it, or at least most of it. You don't know what you may need in the future: better gear for the men, more horses, wood and stone to construct decent buildings. Half of these people are still living in tents."

Octavian rubbed his forehead, and dried blood fell down in flakes. "I—Some of that makes sense, but I'm not sure if it's right. I don't want to become a man who holds gold higher than anything else. I'll have to think on this later. I cannot do it tonight."

"No, not tonight." Sylvain cupped Octavian's cheek in his gloved hand. "You have done enough for tonight, and you must rest now. But until you reach a decision, we should keep this between ourselves."

Octavian nodded, and Sylvain helped him out of the shed. He closed the door and replaced the chain and lock before guiding Octavian to the warlord's hut. Inside, it smelled of the man, but it was warm and bright, thanks to several lanterns and a hearty blaze in the hearth. A large bed covered in furs sat in the corner, and bread, cured meats, cheese, and pitchers of either water or ale sat on a long table. Weapons leaned against the walls, and more furs covered the plank floor. It surprised Sylvain to see dishes and pots and pans on shelves near the inglenook, just like one would expect in a family home, not the den of this depraved monster. Someone had brought a few pails of water, and Myrddin had heated some of it in an iron cauldron over the fire. As he poured it into a basin and scared up a fairly clean cloth, Sylvain helped Octavian to the bed.

"Stinks," Octavian complained weakly as he lay down.

Sylvain smoothed the matted hair off his forehead. "I know. Sorry."

Together, he and Myrddin got Octavian out of his filthy boots and clothes, mostly cutting them away since there was no saving them. Octavian winced when Myrddin lifted the steaming rag to his shoulder and wiped the blood from the shallow cut across the top. His poor body had really taken some abuse. Sylvain had sustained some cuts and bruises, but they covered Octavian's skin. Some scrapes at regular intervals crossed his belly, and they look painful, puffed and red around the edges, but the wound over his hip was the deepest. Sylvain was no healer, but he thought it could have used stitching. Fresh blood oozed from it when Myrddin wiped it, and Octavian stifled a squeal and squeezed Sylvain's hand. He'd been forced to fight without his gloves, and his knuckles wore swollen and shredded.

Sylvain stood. "We should try to find something to keep these from getting infected." He went to the crates and cupboards near the hearth where he'd noticed some clay canisters and vials. Pulling out the corks to sniff the contents, he found most of them were herbs for cooking. Then, toward the back of a shelf, he discovered a crock of salve. He wasn't sure what it was, but the strong scent of pricklefruit told him it would help keep sepsis at bay. He took it to Myrddin to spread over the wounds, and turned away as Octavian cried out at the sting. He found a reasonably clean sheet and tore it into strips, and while Myrddin wrapped Octavian's shoulder, Sylvain wrapped his battered hands. Though Octavian winced now and then, he mostly dozed, eyelids fluttering, snoring softly between moans.

"If he wakes, try to get him to eat something, have some wine," Sylvain said, petting the back of Myrddin's hair.

Myrddin looked up and met his gaze. "Where will you be?"

"Keeping watch. I'm not completely convinced we're surrounded by nothing by loyal converts." Sylvain didn't mention that he wanted to keep an eye on the shed holding a king's ransom in gold and treasure. "Stay with him. Hold him. He'd rather have you with him than me. I don't plan to let anyone other than men I absolutely trust past the courtyard tonight, so you can rest without worrying. If you need me, I'm going to find a perch on the wall."

Chapter Fifteen

Winter clutched like a thief to the lands in the north, close to the mountains. By the time spring unwound its icy fingers from Rosecairn and tufts of green broke through the rime, Octavian's force numbered more than a hundred and fifty men, and the cairn could probably support three times that many. They'd restored the smithy, though they had no smith to operate the forge, rebuilt the stables and armory, enforced the gate with iron bands, and added a pair of watchtowers to the two that already stood. Though they hadn't made as much progress as Octavian would have liked building shelters and barracks for the men, they had torn down the huts in the worst states, as well as walls surrounding the courtyard. The three remaining crossbows had been moved to the front gate. As Octavian had said to the men, he had no desire to live in a camp where he required a barricade to separate him from his own people.

The day was mild, and Octavian turned his face toward the warmth of the late-morning sun. As he surveyed the progress the men had made, he wondered what the best use of his funds would be, and decided decent housing for his warriors would be essential before the next winter came. Cannibalizing the inner walls and the buildings beyond saving had provided some materials, and with what he'd found in the shed and what the company had earned since, he could purchase what he needed and hire craftsman to do the work they couldn't do themselves. He wandered to the center of the compound, where the first buds of roses, red and white, dotted the stones of the cairn. Their fledgling perfume hung sweet in the spring air, and Octavian breathed it deep into his chest. Yes, he could make this into a place men would be proud to call home, a place they would die to defend.

After a few moments, Karl approached him, followed by a group of people Octavian didn't recognize. He clasped Karl's hand; he was glad the loyal man and capable warrior had chosen to stay at Rosecairn. "Beautiful morning," Octavian said.

"Aye." Karl nodded. "The winter lasted too long this year. There are some people here who want to talk to you."

"More hopefuls?" Octavian asked. Their group had already started to make a name for itself, and that drew men seeking to join a lucrative company. While some came with honorable intentions, many others came thinking things would be as they'd been under Brealan Lavock, and they could satisfy their baser desires while earning some coin. Octavian had turned away many more than he'd accepted.

"Some," Karl said. "A mixed batch. I'll let you hear it from them, but I'll stay close by, as a few of them are armed."

"I appreciate it, my friend."

"I haven't forgotten what I owe you," Karl said. "None of us have."

Though he smiled, Octavian shook his head. "You owe me nothing I don't owe you three times over. Please, let's not have debts between us. Let's just say we fought together and leave it at that."

"As you say, Octavian. I'll be over there if you need me." Karl found a place in the shade and a barrel to sit upon, but his sharp gaze never wavered from Octavian and the newcomers.

Reminding himself not to judge these people by the actions of those who had previously come to the Rosecairn, Octavian approached the group. None of them really looked like warriors, but many had thought the same of him, and probably still did. "You wished to speak with me? I'm Octavian Rose. What can I do for you?"

An older man, with a gray beard and wearing dusty, homespun clothes came up to him and extended a hand covered in callouses and caked with soil. Octavian grasped it and returned his warm grin. To his surprise, tears sparkled in the older man's eyes, and he stifled a sob.

Octavian patted his back, feeling awkward. "Have I done something to upset you, tam?"

The man screwed his eyes shut as tears spilled over his dark, wrinkled cheeks and into his whiskers. It took him a moment to compose himself. "Upset me? No, goddesses. They must have sent you themselves. I don't know how I can repay you for what you have done, but I had to thank you in person."

Confused, Octavian said, "Forgive me, but I don't recall us meeting." The man still held tight to his hand. He smelled, rather pleasantly, of warm loam. "Do we know each other?"

"Forgive me." The men let go of Octavian's hand and wiped his palm on his trousers. "We have never met. My name is Rol Billager, and I'm here on behalf of my daughter, Casia. You see, the goddesses blessed us with her late in life, long after me and my wife had given up on having children, so when she was taken by Brealan Lavock, it about ruined us.

"I know what happened to my girl while she was held here. I know even if she won't talk about it. I know from what she screams in the night. She came back to us in pieces, but she came back. She might not talk about what happened, but she tells us over and over again about how the doors to that filthy shed opened, and standing there was the most beautiful man she'd ever seen, covered in blood and bathed in starlight. Those are Casia's words; I'm a farmer, not a poet. She tells us whenever we'll listen about the young man who saw she was safe and fed, who put her on his horse and took it on himself to see she made it home. She says you treated her with respect, but not like she was damaged beyond repair, and she says you killed that whoreson and cut his head off."

"Yes, tam, I certainly did. I wish I could have made him suffer to rival the pain he inflicted on others, but I'm proud to say I sent him to the Shades'."

Rol spat on the ground. "Good riddance. I wish I could have been the one to end his sorry life, but I'm glad someone did it, and I just wanted to say thank you, face to face. Thank you, Octavian Rose."

"Tam, it was truly my pleasure. Now tell me, how does Casia fare? How is your family?"

They wandered to some flattened stones circling the cairn and sat down together. Rol shook his head. "With Lavock and the rest of those savages gone, we've been able to move back into our cottage. It's no palace, but I built it with my own hands, and Casia was born there. We've taken back most of our land, and about a dozen of our sows had litters this spring. We've had some lambs born too. Thanks to you, we're getting our lives back."

"And Casia?"

"She… doesn't like leaving the house. She keeps to herself and her spinning most days, and she sleeps with a kitchen knife under her pillow. She isn't the happy girl I remember, but she isn't dead, and I thank the goddesses, and you, for that. I don't think my girl will ever marry. The talk of being with a man brings her to tears."

"I'm so sorry. I wish I could have done more." Octavian meant it. "I truly hope she can heal, live a full life one day. I hope you'll have a dozen grandchildren."

Rol nodded sadly as he stood and brushed off his backside. "I just wanted to thank you, Octavian Rose. And if you need pork, mutton, or cheese, you come to us. We'll give you our best at fair price, and Casia will be happy to see you again."

Octavian got to his feet and clapped the man on the shoulder. "I'll gladly visit your farm as soon as I get the opportunity. Please give your wife and daughter my best, and if I or my people can ever do anything to serve you, you have only to ask. I mean that."

Rol hugged him, and Octavian returned it. "Thank you, Octavian. My daughter said you were as sweet as a flower and as strong as steel, a vision sent from the goddesses, and I see now she didn't exaggerate. Take care of yourself. This world needs more men like you."

He turned to leave, and Octavian looked over the other three people who had come seeking audience. First he addressed a massive man with close-cut dirty-blond hair, a neatly trimmed beard, and a huge steel hammer strapped to his back. He was attractive, and if Octavian hadn't known in an instant the man had no interest in other men, he might have tried to persuade him to his bed. Instead, he asked, "Who are you and what can I do for you, tam?"

The muscles of the big man's bare arm rippled as he extended his hand to Octavian. "The name's Joaquin Pine, Tam Octavian. A smith by trade. A fair fighter if needs be."

"And what are you hoping to find at Rosecairn?" Octavian asked.

"Ideally, work at a forge. Barring that, I can fight beside you."

"And how do you find yourself without work?" Octavian asked. "Skilled blacksmiths are rarely seeking trade."

"Lavock and the others attacked my village a year and a half ago," Joaquin explained. "Burned my shop to the ground and killed my family and apprentice. I wandered after that, taking what work I could find. When word reached me that Rosecairn had a new master, I made my way here. Met up with these others along the river. All I want is to work, maybe put down roots again, start a new family in a good place. I make damned good weapons and can do repairs. Just don't ask me to hurt innocent people or cause pain for fun. That I won't do, and if that's what you're about, I'll move along."

Octavian smiled wide. "I think we'll get along just fine, Joaquin, and we could really use a smith here at Rosecairn. There's a fine shop just waiting for one to the west of here, down that path, and if you find it sufficient, I personally invite you to build a home nearby. You'll probably make a fair living working for the warriors here, but you're more than welcome to sell your goods elsewhere, provided you don't sell them to our enemies!"

"Can I have a look at the forge, then?" Joaquin asked.

"Be my guest," Octavian said. "Just follow that trail. You'll not miss it. It's an open space beneath a low roof, surrounded by stone walls, probably about knee-high. I'll await your decision."

With a nod of gratitude, Joaquin went to inspect the smithy, while Octavian turned to the two remaining visitors: a pretty young woman and a scrawny youth. "And what can I do for you, my lady?" He extended a slight bow to her as he had at his parents' balls.

The boy, probably Octavian's age or even younger, stepped in front of the woman. "Tam, let me introduce to you Lena, a healer of extraordinary skill and possessed of miraculous talents...." The youth seemed nervous and spoke with an accent—Esperon?—so heavy Octavian had to concentrate hard to understand him.

The woman pushed the young man out of the way. "I thank you, but I can speak for myself, Tam Fabrezio. Greetings, Octavian Rose. I'm here because you and your people are gaining a reputation for being mostly honorable and reasonable to deal with. Like many others, I lost my village to the cruelty of Brealan Lavock, and so aiding the man who rid the world of him appeals to me."

"And you're a healer?" Octavian asked. "We could certainly use that. What of the miraculous talents your companion speaks of? Are you possessed of the gift?"

Her blue eyes, while gentle, made Octavian feel exposed, his every hope, doubt, and fear naked before her scrutiny. Her gaze cut into him like a concentrated beam of light, and he gave up trying to hide. "I see you have a pure spirit. But to answer your question, I am not a mage. I'm possessed of intuition, flashes of truth that come to me unbidden. I can sense the emotions of others, just like right now I know you're suspicious of my words, and that you have a wound on your right hip that bothers you when the seasons change. I can find and relieve suffering in men and beasts, and I can decipher unspoken desires from both. You want to ask me what I seek at Rosecairn. I want to ease pain, and I want to live in safety. I sense you can provide that, and that despite your burning ambition and all you seek to prove, you are a decent man. Or you want to be, and that's the important thing. The striving for it is as noble as the gaining of it."

Octavian almost sputtered at the dagger-sharp truth of her conclusions. She might not be a mage, but Lena had a keen insight into a man's mind. He took her hand and shook it as he would a man's, since he had a strong suspicion kissing her fingers might earn him a bloody nose. "I am a mage, and I would like to learn more about healing. I'm happy to offer you a place here. I would humbly request you share your knowledge with me. Teach me."

Lena smiled and tossed her silvery blonde hair. She wore it short, only to her chin, and it matched her practical brown dress and green traveling cloak "I knew you had a good heart. I'll teach you, and I'll do what I can for your men and animals while I'm here. Both deserve the peace and comfort I hope I can provide. All I ask in return is safety and respect."

"I'll see you have a house and everything you need. Until that time, you can either stay in one of the abandoned buildings or pitch a tent, if you have one. If anyone gives you trouble, come straight to me," Octavian said, his attention focused on the lanky boy, now standing alone in the clearing, his shadow stretching behind him. Their gazes met, and a cautious mutual interest grew between them until the young man looked away. "Tam… what was it? Fabrezio?"

The young man bowed with a courtly flourish Octavian hadn't seen in more than a year. He was thin, but was well proportioned and moved elegantly. "Fabrezio Orvina d'Caelus, at your service, Tam Octavian Rose."

"And you're a warrior?" Octavian raised an eyebrow.

Fabrezio chewed his lips and gazed at his tattered Esperon sandals. "I can't claim that, tam. All I can tell you is, I can learn. I know I'm a risk, but I'll do all I can to be of value to you."

Octavian remembered when, not so long ago, all he had wanted was someone to take a chance on him, give him the opportunity to prove his courage and dedication. He'd been fortunate enough to cross Myrddin's path. He brushed his fingers down the young man's shoulder. "Why don't we sit down and talk?"

They made their way to the stone perimeter of the cairn. Octavian looked at the sword on the other man's back as he asked, "Where are you from?"

"Espero," Fabrezio answered. "The city of Aviertanorra, near the northern coast of the island."

"You're a long way from home," Octavian noted. "Why is that?"

"Just looking to make my own way in the world," Fabrezio said.

Octavian didn't have to have Lena's intuition to see Fabrezio was holding back. He rested his hand on Fabrezio's kneecap and wasn't surprised when the other man didn't recoil from his touch. "Tell me why you left home."

Fabrezio curled his shoulders and rested his elbows on his knees. "I'm not a mage. In Espero, I was a disappointment to my parents. Everyone else in our family had the gift. I tried hard—prayed to have even a little magic, but I just don't. You have to understand, in Espero, there are two types of people: the mages and those who prepare their food and clean their clothes. My parents were humiliated. They're wealthy and powerful and see me as a failure. An embarrassment. They said all I could do was offer myself as a servant, a scribe to one of the mages at the university. I didn't want that, thought I could do better, so I left. I came here on an Emiri ship and made my way up river. I heard the mercenaries of Rosecairn had honor, and I hoped to join. Please take a chance on me. I can learn to fight. I'll work all day until I can be of use to you. I can't just go back to Espero and be a game piece in my parents' power struggles. Give me a chance. If I can't fight, I'll peel the turnips for your supper and clean your stables. I just want to live by my own rules."

"You know, we aren't so different," Octavian said to Fabrezio. "I am my father's eighth child by his third wife. He married all of his offspring to wealthy merchants who could aid his trading business, and he planned to do the same with me. I didn't want to be a piece on a game board either, and so I ran. For a long time, no one would give me a chance, because I was young and lacked experience. I won't do that to you. You have a place here. Honesty is harder to come by than skill, and skill can be acquired, where a strong spirit and a good heart cannot. I expect you to train, and I know you will. I think you are worth taking a risk on."

"I—Really?" Fabrezio looked over at Octavian with wide, dark eyes.

Octavian reached over and brushed a strand of deep brown, almost black hair out of his eye. "Really. Were you expecting me to say no?"

"I just… I suppose I'm not used to people thinking I'm worth much. Bleeding Shades!"

"Here, you can be worth as much as you want to be. This is a place for fresh starts."

"Thank you, Tam Octavian," Fabrezio said. "I'll train hard. I won't make you sorry." He leaned a little closer and said, "I could bloody kiss you, you know. Fuck me."

"We'll see." Octavian patted the back of his hand and smiled wide. "I'll introduce you to Myrddin, and he'll teach you how to handle a blade."

"I cannot express the gratitude I feel for you taking a chance on me," said the lanky Esperon with the dark eyes. "I won't disappoint you. I'll work night and day until I'm good enough to fight beside you. And maybe you can show me a thing or two about handling a weapon. I'd like that. I don't know much, but as I said, I am very eager to learn."

MYRDDIN SAT with Dirk and Quinn outside the warlord's hut, where Octavian had been living since they'd claimed the Rosecairn. True to his word, Octavian had taken a torch to the torture room as soon as he'd been able to rise, and he'd cleared out the other buildings. Now they housed between four and six beds for the men, but Myrddin suspected Octavian wanted to tear them all down and start fresh. He couldn't disagree with tearing away everything Lavock had built, all evidence of the man's existence at Rosecairn.

They were discussing riding to the creek on the eastern edge of the camp to have their midday meal by the water and maybe do some fishing. They'd recently returned from guarding a manor house to the south and apprehending the bandits attempting to burglarize it again, and so they found themselves between jobs.

"Not so long ago, riding out there wouldn't have been safe," Quinn said without looking up from the scrap of wood he worked with his knife. "I must say, it's nice bein' paid for my work and sleeping in my own bed without worrying I'll be killed in it. What about it, Myrddin? Planning to stay?"

"I don't have a better prospect at the moment," Myrddin said, smiling at the new green appearing between the mountain stones. "As long as the work stays steady."

Dirk snorted, and Myrddin knew he'd have tormented him about his commitment to Octavian if they'd been alone. He'd even taken to calling Octavian "the wife," though nothing could be further from accuracy. They'd never discussed exclusivity, and Myrddin didn't mind. It hardly made their time together less enjoyable or their friendship less strong. "No one has chained you to your hut," Myrddin said to Dirk.

Dirk rolled his eyes and signed, *You wouldn't be able to put your boots on without me.*

"So it's an act of charity," Myrddin said.

Of pity, Dirk said. *Though some women around here would be a nice change.*

"You spent two days at the brothel after our last job." Myrddin spoke instead of signing, as it felt less like cutting Quinn out of the conversation altogether.

Dirk sighed. *It would be easier, and cheaper to find a friend like what you have, someone to have fun with now and then, but without the hassle of feeding and supporting them. Without them trying to keep you from others.*

Myrddin did sign his next words. *You fancy the wrong people, my friend. Ladies do not view things as men do. You'll never find a woman who will enter into such an arrangement. Either stick with whores or find yourself a wife.*

Dirk looked stricken. *What, just one? How come you don't have to choose? You have the little wife, Sylvain, and anyone else you fancy. It's like there's a reward for being unnatural. And you get it for free!*

Just then, Octavian came up to them, followed by a young man Myrddin had never seen before, and he would have remembered the willowy lad with the rich, dark skin, warm eyes, and pretty face. He looked up and smiled at the stranger as Dirk signed, *See? What in the Shades'? You've got at least two pretty men to warm your bed whenever you like and he brings you another? Why couldn't he show up with a woman? Would that be too much damned trouble?*

"Not too many mercenary women, friend," Myrddin replied. "You could always switch sides…."

Predictably, Dirk pantomimed being sick between his knees. The new young man looked back and forth as if expecting someone to explain what was going on. Octavian just shook his head. He must be accustomed to the way Myrddin and Dirk harassed each other. When had that happened? It seemed like only yesterday Octavian had blushed and grown defensive at Dirk's mild teasing about him spending the night with Sylvain.

"My friends, I'd like you to meet the newest member of our company, Fabrezio Orvina d'Caelus. Fabrezio, this is my oldest friend, Myrddin, Quinn, who helped me defeat Brealan Lavock, and Dirk, the finest of archers. Speaking of which, where is Sylvain? I'd like Fabrezio to meet him as well."

Oh, there's no doubt they'll get along just fine, Dirk signed. *Can you recruit a pretty girl next time instead of another playmate for the three of you?*

Octavian put his hands on his hips and laughed. "Actually, I already have: a healer called Lena who can sense the thoughts and feelings of men and animals." Dirk perked up, but Octavian said, "Although if you don't treat her with respect, don't come to me for healing when she knocks you to the dirt."

"Aye," Fabrezio said. "That's accurate. Lena's as sweet as honey until you cross her, and then she's a bear. One with the claws to back it up."

Quinn said, "What was your name again, lad?"

"Fabrezio Orvina d'Caelus." He crossed his arm over his belly and bowed.

"Fa—Breeze—What now? Breeze? I'm calling you Breeze. Some of us are about to go fishing. Care to come along? Have a look at the camp and get the lay of the land?"

Breeze looked at Octavian, who nodded. "That sounds great! I see you carry a sword, Tam Quinn. I am interested in becoming a better swordsman. Could I trouble you for some tips?"

"I should say so," Quinn said. "You're part of the company now, which means I might find you watching my back someday soon. You'd bloody well better know what you're doing."

Quinn and Dirk stood. *Are you coming, Myrddin?* Dirk asked.

Myrddin looked at Octavian in his tight leather trousers and white shirt, the sun lighting the planes of his face and gilding his hair. He was smiling, looking light, unburdened by pain or doubt. His hair fluttered in the playful wind. "I'll stay behind."

The three of them departed, and Myrddin reached out for Octavian and wrapped his arms around his waist when Octavian stepped between his legs. Octavian curled against him and raked his fingers through Myrddin's hair. "I have some things I'd like to show you inside my hut."

"I hope so."

"Ass." Octavian swatted him lightly on the back of the head. "That will need to wait. I have some things that I've been working on that are important to me, and I'd like you to see them." He stepped back and pulled Myrddin to his feet. After looking over his shoulder to make sure they were alone, he pressed a soft, chaste kiss to Myrddin's lips. It was enough to make Myrddin's cock stir in his pants.

Octavian wove their fingers together and led Myrddin into the hut. It looked much the same as it had when it had belonged to Lavock, but it smelled cleaner and felt far less foul. They sat down together, side by side, at the long table. Since Octavian had inherited the building, books, papers, and inkwells had slowly crowded out plates of meat and cheese. A carafe of wine remained amidst the sheaths of parchment, and Octavian poured them each a drink before he reached for the scuffed leather-bound journal he always carried. He flipped through pages of neat, rounded letters. Myrddin noticed some delicate drawings among them: Sylvain drawing his bow, a bud unfurling against the stones of the cairn, himself sleeping with his hair tousled around his face. They were beautiful, almost ethereal things with their fine lines meticulously crosshatched to form light and shadow, and he wanted to study each pen stroke, but Octavian flicked past them until he found the page he wanted and turned the book on its side.

"Here is the house I plan to build before autumn." He pointed to the plans he'd sketched. It was a simple home, rectangular and not much larger than the building they sat in, hardly the fortress worthy of the man who'd slain Brealan Lavock and won Rosecairn. There was a large central room with a pair of slashes to indicate a hearth and curved lines to represent a set of bay windows on either side of the door. A short wall blocked the bedroom area from the main chamber.

"And I'll build in a loft above the sleeping area for storage, and a pantry and cold cellar here." Octavian pointed.

"And what did you plan to put here?" Myrddin indicated an area Octavian had scratched out with his quill.

Octavian leaned his back against Myrddin's chest and sipped his wine. "Oh, I had the fanciful idea of making myself a bathtub. One of the things—maybe the only thing—I loved about my life before becoming a sell-sword was bathing. I admit I miss it, relaxing in the hot, soapy water. Lying there in the heat and bubbles helped me think. But it's a foolish fantasy. I would have to hire a stonemason to build it, and I can't justify wasting that much gold on myself when the camp still needs fortification. The rest I can probably do myself."

Myrddin chuckled as he pushed Octavian's hair aside so he could nibble on the perfect ivory skin of his neck. "You'll have your bathtub, my lad. My father was a stonemason, and before I joined the knighthood, I was his apprentice. I may need some tools, but I can do this for you easily. You deserve it, and it would please me very much to make you happy."

"We could spend some time in that tub." Octavian grasped Myrddin's wrists and pulled Myrddin's arms tighter around his waist as he let his head fall back and arched his hips against Myrddin. Goddesses, he was so alluring, and the fact he didn't feign it for effect only amplified his appeal. Myrddin pushed Octavian's shirt aside to nip along his collarbone and lap the sweat from his skin.

"And what is this little area?" Myrddin pointed to a semicircle Octavian had drawn between the bedchamber and the hearth. "An alcove? For what?"

Octavian threw his head back and gasped air through open lips as Myrddin played with his nipple through his thin shirt. "For you. A place for you to keep your books and treasures, to sit when you want to be on your own. We can build a second fireplace here"—he pointed— "and we can even put a bed in the corner in case you're inclined to sleep alone. Or with someone besides me."

The scope of what Octavian proposed washed over Myrddin, and he closed his eyelids against the sting. He hugged Octavian closer and lowered his forehead to his shoulder. "You… you want us to share a home? A bed? For good?"

Octavian jerked out of his grasp and turned to face him on the bench, pressing his hand to Myrddin's cheek in a gesture Myrddin had come to know well and adore. His brown eyes darted back and forth like a scared animal, and Myrddin stroked his cheek with the back of his hand to soothe him. "Myrddin, I did not mean to imply—I mean to say, if you want a house of your own, apart from me—"

Myrddin mashed his lips against Octavian's sweet mouth. "Goddesses, no. I don't want to be apart from you, and I'm delighted you want to live with me. Do you really want to live with me, wake up to my ugly face every morning and fall asleep next to me every night?"

"Yes, Myrddin. Yes. A hundred times yes."

"Goddesses." Myrddin kissed him, licked his lips and swirled their tongues together. "I want you… now and on every day the goddesses grant us. Always."

"I did not mean to presume," Octavian said against Myrddin's lips, his chest heaving against Myrddin. "I just thought—"

"I'll share your house and your bed, Octavian, for as long as you wish it. I'm honored to be asked, and you have drawn plans for a lovely home. We'll build it, bathtub and all. Now, will you take your clothes off for me?"

Octavian kissed him softly, taking his time to nibble along Myrddin's lower lip. "I'll take my clothes off anytime you ask. I-I feel very safe with you, Myrddin, and I desire you. I think—"

"What?"

"Let's just get on with it," Octavian said, and Myrddin couldn't disagree.

AFTERWARD, MYRDDIN rolled off Octavian and onto his side. He propped his cheek in his hand so he could gaze down at him. Octavian never looked more beautiful to him than after they'd made love, with his lips dark and swollen from kissing, his lids languid over his dark eyes, his hair tousled, a rosy glow on his skin, and a sheen of sweat sparkling over his body. His skin wasn't perfect anymore; the wound above his hip had left a glossy, raised scar, and the cuts on his belly had healed to thin white lines. Other small nicks covered his torso, arms, and legs. Some would fade and others wouldn't, Myrddin knew as he circled a raised, round patch of satiny, purplish flesh on Octavian's shoulder. Octavian, in his satiated haze, barely noticed. By now, Myrddin knew just how to satisfy him: a slow buildup, lots of touching, tasting, and exploration. He adored Myrddin's mouth and was anything but shy about asking for what he needed. He liked gentle touches, up until the end, when he didn't. As he usually could, Myrddin had brought him to ecstasy twice, once with his mouth and once while inside him. But that was the benefit of youth.

He also liked to cuddle, and Myrddin opened his arm so Octavian could take his place on his chest. Myrddin liked it too, that connection as he drifted down from his bliss. Sylvain either rolled over and went to sleep or dressed and went to find something else to get up to. He considered lounging around in bed but not fucking dull, and Myrddin felt glad Octavian didn't. As he combed his fingers through Octavian's sweaty hair, he asked, "How old are you?"

Octavian chuckled lazily as he played his fingertips through the hair on Myrddin's chest. "Nineteen."

"And when is your birthday?"

"Why?"

Myrddin traced the knobs of his spine and smiled at the way he shuddered. "Why not? I want to know, but you don't have to tell me if you'd rather not."

Octavian circled Myrddin's nipple with his pinky. "It cannot hurt to tell you. I was born of the twenty-second day of Illira's Moon. The day after I killed Brealan Lavock. I slept through it, if I'm not mistaken. My memories of the days following the battle are still blurry. When is yours?"

"The third day of Sarmine's Moon. And I'm thirty-four years old."

Octavian pecked the underside of Myrddin's chin. "Sarmine's Moon. Then it's no surprise you're such a talented lover."

"And it's no surprise you are a poet and a scholar, my lad. Do you really believe the moon we're born under influences what kind of men we become?"

"No," Octavian said. "I believe we decide that for ourselves, that we must cut our own paths through the bracken. I could have lived as a poet and scholar. All I would have had to do was marry the ugly wife of my father's choosing and see her wealth and connections benefited his trade. You could have been a stonemason, or you could have been a knight, but you chose another road for yourself. Myrddin, why did you leave the knighthood?"

He sighed and rested his cheek against Octavian's soft hair. Aside from Dirk, he'd never met a more trustworthy or honorable man than

Octavian, and he could see no reason not tell him as they held each other in the golden afternoon light coming through the window. Myrddin traced the wavering lines the shadows of the panes left across Octavian ribs. "The short story is I believed in the knighthood when I joined and for a long time after. I believed we were doing good, protecting people, battling injustice. When I could no longer make myself believe that, I left."

"What made you stop believing it?" Octavian asked. "You can tell me, and I'll take your secret to my grave."

"I know, and I know I can trust you, and it's hardly a secret. It's just not something I speak of often. But I'll tell you if you want to know."

"You… trust me?" Octavian sounded skeptical.

"You doubt that? Have you ever given me reason not to?"

"No, I suppose not. Go on."

Myrddin sighed as he dredged up the old memory. He gathered Octavian tighter against him before he began to recount the tale. "It was eight or nine years ago, I think. I was stationed with about twenty other men in a small fortress in Everdale. Our main job was watching the road, keeping it safe for merchants and running off bandits. We were informed some poachers were killing twirl-horn deer in the forest of a wealthy landowner in the area, and we were asked to take them into custody. A simple job. I rode out with eleven other men, thinking I'd be back before supper. But the poachers proved elusive, and the forest was lousy with crude but effective traps.

"After two days of making no progress, I began speaking to the farmers and villagers who lived around the forest, hoping they had seen something. I was appalled at the conditions these people were living under. They were starving, and most of them had families and children. I learned that despite a poor harvest, the landowners had taken nearly their entire yield of meat and grain as rent owed. I learned that the poachers were keeping most of them alive, leaving packages of venison on their thresholds in the night. I shared what I had discovered with my commander and begged him to abandon the mission. He told me we had our orders, and we would either bring these poachers to justice or kill them.

"The 'poachers' turned out to be a single young man, only a little older than you are now. He was the son of a woodsman, living deep within the forest, in a tiny hut where he'd stayed with his father until his death. When we found his dwelling, I saw how little he had—little more than a cot and a fire in a room less than half the size of this one—and yet he risked his life to provide food to people who needed it, and he did it with no hope of reward. I just… I couldn't turn a man like that over to the landholders to be flogged, humiliated, and possibly executed. I tried to convince the others, thought for sure they'd see the justice in letting this man go, walking away. After all, I believed that as knights, our duty was to protect the common people and stand against evil. I could see no evil in a man feeding families. They disagreed. They talked of rewards and moving up the ranks, earning commands of their own.

"When we finally caught up with the 'poacher,' I killed three of my own men, and I took him and ran. Later, I asked him, though it was hardly easy for us to converse in those early days, why he had subjected himself to such risk. He gave me one of his crooked grins and said, 'Women and children were hungry, and I had the ability to feed them. What could I do? What would you have done?' I knew then that what was right wasn't always what was legal, and I knew which side I wanted to be on. I decided some things were more important than rising through the ranks and earning my own command."

"He sounds like a remarkable man, this poacher," Octavian said.

"Aye. No better man to take along when shopping for clothes either." Myrddin poked at Octavian's ribs, making him chuckle and squirm.

"No! Dirk?"

"The very same."

Octavian laughed. "I knew he had a big, soft heart behind that dour façade."

"I don't suggest you say that to him, my lad."

"No." Octavian's tone grew wistful. "He doesn't care for me at the best of times."

Myrddin kissed his forehead. "He worries you'll hurt me."

Octavian sat up and braced himself with his hands on either side of Myrddin's head. That fire burned behind his eyes; Myrddin could almost feel the heat on his skin. He knew this was going to destroy him one day, but he didn't back away. Maybe it was already too late to save himself.

"I won't hurt you," Octavian said. "You're more than a brother to me. I need… I need someone I can be weak in front of, someone I can tell

I'm scared and confused and don't have much idea what I'm doing, that I'm afraid I'll fail, and will still have faith in me. And I need someone who sees worth when he looks at me…. Goddesses, I am so selfish… I need, I need, I need. I am sorry, Myrddin. Tell me what you need, what you want. Ask me anything you want to know, and I'll tell you."

"Come here, lad." When Octavian had sprawled across Myrddin and Myrddin had pulled the furs over them—it was spring, but still too cold to be naked and idle—Myrddin said, "Tell me how you got that cursed knife, as I have often wondered."

Octavian stiffened in his arms. "I told myself I'd never share that story, but since you shared yours…."

"No," Myrddin said. "I told you because you wanted to know, and I trust you. I didn't do it so you'd owe me. Keep your story to yourself if you don't want to share. I have no intention of extorting you."

"No. No, I'll tell you, and not because I owe you, but because I hope there's more between us than spilling our seed on each other, or can be. I believe you can be the person who really knows me and doesn't turn away. I want you to know me, know more than my body… so. It isn't as sordid as you might imagine."

"Ah, a disappointment, then," Myrddin teased, pinching and tickling the cords of muscle at the side of Octavian's waist.

"Oh, I doubt it. It's sordid enough. You know my father is a wealthy and influential merchant and trader. A year ago, last spring, I was kidnapped by a group of bandits hoping my father would pay them to get me back. Instead, in his typical fashion, my father chose to demonstrate his power instead of worrying about my comfort. He hired a… a Cast-Down assassin, a Crimson Scythe, Myrddin."

Myrddin shuddered and glanced around the room, afraid one of those cursed creatures might materialize from the shadows, even though he knew it went against all reason. Like every other goddess-fearing man, he'd been taught not to speak of such things for fear of drawing them, and hearing them mentioned made him shiver.

"I don't know how he did it and I don't want to know," Octavian continued. "The assassin did his work; he killed a dozen bandits on his own. I had never seen anything like it, never imagined a mortal man capable of the skills he demonstrated. I've still never witnessed anything close. This assassin, he was young, maybe younger than me, and beautiful—dark skin like Breeze's. Black hair, and a body forged into a weapon. I… dallied with him. Afterward, when he left me, he gave me that dagger. He told me I was sweet, and that I should hide my sweetness from those who would exploit it. He helped me fake my death to get free of my father, and he said I should have something to defend myself. I like to think, maybe, he saw something in me he didn't want destroyed, but now I don't know. Then again, at that time, I needed badly for someone to see me as worthy, so I might have imagined it."

The thought of Octavian with such a person made cold sweat break from Myrddin's pores, made his gut clench and his mouth go dry, but Octavian had trusted him, and he would not judge. "He had nothing to gain by giving it to you. From what I understand, they do nothing if it doesn't benefit them, so he must have wanted you to live. At least wanted you to have a chance."

"Maybe. It hardly matters now. He gave me my freedom when he could have killed me or dragged me back to my father, and I swore I wouldn't waste it."

"You have hardly wasted it, Octavian. You've accomplished what warriors with twice your experience could not have."

"Because of people like you," Octavian said. "Because of you. You were the second person to give me a chance. I like to think you did it for reasons other than wanting to fuck me. I'm not sure the assassin had nobler motives."

Myrddin didn't tell Octavian he'd done it because he wanted to protect Octavian, keep the pure white light spilling from him untarnished, save him from sacrificing his honor to feed himself. He still hoped Octavian could hold to his ideals, be the good man Myrddin had seen when he'd first walked into the light of his fire. "What was he like, the assassin?"

"Pretty, as I said. Watching him move was like poetry, sparse, elegant, and sharp. Nothing wasted. His eyes, though. He had incredible eyelashes, thick and black, but his eyes were dead, like darkened windows looking out on nothing. When I think of that night, I try not to remember his eyes, but they're what I seem to remember with the most clarity. And when I envision them, I cannot help but think those were not the eyes of a man. So you can see why I don't want others knowing this about me."

"I won't tell," Myrddin assured him, dropping kisses along his hairline. "But I have to ask: Did he force you?"

"No, I initiated it. It was something I had wanted for as long as I could remember. I asked him to take me."

"Did he hurt you?"

"No. He was surprisingly considerate and… and quite competent. I enjoyed myself. Twice."

"Hmm. Better than me?" Myrddin rolled to face Octavian and wedged his thigh between his legs.

Octavian kissed him and then smiled against his lips. He rolled his hips and pressed his fresh erection against Myrddin's belly. Oh, to be so young. "It seems I cannot recall. I may need some basis for comparison."

"I'll give you anything you want." Myrddin hooked Octavian's knees over his shoulders and thrust into him as if he could drive out the memory of that assassin, pound it into nothing. He didn't want Octavian thinking of anyone but him when he felt a twinge as he walked or sat down, and Myrddin might have been old, but he felt confident he'd accomplished his goal by the time they separated, cleaned off, and returned to the bed to nap the afternoon away.

Chapter Sixteen

Octavian Rose's Journal

It hardly seems possible two years have passed since I killed Brealan Lavock and took possession of Rosecairn. Together with the good men I have been fortunate enough to have beside me, we have transformed not just the cairn, but the land for miles around. The farms in the area are thriving, and if they are threatened by bandits, we make short work of them. In return, we receive discounts on meat, cheese, and grain, as well as the loyalty of the locals, which I am sure will one day prove advantageous. Our "camp" is more like a prosperous village now. All of my men have decent shelter, and many of them have houses. I have a bathtub! We have a smith, a healer, and several craftsmen living within our walls, and many others doing business in safety beyond them. We have accomplished the unthinkable, and lucrative jobs continue to pour in, more than I can accept. All of this leaves me to wonder what my next move should be. Should I be content with what we've built and continue improving Rosecairn, or should I seek to secure more territory, make it safe for farmers and artisans? Not even mages such as I can see the future, and I am not sure which course of action would most benefit me and the men who have sworn their allegiance to my banner.

My banner. That reminds me. Maybe it's romanticism or hearing too many stories as a boy, but I want heraldry. Maybe it's just arrogance, but I imagine this camp draped in red banners bearing crossed halberds twined with thorny vines, a single rose above them. I can draw it….

And he did, taking a whole precious page in his rapidly filling journal to sketch out what he hoped would one day be the livery of the Thorns of Rosecairn.

…We are already known as the Roses, and I would be deceitful if I denied drawing satisfaction from the derivation of my chosen name. The men do not seem to mind; they're happy to earn good coin while being part of a respected, and dare I even say feared, company of warriors for hire.

SYLVAIN STIRRED next to him and pawed at Octavian's legs in half sleep. "What are you doing?"

"Just writing," Octavian said.

"Well, go to sleep."

"I am not tired."

"No?" Sylvain sat up in the bed they shared in his house and closed Octavian's book. "I haven't worn you out? I must be losing my touch." He grasped Octavian's journal by the spine and moved it to the night table, next to the candle Octavian had been using to write. "We can't have that."

Octavian sighed. "I'm just restless. I don't know what my next move is. You know I cannot sleep when I have something on my mind. I just need to figure this out. Puzzle through it. Then I'll be able to rest."

"You can do that, or we can make love until you fall to the sheets like a soggy slice of bread, drenched and limp and about to fall to pieces."

"Ugh. Such enticing imagery, Sylvain. Besides, you'll want me to clean myself, and I don't know if I feel like getting up to heat water. I have never had a lover who expected so much cleaning."

"It's nothing," Sylvain muttered against the side of Octavian's chest, where he'd pressed his face and lips beneath Octavian's arm. "You should see what the brothel boys of Elvara did to be pleasant for their lovers."

"You and your whores. I'm not a whore," Octavian said, even as he gave in to his curiosity and the arousal it inspired. "What did they do?"

Sylvain sat up, rested his head on Octavian's shoulder, and combed his fingers through the patch of hair over Octavian's heart. "For starters, they did not eat after the midday meal if they'd be working that night. A few hours before the evening began, they drank a pitcher of warm water infused with various oils and juices, and then they put a mixture of the same into their bodies, sometimes more than once. They did it until the water came out clear."

"And how in the goddesses' names do you know this? You must be worse than Dirk." Octavian asked. "Did you spend that much gold on whores?"

"On one whore," Sylvain said in a whisper. "When I first left home, I gave him every coin to my last. Goddesses, I would have given him anything he asked of me. I visited him every night, and I—"

"You fell in love with him," Octavian supplied.

"I was young, and a fool," Sylvain said, "and he was very good at his job, quite adept at making me think he returned my feelings."

"How do you know he didn't?" Octavian was interested but uncertain. He'd never heard vulnerability or regret in Sylvain's tone before, and he wondered what inspired it. Then again, he didn't want to pry until Sylvain became angry and closed him out, or deflected him with some crude joke.

"Because I asked him to leave it behind. When he worried I'd be killed doing mercenary work, I offered to give it up, take a job in a shop, sow crops, whatever he wanted. In the end, his gold and jewelry and fancy suite of rooms meant more. It was a good lesson for me, though."

"He said those things to you?" Octavian asked, reaching over to squeeze Sylvain's hand.

"No, of course not. He still had coin to bleed from me, so he spun me a teary farce about how I'd one day realize I didn't want to be with a whore, and by then he'd have lost his youth and his ability to make a living. It's no matter, Octavian. It was years ago, and since leaving Elvara, I have met more beautiful and exciting men than can I count."

Octavian could tell it was hardly no matter; that while the wound was old, it still troubled Sylvain. He wouldn't pick at it, so he changed the topic of conversation. "You must have had many adventures before joining the Bitter Tide. If you don't mind me asking, where was home?"

Sylvain moved closer to Octavian and stretched his arm across his belly to hold him closer, tighter, something he didn't normally do, even in his sleep. Octavian ran his fingertips along Sylvain's forearm. Unlike Myrddin, he had little hair on his body, and his arm was smooth, the skin soft over the subtle musculature.

"I come from Foghollow, here in Gaeltheon, to the southeast. I left behind not only wealth, but a title."

"Hmm. I knew that about you the first time we spoke. You're… courtly. You choose your words artfully, instead of just saying what pops into your head like the others. I remember that kind of subtlety and double meaning from my days as the son of a wealthy merchant, when what wasn't said sometimes held more weight than what was. How a calculated barb could be more lethal than shouting. A title is a lot to give up, though. Why did you go? Because of this?" He skimmed his palm over Sylvain's hip and thigh. "Being unnatural?"

"Goddesses, no. You know as well as I do that it's astounding what wealth and power will persuade people to ignore. No, it's much simpler than that. I left because I was bored. Bored with being fitted for clothes, smiling vapidly at feasts, listening to advisors prattle, and dancing at celebrations. I knew the world held more than that, that other men in it had grand adventures. I wanted to test myself, get up to mischief, move on to the next thing when I lost interest in my current pursuit. Yes, I wanted men, but more than that, I wanted exploits and escapades, to be entertained. Stimulated." He kissed Octavian's shoulder. "Why did you leave? So desperate to seek out a gorgeous archer who would school you in the arts of pleasure as only a man who learned from an Elvaran whore is capable?"

Octavian put his knuckles beneath Sylvain's chin, angled his face upward, and kissed him softly. "Not necessarily, though it has certainly been an advantage. No. I left because I did not want to be controlled."

"I cannot imagine anyone daft enough to even attempt it. Do you ever miss that life? Think about going back?"

He chuckled and rolled so he and Sylvain faced each other. After wriggling to get comfortable in his arms, Octavian pressed their foreheads together and peppered kisses over Sylvain's forehead, eyes, nose, cheeks, and chin between his next words. "My father wouldn't want me. I'm damaged goods now. Hardly saleable to a wealthy old woman in search of a husband, not after over two years of being fucked in every conceivable manner by miscreants and rogues." They smiled against each other's lips, and Sylvain's eyelashes fluttered, brushing

Octavian's skin. "What poor woman could stand a prayer of pleasing me in bed after I've been in yours?"

"Aw. Don't you say the sweetest things? Well, my treasure, shameless flattery will get you everywhere." Sylvain twined his fingers in Octavian's hair and inclined his head so he could nibble up and down the length of Octavian's neck, the pressure of his lips and teeth increasing until he sucked Octavian's skin into his mouth with a tingle.

Octavian pressed halfheartedly against his shoulder. "Don't—"

Sylvain sighed, his breath cool against Octavian's wet and heated skin. "Mark you. I know. You are not mine." He lifted his mouth from Octavian's neck, some of his ardor doused, though he held Octavian even tighter.

"It isn't like you'd want me to be," Octavian said. After a few years, he knew Sylvain, knew he took his pleasures with Myrddin, Breeze, and any of the new recruits he could coax into his bed. When what was on offer at Rosecairn grew stale, he rode off in search of something fresh, often disappearing for days at a time.

"Of course not. We're friends. I enjoy spending time with you. What else does either of us need?"

All the things you don't say, Octavian thought. "So you wouldn't work in a shop for me and sleep beside me every night? You only ever met one man worthy of that?"

"Octavian." Sylvain started to pull away, and he looked down, unwilling or unable to meet Octavian's eyes.

"Sorry. I'm sorry, Sylvain." He wasn't really sorry, though. He'd caught a glimpse of a side of Sylvain he'd never known existed, a hidden depth beyond his frivolity he wanted to explore, an intriguing secret place he wanted to know, because he was sure he'd be the first to set foot in that buried place—or at most, the second. "I did not mean to pry. I didn't know your feelings about it were still so tender."

"My feelings are not tender." Sylvain bit off his words, the rawness of his tone answering everything Octavian wondered.

He hurried to change the subject before his digging ruined the evening beyond salvage. No one wanted old wounds torn open, unless there was a chance to heal them, and Octavian knew he couldn't heal Sylvain of this. They were friends, and they had a good time together, but he would never take the place of that brothel boy. He saddened at Sylvain's loss and resisted the urge to tell him to ride to Elvara and try again. Things ended. They died and went to ground, just like the life he'd left behind. But traces of them always remained, because one's experiences could never truly be forgotten. Every man's past became part of him, sometimes in ways even he couldn't see. "I can't say I'm completely without regrets. My actions in splitting from my family were hasty. I saw an opportunity, and I took it. I didn't take the consequences into consideration."

Sylvain chuckled and moved close again, curling around Octavian and resting his cheek on Octavian's chest. Goddesses, the man could move as if his bones were made of pliant cord. "That's something you've done more than once. Like when you walked into the Bitter Tide camp. It was one of the first things that drew me to you. I knew if I stayed close to you, I would be well entertained, and not just because of your beauty, but because you make things happen. You aren't ever content. You stir things up. You're like a firestorm, and who can hope to control that?"

"My father did. He made sure I knew from the time I was able to understand that I'd never be more than a game piece, a soldier in his empire. I thought I could do better. As arrogant as it sounds, I suppose I always wanted my own empire."

"And you took it." Sylvain kissed across Octavian's Adam's apple and over to his ear, where he nipped at the lobe and ran his tongue along the shell. "You take what you want. I like that."

"Yes." Though Octavian enjoyed Sylvain's mouth—always did—something gnawed at the edges of his thoughts, wormed into his mind until its presence distracted him. *Empire*, it whispered to him, trying to communicate its meaning through the twisting of its wormy form within his skull. "Rosecairn isn't an empire," he whispered. "It is the beginning of one, but… I know what I should do!"

He sat bolt upright, startling Sylvain and making him sit as well. Octavian grabbed for his journal and quill and flipped to the first clean page he found. "The Rosecairn is not enough." Furiously he sketched a map of the area beyond their sheltered valley from memory, trying to recall the roads and trails winding across it. "I should construct a series of outposts—" Scrawling notes, he indicated some likely places with a series of *X*s. "The other mercenary bands in the area are small. We can drive out the undesirables and keep those worth absorbing. We can control at least another twenty or thirty miles of land with very little risk or effort. Goddesses, why has this eluded me until now? It's so obvious. It will have the added advantage of putting more farms, homesteads, and villages under our protection. And it will be a good place to send the new recruits to train." He was excited; his heart beat faster and faster as he scribbled his plans across the page and flipped to the next, annoyed at the interruption of dipping his quill in the ink. "After all, anyone I accept should be able to handle bandits and wolves. It will provide valuable experience to them before they join us on the more important campaigns."

"You know, a more sensitive lover might take offense to being ignored in favor of a tattered old book," Sylvain said gently.

"Oh." Octavian closed his journal and set it and his quill on the stand before taking Sylvain's face in his hands and meeting his gaze. His eyes were faceted and gemlike, seeming lit from within. "I did not mean it that way. No breathing man could ignore you. I just… this has been troubling me, what to do next, and the answer came to me so suddenly. I just wanted to record it before it wriggled out of my hands and I couldn't catch it again. What do you think of my plan?"

Instead of pouting at being spurned, Sylvain considered. "If the fortresses are placed strategically, it could be a great advantage to you. You'd rid your lawn of enemies, as you observed, and you'd see trouble coming long before it reached your front doors. Location will be everything. If you're lucky, you might find some intact buildings you can repair instead of building from the ground up. Many things were left abandoned while Lavock reigned. It will be interesting to see what you can discover. The countryside around the cairn is still very desolate. It would also be an advantage to devise a way for these outposts to communicate with each other."

Octavian's thoughts raced, chasing each other, tangling together, and coupling to produce exponentially more ideas until he felt like they'd split his skull. His fingers twitched, and the next thing he knew, Sylvain had opened his journal and draped it over his thighs and pressed his quill against his palm. He began writing, reading over his words, scratching them out, and adding notes in the margins until letters stretched horizontally, vertically, and diagonally over the parchment. The overabundance of creativity both excited and irritated him. It was almost too much to process, so he wrote down everything that came to his mind and every offspring of those ideas. If he told himself he was just observing, just recording for later contemplation, he wouldn't drown beneath the onslaught. By the time he finished, he realized he had a cramp in his hand and a slight headache. He read over what, to anyone trying to decipher it, would look like gibberish, and the idea came to him. "I'll use magic. I'll put something in place so the men stationed at different outposts can send each other at least rudimentary messages with magic. I don't know quite how. Maybe I can use looking glasses, or water, or put a spell in place they can trigger with an ingredient... It will have to be something everyone can use, not just those with the gift...."

"Haven't you done enough for one night, my flower?" Sylvain's breath, warm against Octavian's ear, hauled him out of the maelstrom of his thoughts. The scraps of ideas he'd been jumping up and down so frantically to try to grasp dissipated and drifted away, and Octavian let them go. He was ashamed to admit he'd almost forgotten the other man was in the room, in bed with him, naked. It was no wonder Sylvain entertained no thoughts about settling down with him, or even with their little group of friends and lovers. Sylvain gently closed the book and pinched Octavian's chin, turning his head until their gazes locked. "You must let your mind be quiet sometimes, let your thoughts rest. You're going to burn yourself up. You're young, and you have time. Tomorrow is another day. Tonight, let your head shut down. Listen to your body."

Octavian curled back against the wall, let the nervous energy flow out of him, and opened his limbs so Sylvain could roll on top of him and twist into his arms and legs. His weight and the warmth and texture of his skin felt perfect against Octavian's chest and belly. As they kissed slowly and deeply, Octavian focused on the sensations and let Sylvain's lips, tongue, and the erection hardening against his own fill his thoughts. Tomorrow would wait, and yet.... "Will you ride out with me tomorrow morning? Go exploring? Look for places to build my way stations?"

"Of course I will." Sylvain curved his hips against Octavian, and Octavian bent his to meet him. "Now will you let all this go, just for an hour, and let me make love to you?"

"I'm sorry," Octavian said. "It isn't that I don't want this. I love this. But my head was just so full, my thoughts on fire...."

Sylvain rubbed his lips against Octavian's cheek and moved them against his skin as he spoke. "No need to apologize. I know you."

"You do, don't you?"

He made a soft, rough sound of assent against Octavian's throat, just below his ear, and the noise vibrated through Octavian's throat. Both the sound and the feeling, along with the idea of being known so thoroughly by someone—the scarred and ugly parts along with the beautiful—made Octavian's ass and cock twitch and crave attention. "And do you have more to teach me about the arts of pleasure, or has the student become the master?"

Sylvain licked down Octavian's neck and then across his collarbone, leaving a cool trail on his flushed skin. "The student is very adept, but there's more I could show you. It just depends how, uh… exotic of a territory you're willing to venture into to."

"Tell me," Octavian said as he reached between them to wrap his fist around both their cocks. Almost instinctively, they established a leisurely rhythm that would keep them excited but not push them too quickly toward the edge. "Tell me what you learned in the decadence of the Elvaran brothels. What can you do with me that you haven't already done?"

"So much. I could tie your hands behind your back—"

"Good luck. Not only have I lived among thieves, pickpockets, burglars, and mercenaries for almost three years, I'm also a mage. You think it would hold me?"

Sylvain laughed between Octavian's clavicles and lapped at the divot between the bones. "No, but that's beside the point. *If* I did, I could bring you to the point of release, just to the very edge of ecstasy, before pulling away and leaving you in agony. I could do it four times. Six maybe. You'd be begging me to let you spill. I could get you to agree to anything, because you'd become so desperate nothing else would matter to you. And when I finally allowed it, you'd come harder than you ever have in your life. You'd cry with relief."

Octavian bit Sylvain's lip, just enough to pinch but not break the skin. "You know me. So you should know being told what I'm allowed to do and what I'm not doesn't sit well with me. I've never let anyone or anything tell me what I can or can't do. And beg?"

"I expected that," Sylvain said. "And I wouldn't wish you different. If I might offer an alternative, why don't we roll onto our sides? You can play with my cock and I can play with yours. Equal, mutual pleasure. That's what you like, isn't it?"

"I thought you did too."

"I do," Sylvain said as he disengaged from Octavian's limbs and twined to invert himself next to Octavian. He cradled Octavian's balls and pecked lightly up his shaft. "I like your mouth on me. The way you love my cock. I like making you come, tasting you. I like everything about you. I'll show you how much."

He did, and Octavian gave as good as he got. Afterward, he lay with his back against Sylvain's back, snug beneath his furs, the fire low and bluish in the hearth. Before he knew it or consciously intended it, he closed his eyes and slept in blissful oblivion.

EARLY THE next morning, while the mist still hugged the ground like a lover reluctant to let go and the wet loam and new green life scented the air, Octavian met Myrddin near the center of the camp. Clearly excited, he spoke so quickly Myrddin could barely follow his plan. He caught the bones of it, though, and followed Octavian to the stable they'd only finished constructing the previous autumn. It was an impressive structure with a stone wall, thatched roof, and open front. It held stalls for three dozen horses, with storage for tack and grain at either end. The loft space above held hay and straw. A half a dozen cats—ferals Lena had somehow managed to tame to keep vermin at bay—scattered when they entered the building. Myrddin shook his head. That lass had a way with animals that was almost an arcane ability. A large tabby tom, braver or more arrogant than the others, sat in the aisle with his back leg stretched out, his pink tongue working between his spread toes. He spared Myrddin a disdainful flash of his yellow-green eyes as they passed.

Sylvain and Breeze had already equipped their mounts when Myrddin and Octavian arrived, so they chose horses—a big bay gelding for Myrddin and a jittery chestnut mare for Octavian. He preferred fleet if unpredictable mounts, while Myrddin opted for stout and steady. When they were ready, the four of them left the cairn through the gate and cantered out onto a sea of undulating grass dotted with blue-gray rock. The warm wind felt good in Myrddin's hair, and the blue sky stretching over him felt like freedom. The sun rippled across the plain as if it were water. As he looked at the three men around him, he felt that although he did not deserve it, the goddesses had blessed him. He'd never imagined, being unnatural and a mercenary, that he'd find so much love—or at least deep friendship and physical companionship—as he had with the men riding beside him. As he contemplated how much more satisfying coupling with a partner one knew, one whose preferences he'd learned, one whose pleasure he cared about, could be than anonymous rutting in the dark, he found his attention returning again and again to Octavian.

They rode in a diamond formation with Octavian taking the lead. The easy way his body moved with his horse reminded Myrddin of the way he moved in bed: confident and sure, almost instinctively, and with the grace of a sapling in the wind. Over the past few years, he had grown a little taller and put on probably twenty-five pounds of muscle. Though still lanky, no one looking at him could deny he'd become a man. Myrddin watched his hips rock and his rich brown hair flap in the breeze, wishing he could see his face, knowing his cheeks would be a dusky rose and his eyes would be as sharp as lightning as they scanned the countryside. His nostrils would flare as he took in the pure spring air.

They rode for probably fifteen or twenty miles, going off to explore the overgrown roads and winding trails they encountered. Octavian moved to the back of the group, and as often as not, attempted to ride while writing in his book. His fumbling made Myrddin smile; he should have chosen a more even-tempered horse.

Their excursion proved wildly successful. Not only had they found promising locations for their fortresses, but they'd discovered a few ruined towers and partial walls they could adapt into sturdy buildings. Better yet, after venturing along some rocky paths into the hills, they'd found absolute treasure: a copper mine, a chalk mine, and an ironstone quarry. In the case of the third, which lay farthest to the south, some rusted pickaxes still lay on the ground. The four men dismounted to have a closer look.

Breeze ventured closest to the edge and looked down into the deep pit. "There's a trail winding down, all the way to the bottom." His accent was still heavy, but Myrddin had no trouble understanding him now. "I can see some carts on tracks, and some of them are even filled with stone. If I had to guess, I'd say the workers abandoned this quarry out of fear of Lavock. It wouldn't take much to get it up and running again, just like the mines." He ticked his list off on his fingers. "Workers, obviously. Maybe some equipment, but not much in this case. A couple of our men to keep the workers safe. Maybe a lookout tower. Merchants. Channels to turn the product into coin. Places to sell it."

Octavian nodded as he gazed into the chasm. Myrddin moved closer to him and put a hand on his shoulder. "If you want my advice, it's this. Send men to watch this quarry and the two mines as soon as you can spare them. Put out word that skilled workers will be offered a fair wage. Treat the workers well, let them share in the profit if you're so inclined, but keep firm ownership of these assets. Many men will be happy to make a good living, and the profit the Roses stand to earn might be sizeable."

"Camps, and possibly villages, will spring up around these mines," Sylvain said. "Merchants will come selling equipment, food and drink for the workers, and luxury goods they'll be interested in when they're making a steady living. Taverns will spring up. Women will come looking for men who can support them and their future children. Women and families mean stability, a place men are invested in. These abandoned places will be thriving villages in a few years if you manage them properly. Villages loyal to us."

"I'll have to find buyers for these goods," Octavian mused, crouching to rest his book across his knees and make notes.

"Copper, ironstone, and chalk?" Myrddin asked. "Everyone wants those things. It'll be more a matter of finding the best price. Forgive me, lad, but your upbringing in a merchant family will serve you here."

"We should send men to guard these sites right away," Octavian said. "I don't want someone else claiming them. I have people I can spare. In my hands, these can be places people can build lives. I won't risk them falling under the control of another warlord. We should ride for home. As strange as it may sound considering these mines have been here for years, but now that I'm aware of them, I feel I cannot waste a moment making sure they won't be exploited. I'd like to send men out tonight to watch over them, and start looking for workers first thing tomorrow. I also want to get construction of the fortresses underway."

Octavian's voice had taken on that subdued tone that told Myrddin he was talking to himself, making a mental list of what he needed to do. He mounted up without waiting to see if the others followed. Myrddin glanced at Sylvain, and they smiled at each other. Both of them knew that, at age twenty-one, Octavian didn't have to accomplish his life's work by tomorrow. But they also knew they'd never convince their passionate young leader of that, so they shook their heads and got back into their saddles.

They'd been riding toward the setting sun melting into the mountains and turning the landscape to a fuzzy pink, for about five miles when Myrddin sensed something—an undefined dread that told him they weren't alone. He held up his hand, and the others reined their slowly trotting horses to a stop around him.

"What is it?" Breeze asked, looking around and squinting into the increasing shadows.

"I just have a feeling," Myrddin said. "Warrior's intuition, I suppose. We may not be safe."

Sylvain nodded and took his bow and an arrow from his back. The validation of his unquestioning trust pleased Myrddin, as did his readiness for battle. Aside from Dirk, Sylvain was probably the best archer Myrddin had ever met, which meant he would be Myrddin's second choice to cover his back, but still a damned good risk. Sylvain might like his fun, but Myrddin knew he never shirked his duty or failed those depending on him. He'd come to trust the archer over the years, and it seemed that trust was reciprocated. Myrddin hadn't realized it until that moment, but he didn't have time to dwell on it.

"What?" Octavian struggled to keep his jittery mount under control as the mare, unhappy with standing still, danced over the ground. "What are you thinking? Wolves? Bandits? Why would it be bandits? There's nothing here to steal. There's nothing within miles of here but the occasional family farm. It's not likely bandits have come out here to toil in the mines themselves, if they even know of them. Myrddin, what should we do? Which way should we go?"

Octavian had always believed in him, and the significance of that sunk in as their gazes met in the gloaming. Octavian would act on his word alone, and he had to lead him to the right path. "Let's ride—quietly and discreetly—to the crest of that ridge." Myrddin pointed slightly east, to a knoll ringed in the first of the evening's stars. "It will give us a better idea of what's happening around us."

Silently, the other three men nodded, and in a single-file line, they walked their mounts slowly toward the knoll. The steps of the horses faded beneath the soft night wind in the grass. Myrddin, at the front of the procession, had his sword in his hands, as did Breeze, riding behind him. He knew without looking that he could count on Sylvain's arrows when he needed them. Octavian…. Myrddin had no idea what he might do, but he knew it would be the perfect thing at the perfect moment.

When they reached the top of the hill, a rolling plain studded with rounded stone formations stretched beneath them. About a half a mile away, a single-story cottage stood within a circle of light cast by the lanterns hanging near the front door. Squinting, Myrddin could make out figures, maybe half a dozen, dark swaths against the orange glow. None of them were moving, but he couldn't see exactly why.

Breeze reined his palomino gelding to stop next to Myrddin, and he shielded his eyes with his hand as if it would help him see. After a few moments, he let loose a string of what Myrddin could reasonably assume were Esperon curse words. "Bleeding Shades! Those whoresons! They have children down there at the points of their swords." Breeze shouted, dug his heels into his horse's ribs, and took off like an arrow down the hill, a smear against the darkness. Myrddin hurried to follow. He'd nearly reached the bottom before Myrddin understood what was happening.

Octavian cantered past him, calling, "Time to be good neighbors."

Following his instincts and trusting in his men, Myrddin spurred his horse harder. Halfway down the hill, the scene around the simple hovel clarified. Six bandits had attacked the family. A pair of them, their weapons drawn, had cornered a stout woman with two young children clinging to her skirts. Two others stood over the prone body of what was probably the man of the house. He held a spade in his hand and had clearly fallen while defending his family. Myrddin's blood boiled as it always did when thugs took advantage of the good, solid people who worked the land and sought only to toil in peace. He was out of the saddle and on the ground before his gelding came to a full stop, running for the last pair of bandits, the ones taking everything from preserved meats to chipped dishes from the home. He hit the first of the two in the lower back with the pommel of his sword, knocking the man facedown on the ground and sending the hams he'd had in his arms scattering. Before he could get up, Myrddin kicked him in the base of his skull with his heel, and his face hit the dirt.

The other man dropped the dishes and jugs of wine and ale he carried. They shattered on the ground, which meant little to him but would devastate the family. His hands free, the bandit tried to reach for his blade, but Myrddin beat him to it. Before the ruffian could draw his sword, Myrddin drove the tip of his blade into his shoulder and crippled his arm. When he reached for something behind him with his left hand, Myrddin drove his fist into his chest, and his shabby furs and worn leathers did little to dampen the blow. Gasping for wind, the bandit doubled over and dropped the dagger he'd tried to pull. Myrddin took advantage of his lowered head and drove his knee into his nose. Blood streamed from the man's face, and he lifted his hands to catch it as he crumpled on his side. Not willing to take a chance, Myrddin kicked him in his belly and wrenched his arms behind his back. Despite the thug's screams and protests about his injured shoulder, Myrddin tied his hands firmly. "Remember this the next time you want to take advantage of unarmed women and children, you cowardly slug." Myrddin gave him a hard kick to the hips before turning to see if any of his men needed his aid.

Not surprisingly, the others had subdued the rest of the thugs. Octavian stood with his foot on one's man's chest and his sword—thank the goddesses Myrddin had finally convinced him to stow that damned dagger in a crate beneath their bed—held to his throat. Breeze, on his knees with his blade on the ground beside him, comforted the children while their mother pressed her hands to her mouth and cried. The two bandits who had threatened them lay unmoving behind Breeze. Sylvain hadn't left his saddle, but his arrow protruded from the back of one of the men who'd been beating the farmer. Of all of them, Sylvain had shown the least mercy. The man he'd shot down wouldn't be getting back up, if the rivulets of blood streaming down his sides and pooling around him offered any indication. Six more men, now disarmed, stood huddled together, cowering like the pathetic worms they were.

Myrddin stowed his sword and went to offer his hand to the farmer. Judging by the bruises on his face and the way he clutched his probably broken ribs as he stood, the man had taken quite a beating. It didn't stop him from racing to his wife and children's sides, making sure they were all right. Breeze backed away to allow them privacy as they cried and embraced. He dropped his head and said, "Forgive me. I should have waited for orders, but when I saw those pig-fuckers scaring children and bullying their mother.... Something in me snapped."

Octavian clapped him on the shoulder. "Don't apologize, Breeze. I'd much rather have a man beside me who acts when women and children are in danger than one who hesitates. You showed what kind of heart you have tonight, and I'm proud of you."

"Aye," Myrddin said, meeting Breeze's dark, exotic eyes. "There was nothing else you could have done. You did right. Look at that family embracing. They can do that because you didn't stop to think. There are times when a man just knows what must be done."

"I'll never fault you for defending an innocent," Octavian said. "I'll only fault you if you don't. You did good work here tonight. Go on. I think those people would like to thank you."

"Do you want me to shoot the rest of them?" Sylvain called from his horse. By his tone, he might have been asking if the others wanted another round of drinks.

Myrddin and Octavian exchanged a smile before Octavian turned and said, "Thank you, but I think these weaklings will run away of their own accord. Right, piglets?" He waited for the men who were able to stumble to their feet. "Run, little chicks. Although if they slow down, feel free to put an arrow in their sorry asses. In fact, if a few moments pass and you can still see their worthless carcasses, by all means encourage them to move faster."

Sylvain drew his arm back. "If they stagger or stop to catch their breath, they're mine, then. Go on, then. Run!"

"All yours," Octavian called as the thugs tripped over their feet to gain some distance.

He and Myrddin turned to the family. "I have a plan in place to put this area under the protection of the Thorns of Rosecairn. I can only hope nothing like this will befall your family again. Please accept my apology that we didn't get here sooner. I hope, when we have built our watchtowers along the roads, that will no longer be a worry."

The father, a young man with receding blond hair and a neatly trimmed beard, clasped Octavian's arm. "Thank you for defending my family. Call on me if you need aid in building your fortresses. Lots of men in these parts would be happy to trade their labor for the safety of their wives and children. It's been hard living here for a long time, but you and your honorable friends give us hope. I'll help you if I can."

"I appreciate that, tam," Octavian said. "And if you have skill at building, I would welcome your help, and pay you for it as well."

"I won't take a scrap of copper," the man said. "I'd be honored to work for you. Please, tell me your name."

"It's Octavian Rose, but the man you should be thanking is Fabrezio Orvina d'Caelus."

"Breeze," Breeze said. "And I don't need thanks. Just to know you and your lady and little ones are all right."

"Thanks to you," the man said. "Thanks to you, Tam Breeze. I wish I had something of value to offer you."

"I would refuse it even if you did," Breeze told him with the wide smile that set almost anyone who saw it at ease. Breeze had become an excellent swordsman and had eagerly taken up the crude language of the others, swearing and teasing as if he'd been born to it, but there was very little guile in him, and it took little to make him happy.

By the time Octavian finished healing the farmer, he was groggy and confused. From his ramblings, Myrddin suspected the man's internal injuries had been severe beyond the broken ribs and a bruised belly. Octavian slumped against Myrddin as Myrddin put him into the saddle in front of him. Breeze tethered Octavian's mare to his mount, and she reluctantly accepted being led home. As they rode, Octavian dozed against Myrddin, snoring softly through parted lips. Myrddin held tight to him, proud of him and what they were establishing together—a place ordinary people and families could feel safe—as they made a slow journey back to the cairn.

After they passed through the gates, Octavian startled awake. "I must send guards to the mines and quarry. I should establish a patrol for the countryside. I don't want anyone else falling victim to the kind of thugs we encountered earlier."

Myrddin nuzzled his face into Octavian's thick hair. "Those fools won't dare come back tonight, my lad. Leave it till morning. You need to rest. You've worn yourself too thin today, and if you don't mend, you'll tear. Look, here's the stable. It's just a short walk to our house and our bed. I want to hold you, and I want you to sleep until you can sleep no more. A few days, or even a moon, won't stem your ambitions in regards to the watchtowers and the mines. You deserve a respite."

"But there are farms and families left vulnerable...."

"You have time." Myrddin helped him out of the saddle and practically dragged him to the steps of their house. "All the time in the world. You've already done so much. Sleep in my arms tonight before you wear yourself to nothing with these goals tomorrow. Just give yourself tonight, lad."

Octavian nodded as Myrddin steered him through their door and across the tidy floor to their bed. "One night. Then I'll put it all to rights, and nothing will stop me."

Chapter
Seventeen

A YEAR and a half later, by midsummer, nine of the twelve outposts Octavian had planned had been constructed and staffed with men. The Roses controlled the countryside for forty miles in every direction. As Sylvain had predicted, thriving villages had sprung up like mushrooms around the lucrative mines and the quarry. Houses and shops had been built almost overnight, and families and children had appeared as if by magic to occupy them. A popular inn and tavern had been established about a mile and a half north of the ironstone quarry, and that was where Dirk wanted them all to go when evening came.

Myrddin didn't mind. The spring was warmer than average, and the early blooming flowers scented the air. They'd just completed a profitable job fighting for one noble house of Gaeltheon against another, and they'd not only prevailed, but earned themselves a sizeable bonus. They could afford to spend the evening in the tavern, and a night of merriment would do them all a world of good— particularly Octavian. A son of privilege such as him should have spent his youth drinking and dancing. Octavian had chosen another way, but he should be allowed one night free of worry.

Just before sunset, Myrddin, Octavian, Sylvain, Breeze, Dirk, and Quinn mounted up. Myrddin noticed Dirk had washed and tried to tame his wild red hair into a leather band. He'd shaved, put on a mint-colored tunic and white shirt Myrddin had never seen before, and shined his knee-high leather boots. He smelled as if he'd borrowed some scented lotion from Sylvain. Myrddin said nothing, but he wondered what his oldest friend had in mind. From the time they'd met, their plans had always included each other.

Sylvain dressed in his usual leathers—the man would be devastating in a burlap sack—and Breeze wore a white shirt and tan vest that accentuated his dark skin. Octavian…. Octavian looked like a vision from the goddesses even though he wore only a simple white shirt and his leather leggings. The way those trousers clung to his thighs was like a spell, and the humidity in the air made his hair curl and his creamy, freckled skin glisten. His eyes and lips looked dark and alluring against his pale skin, and Myrddin knew he'd have his fair share of wenches to beat off when they reached the inn. The way Octavian turned to him now and then with a secret smile made Myrddin feel like the luckiest man in the world. The fairest lass under heaven wouldn't keep Octavian from his bed tonight.

The tavern, The Shepherdess's Bauble, according to the shingle above the door, looked nothing like the mercenary dens Myrddin was accustomed to. Dozens of lanterns on the building's exterior and lining the gravel path to its porch bathed it in dancing firelight. On either side of the path, vegetables and flowers grew in abundance. The scent of herbs perfumed the night and combined with the savory smells of hearty food cooking inside. On the porch, a man strummed a lute while men, women, and even children sat enjoying the music. When the Roses dismounted, hands came to take their horses to the stable.

Inside, the Bauble was candlelit and tidy. Spring blooms sat on every table. Myrddin and his companions found seats near the fireplace, and they'd no sooner sat down before a serving girl appeared with three bottles of wine and several chalices. When Breeze reached for his coin purse, the curvaceous lass winked and slapped his hand. "Roses always get the first round free at the Bauble, tam. We ain't been robbed since we opened our doors, and we owe it to you. Go on, then. Drink up. I'll be back in a bit to see if you want anything to eat." She leveled her gaze on Breeze. "If you want or need anything in the meantime, I'm your girl. You call on me, aye?"

Sylvain opened the first bottle and poured them all libation. They lifted their cups and clinked them together. "To the Roses," Sylvain said. "A company I am proud to be a part of." Quinn elbowed Breeze in the ribs, and he sputtered before turning his head toward the young woman watching him expectantly and batting her lashes hard enough to work up a gale. Blushing the color of red clay, Breeze set his goblet down and clasped her hand. "Thanks very much for your attentive service, my lady."

She looked disappointed when he let go of her hand, but with a small curtsey, she left the table to attend to the other patrons. Quinn turned to Breeze. "Are you out of your mind, lad? She fancies you!"

Breeze laughed and took a long sip of his wine. "She isn't my type." Myrddin wasn't sure if Quinn caught the longing gaze Breeze directed at Sylvain, but Sylvain did, and the archer raised his goblet and made a show of mopping the wine from his upper lip with his tongue.

"What in the goddesses' names is wrong with her?" Quinn knew what went on among the four of them; Myrddin knew it for certain. Whether he was teasing, hoping to do the young man a favor by enlightening him to the pleasures of women, or simply unable to believe a young man could look at a plump, red-blooded lass like the serving girl without anything stirring, Myrddin wasn't sure.

Breeze held his hands out in front of his chest and cupped nonexistent orbs of flesh. "It's all those breasts," he said, just over a whisper.

"Only saw two," Quinn persisted. "And a fine pair, if I'm any judge."

"A better judge than I am any day, my friend," Breeze agreed.

Don't knock it until you try it, Dirk said.

Breeze met his gaze and smirked. "I could say the same to you. Aren't you curious?"

No, Dirk signed. *Emphatically fucking no. The only cock I'm interested in is my own, so don't go getting any ideas, you cheeky Esperon ass.*

Breeze leaned across the table. "Oh, but I already have ideas. I've seen you working with your shirt off, your bony body and snow-white skin blinding in the sun. Goddesses, I never knew a man could have so many freckles. I have to ask myself how far down you they extend. And if that wasn't enough, your sweet romantic manner and compassion for your fellow man won my heart."

You ever come near me with my shirt off and you'll get an arrow through your little brown pecker, you dust-colored son of a whore. Dirk leaned back and crossed his arms as if the matter had been concluded. The rest of them roared with laughter.

Octavian squeezed Myrddin's knee beneath the table. "And here is what happens when a man learns our language from such a disreputable mob as all of you. Poor, innocent Breeze. Alas, I worry I have steered you wrong."

One poet is enough, Dirk said. *And unless you plan to bore our enemies to death with your unique talent, you should stem the flowers falling from your tongue, rosebud.*

Octavian winked. "You adore me. You hide it well enough, though I can see the soft heart shining behind the crusty layers of rancor you wear like armor."

What you see is my dinner about to come up, Dirk responded.

"Dinner is a fine idea," Myrddin said, already feeling his face warm and his head going fuzzy. He knew the wine had gone to his head when he almost brushed Octavian's hair aside to peck along the length of his graceful neck. "This tavern's wine is strong. We should get something into our stomachs or we'll all be falling out of our saddles on the ride back to the cairn."

They ordered bread, cheese, pickled beets, boiled eggs, sausage, and a ham, placing the heaping platters at the center of the table so they could share. Their dutiful server replaced each bottle of wine with a fresh one as soon as they emptied it. As the night stretched on, the tavern filled to capacity, with customers who couldn't find seats leaning against the walls. Younger men stood with their arms across the shoulders of their sweethearts, older men holding hands with their wives. The swell of the crowd surprised Myrddin. The tavern was tidy and served good food, but he had to wonder if that alone could draw so many.

A few moments later, the lamps hanging from the rafters dimmed as the tavern workers closed the shutters a little further. Conversation tapered off, and Myrddin wondered if the inn was closing for the night. It seemed rather early. Then chair legs and benches screeched across the floor as everyone adjusted to face the far wall. Onlookers formed a crescent around a man with a hand drum who took a stool to the left and another with a flute who stood to the right. They began playing music unlike anything Myrddin had ever heard: slow but rhythmic, sensual, almost sexual in its tempo. The crowd applauded and cheered as a woman moved to the center of the stage, but they fell as silent as the grave when she began to sing in a lilting, strong, and suggestive voice that not only complemented, but completed the melody of the musicians.

She sang like Myrddin imagined the goddesses might sing. Her voice carried through the tavern until he became so caught up in her song everything else faded from his mind. Even he could acknowledge she was beautiful, with skin as dark as Breeze's, lustrous waves of black hair, and full, wine-colored lips that formed her words as if making love to them. Beads glittered on her full, sky blue skirts, and her billowy shirt and purple bodice accentuated her shape without making her spill out of it like the serving girls did. As she sang with her eyes closed, swaying her full hips and carving circles and figure eights in the smoky air with the motion of her fingers, Myrddin looked around the table at his companions. All of them sat staring, mouths open, as if under a spell. Dirk smiled wistfully and brushed a tear from his cheek.

Myrddin tapped his arm to get his attention and signed, *So this is why you wanted to come tonight, and why the inn is so full. She's a remarkable performer. Who is she?*

With wide eyes and a guileless smile, Dirk stared at the singer. *Her name is Kyrie. I'm going to marry her.*

Oh, indeed? Maybe if you could hear her voice I'd believe you.

Dirk shook his head slowly and pressed his palm to his belly. *I can't hear it, but I feel it. Here. Inside. Here.* He touched the center of his chest.

Myrddin swallowed the taunt he would have normally offered. Dirk sat there staring at the woman, his ribs split open and his heart ripe to be torn out and crushed. He never imagined he'd see his friend so vulnerable, so willing to risk agony on such a slim chance. Had his eyes sparkled like that when he'd first met Octavian? Did they still? For the first time, Myrddin understood Dirk's worry over him being hurt. He loved Dirk, thought him a fine man, but this woman…. Dirk would have a better chance bedding the Queen of Selindria. Suddenly Myrddin hated her, thought her cruel for being so beautiful, and assumed she'd be petty and mean even though he knew he had no right. He didn't know what to say. Had Dirk worried because he'd felt Myrddin wasn't good enough for Octavian, would never stand a chance? And how could he tell his friend he didn't measure up and would be better off finding himself a farmer's daughter?

Women like that are the makings of stories, he signed cautiously, and Dirk nodded. *And in those stories, they destroy kings and level empires. Women like that are dangerous. Trouble. Pain in the making.*

What do you know? Dirk signed without looking away as the trio began their next song. This one had a quicker beat, an infectious happiness, and many couples moved to the center of the room to dance.

Octavian tapped his feet and drummed his fingers on the tabletop. "Did you enjoy dancing?" Sylvain shouted to ask him.

"I did," he said, "even though I didn't necessarily enjoy my partners. Some of the more romantic dances, I could see how they could kindle emotion, but for me, it was always just going through the steps. I often wondered what it would be like to dance with someone I… I've heard it described as losing oneself in one's partner, noticing nothing but their eyes, their movements, the feeling of their body moving against yours, until the rest of the world faded away. I'd like to experience that."

"I'd dance with you, Octavian," Breeze said, "if we wouldn't get thrown out and have our asses kicked in by every farmer and miner in this tavern. It was the only thing my parents acknowledged I did well. But like you, I wanted to do it with someone… else. I never felt a connection, just went through the motions."

Sylvain shook his head, looking serious. "And would the goddesses tumble from the sky if two young men in love danced together? What's the sense in denying their happiness?" He downed his wine too quickly and muffled his belch in his hand.

"Are we in love, Breeze?" Octavian asked with a wink and smile—a smile meant to mask the pain clear in his eyes.

Breeze responded in kind, forcing a laugh. "Ask me when I sober up."

This world is a sorry pile of horseshit sometimes, Dirk said.

"Aye," Quinn agreed. "Don't tell the others, but I'd love to see you two young men get to dance. You should be allowed. I-I'm sorry about teasing you earlier."

Octavian poured Quinn more wine and patted his shoulder. "You didn't offend me. Jesting among friends is different. Now, let's shake off this melancholy. We're here to have a good time, and more importantly, to aid our fine comrade in meeting and wooing his future wife. Now, Roses, I'll hear proposed strategies." His fingers moved against the grain of the table, and Myrddin knew he wished he had his book so he could list all their ideas and compare their merits.

"A good bottle of wine," Breeze said with a decisive nod. "Something… ladylike. Sweet and smooth and flowery. And expensive."

"Not a bad idea," Quinn said, "but be careful. Proper ladies like her are suspicious of men who encourage them to drink too much."

"Besides," Sylvain said, "Dirk will hardly be the only man offering her a drink after her performance."

"What we need to do is devise a way to eliminate the competition," Octavian mused, staring down at the linen napkin over his thigh. "A distraction, perhaps. A way to take the other men who want to speak to her and buy her drinks out of the way. I-I have it, that is, if Breeze doesn't mind a few bumps and bruises?"

"A small price to pay for true love," Breeze said, lifting his glass.

"What are you up to?" Myrddin asked. "You two aren't planning to dance together?"

"No," Octavian said, smiling sadly as he stared into his goblet. "I considered it, but I don't want to tarnish the reputation of the Thorns of Rosecairn. Now, on to our next move. Dirk will need someone to translate his words to Kyrie, and I nominate Sylvain. You have experience flattering women, do you not?"

"All part of my esteemed position at one time."

"Good. This is a solid plan, and it can work. Breeze and I will create a distraction, draw the attention of the other men in the tavern away from Kyrie, and Dirk will buy a good bottle of wine. This far north, they might even have Lockhaven ice wine available, and that's the finest drink under the goddesses' light. You should have it ready before her act finishes. As she takes her final bow, Breeze and I will take position here." He pointed on the napkin. "Myrddin and Quinn should position themselves here, to intercept any stragglers. Sylvain and Dirk, you know what to do."

They waited, having more drinks than were probably wise, while Kylie and her ensemble finished their performance. Myrddin felt a little unsteady as he moved to take his place on the left side of the makeshift stage. Quinn took his position on the right side, and they exchanged a single nod. Dirk and Sylvain moved to the bar, and Sylvain spoke to the serving girl. Dirk's mouth fell open as she dusted off a bottle on her apron. He started to argue over the price, but Sylvain nudged him with his shoulder and shook his head. Dirk handed over his gold as if he were relinquishing his firstborn. Together, they pushed their way through the throng gathering around the performers.

The sound of shattering glass near the center of the room drew everyone's attention. The crowd backed away, even as those who'd gathered around the performers moved toward the excitement. Octavian had stumbled against a table and spilled the drinks of the men around it—probably the only three men in the tavern who looked more like sell-swords than farmers. Myrddin smiled. He was just so good. He wouldn't exploit the common, innocent people as a means to an end, not even for Dirk. Of course, he risked a much worse beating at the hands of trained warriors than shepherds and miners.

Octavian staggered back from the table, hands in the air and tripping over his feet. Myrddin didn't know how much he affected; he'd had a lot to drink. "Beg your pardon."

"You clumsy little fuck," one of the men said, getting to his feet. "You owe us another round of drinks."

"Hold on." The girl who served them pushed her way between Octavian and the big thug, planted her hands on her hips, and looked up to meet his eyes. "Do you know who you're talking to? That's Octavian Rose. He's free to get drunk at the Bauble anytime he chooses, and if you don't like it, there's the door."

"Out of my way, silly bitch." The big man hit her in the face with the back of his hand, and Breeze moved as fast as his name suggested. Soon he and the man traded blows, while Octavian faced the other two. If he was drunk, he didn't fight like it.

The barmaid rose from the floor with a bloody nose and a broken bottle in her hand. With a cry worthy of the battlefield, she slashed at the man who'd hit her, opened a deep gash across his cheek, spat blood on the floor, and said, "Who's the silly bitch now? You picked the wrong bar wench to fuck with, you bastard." She leaped onto the back of one of the men fighting Octavian. Before long, the local men—and most of the women—had joined the fray in support of their local barkeep and friend. Myrddin had no worries about which side would prevail.

A pretty blond lad with a handful of wildflowers, dirt still clinging to their roots, grinned shyly as he approached Kyrie. Myrddin did his part and stumbled into him. He offered the lad his hand, and by then Dirk and Sylvain had made their way to the songstress. Dirk bowed shyly, and his gaze met hers. She smiled and nodded at something Sylvain said. Dirk signed, and Sylvain leaned in to translate. Kyrie looked a little confused, and Dirk turned to swat Sylvain in the shoulder. He took a few steps back as Dirk lifted the bottle of wine and jutted his chin toward an out-of-the-way table. He gestured again, and when Sylvain started to relay his words, Dirk rolled his eyes and shook his head. He threw his arms up and pointed, and Sylvain said a few clipped words before retreating with his head hanging.

Alone with Kyrie, Dirk somehow managed to convey his intentions, and the two of them moved to a table and sat down. When Sylvain moved to join them, Myrddin caught his elbow. He gestured toward the table, where the two of them managed to converse, leaning in and watching each other's faces. "I don't think he needs us. Let him go."

They made their way back to their original table and sat down. Breeze, with a black eye, and Octavian, with a split lip and bruised cheek, soon collapsed beside them. Quinn complained he'd missed all the fun when he joined them, and their dedicated server brought another bottle of wine as if oblivious to the dried blood beneath her nose. "On the house," she said with a wink at Breeze. "We've been keen to get rid of those bastards since they first came in here. That ain't the kind of place we're aiming to run. Though I hope they try coming back in. I'd like another go at that whoreson who smacked me."

Quinn slung an arm over Breeze's shoulder. "Bleeding Shades, boy, that's a woman. If you ain't having second thoughts, you're well and truly hopeless. Goddesses, I think I'm in love."

"She's all yours, my friend," Breeze said.

They sat drinking a while longer as the tavern emptied out. Farmers and miners rose early, after all. Myrddin spared a glance at Dirk and Kyrie. She'd draped her hand over his and spoke animatedly as he nodded. Even when a comely young farmer approached their table, she simply shook his hand, offered a few words, sent him on his way, and returned her attention to Dirk.

"We should be off," Myrddin said.

Sylvain and Breeze, sitting close on the bench, their hands on each other's legs, dangerously close to kissing, nodded with enthusiasm. Octavian rubbed Myrddin's lower back and pursed his lips as he nodded. Together, they left the tavern and collected their horses.

By the time they had their mounts brushed down, fed, watered, and set free into the paddock beyond the stable, Myrddin had sobered up. But then Sylvain went to fetch some fierrine, a wine from the Selindrian side of the bridge, and the four of them shared it as they sat just inside the gate, watching for Dirk's return. As the hours passed, Myrddin became more optimistic.

"A good sign he's not back yet, isn't it?" Breeze asked.

Sylvain clinked his bottle against Breeze's. By now, all of them were drunk and leaning against one another. "If we see the sunrise and he's not back, that means she let him spend the night."

"And if he spends the night," Myrddin said, struggling not to slur his words, "she'll see how much her pleasure means to him. Dirk has always prided himself on his oral skills."

Breeze groaned and collapsed into Octavian's lap, giggling against Octavian's crotch. "That is so going to give me nightmares."

Sylvain reached across Octavian to rub Breeze's ass. "I'll keep those horrible images at bay, my Esperon jewel."

"Yes, all right."

"Go back to Sylvain's house, you two," Myrddin chided. In truth, he didn't mind watching them thrusting their tongues into each other's mouths and pawing at each other through their clothing. Octavian touched the backs of their heads as they slurped and nipped at each other's lips in front of his chest, but his eyes never left Myrddin's gaze.

"I want to wait," Breeze panted. "I want to see if he really did it. I hope he did. Dirk deserves to be happy."

"One night of passion doesn't equate to her agreeing to marriage, Esperon," Sylvain said. "There are a few rare women who like conquest the same as men."

"No, she didn't seem that way to me," Octavian said. "She's an artist, passionate, but that's not the same as a strumpet. She's a woman like… even if she wants only a night of companionship, she'd be particular. And why can't women enjoy coupling the same as us?"

"You're so drunk." Myrddin smoothed Octavian's hair and kissed the part. "We should go home."

"No. I want to see if Dirk accomplishes his mission. Dawn's only an hour away now. If he's not back… if he's not back, then he got somewhere, didn't he?"

So they sat together until the tines of the sun's crown pierced the darkness and dawn brushed pink across the base of the clouds. The light seemed bright as a sword's edge to Myrddin as he roused Octavian, who slept against his shoulder. "My dear love, Dirk is spending the morning with his songstress. You can count tonight as a victory. Come to bed with me. Sylvain and Breeze have already gone to sleep. Come on, my sweet lad."

Octavian nodded without opening his eyes as he clutched Myrddin's waist and let himself be dragged to their home, in the door, and onto the bed. They collapsed atop the blankets and furs, Myrddin above Octavian, wrapped in his arms and legs, too intoxicated to do anything but chuckle against the skin of his neck. Octavian went limp beneath him, relaxed as only an innocent spirit could be, and they slept wound up together, tangled, but secure.

Chapter Eighteen

Autumn berries, garlands of yellow, orange, and burgundy leaves, and some late blooming flowers encircled the center of the camp at Rosecairn. Fires burned in stone-lined pits, tables buckled beneath the food heaped atop them, and casks of ale and barrels of wine sat at intervals so the revelers would never be more than a few steps from their next drink.

The drummer and flutist from the Bauble, along with a girl with a lute, played slow, romantic music as Dirk danced with his bride. He wore a pair of brown trousers, a green shirt, and a rust-colored vest, as all marrying couples should wear red to honor Sarmine, the goddess of love. Kyrie wore a matching green gown embroidered with scarlet flowers, her thick, shiny hair held in a tapered bun behind a golden cage studded with emeralds and topazes. Matching earrings brushed against her neck. The belt of golden medallions Octavian had given her as a wedding gift draped over her hips, obscured in the front by her burgeoning belly. Though she wore more jewels than a princess, anyone could see she was at least five moons pregnant. Not that the mercenaries cared, or Octavian; Dirk and Kyrie looked happy as they gazed into each other's faces, ignoring the rest of the world. That was what mattered—the happiness they'd found in each other.

Octavian stumbled to a bench, and though he already felt warm and floaty, he poured himself another glass of wine. Goddesses, this wedding symbolized everything he'd hoped to achieve. Rosecairn had grown from a place of despair into a place of hope, of children and families, of a future. It pleased him so many farmers and villagers had come to the cairn to attend the ceremony, when a few years ago they wouldn't have ventured within twenty miles of it. Husbands and wives, sons and daughters, enjoyed the music and the feast spread out before them. He smiled and raised his goblet at a quartet of little girls in simple dresses holding hands and spinning in a circle. Beyond the light of the fires, Sylvain danced with Breeze, holding him close like nothing else mattered, Sylvain's face buried in the hair between his neck and shoulder and Breeze clutching the back of his green velvet doublet as if the ground might fall away beneath his feet.

Octavian wanted to dance. He wanted to dance with Myrddin. Raking his gaze over the crowd, he located Myrddin near the edge, between the flickering light and the shadow. He looked amazing in his new shirt, snug trousers, and the bright blue doublet that matched his eyes, but his expression wasn't happy. After watching the cheerful people dance for a few moments, Myrddin set his cup on a barrel and turned to wander into the darkness.

Though he stumbled a little as he rose, Octavian followed, leaving a few dozen feet of distance between them until Myrddin reached their little house and leaned on one of the lintels of the small, square porch. For a few minutes, Octavian watched him, the defeat in his posture and the way his head seemed too heavy for his neck to keep aloft. When he could no longer bear seeing Myrddin suffer alone, he approached, stopped a dozen feet from him, and said his name.

"Octavian, lad." Myrddin opened his arms, and Octavian filled them, clinging to the muscles of Myrddin's back. He grinned against Myrddin's chest as he recalled how much he'd once hated being called lad, how he'd equated it with childish dismissal. Now, the word on Myrddin's lips made his blood sing and his cock harden; it was a nickname of endearment, and he liked being found worthy of protecting and cherishing. But he was not the one hurting tonight.

"What's troubling you?" Octavian combed his fingers through Myrddin's whiskers, and Myrddin leaned in to his touch.

"I'm just being a fool."

"I'm a fool more often than not, and you listen to my nonsense," Octavian said. "Nothing you can say will make me think less of you, so just tell me. You know I'll persist, so don't make me fish for it. I… don't like seeing you unhappy."

Myrddin drew in a breath and then seemed to deflate and sag against Octavian as he released it. He shuddered as he exhaled, and Octavian squeezed his ribs as if it would matter. Myrddin was so much larger than him, so much stronger, but Octavian would hold him up if he had to. "I'm being selfish, lad. I'm happy for Dirk. He's married a remarkable woman and has a child on the way, but—"

"He's moving into the tavern," Octavian offered. "He plans to open an archery shop. He'll only ever be a few hours ride away."

"But I've lost him in a way," Myrddin said in a broken whisper. "I'm glad he's happy, but he was my constant. I thought we would stand together, fight together, until the goddesses called us from the light of the world. And now he's retiring. Abandoning fighting to make bows and raise a family. I feel—"

"Betrayed," Octavian supplied.

"Yes, though I have no right."

"You have every right," Octavian said as he nibbled up Myrddin's neck. "Your feelings come upon you like a storm, and there's nothing you can do to keep them at bay. How you react to them is all you can control, and you have done nothing to disgrace yourself. It isn't like you tried to stop the wedding, or to make Dirk feel guilty for the choice he made."

Myrddin was drunk. Octavian detected it in the way his words slurred into each other. Octavian knew only too well how wine and ale could magnify hurt, weaken the barriers that kept it from flooding out. He didn't know exactly what to do to reassure Myrddin, so he just squeezed him tighter. "He is like a brother to you, and now he'll have people who need him more than you do. You cannot be his main concern any longer, and that's a loss you have a right to mourn. But you aren't alone. You have me. I know it isn't much consolation—"

"Do I really?" Myrddin pushed the hair from Octavian's face and stared into his eyes with his lids peeled back, showing the white around his irises.

"Of course you do. Always. I would have nothing if it hadn't been for you."

"Always?"

"Yes, Myrddin." In a way it surprised Octavian that he meant it; he wanted to stand beside this man, share in his happiness as well as help him shoulder his pain, do what he could to make him happy. He realized he trusted Myrddin in a way separate from the others. Myrddin would never exploit the cracks in the armor Octavian revealed. He needed that, and he needed to reciprocate it, show Myrddin he could also help him carry his burdens. "I cannot imagine being without you. You… you're the only one who spares me being completely alone. I hope I can be that for you too. A shelter. A bulwark if you need one. Just a flicker of light when everything seems drowned in darkness."

"A flicker," Myrddin repeated as he pulled Octavian closer, pressing his hands against the small of Octavian's back to guide Octavian's belly and groin against him. "You—you're the sun."

"The sun can be trusted," Octavian panted at the corner of Myrddin's jaw. He had things he wanted the other man to know, things he had to verbalize before lust scorched them from his brain. "It is a constant. There every day. Goddesses, if you can trust in nothing else, you know the sun will rise in the sky every morning… warm your shoulders… kiss your cheeks and dance across your hair…."

"The sun is also far away, my boy. Beautiful from a distance, magnificent, but hardly something a man can hold in his hands and call his own. The whole world needs the light of the sun. Only a bastard would hoard it. Try to call it his. And if he did, its light would burn him to nothing."

Octavian cursed himself for drinking too much, again. The words he needed slithered through his fingers, and even when he caught one, the others he needed to form something coherent had long since escaped. "I am not far away. I'm here. Here. Solid and flesh and wanting you very much."

"I'm here too, Octavian." They pressed their lips together and bumped and slid their tongues along each other's clumsily, wetly, in a messy but miraculous kiss. Myrddin pulled Octavian taut against him, and Octavian dragged fingers that desperately wanted to sink into something warm and yielding up the back of Myrddin's shirt. They pressed their erections together, moving to the faint melody coming from the center of the camp. Myrddin broke away and spoke against Octavian's lips. "I want you too. Always want you. You are my sun, and I move around you. I want to be within your fire. I don't care if I burn."

Octavian tingled from his toes to his eyelashes as he melted against Myrddin, let Myrddin's hands above his hips support him. "I'm so—so aroused," he panted against Myrddin's mouth. "I need…. Goddesses, I need you."

Myrddin, still holding Octavian, kissing him and cradling the back of his head, reached for the door to their home. The hinges squealed and the door scraped against the stone floor as Myrddin threw it open with his elbow. Walking backward, he pulled Octavian over the threshold and into the kitchen with its smells of charcoal and burnt fat. The fire they'd built before the ceremony burned low, casting the room in fuzzy, flickering light.

Home, Octavian thought. Home was bacon grease and bed linens that smelled of their hair. Their dirty boots—leather and foot sweat—stacked by the door. The stew pot over the fire, the contents boiled to the thickness of clay. Dirty chalices near the sink. Myrddin's stockings strewn on the floor in front of their bed, yellowed at the heels. Worn thin at the balls of the foot. Threadbare, and yet so precious. Like the empty oil vials discarded on their bedside table, their corks littering the floor. In that moment, it all seemed like treasure scattered at his feet, and he blamed the wine. *What a mess. My mess. My home. My man....*

He loved it, the mingling of their scents, their messes, their lives. It was all sloppy and tangled, hard to define, but still good. Better than good. Better than he'd ever hoped for. Thirteen Sisters, he was drunk. He just wanted to kneel at the foot of the bed and let Myrddin push inside him, let Myrddin make sure he felt good. He trusted him with that, and with so much more. That trust, it felt like flying, being weightless and buoyant and drifting along, yet knowing someone held the end of the rope, someone who wouldn't let him be lost. Myrddin would hold on. No matter where Octavian drifted, he'd hold on, and he'd bring him back to the ground. Goddesses, knowing someone held the end of the tether meant he could soar.

Myrddin carefully removed Octavian's clothes. He'd dressed properly for the wedding, especially since Dirk had asked him to officiate the ceremony, in a pair of dark brown trousers and a deep red vest. The garments fluttered to the floor and landed in soft heaps, until he and Myrddin stood naked, facing each other, touching each other as if it were the first time. Myrddin's thick muscle, his skin and the light dusting of golden hair over his ass, the backs of his thighs, his groin, and his belly felt so novel and forbidden beneath Octavian's fingertips that he trembled, wondered if he'd fallen into a dream. He just stood watching Myrddin's face as he moved his fingertips along the ridges of his belly, along the thatch of hair between his legs, over the girdle of sinew between his waist and hips, down the firm crescents of his ass. He didn't think he'd realized how beautiful Myrddin was, especially when his eyelids sagged and his lips parted at Octavian's touch.

"Is there room for, and interest in, another here?" Sylvain asked as he quietly closed the door to the quaint hut behind him.

His voice startled Octavian. He'd been so lost in his dreamlike fugue he hadn't heard Sylvain enter, not that he minded. They shared everything, including their homes, and Octavian didn't expect Sylvain to knock. Slowly, Sylvain's offer percolated down through the layers of Octavian's inebriated and distracted mind, and he looked at Myrddin for confirmation. Their gazes met, and Octavian found no envy or resentment in Myrddin's expression. His skin was pink, his lips swollen and eyes glazed and dark with lust.

"Do you want this?" he asked Octavian.

"I think… yes. I think this will be fun."

Sylvain slowly unlaced his doublet and let it fall behind him. The muffled brush of fabric was loud in the nearly silent room. He toed off his boots and discarded them as he took a step closer to Octavian and Myrddin. Before he reached them, he shrugged his shirt off his shoulders. The snug leather trousers he wore did nothing to conceal the swell of his cock as he narrowed his eyes and looked between them with the mischievous grin Octavian knew so well—like the proverbial cat who'd just eaten the songbird. One at a time, he opened the buttons on his pants, and then he pushed his hands into them to slide them down his legs. Naked, he stood next to them and put a hand on each of their shoulders. He leaned in to kiss Octavian, drawing his lower lip into his mouth and running his tongue over it. Octavian was too drunk to match his artistry, but he surged his tongue into Sylvain's mouth and gave him a wet, messy kiss full of need, if not perfect in technique. Sylvain didn't seem to mind as he let his jaw go slack to accept Octavian's onslaught. Then he broke away to kiss Myrddin, and as their cheeks hollowed and undulated, Octavian couldn't resist reaching down to stroke himself.

"Do you want to watch?" Sylvain panted, turning to Octavian when he broke from Myrddin's mouth. "What do you want to see?"

Octavian bit his lip and concentrated on the pain. He didn't want to waste this opportunity, but he was so excited by seeing Myrddin's creamy skin and golden hair against Sylvain's dusky skin and dark hair that his cock dripped onto the floor. "I-I want to see what the two of you do when I'm not there."

"He wants to see what we do," Sylvain murmured as he pecked lightly across Myrddin's lips.

"All right, then," Myrddin said, moving his hand into Sylvain's hair. "For now."

Octavian had heard from both of them the details of their dalliances, how they involved mostly play—hands and mouths—since neither of them especially enjoyed being entered. He'd often tried to picture what it would look like when he pleasured himself, but the real thing took his breath away. They stood with a few inches between them, kissing deeply but slowly, tracing their hands along each other's backs, thighs, asses, and chests. Their cocks pointed out and crossed, reminding of Octavian of the halberds in the livery he'd drawn, and then he wondered what was wrong with him that he'd think of something so absurd while the two beautiful men in front of him put on such an enticing show. They touched each other differently than either of them touched him; Sylvain's caresses to Myrddin were guarded, almost cautious where they were more than confident with Octavian, and Myrddin was more rough, certainly not intending to hurt, but more aggressive than with Octavian. Octavian wondered if Myrddin found him more fragile, but decided Myrddin just knew him and knew how he liked to be touched. They both did. They also seemed to know how to excite each other.

Myrddin took Sylvain's hair in both hands and pulled it back from his face. Then he just stood looking at him, breathing through slightly parted lips. "There's no denying you are a beautiful man, my friend." He moved his hands down Sylvain's neck, down the sides of his lean arms, until he grasped them just above the elbows and urged Sylvain to kneel in front of him. Sylvain looked up at him a little defiantly, his cheeks dark and lips swollen with arousal. With their gazes locked, Sylvain flicked his tongue out to mop up the bead of precome glistening on Myrddin's tip. Myrddin groaned and buried his fingers in Sylvain's hair. Sylvain didn't taunt and torture him quite as long as he did Octavian before letting him push between his lips and into his mouth and throat, but he did enough to drive Myrddin to the edge. Octavian knew by the way Myrddin tossed his head back and moved his lips but made no sound. He held Sylvain's cheeks in both hands and rocked his hips in tiny increments, though he clearly wanted to thrust. When his belly muscles trembled and his breath came in short, needy bursts, Octavian knew he'd crested, and Sylvain groaned with pleasure as he took everything Myrddin offered.

They tasted a little different: Sylvain more tart and Myrddin heavier, more meaty. Octavian wanted to taste him, needed it. He knelt on the floor next to Sylvain and licked a dribble from the corner of his mouth.

"Goddesses," Myrddin moaned, and his body tightened and spasmed again, another spurt of seed making Sylvain gag. As soon as Sylvain released Myrddin from his mouth, Octavian took hold of his face and pressed his tongue past his teeth, lapping up the vestiges of Myrddin's flavor on the roof of his mouth, the silky insides of his cheeks. Sylvain kissed him back as he reached down to cradle Octavian's balls in his warm hand.

"So desperate to taste come, my treasure?" Sylvain panted against Octavian's lips. "I can accommodate you, if you like."

Octavian looked down at the streaks of seed on Sylvain's purplish brown erection. His mouth watered. Maybe the wine gave him false confidence, but he felt sure that tonight, finally, he'd be able to take that monster all the way to the base. He turned and looked up at Myrddin. "Do you want to watch me suck his cock?"

"I want to see you happy," Myrddin said. "It's all I ever want. So if you'll enjoy it, I'll enjoy watching."

"You can do more than watch," Octavian said. "I have the most brilliant plan. We should move into the bedroom."

Myrddin offered his hands to both of them to help them to their feet, and when they reached the bedroom, Octavian lit the lamps on the tables on either side of their bed. Taking Sylvain's hand, Octavian guided him to perch on the edge of the mattress, and then he pushed his knees apart. On his hands and knees, he ran his lips along the length of that big cock, tugging on the foreskin with his mouth, pushing it back and forth over the crown. He arched his back and walked his knees apart, spreading his legs a little wider. Myrddin knew him, knew him better than he knew himself sometimes. He'd know what Octavian wanted.

Cool, thick oil ran between Octavian's cheeks as he skimmed his teeth over Sylvain's cock. Sylvain shuddered and propped his hands on the bed behind him. He liked a little bit of teeth, and he liked his nipples touched. Octavian reached up to capture one between his thumb and finger as Myrddin traced around his rim with his finger. Octavian pushed back against him as he opened his mouth around Sylvain's crown and sucked it in. He slid down the length, slowly, accommodating to the girth at the center, as Myrddin pressed a finger inside him. His body clenched around it as he struggled to take the last few inches of Sylvain's erection into his throat. Sylvain lifted his hips a little, and Octavian's nose brushed the sparse trail of hair on his belly. At first he gagged, but after a few moments of holding still, breathing, and closing his eyes, the reflex subsided. Just as Myrddin pushed another finger into him, sending jolts of pleasure up his spine, he swallowed around Sylvain's cock.

Myrddin kissed up and down Octavian's back as his fingers found that magical place inside and rubbed against it, making Octavian growl around Sylvain's cock. Normally Sylvain would have asked him to move by now, but he just sat looking down at Octavian with an expression Octavian couldn't place. He reached down and swiped a tear from Octavian's cheek with his thumb. "Octavian Rose…."

They moved together as smoothly as Octavian did with either of them separately. As Myrddin thrust his fingers in and out of him, Octavian slid his mouth back and forth over Sylvain's cock. He'd learned to alternate his strokes between long and slow, tip to base, and short and quick, working his tongue against the sensitive groove on the underside of his head. Likewise, Myrddin knew to pull his fingers out, twist them, and push them in hard. When he hit Octavian's sweet spot, it felt like he pushed his seed out from the inside. Combined with Sylvain's taste, the feel of the thick veins on his shaft against Octavian's tongue, Octavian couldn't last. His whole body tingled and tensed, winding up so tight he had to release it. He swiped his tongue over Sylvain's slit and squeezed his muscles around Myrddin's fingers.

"Don't," Sylvain panted, reaching over Octavian to grasp Myrddin's shoulder. "Don't make him come."

"Goddesses, why not?" Myrddin asked.

"Because." Sylvain cupped Octavian's chin and slid back on the bed, leaving his mouth with a wet pop. He lay down and lifted his heels to the edge of the mattress, propping them next to his asscheeks. He grazed his cleft with his fingertips as he met Octavian's eyes. "Octavian, I want you to fuck me. Would you like that?"

Octavian's thoughts swirled as he looked down at Sylvain, spread open and offering himself in a way he never had before. He missed the fingers Myrddin had withdrawn from his body, and he felt unsure. "I have never done that. What if I'm not any good?" Having Sylvain's pleasure as his responsibility seemed daunting.

Sylvain reached up to stroke Octavian's cheek. "My flower, my sweetness and light, you have excelled at everything you've ever tried. Why should this be different? I want you, want something of you to keep with me. Something of you inside me. Octavian, will you really make me debase myself and beg, or will you give me your cock?"

Sisters, he loved him. Loved the rare honesty shining in his green eyes, loved how vulnerable he looked stretched across their bed. Loved the trust he placed in Octavian to see to his needs, hold the end of the rope while he flew. Octavian bent down and swiped his tongue over the wrinkled opening that looked too small to even get his finger inside. It contracted beneath his ministrations, and it tasted divine: salt and earth with a finish of honey. He pressed the tip of his tongue past the ring of muscle, and Sylvain trembled. "Octavian…."

"Yes, all right. Whatever you want." Octavian fumbled for a vial of oil on the night table, but Myrddin pressed one against his palm. He worked the cork free and drizzled the amber liquid over his fingers and Sylvain's crease. With his finger, he circled the taut rim before preparing to delve in, open Sylvain up as Sylvain always did with him.

"No," Sylvain gasped. "Don't prepare me. I want to feel it, feel it for days."

As always, Octavian looked to Myrddin for guidance. Myrddin nodded once and kissed him, so Octavian lined himself up with Sylvain's opening and pushed. At first it seemed nothing would happen, but then resistance broke and hot, tight heat enveloped him. Goddesses, he'd never felt anything like it. He swore he could feel the beat of Sylvain's heart as his ass clenched and undulated around his cock. He watched Sylvain's face, noting the crease between his brows; he wanted to make sure he wasn't hurting him. Sylvain looked rapt as he tossed his head from side to side, spread his arms, and gripped the blankets and furs on the bed. His back bowed up off the sheets. Octavian buried himself to the hilt and began a slow rhythm, pulling almost completely out before thrusting back in in. Sylvain muttered words of encouragement as he held his knees against his chest.

"Myrddin, love…." Octavian hadn't even realized he'd spoken aloud before Myrddin was there, kneeling on the bed beside him and encasing his head in his arms and kissing him gently. As he thrust into Sylvain, Octavian nipped and suckled down Myrddin's chest, nibbling on his nipples and tugging at his chest hair with his teeth. Finally he managed to move Myrddin into a position on the bed where he could suck his cock while he made love to Sylvain. He could hardly believe this was happening to him, his dick in Sylvain's ass, giving him what he needed, while Myrddin's cock twitched and leaked against his tongue. Both of them muttered his name, encouraged him, and Octavian tried to last long enough to please them both, but he'd never been so aroused or felt so complete.

When Sylvain started to stroke himself, Myrddin reached down to move his hand away and take over. Even with his limited range of motion, Octavian could see the rivalry in the way they looked at each other, along with the fondness. After half a moment of hesitation, Sylvain sprawled back out and let Myrddin attend to his pleasure while he met Octavian's thrusts. Myrddin pushed into Octavian's mouth, the slickness of his seed coating Octavian's tongue. It was almost perfect, almost Octavian's fantasy. For a fleeting moment, he wished he had something—someone—inside him, but the flesh of the men moving against him soon brought his mind back to the present. On the bed, Sylvain and Myrddin held hands, their fingers laced together. Something about the intimacy of that gesture drove Octavian over the edge. He fell forward across Sylvain's chest and caught his lips with his mouth. As they kissed with wet, chaotic abandon, Myrddin stroked himself until he came across Octavian's back. With a truncated cry, Sylvain shot over his stomach, his muscles hugging Octavian's cock in rhythmic waves.

They collapsed in a heap, gasping for air, Octavian and Sylvain chest to chest, still connected, and Myrddin stretched over Octavian's back and kissing Sylvain softly—slow, languorous, satisfied kisses. After they came back to their senses and drifted down from the pinnacles of their bliss, they broke apart and lay close. The autumn air had a bite, and Octavian felt wonderfully cozy and secure pressed between Myrddin and Sylvain as they held each other over him. He drifted, content, drunk, and sleepy. He couldn't believe he'd made love to Sylvain, and it surprised him how much he'd enjoyed it. He hoped they both had. Goddesses, his life was good—full to overflowing.

Octavian had been hoping to just fall asleep, safe in the arms of his friends, but of course Sylvain couldn't be content. He rose to find a bottle of wine, opened it, and filled one of the rare clean glasses he found in the cupboard. Then he returned to perch on the edge of the bed. "You know, I think it's time for me to be moving on."

Octavian felt like he'd been doused with a pail of cold water. He sat up in bed and said, "What? What are you talking about?" He could only hope and assume Sylvain was talking in abstracts. He wasn't ready to lose him.

Without turning to look at Octavian, Sylvain said, "Things here at Rosecairn have become orderly. The work is steady and safe. I'm beginning to grow restless, to feel the need for adventure."

Octavian reached out to touch his curved back, placing his hand between Sylvain's shoulder blades. "Perhaps the hollowness you feel has less to do with danger and more to do with missed opportunities. Maybe you should return to Elvara."

Sylvain shook his head. "There are no such things as second chances in this life."

"That isn't true," Octavian said, curling his fingers around Sylvain's shoulder. "My whole life is a second chance. Rosecairn is a second chance, and not just for the men here, but for everyone in the area. There's always a chance to try again."

Finally, Sylvain turned and looked at Octavian with an expression of deep regret, his forehead wrinkled and his eyes wide and sparkling. "You are too wise for your age, Octavian Rose. You are a force, and a beacon of goodness in a wicked, rotten world, and I'm going to miss you very much. But you don't need me any longer."

"Yes, I do," Octavian said in a broken whisper, his chest constricted and his hands numb and trembling, too weak to hold on to Sylvain.

Sylvain flashed him a watery imitation of his signature cocky grin. "You don't. You are the lord of all you survey, loved by everyone who knows you. I'm glad I helped you get here, but my work is done. It's time for me to find something else to get up to, my treasure. Time to stir something up. You'll be fine—brilliant—without me now."

"But I—" Octavian screwed his eyes shut; the sight of Sylvain grinning like this was no major affair was too much for him. It hurt that he'd never hold him again, kiss him, make love to him, or share his plots and dreams, but Sylvain had a right to be happy. "I understand. I'll miss you very much, and I appreciate everything you have done for me."

"I must admit I'll miss your slatternly ass myself," Myrddin said.

"Just my ass?" Sylvain asked as he leaned down to trace the lines of Myrddin's jaw. "You've never had it, but the night is young."

Myrddin clasped his hands and kissed along the ridges of his knuckles. "I'm going to miss all of you, you cheeky bastard. It's been good, Sylvain."

"It has," Sylvain said, "but it's time."

"I wish it wasn't," Myrddin said, "but I'm sure you have your reasons."

"Life here is just becoming too predictable," Sylvain said with a shrug. "I need challenges and surprises to occupy my mind."

Octavian's heart hurt, less because Sylvain was leaving than because he clearly couldn't see the source of his own restlessness. Until he reconciled it, Octavian doubted he'd find happiness or contentment, and that made him sad. He hated to think of Sylvain never finding what he needed. "When are you planning to leave?"

"Not tonight," Sylvain said, kissing Octavian's forehead. "We still have fun to have together, and tomorrow, and maybe the next day, I have to say my farewells to Breeze."

"He's become quite fond of you," Myrddin said. "He may not take this well."

Sylvain stretched across the edge of the bed next to Myrddin and set his cup on the floor. "Breeze understands the nature of our friendship."

"He's also young," Myrddin said, meeting Sylvain's gaze. "Things like this feel more profound, hurt more, in youth. Be careful with him."

"I'm careful with all my lovers," Sylvain said as he rolled to his side to kiss Myrddin. "I'm more than happy to show you."

The three of them made love twice more that night, and Octavian woke in the afternoon to find Sylvain gone. He wriggled closer to Myrddin and held him tight, reassuring himself this man—his man— wasn't going anywhere. It was enough, he decided as he eased back into sleep. Sylvain would leave to pursue his needs, and Myrddin would remain beside Octavian. He accepted that, and though Sylvain's loss pained him, he would be all right. With all his heart, he hoped Sylvain would secure what he needed to be content. Octavian knew all too well how it strained a man's spirit to always seek for more. In the moments he spent safe and satisfied in Myrddin's arms, Octavian decided he wouldn't ride out to bid Sylvain farewell when he left. They'd said everything they needed to say to each other, and it was done. Some things ended, went to ground, and part of living was accepting that. Octavian had the man who meant the most to him in his arms, in his bed, and it was enough. More than enough. He kissed Myrddin's sleeping face, nestled closer to him, relishing the weight of his arms, the warmth of his skin, and the softness of the hair on his chest and belly. He tucked his head under Myrddin's chin and went to sleep with his face against Myrddin's chest, thinking as he dropped into oblivion, *As long as I have you….*

Chapter Nineteen

OCTAVIAN ROSE'S Journal

Winter descended early and hard on Rosecairn this year. By the twelfth moon—Illira's—over a foot of snow and thick ice lay over the camp. I'm glad everyone has sturdy shelter and that we have stocked plenty of firewood, cured meats, cheese, and grain to get us through the lean months that can feel eternal here in the far north. It will save us the added nuisance of braving the roads for supplies.

I have much to be thankful for today, on the day of my twenty-third birthday. From the window I am sitting beside, trying to take advantage of the sun that graces us with its light so briefly on these winter days, I can see my scarlet banners hanging from the buildings. They, along with the triangular flags atop every house and shop, bear the crossed halberds and single rose I designed as the livery of the Thorns. We have fifteen outposts beyond the cairn, each staffed with fifteen to twenty men, bringing our force to a total of more than 650 warriors. I'm happy to report many of them have taken wives and started families. Traders, shopkeepers, and artisans of all kinds have chosen to make Rosecairn their home, and my mines and quarries are flourishing. The Thorns control the land for sixty miles in every direction. Our territory rivals that held by many noble families.

We have been kept busy through the cold months with many lucrative jobs, mostly far to the south, as our territory is safe and secure. But the lands beyond ours, on both sides of the river, are still in constant flux, passing from the control of one warlord or mercenary leader to the next. We fight beside whichever offers the most coin, though I am still particular about which jobs to take. I refuse to take gold to harm innocents, and I won't have men beside me who disagree.

I have managed to achieve all I'd ever hoped and much more while being true to myself. I did this, and I remained myself. I did not win by being ruthless, or callous, or lowering my personal standards, or exploiting the weak. I won by being better than the men who wanted to kill me. I don't feel I have sacrificed anything.

Yet all of this pleases me less than it should. I am melancholy, watching the shadows cast by the mountains swallow up the camp. Something is still missing. It wiggles and scratches at the edges of my mind, whispers in a language I cannot comprehend. It calls to me, taunts me, and yet just when I think I have grasped it by the tail, it slides through my fingers. Sometimes I lie awake at night, worrying I will never find satisfaction in this life. I don't even know what I'm seeking. I wonder if I should share my troubles with Myrddin, and how to phrase it. How do I tell him I desire, even need, something, but that I don't know what it is? Sometimes it is just wine. At least, a good quantity of wine allows me to ignore those crawling, burrowing things at the edges of my thoughts.

I miss fighting beside Dirk. I even miss him rolling his eyes at me and showing me his middle finger. I miss Sylvain much more than I expected to, much more than the casual friendship he insisted we restrict ourselves to would dictate. There are times when I still expect to see him, reclining in some feline pose in some dark corner of the camp, his green eyes sparkling, and that up-to-no-good grin on his face. I often wonder how he is, where he is, what he's "found to stir up." I wonder if he might find his way back here someday, if he thinks of me as I think of him. But it is done. Things end, and accepting that is part of life. I can only try to convince myself a day will come when I won't look for him, or wake from a dream of him to pain too raw for the loss of such a superficial association.

I am tired of these lifeless pages. They bring me less comfort than they used to, and they bring me no closer to figuring out the hunger eating me up inside.

AFTER HIS ink dried, Octavian closed his book and reached for the wine bottle. Even after draining it, his thoughts were still running amok like spring hares, crashing into one another. His stomach rumbled, reminding him he hadn't eaten all day. A basket of eggs sat on the counter, dried pears and apples hung in a garland in front of the hearth, a half loaf of bread, jars of jam and chutney waited on a shelf, and dried meats hung from the ceiling. It wouldn't be hard to fix himself something, but he couldn't muster the ambition. Instead, he decided to go to the rack and find another bottle of wine to open. He had every right to have a drink on his birthday, after all, even if everyone else had forgotten it and he was alone. On his way, he used the small knife he kept on his belt to slice off a few strips of bacon for the scrawny tortoiseshell cat that had decided she would live in their house. The little beast still hissed and raised her hackles whenever Octavian came near, but Myrddin had managed to coax her into his lap and had taken to calling her Snippet. Snippet yowled at Octavian as he dropped the meat to the floor in front of her, then sniffed at it, arched her haunches into the air, stretched her front legs out, and ignored him in favor of her supper.

Octavian chose a bottle of wine and removed the cork. Where had Myrddin been all day? He'd been gone when Octavian woke. Not that Octavian had any right to feel resentment. Myrddin didn't owe him an explanation; he was free to come and go as he chose, and he hardly had to report to Octavian. Since the little house suddenly felt very dark and very lonely, Octavian decided to take a walk and shrugged on his fur-lined cloak.

Outside, the camp was unnaturally still and quiet. Maybe the cold was to blame, but the typical sounds of men drinking, feasting, and engaging in good-natured combat around the fires was missing. As Octavian wandered toward the center of their village, smoke curled lazily from the chimneys of the humble but well-built homes. Now and then the smell of something savory cooking reached his nose but didn't whet his appetite. Even the animals—the goats, sheep, milking cows, horses, and regiments of cats Lena had somewhat tamed—seemed to have found warm places to bed down for the night. Octavian made his way to the cairn and looked up at the ancient monument. An almost full moon, smudged by the clouds in front of it, provided a hazy silver light. Snow and rime coated the stones of the cairn and the dark, gnarled vines twisted around it. Some of the vines were as thick as Octavian's arm. They had been there long before him, and they'd continue long after he was gone, buried, and forgotten. What would all his exploits mean in a hundred years? In five hundred? Would anyone remember his name? Leaning against the cairn, he looked up at the stars struggling to shine through the thick white veil, and he felt very small, very insignificant, and very alone.

Octavian didn't know how much time he'd spent leaning against the smooth boulders and nursing his wine before he heard the muffled sound of boots shuffling through the snow. He hadn't realized he'd closed his eyes until he opened them and even the subtle moonlight seemed as bright as dawn. Myrddin stood backlit, but Octavian recognized his silhouette: the shape of his shoulders, the way he held his head, how he stood with his feet planted far apart.

"Where have you been?" Octavian didn't know if the bitterness he felt came through in his tone; he'd drank too much to parse his actual response from his intention.

Myrddin stepped closer, close enough to touch Octavian, though he didn't reach out. "I had matters to attend to. What are you doing out here? It's freezing, and the snow has started again." He brushed away what had accumulated on Octavian's shoulders.

"Has it?" Octavian looked up at the fat flakes spiraling slowly down. One landed in his eye, and he blinked away the cold tickle. "Where have you been all day? What matters did you have to attend to? Goddesses, never mind. Ignore me. I'm not your wife, no matter what Dirk says. Do you want some wine? Oh… oh, Shades. Never mind. Seems I've finished it."

Did Myrddin look disappointed as he pried the bottle from Octavian's fingers? Octavian couldn't be sure. He'd been angry with Myrddin, but now… now, with the man in front of him, snow in his golden whiskers, his breath warm on Octavian's face, his blue eyes bright in the gloom… now, he just wanted him. Just looking at him sent Octavian's blood rushing to his root. "Myrddin…." He grasped Myrddin's hip and tried to pull their groins together, tried to stretch his neck to catch Myrddin's lips with his own.

"Let's get you out of the cold." Myrddin dodged Octavian's attempts at kissing and groping and took his hand. Octavian staggered a little as he attempted to follow. "Let's get home. I have some things to show you."

"I hope so." The wine had driven out all Octavian's doubts, all his anger, and now he just wanted to get into bed. As they trudged slowly through the new-fallen snow, he struggled to drive the inebriation from his mind so his senses wouldn't be dulled when they joined. The way he tripped over his own feet even though he put all his concentration into walking a straight line proved his failure. It didn't matter; Myrddin would take care of him. In that moment, it was a revelation. Myrddin would take care of him; he could stumble and fall and make a fool of himself, and Myrddin would help him up without judging him. He had never had anyone to do that for him before, and Octavian knew he'd taken it for granted.

When they reached their house, Myrddin steered Octavian through the door and to a seat at the table. It took Octavian a few moments to realize the house wasn't as he had left it. The mess of papers, maps, scrolls, and notes had been removed from the table and organized into a neat pile on a stand nearby. The dishes were clean and the floors swept. The clothes that had been draped over the furniture or hanging from the ceiling to dry had been folded and put away. Even the boots in front of the hearth stood in an orderly line. The bed had been made, the pillows fluffed. Octavian blinked hard, trying to stop the spinning of the room so he could appreciate it all. Something that smelled delicious boiled over the fire, and bread and cheese sat on a platter in front of him. Wine, too, but Myrddin quickly whisked that away and poured cold water from a clay pitcher.

"What is all this?" Octavian asked, hoping he hadn't slurred his words.

Myrddin sat at the table across from him. "It's your birthday, my lad. Did you think I had forgotten? I went to one of the nearby farms to buy fresh beef. I know you love a good stew. I got bread and cheese to go with it. I wanted you to have your favorite meal. I cooked it myself, so I hope it will be adequate. I'd hate to celebrate by poisoning us both."

"I—" Octavian choked. Whether he had admitted it or not, he'd been hurt by Myrddin being away for his birthday. He tried to get up from the bench, but his ankles crossed, and he would have tripped if he'd not gripped the edge of the table in time. Walking proved an effort, but he managed to get to Myrddin, drop to his knees, wrap his arms around Myrddin's waist, and press his face against his belly. "You did things for my birthday."

"Of course." Myrddin smoothed his hair before gripping Octavian beneath his arms to help him back to his feet. "Let's get some food into you, all right?"

The stew was delicious, the bread fresh, and the cheese sharp enough to rouse Octavian's senses. After the meal and a few full goblets of water, he felt better, his mind more clear. He reached across the table to drape his hand over Myrddin's. "Thank you for this. It means a lot. I-I thought you had abandoned me. I had no right to feel that you owed me anything, but…."

Myrddin laughed. "If anyone has cause to thank the goddesses for the day you were born, it's me."

"Why?"

Myrddin tilted his head and squinted at Octavian. "What do you mean, why?"

"Why are you so happy I was born?"

"Oh, my lad. I needed you, needed you more than I even knew. I was drifting along, just keeping myself alive, without any purpose. Then I met you, and I wanted to keep you safe. Keep you pure. Keep the light inside you burning. Now you and I do important work. I feel alive again, feel like I'm making a difference again. And I feel rejuvenated. Every time I look at you, my body, every inch of my skin, trembles with life. You make me feel young, like everything is possible and within my reach. Goddesses, Octavian. I love you."

Octavian rose from his seat, a little steadier with the food and water in his stomach. He fell into Myrddin's arms, practically knocking Myrddin from his bench. He burrowed his face into Myrddin's neck and the hair hanging in languid waves around it. With his lips pressed to Myrddin's skin, he mumbled, "I love you too. I always have."

Somehow, they ended up on the floor in front of the fireplace, Myrddin on top of Octavian. Shedding their clothes proved a messy, clumsy affair, but they managed. Lying skin to skin, looking into each other's eyes, Octavian and Myrddin kissed softly and slowly as they ran their hands over each other's bodies. Though they'd lain together more times than Octavian could count, this felt new, different. They kissed and caressed each other for long moments, neither of them needing anything else. When they finally joined, they moved together slowly, looking at each other's faces, in no hurry to rush to release. Finally, Myrddin came into Octavian, whispering words of love and devotion, promises of future loyalty. Octavian responded without thinking, letting his declarations of commitment fall from his lips as he rocked up against Myrddin and squeezed his muscles around Myrddin's cock inside him. His release tore from the core of his being, making him shake from his toes to his shoulders as he wrapped his limbs around Myrddin. It felt like they melted together, shared each other's sensations, became a single being. Octavian had never felt anything so profound, and he knew the connection between them fueled the fire engulfing them. It might have burned hot, but it would last, as it had plenty of fuel.

Myrddin touched Octavian's cheek with the back of his hand. "Are you all right?"

"Why wouldn't I be?"

"Your eyes rolled back, and it seemed like you'd passed out," Myrddin said.

Octavian drew in a breath and let it out slowly. He was… calm. His body and mind held no tension. "I—It's never been like that for me before. It… wasn't just our bodies."

"No. I hope not."

"Myrddin, do you really—"

"Love you? You think that was just a hard cock speaking?"

"It's happened," Octavian said.

"Not this time. I do love you, Octavian Rose. Very much. I never imagined sharing my life with a man like you. I…. It's hard to express."

"For me too. But I… I love you, too. If everything else falls apart, you'll be there. If it all goes to the Shades', and you're there, nothing else matters. Myrddin, I'm sorry you haven't found me at my best. I'm sorry I drank too much. There's a tangled mess inside my head, but this is one thing I see clearly. I know… I know me and you belong together, and we can do anything if we stand side by side. Me and you, yes?"

"Yes." Myrddin lifted off Octavian and withdrew from Octavian's body. It left Octavian needy and bereft. Myrddin went to the kettle over the fire and poured warm water onto a cloth to clean himself. Then he knelt next to Octavian and wiped the dried come from Octavian's belly. "Me and you. Nothing would make me happier."

Myrddin lay down on the stones on the kitchen floor and wrapped his body around Octavian's. Despite the cold hardness beneath him, Octavian began to fall asleep in Myrddin's arms, feeling safe and replete. Just when he'd dozed off, Myrddin roused him by shaking his shoulder. "Octavian, I have a birthday gift for you."

"I thought you'd already given it to me," Octavian teased as he sat up. "You've given me so much already."

"There's more." Myrddin smirked like a boy who'd stolen a biscuit as he stood and offered his hand to Octavian. Together, they went to a table by the wall. A thick white fur covered the stand. "You are always cold, so I got you a blanket made from the fur of northern foxes to put across your bed."

"Those are clever and elusive creatures. Did you kill them?"

"I did," Myrddin said, "with Dirk's help. Lift it up."

Octavian lifted the fur with trembling hands. Beneath it, he found a beautiful breastplate, bronze—almost golden in color. Delicate etchings in the shapes of vines and tendrils ornamented the metal, and at the center of the chest, carved deep and accentuated with gold and silver, was the heraldry of the crossed halberds, executed in perfect detail. Octavian traced his fingertips along the lines, his breath catching in his throat. It took a few moments before he noticed the matching pauldrons, greaves, and bracers and the chain-mail tunic with links as fine and light as spider silk to wear beneath them. He looked at Myrddin with stinging eyes. "This—It's armor fit for a king. This is for me?"

Myrddin chuckled as he pulled Octavian's back against his chest and pecked along the globe of his shoulder. "My dear lad, you are the commander of the Roses. Don't argue—I know you have no wish to place yourself above anyone else, and that's part of the reason these men hold you in such esteem. But the fact is, whether you or anyone else will say it aloud, you are. It's time you looked the part, if you ask me."

Octavian lifted the breastplate and marveled at the intricacy of the details. He knew a set like this would cost hundreds and hundreds of pieces of gold. The Roses prospered, but even he would be hesitant to spend such a vast sum. "How…."

"Joaquin made it. So don't worry over the cost. He gave me a good discount."

"But the materials alone…," Octavian protested.

Gently, Myrddin uncurled his fingers from the blunted metal at the edge of the breastplate. He took it and set it carefully atop the rest of the pieces and then took one of Octavian's hands in each of his. "I wanted you to have it. What you have achieved here is miraculous, and you are a leader. Now, when you ride into a village, everyone will gather round and whisper, 'Look, that's Octavian Rose.' That's as it should be. You have earned this. Besides, it might be pretty, but it's also sturdy, so it will keep you safe, and that's important to me. I'll feel better going into battle knowing you're wearing this."

"Myrddin." Octavian pivoted on the balls of his feet and spun to face him. "Thank you. Thank you for seeing such potential in me. I hope I can live up to it."

Myrddin kissed him at the corner of his mouth. "You already have. Your light, your idealism, is as bright as the day you walked into my camp. I thought it would go out, traded for wealth and power, but if anything, it's stronger. It has shone out from this cairn and bathed the land in its goodness for a hundred miles. Lad, do you even know how many lives you've touched? How many people are leading good lives because of your protection?"

"I'm just a sell-sword. We all are."

"That's the thing, Octavian. We're more. We're more because you have lifted us higher. I'm a better man for having met you. You reminded me what was important. Gold is left behind us when we meet the goddesses. When the sisters judge us, it will be on our deeds."

"But we should not do good because we'll be judged," Octavian argued halfheartedly. "We should do good just to do good." He laughed. "Though I must point out, none of us are temple acolytes."

"No, but we're at least as virtuous as the best of the aristocracy." Myrddin brushed Octavian's hair aside to nip up his neck and along the shell of his ear.

His cock hardening, Octavian let his head fall back onto Myrddin's shoulder. "A low standard you set. Most of the nobles are bigger crooks than the lowliest pickpocket. Strange, isn't it, how cutting a purse will land a man in prison but robbing dozens of families of the food they need to keep their children alive is considered the landholders' due?"

"Stop worrying over it, love."

"Someone needs to change this world. Burn it down and start over."

"Hush, Octavian. Let your mind be still. Good lad. Now put your hands against the wall and open your legs a little bit more."

They made love—an expression Octavian had used before but only now truly understood—and then they ate more stew, fed each other rounds of bread smeared with melting cheese, drank a little wine, made love again, and ate more. Lying across Myrddin's chest, Octavian saw the sky lightening to lavender gray beyond their window, and he sat up in bed. With a snort, Myrddin woke and reached for him. "Lad?"

"Do you love me?"

Myrddin scrubbed his hand over his face and bent his neck from side to side to work out the stiffness. "You know I do."

Octavian bent down to kiss him. "Get dressed for me."

"Dressed? What in the Shades'?"

"Myrddin, please do this for me. The sun is about to come up, and I want to walk to the cairn."

"Why?"

"I just do, and I need you to come with me."

Groggily, moving slowly, Myrddin pulled on his trousers, shirt, doublet, boots, and cloak. Octavian watched him as he dressed, enjoying the compact way he moved, so different from Sylvain's liquid motions. Part of Octavian still missed Sylvain, but Myrddin's words and actions had bandaged the raw wound. Of course, he still wished Sylvain well, but if their paths led them in different directions, Octavian could accept it. He would cherish the brief moments their lives had intersected, but he wouldn't mourn any longer. Sylvain had given him much, taught him many valuable things, but what he'd said had been true in a way: Octavian no longer needed him. Sylvain had never been his as Myrddin was his.

Hands joined, they trudged sleepily through the swirling snow as the sunrise turned everything a muted pink. The snowflakes could have been rose petals eddying around them. Nothing else, not even an animal, stirred in Rosecairn. Mauve-gold light danced along the edges of the stones when they reached the ancient monument. Octavian turned to face Myrddin and smiled.

"Why did we have to come out in this horrific cold?" The wind had nipped Myrddin's cheeks as red as an autumn apple, but the soft light gilded the hair of his whiskers and made his eyes sparkle.

"I wanted a witness," Octavian said as he took Myrddin's hands and pulled them to his chest. "I want the goddesses and the honorable dead to hear what I want to say to you. I want the cairn to observe this covenant I'll make with you, if you'll have me."

"Go on."

"Me and you, Myrddin. No matter what happens. Even if all of this falls to ash, if nothing remains but echoes of what we have done, I swear to stand with you. I want to spend my life beside you, supporting you, doing what I can to help you realize your dreams. The rest of it—the gold and glory—might be fleeting, but if we can hold on to each other, well, that's the important thing. We'll always be rich. Will you make this promise with me, to stand side by side against anything the world hurls at us?"

"Yes. Does this mean we're truly wed?"

Octavian chuckled and shook his head. "I don't need that. I don't need to prove anything to anyone else, but if you want that…. Goddesses, can you imagine? You and me taking vows before the goddesses? Even our staunchest allies would turn their backs on us. Myrddin, I just want you to know. I want to make this promise to you."

Myrddin blinked rapidly and dropped his forehead against Octavian's. "Me and you, Octavian. Always. I swear it. Nothing would please me more."

They kissed as the spines of the sun's crown wreathed the pinnacle of the cairn. Though nothing but the old stones had witnessed their covenant, everything between them felt different, more profound, as they made their way back to the little house they shared. Once inside, cozy and secure in their blankets and furs, a hearty new blaze in their hearth, Octavian entered Myrddin's body for the first time, cementing their connection. Afterward, he slept with his face against Myrddin's chest, the niggling doubts in his mind silenced, the burrowing worries still and content. He had never known such peace.

Chapter Twenty

LOOKING BACK over the past two years, Myrddin could only describe his life as quiet. Since his promise to Octavian, he'd entered into a soft and easy period, a period of contentment he never expected to find in life. They still made their livings with their swords, but Octavian's model had proved viable. Some men went on missions while others stayed to watch the cairn or guard one of the outposts. Together, he and Octavian had devised a rotation all the men accepted. It allowed them all to make a good amount of coin while having plenty of time free from conflict. Like the rest of them, Octavian took his turn at the way stations or fighting on less important jobs. The love and respect the men held for him swelled, and Myrddin loved him more every day, though he never thought it possible to cherish him more. But with every new dawn, his devotion to his lad doubled. His lad. Goddesses, Octavian was twenty-five, but Myrddin thought he'd be calling him his lad at sixty, when both of them were sagging and gray.

Of course, he would be far grayer and baggier than Octavian by then, though Myrddin suspected Octavian wouldn't mind any more than he did. Octavian's nights with Breeze, or the nights Breeze shared their bed, or one of them sampled the favors of a new recruit or enthusiastic villager, didn't diminish their commitment. Lying with others didn't lessen their love. Both of them accepted that what they shared was more than physical, and they didn't need to place restrictions on each other to be certain of the other's devotion.

They hadn't exchanged rings or vows in front of a priestess, but Octavian had wanted a physical symbol of their commitment, and he had found something more permanent than a trinket. Myrddin turned his left hand over in his lap and looked at the inside of his wrist. As he traced the inked lines of the halberds and rose, he remembered how much it had hurt when the Emiri artist had engraved the heraldry into his skin. He remembered Octavian's eyes going wide as he took his turn. Neither of them had expected the pain, but then the natives of Selindria and Gaeltheon didn't often put permanent paint to their skin. It was an Emiri custom and therefore indicative of pirates and criminals. Not surprisingly, Octavian didn't care. The lines of Myrddin's paint had smudged slightly over the past two years, but as the Emiri artist had promised, the colors remained vibrant, especially the red of the rose. Since then, many of the men in their company had acquired similar paint as a symbol of allegiance, and Octavian had been delighted.

Today Octavian sat by the window writing in his book, as usual. The shutters were open, and the air coming from the west, off the river, was warm with the promise of spring and heavy with the scent of rain. Myrddin paused in polishing his armor and looked up to watch him. The years of combat and worry showed in the deeper lines around Octavian's mouth and eyes, in the scars on the side of his neck visible beyond his collar. All the roundness of youth had left his face, leaving him with a beauty that was carved and masculine without being severe. More than that had changed since the night at the cairn, though. Octavian was more at ease; still driven, but not as frantically obsessed. Myrddin saw it in the way he wrote in his journal, working at a deliberate and steady pace instead of scrawling furiously with his eyes so wide he looked half-mad. He had nearly filled the thick book and would soon need another, because Myrddin thought he would lose his sanity without the outlet of forcing his thoughts into the orderly boxes of words and pictures. He'd lost count of the number of times he'd seen that battered old book lying on the table and almost picked it up, glanced through that peephole into the recesses of his lover's mind and spirit. In the end, though, it felt dishonest, too much of a violation, and Myrddin didn't want any part of Octavian not freely given.

Myrddin knew Octavian was trying to work out a way for the outposts to communicate with one another through magic. It was something he'd been trying to put into practice for years but had never settled on the exact formula. Currently they signaled each other through large crossbows, similar to those over the gates of Rosecairn, affixed to each fortress. The flaming arrows they shot into the sky could be seen at least by those way stations closest. It worked well enough in

Myrddin's mind, but of course Octavian wanted more, wanted to improve the system. He squinted at his pages with a little furrow between his brows, but he seemed… calm. He had seemed more at ease for the past two years, and Myrddin wasn't sure if Octavian finally felt he'd proven himself, but clearly he had found something he'd been seeking. Some of the hollowness within him had been filled, and it showed. The hunger in his eyes wasn't as feral as it had been.

A soft knock on the door broke Octavian's attention. He lifted his head, blinked hard a few times, and said, "Yes?"

The door opened and one of the newer recruits entered the house. "Sorry to bother you, Octavian," the dark-haired young man said as he handed Octavian a scroll. "A messenger brought this to the gate. He said it was urgent and for your eyes only."

"It's no bother," Octavian said with a smile. "Thank you."

The young man nodded and returned the smile before leaving the house.

"Urgent," Myrddin repeated. "What do you suppose it is?"

Octavian shrugged and traced his fingertip around the wax seal holding the parchment together. "Probably just a job offer. You know how the nobles are, always thinking their affairs are of the utmost importance and must be kept secret. Some of them are ashamed of their need to hire mercenaries. If I suspect that's the case, I'll charge them extra." Octavian grinned and winked at Myrddin. His smile still made Myrddin's heart flutter as if he were seeing it for the first time.

As Octavian read, the amused expression fell from his face, and his lips turned down.

"What is it?" Myrddin asked.

"I'm not sure." Octavian rolled the scroll back up and stood. Myrddin could almost see the thoughts and questions rising and spiraling behind his eyes as if someone had kicked a hornet's nest inside his head. "Let's go find Quinn, Karl, Eduard, and Breeze. I want to see what they make of this. Something feels off-kilter to me."

Since it was just past the midday meal and the day was one of the fairest of the year so far, Myrddin suggested they try the center of the camp. The area around the cairn had become their version of a village square, lined with shops and frequented by traveling merchants who came to the prosperous camp to hawk their wares. Of course, the heavy northern snows had only melted enough to make the roads passable a few weeks ago, and it would probably be another moon before peddlers appeared at their gates. Myrddin looked forward to it; he wanted to buy Octavian another book, and some of the traders offered exotic gifts, maybe something he could really surprise his lad with. Nothing made him happier than making Octavian smile.

They found their friends and comrades around a small fire. Eduard, one of their newer members but a brave and able soldier, and Karl sat on a bench dipping loaves of bread in bowls of stew while Breeze and Quinn engaged in a good-natured duel. Not wanting to distract them, Myrddin caught the hem of Octavian's shirt and held up his hand. Together, they stood at a distance as the two men's steel met.

Though it was a friendly competition, both men's features were set in hard lines, and sweat soaked their shirts as they traded blows. Breeze struck and Quinn dodged; Quinn struck and Breeze parried. They met each other blow for blow until both of them heaved to catch their breath.

Myrddin leaned down to whisper in Octavian's ear. "Our little Breeze has come a long way."

"I would hope so," Octavian said under his breath. "The goddesses know he trained until he fell over with exhaustion when he first came to us. It looks like it's paid off. Let's see who'll be the victor."

"Agreed." Myrddin turned his attention back to the duel in time to see Quinn swat Breeze in the shoulder and knock him off-balance. Breeze staggered back a few steps, and Quinn lifted his blade to tap him on the shoulder and deliver the symbolic finishing blow. Breeze dropped to a crouch, grasped the hilt of his sword in both hands, and lifted it over his head just in time to catch Quinn's blade. The two of them struggled for a few moments, gazes locked, before Breeze managed to push Quinn off and get to his feet. Breeze poked at Quinn's ribs with the point of his blade, but Quinn swiped his sword away with a quick flick of his wrist. Like Myrddin, Quinn detested flourish and believed in economy of movement. Breeze had learned well from both of them. He feinted to the left and diverted Quinn's attention. Then he kicked out at his opponent's ankles, and Quinn landed hard on his back with a grunt. With a huge grin, Breeze leaned his sword over his shoulder and offered Quinn a hand up.

Octavian clapped. "Nicely done. Can I take this to mean our drinks tonight will be Quinn's treat?"

Quinn snorted. "Breeze's drinks are my treat, you shameless blackguard." It surprised Myrddin when Quinn offered the young Esperon a fond smile. The two of them shook hands. "Well fought, boy. At least you can't drain a wine cask by yourself. Octavian's tab would send me straight to the poorhouse."

"That's a gross exaggeration," Octavian protested without much heat. He and Myrddin went to sit down with the others.

Karl grunted. "I for one would sooner challenge our fearless leader to a duel than a drinking contest."

"Aye," Eduard said. He scratched at his silver-streaked brown beard. He was an older man, and Myrddin had wondered more than once where Eduard had trained, but he never asked. Rosecairn was a place to leave the past behind and start over. "So long as he doesn't use magic."

"A magical attack is the same as any other," Octavian said. "Defeating magic-users just takes the knowledge of their weaknesses. Mages must concentrate to cast spells. If you interrupt them, they're as vulnerable as any other warrior."

"And we can distract our beloved mage with a bottle of wine and a comely young man," Breeze said. All of them laughed. Karl offered Myrddin and Octavian stew from the cauldron over the fire and what was left of the bread. Myrddin hadn't realized he'd been so hungry.

After they ate, Octavian passed the scroll to Quinn. "Tell me what you make of this."

Quinn lifted his patch and rubbed the socket of his missing eye before reading it over. "I'm not sure what you're asking, Octavian. From what I can tell, this Captain Julien Cassis needs your help, and you owe him a favor. All he's asking is for us to meet with him. What's the problem?"

Myrddin dropped his elbows to his knees. He'd hoped that long-ago bargain wouldn't come back to bite them in the ass, but it had—and he had no doubt as to how Octavian would respond.

"I did swear an oath to this man, and if he needs me, I'll fulfill my bargain. It's just—" Octavian chewed on his lower lip. "These words, the pattern of the speech, it doesn't sound like the man I spoke with. It's rather inelegant. Captain Julien is a raider—unabashedly so—but he had an elevated way of talking, rather like Sylvain. This cadence feels wrong, but then it's been probably six years since I spoke to the man. Perhaps I'm reading too much into it."

"You should trust your instincts," Myrddin urged. Octavian was the smartest man he'd ever known, and if something smelled rotten to him, Myrddin had no doubt there was some refuse hidden somewhere between the words of that scroll.

"Are you suggesting I just ignore his plea for aid?" Octavian asked. "That I break the oath I made to him? That's not the kind of man I want to be. That's not want I want the Thorns of Rosecairn to be: men who don't honor their promises."

"Give it here." Karl reached for the scroll and looked it over. "All he's asking is for you to bring a few trusted men to meet with him. We'll have to cross to the Selindrian side of the river, and we'll pass through some hostile territory, but it shouldn't be anything we can't handle. I volunteer to join you, if you can use me. The place where he proposes to meet is rather secluded, and I would recommend we scout the area before entering the valley, but other than that, I cannot see the harm in hearing what this man has to say. There could even be some profit in it for us."

Octavian still looked troubled, and Myrddin wondered if the others knew him well enough to see it. Still, he nodded and said, "We should ride out in the morning, then. It will take several days to reach the place where Captain Julien has proposed we meet. He's requested a small group of trusted men, and I'd like it to be all of you: Myrddin, Karl, Quinn, Breeze, and Eduard. Six of us. That should be enough to defend ourselves if we encounter trouble, but a small enough party as to not attract attention. Pack lightly. I'd like to bring Lena in case we need a healer. I'm good, but she's better. Her safety would be a priority, though."

"We can see she's protected," Quinn said. "She'd certainly be an asset."

Octavian turned to Breeze. "Will you speak with Lena? Don't hide that I'm uncertain about this mission, and don't pressure her if she's reluctant to join us. If she says no, leave it."

"I'll see what she has to say," Breeze replied, standing. "I'd wager she'll be up for some excitement and then some, though."

"Make sure she knows it might be dangerous," Octavian called as Breeze walked away. Breeze just wiggled his fingers next to his head as he made his way toward the stables where Lena usually spent her time caring for the animals.

"The rest of us should gather our gear," Karl said. "We'll be ready to ride at first light." He and Eduard left after kicking dirt over their fire.

Quinn stayed on the bench, nursing a mug of ale. "I'm not as young as I used to be, Tam Octavian."

Octavian reached over to pat Quinn's shoulder. "Shut up, will you? This cairn would not be ours if you hadn't aided me, and there's no man I'd rather have at my back. But if you prefer not to come, I'll find someone else."

Quinn patted Octavian's hand. "I'll be there. It sounds an easy job, after all. When it's over, I might consider retirement, though. I'm getting too old for this shit. A farm and a nice fat wife are looking better and better each day."

"You will always be part of Rosecairn," Octavian said as Quinn stood. "Whether you fight or not, you're family."

Quinn nodded as he made his way up the path. Finally Myrddin and Octavian were alone.

"You're troubled," Myrddin said.

Octavian moved closer to him and draped his hand over Myrddin's knee. "I have a bad feeling about this. Goddesses, what's the use of being a mage if I cannot foresee harm to my people? I don't want to lead men who trust me into something they aren't prepared for."

"You care about them, and that's why they're so willing to follow you," Myrddin said.

Octavian shook his head. "Their safety is my responsibility."

"Do you think they won't be safe? Forgive me, but I don't see what has you so upset."

"I don't know, Myrddin. I owe a debt to Julien Cassis, and I'll repay it. Anything less would be dishonorable. I'm choosing my oath to him over the men who trust in me. Leading is a terrible burden."

"It is, my lad. And the choice has to be yours."

Octavian pressed the heels of his hands to his temples. "There's no choice. I swore to Captain Julien I would return his aid if I ever had the opportunity. I am a man of honor, of my word. I want the Thorns to be known as dependable men who keep their oaths. I—we must do this."

"I'll be beside you," Myrddin offered, though it seemed feeble and little comfort.

Octavian took his hand and brought Myrddin's knuckles to his lips. "You're all I need. Do you know that? Myrddin—as long as I have you beside me—"

"You think too much of me, lad."

Octavian got to his feet. He dug his fingernails into his arms as he began pacing. "No. No, my love. It's you who sees too much in me. Goddesses, if I could be half the man you see when you look at me...."

"We're meeting with the captain, and that's all," Myrddin said, laying his hands over Octavian's to still their scratching up and down his arms. "We can always decline if we don't feel we can do the job he's set for us. We—you, Octavian—are far greater than the Bitter Tide now."

"Our company is larger, but we would have nothing if Captain Julien hadn't taken a risk and helped us all those years ago. We'd probably be dead at the hands of the Crooked Tooth company. And that victory is a large part of how I convinced the men of Rosecairn to trust in my plan. Goddesses, I wish Sylvain was here. He knew Julien better than I do. He would know if there was something amiss here."

Myrddin smiled. "I miss the alley cat myself. More than I expected to. But he isn't here, and we have no way of knowing where he might have gone. This is on us. All you need to do is say the word and we'll cancel this journey. Send a message to the Bitter Tide if you feel better. Ask Captain Julien to meet with us here."

Octavian moved his fingers as he always did when he thought things over. Then he chuckled and said, "How would that look? Octavian Rose, cowering in his fortress, too afraid to set foot outside his gate. I'm being foolish. What can we possibly encounter on the road that will be a match for seven of the Roses? I am too accomplished to let something this simple rattle me. I'm the commander of the Thorns of Rosecairn. The greatest threat I face is probably boredom. Come on, let's get our gear ready."

THE NEXT morning, they left the cairn at dawn. Lena rode with them, staying close to Octavian and watching him the entire time. At first, Myrddin had doubted her claims of sensing fear and emotion, but over the years, he'd seen the proof time and time again. He wondered if she sensed something in Octavian he couldn't unravel. Part of him wanted to ask her what she discerned. He didn't like seeing Octavian uncertain, and though it might upset his lad to hear it, Myrddin still considered it his responsibility to protect Octavian and see to his happiness. He had to do it subtly, but having someone to protect over the past few years had been just what he'd needed to feel fulfilled.

They crossed the Starlight Bridge and soon passed into the valenny of Lockhaven in northern Selindria. The journey was not only uneventful but rather enjoyable with the new spring grass bright along the sides of the road and the first flowers scenting the balmy air. As they turned and rode south, the air grew so warm they cast off their cloaks during the day and slept with only light blankets at night. Five days after they'd departed, Myrddin felt frustrated. He hadn't realized how comfortable his life had become. Many of their jobs lasted only a day or two, and after that, he and Octavian were back in their bed enjoying each other. This was probably the longest Myrddin had gone without lying with Octavian since their covenant at the cairn. As he watched Octavian rocking in his saddle, the light pulling the red and gold in his dark hair to the surface, the sun and wind pinking his cheeks, Myrddin thought he'd lose his sanity if he couldn't touch him soon. He was just so beautiful, such a good man, and Myrddin wanted to confirm that Octavian was his. From the enticing secret smiles Octavian shot over his shoulder, Myrddin guessed his lad also noticed the lack of their regular trysts.

That night, after the tents had been pitched and the food cooked and eaten, Karl, Quinn, Eduard, Lena, and Breeze settled on a blanket to share the last of the wine and play a card game. Octavian stood, caught Myrddin's gaze, and canted his head toward the copse of trees atop a knoll a few hundred feet in the distance. Myrddin couldn't misinterpret what he saw burning in Octavian's eyes beyond the firelight they reflected. He mumbled an excuse as he stood to follow Octavian, but the others barely acknowledged him as they concentrated on their game. A few coppers—and bragging rights—were at stake, and Myrddin had no doubt Lena, with her ability to read emotions, would clean up. It was a strange thing to feel completely comfortable leaving an unarmed woman alone with four men without worrying for her safety, but that was the way of the Roses—the company Octavian had built. For a fraction of a moment, Myrddin regretted that he'd miss seeing her knock the boys down a few pegs. His disappointment passed quickly as he watched Octavian's white shirt, bright against the evening sky and looking disembodied as Octavian drifted toward the woods.

As Myrddin followed, Octavian walked slowly, swaying his slender hips and brushing his fingers over the brush and bracken growing between the trees, releasing little clouds of pollen. He didn't look back, but Myrddin had no doubt Octavian knew he was following. When he reached a small round clearing of soft grass and lush moss between a ring of white trees, he wiggled his fingers, and dozens of glowing orbs, each the size of a berry, pink, pale blue, and soft white, sprung alight around the glade. Myrddin gasped and smiled as they flitted through the interlaced branches, coloring the leaves with shifting pastel hues. The wonder of the sight lifted years from Myrddin's heart, and he felt all the enchantment of a boy. Octavian turned to him, smiled, and reached out a hand.

"Dance with me, Myrddin."

Though there was no music, no sound at all besides their breathing and the soft rustle of the wind in the trees, Octavian wrapped his arms around Myrddin's waist and rested the side of his head on Myrddin's shoulder. Myrddin crossed his arms over Octavian's back as they swayed together. Despite how much Myrddin missed coupling, he didn't want to rush this; he'd be content if it lasted forever. Octavian pressed so close Myrddin could feel the heat from his skin through their clothes, feel Octavian's heartbeat against his chest. Octavian moved his hands up Myrddin's back and curled his fingers into Myrddin's shoulder blades, his need clear in his desperate clutching. Then he looked up and their gazes locked. Octavian's little lights danced across the surface of his eyes, and he smiled. "I have missed you, Myrddin. Missed being home. I suppose I took being with you for granted, but I realize now how much I need you. I have felt… empty. Hungry. Not myself, because you're part of me now. I feel incomplete, unfinished when we can't touch each other."

"Goddesses." Octavian looked so earnest, so vulnerable with his heart and spirit flayed open before Myrddin. Myrddin didn't know if he deserved it, but he had been given that good heart and shining soul, and he would fight until he could fight no more to keep them safe, keep them pure. "I would do anything for you."

"I know. Kiss me now. Touch me. You know just how to touch me. You understand me in a way no one ever has. You *know* me."

"And love you." Myrddin combed his fingers through Octavian's thick hair as he nibbled his lips, his chin, his neck, and his ear.

Octavian arched his spine and pressed his belly and root against Myrddin. As Myrddin watched, all Octavian's defenses lowered. His face was completely unguarded as he looked at Myrddin, and his body was pliant and willing in Myrddin's hands. Everything in him, body and spirit, stood bared before Myrddin, because Octavian trusted him with it all. Myrddin realized he'd never seen Octavian expose himself or lower his walls for anyone else. Goddesses, Octavian needed someone he could trust, and Myrddin was glad to have been chosen. "I love everything about you. I want to please you. Tell me how."

Octavian shrugged off his shirt and let it flutter to the ground. Taking a few steps back, his skin glowing in the magical light, he said, "I want you to make love to me." Octavian looked down, closed his eyes, and then opened them slowly. Faith and expectation radiated from his gaze as Myrddin toed off his boots and pulled his shirt over his head. Myrddin trembled like an innocent as he looked at Octavian. He had never seen a man so beautiful inside and out. Then Octavian closed the distance between them, and they kissed: a slow and gentle meeting of lips and tongues Myrddin felt deep in the base of his chest. He ran his hands up Octavian's soft back, over the scars he knew in his sleep, and it seemed surreal. Octavian seemed surreal—perfect in his imperfections, the record of his life there on his skin beneath Myrddin's fingers. "Make love to me, Myrddin."

They dropped to the dewy grass and got out of their trousers. Octavian felt indescribable beneath Myrddin, all warm, satiny skin and bunching and stretching muscle. There was trust and love Myrddin had never experienced in the way Octavian spread his legs and opened to him. They lay flush, kissing and caressing, for long moments before Myrddin entered Octavian in a slow slide of flesh against flesh. He lowered his face to Octavian's neck and breathed the scent of his skin mingled with the dewy grass and wet soil as Octavian trembled pleasantly at the penetration. When the tension bled from his body and Myrddin knew he'd be comfortable, he pressed in farther. Octavian cried out when Myrddin hit the sweet spot inside him, and then he locked his legs over Myrddin's back and kissed him hard.

They moved against each other slowly, drawing out the experience as they looked into each other's eyes. The luminescence allowed Myrddin to see every subtle expression as it crossed Octavian's face and respond accordingly. He knew just the moment to wrap his arms around Octavian's ribs and drive into him—the moment to stop being gentle. Goddesses, no matter how deep he got, he wanted more, wanted to be closer to him. He wanted to sink into Octavian's being and bask in the brilliant light of his spirit. Myrddin might have muttered something to that effect as he snapped his hips, wanting only to please Octavian. Octavian met him thrust for thrust, panting into Myrddin's mouth until they satisfied themselves. Afterward, they lay in a sweaty heap, covered in the evening dew, still joined, trading sloppy, slurping kisses.

"I love you," Octavian whispered close to Myrddin's ear. "I'd be so lost without you. You're as virtuous and beautiful on the inside as you are on the outside. I can't help wondering why you chose me."

Myrddin felt a pain like a cramp in his chest. "Don't you know how wonderful you are? What you are to me? Goddesses, Octavian, I watch you riding, or moving around the camp, or sleeping or writing in your book by the window, and I'm sure I'm dreaming. You're too good to be real, and yet you chose me, a failed knight and mediocre mercenary. You deserve a prince, and you chose me."

"Most princes are twats." Octavian squeezed Myrddin's nipple and bit his bottom lip. "I've met a few. A good, honest man—a man like you—is worth a hundred of them. You're the best man I have ever met. I don't know how I can thank you for loving me as you have. You have made me happier than I ever expected."

"You have done the same for me."

"I suppose we can call it even, then," Octavian said, "though I still feel I owe you something I'll never be able to repay."

Myrddin closed his arms around Octavian's smaller body and felt his muscles and bones beneath his embrace. "You owe me nothing. You've given me more happiness than I'll ever be able to express to you. You gave me a purpose and a reason to fight beyond gold. You say I'm a good man. If that's true, it's only because you gave me the opportunity."

"You have done the same for me," Octavian said sleepily as he nestled against Myrddin. "You have allowed me to experience love. If I'm a good man, it's because I want so much to live up to what you see in me. I want to be the man you think I am. Everything I do, I do it with that in mind. I don't want to let you down. Not ever."

After a few moments passed, he was asleep. Without his concentration to maintain them, the little gossamer lights fizzled out one by one. Soon only the irregular moonlight filtering through the leaves lit the side of Octavian's face. Though he couldn't see much, Myrddin lay holding him for a long time, running his fingers down the back of his arm and listening to him breathe. Then, late, after the moon had gone down and left the world black and silent, Myrddin shook Octavian awake and urged him to dress. They stumbled sleepily back to their tent and lay wound in each other's limbs. Depending on what they learned when they met with Captain Julien tomorrow, it might be their last night of bliss and peace for a while.

Chapter
Twenty-One

BY SUNSET the next night, they'd reached the narrow valley where Captain Julien Cassis had requested they meet him. Octavian didn't like approaching it in the gloom of the evening, when visibility would be low, and he didn't like the narrow grotto at the end of the passage—barely wide enough for three men to ride side by side—surrounded by high, steep cliffs. But this was the time Jule had specified they meet in his missive to Octavian. Squinting into the darkness, Octavian saw nothing but some stunted trees fringing the crags. He held up his hand, and his people reined their horses to a stop behind him.

Octavian dismounted. "I'm going to scout ahead on foot."

"What for?" Karl asked. "We've been scouting the countryside all day, and we haven't seen another soul. This place is desolate and wild." As if to echo his words, a harrow-wolf howled somewhere in the distance.

"I would feel better getting the lay of the land before we all ride into a place where we could easily be flanked and become trapped," Octavian said.

"Flanked by who? The damned deer, or a herd of goats?" Quinn sounded incredulous, and Octavian began to regret the way he'd always encouraged his men to speak their minds. He had never given Quinn a sliver of a reason to doubt his leadership. "Besides, do you have any reason to mistrust this man? From what I understand, he risked himself and his company to help you. Do you think he'd betray you now?"

"No, but it cannot hurt to be cautious. Wait here until I return or signal you." He handed his horse's reins to Breeze and turned toward the fuzzy orange light he thought he saw in the distance.

Myrddin landed on the ground with a soft thud. "You're not going alone."

"I thought none of you suspected any danger." Octavian spun on the ball of his foot and faced his friend. Of all of them, Myrddin should support his decisions. Despite the others watching, he grasped Myrddin's hand and looked into his eyes. "Do you really think I'm incapable of looking around?"

"I don't think you are incapable of anything," Myrddin said, "but I want to be beside you. Is that so bad?"

Though he understood the sentiment, Myrddin's coddling irritated Octavian. It made Octavian look weak in front of the others. He thought they'd gotten past this, that he'd finally proven himself. "I am perfectly able to do this on my own. Just wait here, and keep an eye on the others. If anyone does try to flank us, they'll approach from behind your position." Myrddin opened his mouth to argue, but Octavian raised his hand. "I really can scout this area and report back on my own. Goddesses, I'm Octavian Rose. I—I'm asking you to do as I say." Without waiting for Myrddin to protest, Octavian stomped away.

He'd gone a few hundred feet before his annoyance gave way to caution, and he moved to hide himself in the shadows cast by the bluffs. His senses sharpened as he concentrated on placing his feet lightly so he wouldn't reveal his position. Soon, a pair of tents came into view. They looked like they'd been there a long time; one of them leaned crooked on its poles and the other had been shredded by the mountain wind. A fire burned between them, and a strip of torn canvas flapped loudly and rhythmically. Octavian crouched just beyond the circle of light and strained to detect any sound over the wind and the call of wolves. He couldn't imagine Jule would have come alone, but he didn't hear any conversation. No light came from inside either structure, and by all observation, they'd been abandoned for weeks. Yet someone had been there recently and lit that fire. It made little sense.

Drawing his sword, Octavian crept a little closer. His chest felt tight as he strained to hear anything but the soft crackle of the dying fire. When he didn't, he stabbed at the torn entrance flap to the wind-damaged tent and pushed it aside with his blade. He tensed, ready to face whatever waited within, but he found the tent empty; not even a bedroll stood inside.

The fine hair rose on Octavian's arms and the back of his neck as he stood, sprinted to the other tent, and smacked it open with the back of his hand. Empty. If anyone had ever used these structures, they'd departed long before he'd received the message from Jule. Jule wasn't here, had probably never been here. Where was he, and why would he lure Octavian and the others to this forsaken place? It didn't matter, not now. Something was terribly wrong, and Octavian had to get back to his men. If anyone was a target, it would be him, and through his arrogance and stupidity, he'd left himself alone and vulnerable.

Octavian turned and ran back toward the mouth of the valley. A hazy lilac moon had just risen, and the light distorted the landscape around him and played tricks on his perception. A rise in the path that seemed farther away tripped him and sent him sprawling on his stomach and gasping for breath. Thankfully the attack he anticipated didn't come, and he got to his feet, ignoring the cramps in his stomach as he willed his body to move faster and reach the others. Finally the silhouettes of his people and their horses came into view. They weren't alone, though. Probably two dozen people scuffled at the limits of his vision. He ran harder. Where had they come from? They'd checked everywhere. Who were they? Simple bandits? His warriors were well trained, skilled, and well armed, but they were severely outnumbered.

As soon as he got within range, Octavian aimed a burst of magic at the four men who surrounded Breeze. He'd perfected the simple spell over the years, and it not only knocked the quartet of enemies down, but sapped their energy while stinging them with small jolts of lightning. Breeze called his name as his enemies lay twitching on the ground, and the terror in his voice almost stopped Octavian's heart. He ran beyond what he thought his body could endure as more men flanked his small party and surrounded his people. Another burst of arcane power toppled three more enemies. Lena, armed with only a small dagger, kicked a man in the groin before backhanding another across the face and running to stand next to Breeze. They fought back to back, protecting each other from enemies who seemed to multiply out of thin air. Goddesses, Lena abhorred violence, but she would defend herself and her friends. Octavian refused to let his kindhearted healer become a killer out of necessity. He didn't want Lena to have to look at the hands that eased pain and see blood, not ever. He drove his sword into the back of one of the men facing her. His hands were already stained, so it didn't matter.

The other man turned toward Octavian with his sword raised. Giving him a quick glance, Octavian didn't recognize livery or the symbol of any faction. The thug wore decent but indistinct armor; he wasn't Bitter Tide, and that gave Octavian some hope. Jule might not have betrayed them, but they faced a superior force. They had to even the odds, and fast. With a quick swipe of his arm, Octavian cut the throat of his adversary. He kicked the body out of his way as he pushed Lena out of the battle. "Run. Get out of here. Breeze, keep her and yourself safe."

"But Octavian—" Breeze began.

"I can fight if I have to," Lena shouted at the same time.

"No! Both of you, get out of here. I'm ordering you, and I am in command. Find a safe place and look out for each other." Thank the goddesses, they didn't argue and ran for the shelter of the bluffs. Three men pursued them, and Octavian swung his sword at one, caught him in the belly, and drove his blade into the enemy warrior's back when he doubled over. Lena picked up a rock and threw it, striking another opponent in the side of the head and leaving him unconscious. The third man hesitated, and then blood burbled from his mouth, and he fell facedown.

"Octavian!" Myrddin pulled his sword from his enemy's back. "We have to get to Karl, Eduard, and Quinn! They're being overwhelmed." He pointed with his sword to where over a dozen men surrounded their three friends.

"Stay here," Octavian said to Breeze and Lena before jogging toward the fray behind Myrddin. Adversaries surrounded his men three thick. He attempted to use his spell to hurl them out of the way, but his magic, or his will to channel it, was wearing thin, and he only managed to knock two men to their knees. It gave Myrddin an opening, though, and he charged into the battle with his sword raised above his head. Before Octavian could track him, the opponents closed behind him and blocked him from Octavian's view. He saw only shuffling, shadowed bodies and heard the clang of steel against steel. He tried to break through with a gout of flame, but the thin arc of fire he managed barely disturbed the men. In desperation, he hacked past them until he reached Myrddin.

Myrddin faced four men; Karl, Quinn, and Eduard fought others beyond Octavian's vision. He heard them, saw flashes of movement, but couldn't discern the details. All he knew was that Myrddin was slowing, struggling to lift his blade against overwhelming opposition.

Two warriors blocked Octavian's path to Myrddin, and with a shout, his magic sent them flying from the ground as if it had a will of its own. He drove his sword into the belly of the next enemy to stand in his way and left him bleeding out on the ground as he called Myrddin's name. He just wanted to get to him, stand beside him as he should have from the beginning. Layers of men stood between them. Octavian used his magic and his sword without much conscious effort, cutting a path to Myrddin in any way he could.

Octavian swiped his sword across the back of a man's legs, slicing the muscles and tendons and sending his enemy facedown on the ground. He finished him with a stab to the back of his skull. As he ran to reach Myrddin, one of the enemy warriors struck Myrddin in the back of the head and sent him to his knees. Time seemed to slow as Octavian ran with his sword raised, but his body just couldn't cross the space as fast as he needed it to. The warrior in front of Myrddin kneed him in the face, sending him sprawling on his back. Myrddin lifted his sword, but the enemy swiped it away and drove his blade into Myrddin's belly—again, and again, and again. Blood fountained from Myrddin's lips, and Octavian screamed. As blood spread in a pool around Myrddin, the man looked at Octavian and smiled. His was a face Octavian knew well and had hoped to never see again: Eric Beasley.

Power flooded Octavian, seeming to flow in through every pore in his body until his entire being vibrated with it. The magic pulsed inside his skull until white flashes appeared in his vision. He didn't think as he lifted his arm to release the energy, just let his rage, pain, and fear transform into whipping blue cords of arcane might. Men flew feet into the air when it reached them and landed feet away. When they got back to their feet, those who still could, ran. As he ran toward Myrddin, Octavian let his magic do what it wanted. The world felt gray and insubstantial, the ground beneath him undulating and thin. Before he realized what he had done, all the enemies either lay dead or had fled. Eric Beasley ran for some horses tethered a few hundred yards in the distance, and Octavian almost went after him. He wanted to make Eric suffer until he begged for death, but pursuing him would mean leaving Myrddin to bleed out on the ground.

He skidded to a stop beside his love and dropped to his knees. As he tried to press his hands to Myrddin's wounds and stop the blood, the others gathered around, Lena and Breeze arriving last. Lena knelt down on Myrddin's opposite side as Octavian looked in horror at the blood on his hands, the blood he couldn't stop from pouring out as the man he loved grew paler and paler.

"No," he whispered. "No, no, no, no." This could not be happening. He couldn't lose Myrddin. He put his hand behind Myrddin's head and lifted it so he could look in Myrddin's eyes. Goddesses, he needed Myrddin to tell him it wasn't as bad as it looked, to comfort him and tell him not to worry. But Myrddin's eyes rolled back, and he moved his lips without making a sound beyond a pained gurgle. A glob of blood shot out and splattered over his chin. Octavian shook so hard he could barely get Myrddin's armor and clothing out of the way to look at his wounds. When he managed it, bile rose in his throat at the lacerated skin and muscle that revealed the innards and pumped life's blood and fluid onto the ground.

"I will not let you die," Octavian said. He blocked out the rest of the world and focused on the magic around him. His earlier efforts had left him weak, but he took the energy into himself even though it felt like it would break him apart. He wrestled it down, made it do as he commanded, and sent the energy into Myrddin. By the time he opened his eyes, not realizing he'd screwed them shut, Myrddin's blood flowed slower, and he looked less ashen and more alert.

"My dear lad," Myrddin choked, reaching up to touch Octavian's cheek, smearing Octavian's face with his blood. "You must not let this ruin you."

"Nothing is ruining either of us." Octavian siphoned more energy; at this point, he didn't care where it came from. If he stole it from the life around him or relinquished his own vitality, it didn't matter as long as he healed Myrddin. But no matter what he did, the horrible gashes crisscrossing Myrddin's chest and belly didn't close. His stomach swelled as the fluids filled it, and between brief moments of lucidity, he fell into unconsciousness. Octavian dug deeper, pulled from everything he could feel with his perception, and channeled it into Myrddin. A little color returned to Myrddin's cheeks, and he opened his eyes again.

"Octavian… you have to let me go. Tell… tell me good-bye, and that'll you'll be all right without me."

"I won't be!" Octavian delved deeper, sucking the life from the grasses and trees, the wind, the sky, everything he could find to steal from. For a few moments, his efforts revived Myrddin, but before long he started to fade again. Blood and phlegm flecked his lips. The anguished grimace Myrddin made as he coughed hurt Octavian more than any blade that had ever penetrated his body, and, coward that he was, he had to look away until the spell passed. He couldn't bear seeing that pain on Myrddin's face.

"Please, please my lad. Don't let this turn you into something you aren't. Don't let it douse the light inside you. Promise me it won't, and tell me it's all right for me to go. It… it hurts so much, Octavian."

"No! No, I'm going to save you."

"There's… there's no saving me, love. I'm glad you're the last thing I'll see."

"I won't be," Octavian insisted. "I don't care what I have to do. I won't let you die!"

"Things… all things end, lad."

"Not this. I won't let it." Octavian scraped every sliver of life from the land around him; he could feel the forests and plains dying as he transferred their energy into Myrddin. It revived him for a few moments, but then he went limp in Octavian's arms again. "Stay with me."

"I can't, my love. It hurts. Tell me that you'll remain Octavian, and that you can make it without me. I need to hear you say it before I can find peace, find some relief from this pain. Tell me, and kiss me good-bye. Please, lad. Please let me go. Let me go knowing you'll always shine. I… I would hate to be the thing that made you compromise."

"No," Octavian said. "You're going to be all right. You'll heal. I-I—"

"I love you, Octavian."

"You are not going to die!" Octavian had no energy left to draw on but that keeping him alive, so he delved as deep as he dared and gave it to Myrddin. Blood spurted from his nostril and flowed over his lips and chin, but he ignored it, along with whatever had broken in his head behind his left temple and made his vision fuzzy in that eye.

"Let me go," Myrddin pleaded. "Tell me you'll be you, you'll be fine without me. You… don't need me anymore."

"No! I will not accept this!"

Lena reached across Myrddin and grasped Octavian's wrist in a surprisingly forceful—almost painful—grip. He looked up and met her serious gaze. "Octavian, he cannot be healed. The damage is too much. You need to let him pass to the next world peacefully and without guilt.

Keeping him here through your arts is only prolonging his pain. You're making him suffer to assuage yourself. Is that what you want?"

"I… no. No, of course not."

"I know this hurts, my friend. But you need to let him move on to his next plane of existence," Lena gently urged. "It's his time, and it's time for you to say good-bye. If you don't say it now, while you have the chance, you'll regret it for the rest of your life."

"Myrddin, I love you more than I can express in words…. There's so much I need you to know… what you have meant to me… what our life together has meant…."

"I-I know, my lad. I hope you'll love like this again one day."

Octavian didn't say he wouldn't even though he knew he'd never feel anything this profound again. "I will never forget you. I—"

"You are ready. Ready to go on without me. Just… just promise this won't make you turn from honor. You're the… the best of men. Don't sink to the level of the men who did this. Promise me that. I don't want to be what made you not be Octavian Rose."

Octavian laid his head on Myrddin's chest, ignoring the blood soaking his hair and the side of his face, and Myrddin wrapped an arm around him. Octavian couldn't hear Myrddin's heart, couldn't detect the steady rhythm that always made him feel so safe and loved as he fell asleep. The absence of the soothing sound drove the truth home for Octavian. Myrddin was dying, and in mere moments, he'd be gone from Octavian's life and nothing would bring him back. This was the last chance they would have to speak until they found each other in the next life. Octavian didn't know if he believed in such things, so he spoke quickly. "I'll try to be the man you think I am. I'll live to make you proud."

"You made me proud. And happy. And I love you more than I ever thought possible. My lad…. Good-bye, my Octavian."

"Good-bye, my dearest friend. My love." Octavian held him as he twitched and convulsed, as the last broken breath left his lungs. When he didn't draw another, Octavian cried and whimpered against his ravaged body. He didn't care who saw. Pain like nothing he'd ever experienced tore through his body, fresh waves shredding him every time his face brushed against Myrddin's whiskers and he knew he'd never feel them against his chest or belly again; every time he noticed Myrddin still and cooling beneath him and knew he should be warm, breathing, but would never take another breath. Octavian lifted his head. At the sight of Myrddin's lifeless eyes and ashen lips, at that face that had looked at Octavian like he held the sun aloft, Octavian threw his head back and screamed. He didn't know what else to do, owned no words to make sense of this or ease the agony, so he beat his fists against the ground and screamed until he lost his voice.

By the time he wore himself out, minutes or hours later, and dropped his forehead against Myrddin's body, the others had gathered in a circle around him. Lena and Breeze held hands, both of them watching him like some unpredictable wild beast that might attack them. He didn't care what they thought, but he didn't think he'd ever find the strength to lift himself off the ground. He didn't want to; he didn't deserve to after what he had let happen.

Karl, Quinn, and Eduard traded glances as if trying to decide what they should do about Octavian, if it was worth risking speaking to him or trying to comfort him. Judging by the looks on their faces, they wanted to back away from him like a drunkard in an alleyway and hope he didn't notice them. Well, let them. He didn't care.

Octavian closed his eyes. After a few moments, he felt restored. Myrddin couldn't really be gone; that was impossible. He just couldn't. Maybe Octavian had hit his head or been the victim of a foul spell. He'd heard of magic that could make a man believe he was trapped in his worst nightmare. When he fought his way back to reality, Myrddin would be there, smiling, shaking his head at Octavian's nonsense. Then they would go back to the little house they'd built together and grow old and fat just as they'd always planned. Myrddin wouldn't leave Octavian alone in the world, not when all he'd ever wanted was to protect him. He wouldn't leave knowing he was the only man who saw the real Octavian. That had never been their plan; it couldn't happen that way. He wasn't gone. He couldn't be.

But when Octavian lifted his head, blood still matted his hair and coated the entire front of his breastplate. The metallic smell clung to him. Myrddin's still, clouded eyes reflected the starlight as he lay unmoving, his lips turning blue. Octavian reached up and shook his shoulder. When he didn't move, he grasped the other and shook them both, hard. "Myrddin? Myrddin, you must wake up. You must come back to me. You told me you would do anything for me! You promised! Myrddin?"

Myrddin's body was growing rigid, and panic rose in Octavian. It couldn't be too late. He was a mage; there had to be something he could do. Thinking he couldn't do anything, that he'd missed his chance, terrified him beyond anything he'd ever know. His heart beat so hard he thought it would explode, and his hands shook uncontrollably. Magic could fix this, couldn't it? If he could defeat the Crooked Teeth and take Rosecairn, he could fix this, couldn't he? Goddesses, what if he couldn't? What if he'd really lost the only thing that had ever mattered to him, the one thing he could depend on?

"Goddesses!" Though his legs felt like porridge, Octavian got to his feet. The stars looked like pinkish smears against the colored lights of the northern sky. Nothing felt real. How could the ground be solid beneath his feet and the sky sliding past above him as if nothing had happened? The world—his world—couldn't go on without Myrddin. "Give him back to me!" he yelled at the Thirteen Sisters. "Please. I'll do anything. I'll live out the rest of my life in a temple. I'll donate every coin I have. Please!"

He felt alone, surrounded by the cold indifference of the firmament and the distant stars, until he felt hands on his shoulders. Octavian's first instinct was to ball his fist and strike out against whoever had dared to interfere with his grief. Breeze never flinched from Octavian's hand. He met Octavian's gaze with his exotic dark eyes as tears spilled over his cheeks. "Octavian, I wish there was something I could do for you, but there's not. There's nothing I can do. I… I'm sorry, my friend. I'm here, for whatever that's worth."

"Breeze." It felt good having Breeze close, letting him hold him. Octavian collapsed against him and dropped his forehead to Breeze's shoulder. Breeze held him up as he shuddered and sobbed. Octavian couldn't hold it in. It hurt so bad, and he was so afraid.

"We should take him home." Breeze held Octavian's cheeks and kissed his brows. "I think that's what he would want."

Octavian, drained to his core, just nodded. He understood action, the steps necessary to achieve a goal, and so he went to retrieve Myrddin's horse. The smells of blood and death made the animal skittish, but Octavian urged it forward. He lifted Myrddin's stiff, heavy body into the saddle and mounted up behind it. Without waiting for the others, he wrapped his arms around Myrddin's waist, remembering a time when he was just a farmworker without a horse of his own. Myrddin had let

Octavian ride with him then. Octavian had denied it at the time, but he'd liked riding with Myrddin, feeling the solidity of his body and the shelter of his arms. Goddesses, how was he going to live without that?

Octavian shut his feelings off, forced them into a box, locked it tight, and buried it. Things needed to be done. First, he needed to get Myrddin home. If he had been in Myrddin's place, Myrddin would have seen he got home, and so Octavian held his body, driving away that it would be the last time he felt Myrddin's flesh against him, and rode hard. He had a goal now, a mission, and he would accomplish it. Nothing else could influence his thoughts.

With little regard for the others, Octavian pushed his mount toward the Starlight Bridge and home, stopping only long enough for his horse to rest. He had something to accomplish, and he needed to shut everything else off, so he did. He didn't bother changing out of his bloody, reeking clothes, he didn't eat, and he barely slept. He reached the gates of Rosecairn two days ahead of the rest of his party, and he rode to the center of the camp.

By now lush leaves, fat, green vines, and abundant white blossoms covered the stones of the ancient monument. Octavian could barely see the smooth rocks beneath the greenery and flowers. Blinking against the sun and scrunching his nose against the heavy perfume of the roses, Octavian carefully dismounted and eased Myrddin's body off the horse. He tried to pose Myrddin peacefully. He looked like a child with his knees curled almost against his chest, but his skin was gray and sagging. Octavian had a job. Almost without thinking, Octavian began shifting rocks that probably weighed as much as he did. After he cleared a patch and lined it with the stones he'd shifted, he dug his fingers into the soil. Handful by handful, he moved the dirt until he'd made a deep hole. It took him the better part of a day and a night, and his body trembled so hard he thought he'd fall over. He almost wished he would, to spare himself the pain of what he had to do next. He looked into the grave he'd dug, at the protruding roots of the roses and the worms wriggling in the disturbed soil, and he didn't know if he could push his Myrddin into that pit. Octavian wanted to take him home and wrap him in their bedclothes, curl around him and let him know he wasn't alone. But he couldn't. His Myrddin no longer existed in that body; his Myrddin was gone and would never return. Octavian bent, lifted the body, and dropped it into the hole. It all seemed so unworthy of Myrddin, curled so ungainly in the dirt. But death was not pretty, and the rotting flesh in the grave was not the man he had loved—still loved. Would always love.

Though his nails were broken and bleeding and his fingers worn almost to the bone, Octavian scooped the soil over his lover. He thought he'd die as the first handful of dirt splattered Myrddin's face— and death would have been a mercy—but he kept going. After he filled the grave, he dragged the stones of the cairn overtop to mark it. Then he stretched over the rocks and shook with sorrow. Though he'd been awake for days, instead of resting, he passed between a waking nightmare and a sleeping one, always seeing Myrddin's face, hearing Myrddin tell him good-bye, crouching next to him, helpless. He didn't care if he ever rose, and he might not have if Breeze hadn't touched his back and asked him what he planned to do next.

Octavian touched the stones he'd laid to mark Myrddin's resting place. "I'll make you proud, my love. I'll try to be the man you saw when you looked at me. I will. But for now, Myrddin, I need you to look away."

Chapter
Twenty-Two

OCTAVIAN DIDN'T bother washing after he buried Myrddin. The blood on him was Myrddin's, and he wanted it with him. It would be like having Myrddin by his side one last time as he did what he had to do. Myrddin might not approve, but Octavian had to do it. He went back to the house and tried to ignore Myrddin's shirt drying over the back of one of the kitchen chairs and his warm cloak at the foot of the bed as he took his old dagger from the chest beneath it. He tucked it into his belt and went to find a fresh horse.

Breeze met him at the gate on a dappled gray mare. To Octavian's surprise, Dirk also waited on a horse, his bow in his hand. *He was more than a brother to me*, Dirk signed. *Let's make this right.*

"I do not intend to make anything right," Octavian said, his tone as sharp and frozen as he felt inside. "This is vengeance, and it will be ugly. I doubt either of you want to be beside me for this."

Dirk and Breeze both just nodded and heeled their mounts behind Octavian's. None of them spoke as they made their way west, toward the river. Instead of crossing the bridge back into Selindria, Octavian stopped in the roughest and most dangerous settlements along the banks of the Kanda. Through either gold, his fists, his blade, or his magic, he soon gained a rough idea of where he could find Eric Beasley and the men who'd assisted him. After they crossed the river, he used the same tactics and even some harsher ones to learn the location of Eric's camp. He didn't care if the mercenaries and thugs he'd strong-armed warned Eric that he was coming. Nothing Eric could do to prepare would stop Octavian. The goddesses themselves wouldn't stand in his way. It hardly mattered to him if he came back, but he'd drag Eric and every man who'd fought beside him down to the Shades'

Abode right beside him. He didn't plan to let a single one of them stay in the light of the world while he still drew breath, and he'd deal with the consequences when he had to.

They rode northwest for days, skirting the edge of Estrella Lake between Everdale and Lockhaven. Eric Beasley and his men had holed up in some caves near the foothills. After Octavian had broken his nose, an oily little merchant fencing stolen goods had been kind enough to draw them a map, so Octavian knew he'd find Eric near a tributary coming off the lake, and he knew to expect about two dozen men. When they came within a day's ride of the caverns, Octavian reined his horse to a stop, dismounted, and waited for Breeze and Dirk to join him.

"I need to give both of you a last chance to turn your backs on this and go home," he told them.

Dirk shook his head and rolled his eyes at Octavian as he'd done since they first met.

Breeze reached out and squeezed Octavian's wrist. "You think we're going to abandon you now? Why would we do that?"

Octavian squeezed his eyes shut and pinched the bridge of his nose. He hadn't noticed how badly his head hurt over the pain in his chest and the simmering rage in his belly. He probably needed water, and he knew he needed sleep. But he would worry about that later. Now he needed Breeze, who'd retained a bright streak of innocence and optimism despite becoming a capable sell-sword, to understand. "There's no virtue in what I mean to do. There's no profit in it either. What you're going to see if you stay here will likely haunt you for the rest of your life. Being a part of it isn't something I can ask you to do, because you'll never be able to forget it."

"And what about you?"

"I don't want to forget," Octavian said, grinding his teeth together. He wanted to look into Eric Beasley's eyes as he killed him and always remember it.

"Will this really do any good, Octavian?" Breeze asked. "I mean, I hate to say this, but it won't bring him back, and I don't know if Myrddin would want—"

"I want it! I can't just go back to my life as if nothing has happened. I can't let those bastards who took my—I can't just let them go on living, get away with it!"

"All right," Breeze conceded, though he looked like he might be sick. "I'm not going to let you face them all alone."

Octavian shook his head and touched Breeze's cheek with his fingertips. "I don't plan to face anyone. I plan to slaughter them—every person. I don't know which of them had a hand in this and which of them didn't, and damn it, Breeze, I don't care. Do you see now why I can't ask you to come with me?"

"I won't turn my back on you," Breeze said. "But I don't know. What makes you think this won't gnaw at your spirit in the years to come? Maybe you should wait. Get some rest. Think about this when your head is clearer. Maybe then you won't think this is the best thing to do."

"No. I will do this. But it doesn't mean you have to."

We should get on with it, Dirk said.

Breeze turned to him. "Dirk, you have a wife and family!"

I wouldn't even have my own scrawny neck if it hadn't been for Myrddin, Dirk answered. *He deserved better.*

"But this won't make it better," Breeze argued.

Dirk shrugged, and Octavian said, "Neither of us will think less of you if you turn around and go home. I'll respect your decision and still consider you a friend."

Breeze squeezed his lips into a taut line. "If this is what you need, I'm here beside you."

Octavian nodded a little sadly. "Then we do this my way. Cover me and defend yourselves, but I cannot ask you to kill if you're not threatened. I'll bear the weight of that. And Eric Beasley is mine."

Dirk patted Octavian's shoulder. *Let's go.*

They found a safe, sheltered place to tie their horses and continued on foot, walking through the night. By daybreak, they were within a few miles of the caves. For the first time in probably a week, Octavian considered what he must look like, covered in filth and dried blood and wearing the same armor and clothing he'd worn on the night of the battle. Rusty smears streaked every inch of exposed skin, and his hair hung in tangled, fouled clumps. He probably appeared more barbaric and mad than any warlord in either kingdom, and he smelled like death itself. Good. His appearance matched the filthy, knotted mess inside. There was nothing beautiful left in his spirit, and he was ready to show his enemies. He took his cursed dagger in one hand and his sword in the other as he dredged up the boxes holding his pain and anger and threw open their lids. Rage and anguish pumped through his veins and flooded him as he approached the camp.

As the sun rose a little higher, the mouths of three small caverns became clear. Outside them stood some ale kegs, fire pits, spits for roasting, cauldrons, and crude benches. No one appeared to be awake yet. Octavian held up the hand holding his dagger, and Breeze and Dirk halted behind him and knelt to conceal themselves behind a cord of wood. Dirk drew an arrow and held it ready as Octavian continued to the entrance of the smallest and closest cave alone. He recognized the smell inside from long ago, when he'd been eighteen and kidnapped by bandits: mold, body stink, garbage, and old ale. A crude fire sputtered in the center of the cavern, adding the acrid bite of smoke to the other odors. Still, it allowed Octavian to see. A few of the men had made it onto cots or piles of fur to sleep, but at least four of them had passed out on the ground, still clothed, some still clutching bottles as they grunted and snored.

Octavian curled his lip. These pigs had no right to even look at Myrddin. There was no justice in letting them continue to live while Myrddin lay beneath the ground, and Octavian would remedy it. He approached a man sprawled on his belly and kicked him in the ribs, flipping him onto his back. The man barely managed a shocked breath before Octavian plunged his dagger through his throat. A savage grin spread across Octavian's face as blood burbled up between the man's teeth. He went through the cave from man to man. He could have killed them while they slept—it would have been easier and more efficient— but this was not a job. This was personal, and he wanted his blood-smeared face to be the last thing every one of the bastards saw before they felt his blade, so he shoved or kicked each one awake and give him a moment to know he was going to die. Blood dripped from his hands and ran down the front of his breastplate by the time he reached the back of the grotto. He hadn't been quiet or cautious, so he couldn't be surprised when three men, groggy with drink but holding weapons, faced him in a dark fissure.

Because of these men, Myrddin was gone, and Octavian would never hold him, see his smile, or hear his voice. With a ragged cry, Octavian gripped his dagger and swung his arm toward the trio of enemies, lashing out with his magic. He hit them even harder than he'd intended, and the sounds of their heads and bodies smashing against the wall made his gorge rise even as it satisfied him. The man on the far left lay in a heap, his head jutting at on odd angle, but the other two managed to grasp the wall and haul themselves up. One of them swayed, unsteady on his feet, but the other squinted at Octavian and said, "You… you ain't a regular burglar."

"I am no burglar at all, you piece of filth. I am Octavian Rose. Didn't Eric Beasley tell you of me? Didn't he warn you what would happen, what happens to pigs like you who dare to attack my people and take things precious to me?"

The stumbling man advanced, and Octavian directed a stream of energy down the blade of his sword, hitting him in the chest and knocking him back against the cavern wall. For good measure, Octavian lifted his body and slammed him down again, and again. Finally he stopped moving, and Octavian turned his attention on the other man. "It's time to pay for what you have done. You made the wrong choice in listening to Eric Beasley, and now you have to take your medicine."

The man, big, hairy, and dirty, but probably not much older than Octavian, dropped his mace with a clang and held up his hands. "Look, friend. It was just a job. All Eric told us was what we were being paid and what he wanted us to do. I've heard of you, sure I have. Commander of the Roses. You and me ain't no different. We're sell-swords, and that means fighting for pay. That's all I done. Same as you do."

In a few strides, Octavian closed the distance between them and pressed his dagger to the man's throat. "How dare you compare yourself to me? If you can't be bothered to know what you're doing, who you're hurting, then you deserve this and more."

"No, please. I-I have some gold… It's yours if you let me go."

"Where is Eric Beasley?" Octavian pressed his blade into the man's neck enough to draw a thin rivulet of blood.

"Here! Here in the camp. He stays in the third cave with some whores and a couple of his favorite men. You'll find him there, probably sleeping off last night's drink. Let me go, tam. I beg you."

Octavian met his frightened brown eyes. "If you had bothered to learn about the job you'd been offered, if you'd had honor enough to refuse, my friend might be beside me right now. May the goddesses forgive you, because I can't." Octavian cut his throat before he could draw in a breath to protest further, and left him bleeding out on the floor of the cave.

The sun outside pierced his eyes and made him squint. Breeze and Dirk flinched at the sight of him when he went to check their position, and Octavian looked down at himself. He looked like he'd emerged from a lake of blood; not an inch of him from his face to the toes of his boots wasn't covered in sticky red. Seeing Breeze and Dirk safe, he turned and strode toward the second cave, stopping a few hundred yards in front of the mouth. He drew in a surprisingly calm breath and let the magic in the ether fill him until he lost track of where the power ended and his flesh began. He thought of Myrddin in his last moments, the pain on his face as he told Octavian good-bye. Reaching out with his arm, Octavian shot a dozen boulder-sized balls of white-hot, magical fire deep into the second cavern. With a whoosh, everything within caught. Flames and smoke spilled from the irregular entrance. Octavian watched, feeling strangely detached and numb, feeling nothing, even at the horrible screams coming from inside. He raised his arm again and struck at the arch of the entrance. It crumbled and fell, followed by chunks of rock from above. In moments, the rockslide had sealed the opening. It muffled the screams but didn't silence them.

Breeze stood and jogged from his hiding place to grasp Octavian's shoulders and shake Octavian until his teeth rattled. Breeze looked frantic, his eyelids peeled back to reveal the whites of his eyes, his dark skin pale and grayish. "What in the fucking Shades' are you doing? You don't even know who was in there! Octavian, this isn't battle! This is—Goddesses, I don't know what this is!"

"I told you what I meant to do," Octavian said, his voice sounding faraway to his own ears, as dispassionate as if he recited a lesson. "You can still turn back."

"Don't you feel anything?"

Octavian tilted his head and considered. "No. Nothing beyond the need to finish what I started."

Before Breeze could argue, five men and three women, all of them in various states of undress, rushed from the third cave, no doubt roused by the quake Octavian had caused. One of them ran toward Breeze's back with a sword drawn, but before Octavian could prepare a spell, an arrow pierced his forehead and he dropped. The women shrieked and huddled together, trying to cover their bare breasts, as the other four men converged on Octavian and Breeze. Breeze ran to face the one nearest him, and their swords met with a resounding clang.

Octavian turned to Dirk and shouted, "Leave Eric Beasley! Eric Beasley is mine!" Through the smoke and chaos, he sought the man and found him near the far end of the camp, trying to escape with two of the women in tow.

Shouting his enemy's name, Octavian ran after him, ignoring the other three man. Either Dirk would see to him or he'd flank Octavian; Octavian didn't care. Nothing, no wound, would keep him from his vengeance. As he raced across the hard-packed, dry ground, he collided with one of the whores, and both of them landed on their sides. Octavian drew his dagger to strike, and the woman—or the girl, she couldn't have been more than fifteen or sixteen—squealed and shielded her face with her forearms. He wanted to run her through for holding him up, possibly giving Eric the chance to abscond. He wanted to cut her throat for selling herself to a man like Eric Beasley. She was no different from the men who'd fought beneath his banner; she hadn't bothered to find out who she was lying with. Octavian lifted his dagger. He couldn't forgive it. He'd been hungry and desperate too, but he'd never stooped so low.

At the last moment, he looked at her round red face, the tears spilling from her blue eyes, her running nose and quivering lips, and he stayed his hand. He hadn't compromised himself before, and he wouldn't sink to murdering a half-naked, unarmed girl. "Get out of my way," he snarled. He didn't wait to see if she ran, or where. Through the thickening haze, he located Eric Beasley, and with a swipe of his hand, Octavian cleared the smoke so they could face each other.

Eric grabbed one of the whores by her arm and held the point of his sword to her belly. "Turn around and get out of here, Octavian. Leave me alone or I'll kill her."

"And when you're finished, I'll kill you. I can wait while you kill the other one as well, if you have not sufficiently proved what a slithering coward you are. I don't want to see those women die, but it won't stop me. You took something from me, and I'm going to make you pay for it."

"You took something from me, you unnatural little harlot! My brother!" Eric flung the girl away from him, and she landed hard on her hip. The other woman hurried to help her up, and the two of them ran for a copse of stunted trees in the distance.

Octavian didn't bother explaining himself. He didn't care if Eric realized he'd been defending himself and that his brother had been an ass.

It didn't matter at this point. "I won't ambush you based on a lie, Eric. I'll give you the chance to behave as a man for once in your life and face me."

Eric looked from Dirk to Breeze, who stood behind Octavian, and he snorted. "So your friends can finish me off as soon as I best you?"

"No. This is to the death, and I give you my word, on Myrddin's grave, that if you kill me, they'll let you go. Unlike you, I'm a man of my word. Everyone knows it. Come on, then, Eric. You always thought you were better than me and now is your chance to prove it. Imagine the boasting you can do if you kill the commander of the Roses in single combat. But if you are too craven, I'll kill you where you stand. The only way out of this for you is over my body. Make your choice."

"Fine." Eric cut an X in the air in front of him.

"With honor, Myrddin," Octavian whispered to himself. "For you."

With his dagger in one hand and his sword in the other, Octavian pushed his right leg out behind him and sunk into a crouch. Eric's arrogance would compel him to attack first; he wasn't a man for strategy or analyzing his enemy's mind, and so Octavian waited. Eric didn't disappoint him. He charged Octavian with his sword raised above his head, and all Octavian had to do to avoid the blow was pivot the ball of his back foot slightly. Myrddin had taught him to fight efficiently and not waste his energy, and he had taken those lessons to heart. His attack dodged, Eric pitched forward, off-balance. Octavian spun, lifted his right leg, kicked him hard in the ass, and sent him facedown in the dirt. He could have finished him, but he took a step back and waited for Eric to scramble to his feet. Octavian wasn't prepared to let him off that easily.

Eric wiped the soil from his chin as he scowled at Octavian. He held his sword diagonally across his chest as he advanced, a little more wary this time. Octavian waited. He swung wide toward Octavian's belly, and Octavian deflected with his dagger. At the same time, he swung his sword and opened a superficial gash across Eric's thigh. Eric stabbed at his chest, and though Octavian hit him in the forehead with the pommel of his sword, Eric's blade dented his armor. Eric staggered backward, his hand pressed to his face and his sword dragging on the ground. Octavian took advantage of his distraction, dropped down, and kicked at Eric's ankles. Eric fell with a grunt to his back.

Octavian wanted it over. He stood over Eric, ready to drive his dagger through his heart. He couldn't wait to see his face twist up, see the fear and agony in his eyes that he'd seen in Myrddin's. He struck, but Eric raised his sword in time, and then he took advantage of Octavian's shock and kneed him in the groin. Even through his chain-mail tunic and leather leggings, pain exploded across the root of Octavian's body, and he fought to stay on his feet as his stomach clenched. He backed away from Eric, crossing his blades in front of his face in time to catch Eric's sword. He tried to return the favor and drive his heel into Eric's balls, but Eric avoided it with a step back and a lob of spit toward Octavian.

Octavian refused to let his anger distract him or make him sloppy. He let Myrddin's tutelage guide him as he watched Eric's face to predict his next move. Though Eric lifted his sword and feinted to the right, toward Octavian's shoulder, his eyes darted to Octavian's legs, and Octavian was ready to deflect the slash aimed at his knees. As they pushed their blades together, struggling to get the upper hand, Octavian drove his forehead against Eric's. Eric buckled, and Octavian punched him in the stomach. He doubled over, and Octavian hit him in the temple with the hilt of his sword. Goddesses, he couldn't deny it felt good to make Eric Beasley suffer. He was torn between wanting to make it last longer and finally ridding the world of the bastard. Eric's ankles crossed, and he fell on his side. When he raised his sword to protect himself, Octavian knocked it from his hand. Then he kicked him in the ribs and onto his back. He looked down at Eric's face. "This is for Myrddin, you son of a whore."

Eric reached for a small knife near his hip. Octavian brought his sword down and cut through his arm, severing it just below his shoulder. Blood spurted from the wound as Eric howled and writhed on the ground. Octavian watched, the satisfaction and redemption he'd expected absent. Kneeling, he poked his dagger into Eric's belly, and then into his chest. He watched his face contort with pain, watched his mouth gaping as he cried out, but it didn't negate Octavian's pain as he'd thought it would. He observed the man shrieking and bleeding in front of him, trying to feel anything at what he saw, before he raised his sword and decapitated him. Even the sight of Eric's head rolling away from his neck didn't satisfy Octavian. He sheathed his sword and dagger and walked away.

"What now?" Breeze asked.

"Nothing," Octavian said. That was what he felt: nothing. "Let's go home."

"And then?" Breeze persisted.

"And then nothing, Breeze! Nothing! None of it mattered. Nothing mattered. Just leave me… I need to be alone."

Alone, Octavian walked the few miles back to his horse. He barely noticed his surroundings, barely felt the ground beneath his feet. He didn't know what he'd expected to feel after killing Eric Beasley, but it wasn't this emptiness. Forcing his questions down deep, burying them, he gave his horse some oats and water before mounting up. Then he just let the horse walk as he slouched in the saddle. He didn't care where the animal wandered. It didn't matter. Nothing did.

Chapter
Twenty-Three

AFTER HE returned to the camp, mostly through the grace of his horse knowing the way home, he stumbled to the cairn and collapsed across the stones he'd laid as Myrddin's marker. He wanted to tell Myrddin about the battle, confess what he had done and how awful he already felt. He regretted everything and hoped wherever Myrddin was, he hadn't seen it. It would break his heart to see what Octavian had become only days after swearing to Myrddin he wouldn't. He couldn't tell Myrddin how he'd found no satisfaction in his vengeance or how hollow it had left him. His heart felt cold and decimated to ash. Aside from loss and pain, he couldn't imagine ever feeling anything again, but maybe that was for the best; maybe he deserved it. Octavian knew he was wallowing in self-pity, being selfish and pathetic, but what did it matter?

He went to one of their storehouses and opened a cask of strong wine. After filling his skin and returning to the ancient tomb, he started drinking. He didn't remember much after that.

He didn't remember how he'd gotten home or why he was lying on the kitchen floor with his shirt off. His head throbbed above his left eye, and when he reached up to touch his brow, flakes of dried blood fluttered down. Octavian dropped his head back to the floor harder than he intended, and his head vibrated with the impact. He screwed his eyes shut and waited for the spinning in his skull to wind down. Then he rolled onto his back and stretched out his arms and legs to take stock of injuries he had no idea how he'd sustained. Soon he realized he wasn't just missing his shirt but his trousers as well; he was completely naked. And he hurt everywhere. The sides of his ribs felt bruised; his knees and elbows were scraped raw. His tongue felt thick in his mouth and his throat felt like he'd swallowed gravel. Needing something to drink, he grasped the side of the table and hauled himself up. Bad mistake. The whirlwind in his head kicked up again, followed shortly by the lurching of his stomach. He hunched over and the contents of his stomach spattered the smooth stones of the floor.

He felt sick and wanted to get into bed. On his way, he tripped over his discarded breastplate, fell, and cut his chin open on the corner of a stand. He tried to catch the blood in his hand, but the sight and smell made him retch again, even though nothing remained to come up. Goddesses, where was Myrddin? Octavian called out to him, but he didn't come. Where was he? Holding onto the walls to steady himself, Octavian searched for him. He didn't feel well and wanted to be held and coddled, and he only trusted Myrddin with that weak part of himself. Why wasn't Myrddin here to take care of him?

Even though it hurt his head and made him dizzy, he looked around the room. The place was a disaster, dishes broken on the counter and spilling over to the floor, dirty clothes everywhere. Flies buzzed around a gnawed slab of ham on the counter. Myrddin's shirt hung over the back of a chair, and some of his socks littered the floor, but Octavian didn't see his armor or cloak…. Then he remembered where they were: in a hole in the ground, rotting. Gone. Gone, gone, gone. Octavian dropped to his knees and cradled his head in his hands, sobbing. He needed something to take the edge off this pain, needed some wine….

OCTAVIAN WOKE on the bed and reached for Myrddin. Why was he alone? He could smell Myrddin on the pillows and furs. He called out for him. Called again. Then he remembered, and though the first gulp of wine made him throw up, Octavian kept drinking.

SOME TIME later—he had no idea how many hours had passed—he heard Myrddin in the kitchen, humming softly as he often did as he cooked. The ladle clicked rhythmically against the pot as he stirred whatever he was making. Octavian smiled and stretched. His body still hurt and his nausea persisted, but at least all was right in the world again. Myrddin was home, making their dinner. He was where he belonged, where they'd promised each other they'd live and grow old. The little house they'd built together. The life they'd built. Thinking of simple things like sitting in front of the fire and darning their socks, sweeping the floor while Myrddin washed the dishes, facing each other in the bathtub while the spring scent drifted through the open windows, and sleeping late beneath layers of furs in the winter made Octavian weepy and emotional. He could tell Myrddin how those images in his imagination affected him. He could cry in front of Myrddin, and Myrddin wouldn't mock him; he'd hold him and kiss him and tickle his ribs until they stumbled into bed with Octavian smiling. He needed to smile. He hardly remembered how it felt.

Though he couldn't hear Myrddin anymore, Octavian swung his legs over the edge of the bed. After sparing a moment for his dizziness to pass, he rose and made his way toward the kitchen. He found it chilly and dark, stinking of rotten garbage. Snippet yowled and swatted at his feet; she was Myrddin's cat through and through. Why wasn't she perched on the table or a shelf begging for some of the scraps Myrddin always provided?

"Myrddin, love? I had the most terrible nightmare. Where are you? Come to bed, please. I need to be near you tonight, feel you next to me. Myrddin?"

The house was as quiet as a tomb, quieter than Octavian ever remembered. The walls didn't even creak in the breeze. No fire crackled in the hearth. The garland of dried herbs didn't rustle.

"Myrddin?" Octavian needed light, and he was too disoriented—too drunk—to feel out the flint and tinder, so he used magic to conjure some flickering pastel lights. They reminded him of the night in that little forest, and he expected to see Myrddin in front of him, smiling gently and looking at him like he was worth all the world and more. He saw only distorted images of dirty clothes, broken dishes, and bad food either he or the cat had left half eaten. He took a few more steps and shards of ceramic sliced the soles of his feet, but the pain was dull and distant. Myrddin had been here; Octavian was sure. Now he wasn't, and he never would be. Octavian stumbled to the table. His journal lay open to some foolish nonsense about communication between the way stations beyond the cairn. It was hard for him to believe he had cared so much about creating that system. When he tried dipping his quill, he spilled the inkwell, but he managed to crosshatch over the exposed page and flip to a clean one. Writing in big, crooked letters, he scrawled *Doesn't matter. Doesn't matter. No sense to it. No reason. No order from chaos. Fuck it. FUCK IT.*

Quite a few of the dozens of bottles lined up on the table still contained wine, much to Octavian's gratitude.

A LOUD sound, like the Shades pounding against the entrance to their cursed abode, woke Octavian and renewed the hammering in his skull. His eyeballs throbbed and his mouth tasted bitter. It took him a few moments to realize he was on the floor in the kitchen with something sharp poking against his waist. Twisting, he discovered the leg of a broken chair stabbing into his flesh. The thunderous pounding continued, and Octavian covered the back of his head with his arms and waited for it to go away. When it did, a wall of light struck Octavian in the face like sword of the goddesses. He winced away from the hurting radiance and threw up down his chest.

"Good goddesses, look at you." Octavian recognized the voice, though he didn't know why Breeze had to speak so loudly. He tried to shush him, but Breeze kept talking, his words bouncing off the walls and echoing in Octavian's aching head. "Fucking Shades. The smell in this place. It's disgusting. I might puke myself."

"Breeze?"

"Oh, very good. Do you know your own name too?"

Octavian hurt. His head throbbed and his heart raced. His body felt bruised and battered from forehead to foot. "Breeze, I want to go to bed." Octavian tried to stand, staggered, and smacked his face off the table. His jaw pulsed and swelled where it had struck the wood, and he had neither the strength nor the desire to get up. Strong lean arms encircled his waist and pulled him toward his bedroom. Octavian let himself be dragged, let himself be dropped onto furs stinking of vomit and urine. He didn't care; it felt too good to curl up in the warmth and softness, to be still and let the throbbing and whirling in his head subside.

"You sleep, Octavian. Sleep it off. I'm going to clean this disgusting shit-hole, and then I'm waking you up, so be ready."

OCTAVIAN WOKE to the scent of citrus, bright light, and Breeze shaking his shoulder. When he sat up in bed, his head spun and he threw up a little: a spoonful of foamy burgundy that dripped down his chest. He swiped the back of his hand over his mouth and waited for his vision to focus before cautiously looking around. He hardly recognized the place. The dirty dishes and clothes were gone, and everything had been polished to a sheen. Beyond the stink of his bed, the house smelled fresh, and the windows stood open, letting in the summer air. But Octavian flopped back down in his fouled furs. "I don't want to get up."

"Too bad." Breeze whisked the coverings off him and exposed his skin to the bracing air.

Octavian tried to curl up, drawing his knees to his chest, but Breeze tugged on his wrist. "A few more minutes," Octavian pleaded, burrowing his head into the pillow.

Breeze swatted his bare ass, not playfully. It hurt. "You've had nine days. Get your sorry arse up."

The sting of that smack stirred something Octavian had ignored, and his cock bucked. He rolled to his back and looked up at Breeze. Goddesses, he was beautiful with his thick black lashes and honey-colored eyes. His lips like wet brick. "Breeze." Octavian reached for him, tried to pull Breeze's mouth toward his own.

Breeze slapped him hard and sat up. "You think I'm going to make love to a man covered in his own vomit? Think again. You're not touching me, the way you smell. Come on. I drew you a bath. Luckily, I guess, you're already naked."

Breeze hoisted him from the bed and dragged him to the tub. The tub Myrddin had built for him. He didn't want to go into the bath, but Breeze forced him. He also forced him to drink tepid water from a clay cup when Octavian wanted wine. Breeze dipped a pitcher into the bathwater and poured it over Octavian's head. "You stink," Breeze said. He pressed a cake of yellow soap into Octavian's palm. "Wash yourself. I'll make something to eat."

Octavian dragged the soap clumsily over his body. He had no idea if he was doing a good job, washing properly. It took all his concentration to rub the yellow bar along his skin. The bubbles it formed in his chest hair distracted him. There were so many shifting colors in each little dome. Watching the teal and pink undulate over the bubbles fascinated him even while it made him sick. He looked away and slid down beneath the water, holding his breath. When he released it, some misshapen silvery bubbles zigzagged to the surface. He sat up and raked his fingers through his hair and over his face. When had his whiskers come in so thick? He'd have to shave. Myrddin liked him better—

"Breeze!" Octavian shouted. "Breeze, bring me some wine."

A moment later, Breeze scowled down at him. "You're bleeding fucked in the head if you think I'm letting you have any more wine, mate. Get out of the tub."

When Octavian hesitated, Breeze grasped both his hands and pulled him to his feet. He guided Octavian out of the water and handed him a towel. Dazed, not sure what was happening, Octavian dried off and wrapped the towel around his hips. Breeze took his elbow, led him to the table, and made him sit down in front of a plate of bacon, eggs, fried mushrooms, and toasted bread. Turning away, Octavian struggled not to throw up.

"Eat it," Breeze insisted.

"I-I can't."

"Do it anyway," Breeze said, touching the hilt of his sword near his hip. "And drink the water. Goddesses damn it, Octavian, I'll use force if I have to. Fucking eat."

Octavian took a few cautious sips of water and battled his gag reflex. He nibbled at the edge of the toast slathered in butter. After his stomach settled, he realized he had never been so hungry. He cleaned his plate, and Breeze scooped more meat and eggs onto it. Octavian ate until he couldn't force another bite down his gullet. The food and water cleared some of the haze from his head, and when he looked around his tidy kitchen, with the dishes stacked just the way Myrddin liked them, he started sobbing, pain racking his body.

Breeze pulled Octavian to his feet and folded Octavian in his arms. Octavian clung to him and cried. The pain was too much. He needed it to go away. Goddesses, he needed something to dull this agony. "Can I please have some wine?"

Breeze chuckled without amusement. "When the Cast-Down fuck the Mother Goddess like a street whore. I'm not letting you stay in this house and drink yourself to death. Bleeding Shades, mate. Do you think that's what Myrddin would have wanted?"

"What does it matter what he once wanted? He's gone." Octavian's voice caught in his throat. "Dead."

"But he left a legacy," Breeze said. "He left you. He changed the way you are and the way you see things. So either acknowledge he left the world a different place or tell me he contributed nothing, and that his life didn't matter."

Octavian wanted to beat Breeze to a pulp. "How dare you say his life didn't matter?"

"You're acting as if it didn't. Is this the man he taught you to be? Would he be proud, looking down on you now?"

Pushing Breeze away, sober enough to be angry, Octavian shouted, "You don't know! You don't how much this hurts! It's more than I can endure."

"I bet it is, and I don't know, not really," Breeze conceded. "But I know this. Myrddin would want you to live. Nothing would hurt him more than knowing you crawled into a bottle and never came out because of him. You know I'm right, and you know you have to lead this company. Men—families—depend on you now."

"How can I lead them?" Octavian stumbled to the wall, slid his back down, and leaned against it, and Breeze crouched down next to him. "All he wanted was to be at my side, and if I'd let him, if I hadn't fought like a child and guarded my stupid pride—"

"I know," Breeze said, resting his head on Octavian's shoulder. "Hindsight and all that. Fucked if I know what it all means, but I do know this: you're still alive, and you have to live. Live as a tribute to him. Let all the men and women and children who are safe and happy be his legacy. If you don't, this place is going to fall apart."

"How can I lead men, Breeze? I should have known what we were riding into. I did know, on some level, but I let arrogance cloud my instincts. He-he just wanted to come with me. Why didn't I let him come with me?"

"It's done, Octavian. The question is what you'll do now."

"I don't know if I can do it. I-I'm broken, Breeze. In a way I don't know if I can mend. What should I do? How can I live the rest of my life hurting like this?"

Breeze squeezed his shoulder. "I wish I knew what to tell you. Maybe don't think about it like that. Think about getting through the next few moments, making it to the end of the day. Getting through the night."

The thought of getting through the night made Octavian tremble. Nights, alone in the dark and the silence, were the worst. The only way he managed to sleep at all was by drinking until he passed out. The worms that had always wriggled at the edges of his thoughts had become serpents, wyrms worthy of legend, and they tore through his head, ripping with teeth and poisoned claws until he drowned them in wine. "Breeze, I…. Everything I see, everything I think about reminds me of Myrddin and what I've done." He paused, because his chest tightened and he had a hard time catching his breath. Repressed sobs shook his body. "I can't even think his name without crying."

"Cry, then," Breeze said. "There's no shame in it. The shame's in running away, hiding from the pain instead of facing it like you've always faced everything else. You're the bravest and strongest man I've ever met, the man who showed me what I wanted to strive for. You took a hit, a bloody bad one, and you're wounded—I know it—but you can either fight through it or you can lie on the ground and bleed."

"And what if I want to lie on the ground and bleed?"

Breeze raked his fingers through Octavian's damp hair and pushed it away to kiss his temple. "Lying there bleeding isn't in your nature. You've never given up on anything in your life, and because of that, you've done things the average bastard could never have dreamed of. What you're made of, the man you are, it's in your nature to fight. You have to fight now, mate. But you don't have to do it alone. I know I can't take his place, but I'm your friend, and I'm beside you. This place needs you. You can't let everything you and Myrddin built fall apart. He's gone, but he left something grand behind, and now it's up to you to look after it."

"What should I do?"

"Rest tonight. I'll stay if you want me to. We can talk, if you want, or you can tell me to shut my bloody fat mouth, and I'll do it. Tomorrow, you've got to get up and get dressed. Let the men see you're all right. Then, if you can, you should have a look at all the jobs that came in for us. I read over them, and I think if we divide up the men carefully, we can take most of them on. But I'll leave that for wiser heads. I'm only here to swing a sword."

Octavian shook his head, hugged Breeze, and chuckled for the first time in days or weeks. "You're as important to this place as I am. Nobody else had the stones to come here, drag my sorry ass out of bed, and tell me to stop drowning in self-pity and being a child. I can't promise you I can do it, but it means a lot that you care what happens to me."

"You can do it," Breeze said. "I'll see to that. I'm here to kick your ass if you try to crawl back in that bottle. I've still got my sword on me."

Octavian felt better than he had since before they'd left on that disastrous mission to meet with Captain Julien. He still hurt, still perched on the verge of breaking down, but he managed to enjoy being with Breeze, the warmth coming off his skin, the strength of his arms, his scent, and the comfort he provided. He knew if he asked Breeze would sleep next to him, and Octavian thought he would ask. Lying alone in the silent blackness terrified him more than any battle he'd ever faced, and the thought of turning in the night to find someone next to him made it a little less frightening. While he'd miss Myrddin every day of his life, it felt good to know he wasn't alone. Breeze would watch his back, help him up if he stumbled, and goddesses, he would need it. Coming back from this would be the greatest struggle he'd ever faced, and Octavian didn't know if he'd be victorious this time.

Chapter
Twenty-Four

OCTAVIAN ROSE'S Journal

Myrddin,

I miss you, my love. More than a year has passed, and I still expect to see you sitting at our table or sleeping in our bed. I look for you everywhere, and it's hard for me to accept that you're gone. I have been getting by, though I cannot say I am happy. I don't think I'll ever be happy in the way I was when we were together, but I face each day as it comes. My life without you is—the only adequate word is "diminished." Some days it's very hard to deal with a diminished life, with having so much less than I had before, but I force myself to go through the motions. Often, it feels like that's all I'm doing, but I must do it. So many people are depending on me.

The camp here at Rosecairn is always evolving. So many of the men have wives and families now that it barely resembles a mercenary fortress at all. There are houses, shops, children running and playing in the lanes, dogs and cats. Dirk recently welcomed his third child: a son. I am sorry you didn't get to see his twin daughters born. He named them Myrdda and Octavia, and they're beautiful, with the rich, honey brown skin of his wife and Dirk's red hair. Goddesses help him when those girls come of age! His newborn son is called Gale, because, in Dirk's own words, Flowers will bloom in the Shades' Abode before I name my son Breeze. I thought it would please you to know your old friend is doing so well. He misses you, of course, as we all do.

Jobs are going well. We have a full company of capable and honorable warriors under our banner now, love. I would not be boasting to say we probably have the finest force in Selindria or Gaeltheon, and the men are willing to fight for their home, for Rosecairn. By giving them something worth defending, we have ensured their loyalty. I always knew loyalty earned through love would be stronger than loyalty earned through greed or fear, and I'm happy to be proven right. Our men will fight because this is a good place for their families, a place they care about. To me, nothing could be nobler.

Now that you're gone, my love, these pages are again my only solace—the only place I can show weakness. And I feel very weak sometimes. I'm still lost without you, and maybe I always will be. But I have obligations, men to lead and families to support, and I am fulfilling my obligation. I want you to be proud of me. I want to be the man you saw when you looked at me, and I'm trying. Sometimes I don't know why, but then I think of what you would want, and I try to live. It's an odd existence, though. I feel trapped between the light of the living and the world of the Shades, but I go on, because I don't know what else to do. I wonder if one day the pain will fade and I'll be happy again. As always, I love you with the entirety of my spirit, and I will talk with you again soon. My heart is with you.

SUMMER FADED to fall and then to winter. The people of Rosecairn stockpiled supplies, and Octavian and Breeze rode out to check on the farmers living in their territory, making sure they had everything they needed to survive the cold, lean moons. Under the protection of the Roses, the properties in the area had prospered, and Octavian returned home secure in his belief that all of them would be fine through the winter. For the mercenaries, the dark part of the year meant fewer jobs and an opportunity to rest. Octavian thought he'd return to the perplexing problem of finding a way for the outposts to communicate through magic.

As the weeks and months passed and the world grew grayer and bleaker, Octavian assigned men to the jobs that came in. He went on a few himself, and in the long days between, he worked on his signaling system. He spent some of his nights with Breeze or one of the other young men new to the company, but he passed many of them alone, writing in his book or just staring into the fire in his hearth, thinking and remembering. He wished he'd known what he had with Myrddin when he had it. Maybe then he wouldn't have taken it for granted, would have cherished the connection they'd formed. He doubted he'd find anything as profound with another man. But he had friends to support him, and so he did the best he could.

LATE IN the winter, when all the men beseeched the goddesses to let the sun return and melt the snow, a quartet of messengers arrived at Rosecairn's gates. Karl led them to the center of the camp, and Octavian went to meet them with Breeze by his side. Their light leather armor, bows, and daggers marked them as scouts, while the quality of their gear and the horses they rode told Octavian they were part of the royal, or at least an aristocratic, force. He treated them accordingly.

"Please, honorable tams. My people will take good care of your horses. In the meantime, please come to my home for some refreshment."

When the four men had followed him and Breeze to his house and sat down at his table, Octavian sliced bread, cheese, and cold sausage and placed it on a platter for them. He opened a few bottles of wine and filled the four men's cups. "This fare is probably not what you're accustomed to, but I hope it will be welcome after a long ride."

"The food is appreciated," said one young man, "but we have little time to linger over it. We are in urgent need of your assistance."

"What are you hoping the Roses can do for you?" Octavian asked.

The young leader took a healthy gulp of his wine before speaking, and Octavian took a drink to brace himself. "Time demands I give you an abridged explanation, Commander of the Roses. The short version is that a group of traitors is camped outside L'Estrella Castle in Lockhaven, waiting to attack the fortress with King Agarick and his queen inside. The turncoat is trying to take the throne, and he commands a force far superior to our own. Within days, the enemy will attack, and we desperately need to augment our army. As it stands, we're hopelessly outnumbered. How many men can you have ready to ride out in the morning?"

Octavian held up a hand. "Don't get ahead of yourself. We don't take every job that's offered. First things first. What's the pay?"

"I can offer twenty-five gold per man per day," the scout said.

"How outnumbered are you?" Octavian asked. Then he used a ruse he'd employed successfully in the past. "And don't lie to me. I am a mage, and I'll know."

"Three to one," the young warrior said, hanging his head and focusing his gaze on the uneaten food on his plate. "We're desperate."

"In that case, our price might be higher," Octavian said. "Supply and demand. You understand."

"I was told this was a company of honorable men! Not money-grubbing—"

"Watch yourself." Breeze stood and put a hand on the hilt of the sword by his hip.

"We have honor, but we're still sell-swords," Octavian said. "Surely you knew that when you came here. I have men with families that need to be fed. This is not a charity."

The young warrior's face reddened and his lips twitched. "Tam, it seems you don't recognize the severity of this situation. Perhaps I have not been clear. A traitor is trying to overthrow the rightful king of Selindria, and he is close to success. Hearing that cannot mean nothing to you. Surely you want to aid your king and country!"

Octavian wondered if he'd been that idealistic a few years ago, his skin glowing and his eyes burning with the surety of his righteousness like this young man's did as he set his mouth into a hard line and stared at them. He still tried to be a good man, as he'd promised Myrddin he would, but he'd learned the value of practicality. In a battle like the one the scout had briefly described, some of his men wouldn't return. He had to at least provide for the families they'd leave behind. "The truth of the matter is, Gaeltheon, and not Selindria, has been my home for many years. Even if I still lived across the river, it matters little to me who rules. My day-to-day life and the lives of my men will not change if a different ass sits on the throne."

"Goddesses, have you no respect?" one of the other scouts said.

"I give respect where it is earned," Octavian answered. "I respect the lives of the men who have saved my life and fought beside me for years over some distant monarch who's never done anything for me and likely never will. If that's a truth you cannot handle, perhaps we have nothing more to say to each other. The Roses are hardly desperate for gold. However, if you'll hear my terms, if we can reach an agreement, you'll have the finest fighting force in either kingdom standing with you, and we'll fight for all we're worth. But I won't ask my men to enter into a difficult—if not impossible—conflict without suitable compensation."

"So your loyalty can only be bought," the leader of the scouts said, shaking his head. "Sad."

"I've had about enough of you, friend." Breeze took a few steps closer, moving around the end of the table to glare down at the other young man.

"Peace," Octavian said, touching Breeze's back. "Let's hear them out. If we don't like what they have to say, we'll send them on their way. After all, they cannot stop us. There are over four hundred men at the cairn, and probably two or three hundred others at outposts throughout our territory. They'd have to ride seventy-five miles to escape the Roses."

Breeze nodded though he neither sat down nor removed his hand from the hilt of his sword.

"Six hundred men." The scout blew air out between his teeth. "Goddesses, six hundred trained men might give us a chance. What is your price?"

"First off, I won't leave Rosecairn, the women and children who call it home, or our friends on the nearby farms, unprotected. If the battle will be a brief one—and it sounds as though it will—I can muster between 450 and 500 men… for a fee of fifty gold per man per day of fighting, and ten gold per day of traveling."

"That's an outrageous sum!" one of the men said.

Their leader rubbed his forehead with his finger and thumb. "Yes, but it's one our king will pay if it means the safety of his family and the security of his throne. Five hundred men will mean many less dead on our side. I-I'll agree to this if you can gather your force and be ready to ride in the morning. The time is short, and we might already be too late."

Octavian stood, and the two men clasped each other's arms over the table. "Every man under my banner is an elite warrior, tam. Every one is worth five ordinary soldiers at least. Our horses and equipment are second to none. You've made the right decision. Please finish your meal, and I'll find a place where you and your men can be comfortable for the night." Octavian turned to Breeze. "We must act quickly. Gather the men here at the cairn, and then send riders to the outposts. Tell them to leave two or three men at each station, and order the rest to arm themselves for battle and report here. Every man who wishes to go on this mission needs to be at the cairn by dawn."

Breeze left, and Octavian sat back down at the table. "Now, I need every scrap of information you have about what we'll face. Tell me the lay of the land, who is fighting, and the position of the soldiers to the best of your recollection. Tell me what kinds of weapons both sides are wielding. I won't let my men go into this at a disadvantage. It's my duty to see as many of them survive this conflict as I can, and I must devise a strategy."

THOUGH OCTAVIAN had stayed awake all night, studying the information the scouts had provided and formulating strategies and counter strategies until he felt sure he'd planned for every contingency, a few hours before dawn, he put on his armor and readied his two swords and his trusty old dagger. His blood hummed with excitement and his stomach flipped and twisted, so he ate only a few slices of bread dipped in mulled wine before making sure his surly cat had food enough for at least a few days and leaving his house.

At the center of the camp, hundreds of men surrounded the ancient monument, their ranks not only filling the clearing around the cairn but spilling to the spaces between the houses and buildings. They shuffled apart to allow Octavian to pass, and he found Breeze waiting for him at the center of the throng. After patting Breeze's shoulder, Octavian climbed a few feet up the cairn so he'd be seen and heard by all his men.

"This is probably the largest battle the Roses have ever taken part in," he told them, his breath as bright and glowing against the darkness as the snow around them. "All of you are my family, and I have never been dishonest. That doesn't change today. The truth is, we'll be outnumbered when we reach Lockhaven. We'll be fighting at a disadvantage, but it will not be the first time. There's not a man among you who I wouldn't trust with my life, and I don't exaggerate when I say that you are the best-trained and deadliest force on either side of the river. Uphill battles are nothing new for any of you, or, for that matter, our predecessors here at Rosecairn.

"Most of you know the story of the monument behind me, but it bears repeating now. A castle once stood on this ground, and inside it lived Lady Philomene, a kind and beautiful woman cursed with a husband as cruel as he was ugly, a bitter old man who could not even make love to his wife. Out of loneliness and despair, Philomene spent her days staring out the window of the tower where her lord kept her prisoner. One day she saw a handsome young soldier with kindness in his eyes, but he was a lowborn soldier, a common fighting man like all of us. Still, the lady vowed to meet him and speak with him if she could. Somehow, she managed to convince her husband to let her clip roses in the garden to decorate and perfume her quarters. That soldier's name is lost to history and legend, but this much is known: Lady Philomene saw beyond his station, saw his courage, his goodness, his humility, and his honor, and they fell in love.

"When the lady could sneak away to meet with her lover, she dropped a white rosebud from her window for him to find. It was a dangerous risk, but in that man's arms, she found the only happiness she'd ever experienced." Octavian's voice hitched a little as he remembered his happiness in Myrddin's arms and how he hadn't known what he'd found until he lost it. After taking a deep breath, he continued.

"The lady grew plump with child, a child her impotent husband knew didn't belong to him. No one had the courage to stand against him as he dragged Philomene to the block and beheaded her, ending her life along with the baby in her belly. One man, at least, had the courage to stand against the wealth and power of that cruel lord: her lover. And he was not alone. The warriors who fought with him joined his crusade, and outnumbered three to one, those twenty-one prevailed against the superior force. Honor, courage, and dedication brought them victory over numbers and gold. Though they knew none of them would survive their injuries, through sheer will alone, they razed the castle to the ground and used the stones to construct this cairn as a monument to Lady Philomene and her lover, a man who valued bravery and commitment more than his own life. That day, those men proved that a small group of men fighting for something they believe in can overcome three times the number of soft, spoiled aristocrats. The goddesses saw their sacrifice and could not let it go unnoticed. Roses grew from the stone even as the men lay down and breathed their last. The briar fronds wreathed their bones, and blossoms opened in the sightless hollows where their eyes had once beheld the true meaning of honor and courage.

"We of Rosecairn carry on a legacy—a legacy of simple soldiers who know victory comes from strength, skill, and dedication, and not from a meaningless title. The bones of those brave men—their blood—

feeds this ground and these flowers. The best and bravest men who ever walked in the light of this world rest below those stones, and one day, all of us will join them there. We must be worthy. We'll be fighting superior numbers, just as they did, but as they did, we will succeed. We'll succeed for the future generations who will hear our story and draw inspiration from it. Today is our day to show what ordinary men can do when their spirits are strong and their motives are noble!"

Octavian raised his sword above his head, and the thunderous cheers of his men answered him. For the first time since he'd lost Myrddin, Octavian felt some of the old fire to prove himself, to show the world what he and his men could do. He felt confident, felt the lust for battle surging through his veins. "To battle!"

"To battle!" the warriors repeated.

"For Rosecairn!"

"For Rosecairn!" the men echoed.

Before the momentum he'd built fizzled out, Octavian went to his horse and mounted up. Waving his sword, he rode through the camp and out the gate, with his army cantering behind him, toward the greatest test they'd ever faced.

Chapter Twenty-Five

AFTER RIDING hard, the Roses crossed the Starlight Bridge into Lockhaven on an overcast, blustery day. The air was cold, dry, and as sharp as steel as the wind pushed the powdery snow in serpentine trails and pelted their exposed skin with icy crystals. When they came within a few hours' ride of where they suspected the battle would take place, Octavian stopped to confer with Breeze, Karl, and the other men who led the infantry when they caught up with him.

"There's something very important I need to tell you." Octavian looked at the scouts—soldiers of Lockhaven, he'd learned—on their horses a few hundred feet away. He wanted to make sure they weren't overheard. "The royal forces have a plan in place, a sort of last resort, in case the battle can't be won. I haven't been able to pry many details from the scouts, but I do know it's some sort of devastating magical spell, one that will endanger allies as well as enemies. I can already feel magic at work—something… something unlike I have ever imagined. Raw power without a will to control it. Now, we're here to do a job, and we'll do it to the best of our ability. We'll fight hard. That said, the lives of all of you and the rest of these men mean more to me than any amount of gold." Octavian touched the ram's horn hanging from his belt. "If I think this company is in trouble, I'll sound the retreat. We all know what a group of mercenaries are worth to the nobility. They don't care if we're wiped out, but I do. The lives of my people are my priority. So if I sound the retreat, I'm counting on you to get our men out of there. Look to me and me only, because these others do not have our interests at heart. They'll sacrifice our whole company if it means a victory for their king."

The others nodded, and Octavian studied their eyes to make sure they understood. "No matter what, retreat if I signal it."

After they agreed, swore their compliance, they rode the last few miles toward L'Estrella Castle.

MYRDDIN, LOOK at it. Goddesses.

Octavian had never seen anything like the battle they approached, already raging on the chilly moors in front of the castle of the valen of Lockhaven. Thousands of men clashed, stirring up dirt and snow, their blood already soaking the ground. Amidst the chaos, it was hard to tell what was happening, but as Octavian reined his horse to a slow trot, he got a vague idea.

The enemy fighters had those loyal to the crown almost completely surrounded, boxed in on all sides by the superior force. From an outcropping above the battlefield, royal archers did their best to make an opening for their comrades. Octavian sensed a wellspring of arcane energy coming from that direction, magic burbling up, unable to be contained. Soon bolts of bright blue lightning struck the enemy force, opening pockets for their allies to escape. As Octavian watched, their adversaries figured out their tactic, and a large group of them advanced on the archers and the mage atop the bluff. A big knight, fighting like a man possessed, carved a path through the enemies, calling for his warriors to protect the archers and the mage. His fighting skills impressed Octavian; he actually managed to fight his way through heavy resistance and up the hill.

The time had come for the Roses to join the battle. Most of their enemies focused on the archers and the mage, while the rest faced the pocket of resistance they'd corralled between them. Octavian thought they could flank them, take down dozens of men with their backs turned, before the enemy even became aware of their presence. He gave the order, and the Roses rode forth. Octavian's strategy served them well, and they sank their swords into the backs of enemy warriors before they had a chance to turn around. The Roses cut through one layer of the ring surrounding their allies, and then another. They had almost reached those they'd been hired to fight beside when their opponents realized the Roses posed a greater threat than the archers on the crag. With a motion like the swell of a wave, the enemies turned and surged down the hill toward Octavian's fighters. He yelled to the men at the back of their group to protect their flank. He didn't want to end up surrounded like his allies had been when they'd arrived, and he wanted the way clear in case they needed to retreat.

Though Octavian wanted to keep an eye on the bluff—something about the magic coming from it felt terribly wrong—adversaries trying to cut him down soon commandeered his attention. A man in heavy plate and a yellow cape—Windwake bairny?—grabbed Octavian's ankle and tried to pull him from the saddle. With a slash of the sword in his left hand, Octavian severed his arm. The man fell, and Octavian's horse reared in terror at the blood and chaos around her. He managed to bring her under control and urge her forward, through a few more knights on the ground, hacking and stabbing at enemies as he went. He and the Roses had almost opened a channel for the royal forces to escape; something told Octavian they would need to run from this battlefield sooner rather than later. The magic in the air grew so heavy that Octavian felt it pressing down on him, pulling his senses in every direction, making his teeth hum and his spine wiggle inside his body. Sparing a glance, he saw a peculiar, bluish silver aura surrounding the mage on the outcropping.

A mounted man swinging a flail drew Octavian's attention. He raised the sword in his left hand to deflect the knight's blow while he drove his quick, sharp dagger into his body below his breastplate. The thin, sharp blade cut through the man's chain mail and sank between his ribs. Octavian drew it back as fast as he could and drove the point into his enemy's belly. The man fell from his horse, and Octavian turned to face his next opponent, arcing his sword to deflect the man's weapon. They scuffled, trading blows, their horses dancing beneath them, until Octavian finally saw an opportunity and drove the point of his dagger through the other warrior's eye. He slumped to the foul, bloody ground, and Octavian urged his mount on.

Octavian didn't want to put himself or his men into a position where they couldn't escape if they had to. He didn't want them surrounded, so instead of charging forward, he moved to the right, trying to chip away at the enemy force still surrounding their allies. The Roses followed his lead, but a big man on a black charger swung a club, hit Octavian in the chest, and sent him over his horse's haunches and to his back in the bloody snow, gasping for breath. He managed to roll out of the way of the blow meant to shatter his skull and get to his feet with his lungs starving for air. He raised his dagger, repelled his enemy's blow, and kicked the man hard in the knee. His horse reared and threw him, and the big knight barely escaped the frantic animal's hooves by rolling free. Octavian drove his elbow into another enemy's face and hurtled a body to reach his adversary. When the other warrior rose into a crouch, Octavian drove his blade into the back of his skull and left him twitching and bleeding at his feet. Another fighter took his place; they seemed endless, and Octavian realized how outnumbered they were. He raised his hand, summoned his magic, and sent every man within ten feet of him sprawling, numb with lightning, and sapped in strength. It gave him an opportunity to survey the field and catch his breath, even if it did draw attention to him and mark him as a threat.

Most of his men still stood. They could break through the resistance and join their allies, but something was wrong. The cords of magic winding through the ether converged above the bluffs where the archers stood. Octavian had never felt anything like it. If his power was a swiftly flowing stream, then this was an ocean that could tear down the mountains. His teeth, every bone in his body, shook with the power saturating reality. After fighting through a few stragglers, he turned and ran east toward the edge of the fray. Octavian sheathed his blades, raised the horn to his lips, and sounded the retreat. Nearby, a riderless white horse picked around some fallen men. Octavian caught the horse's reins and swung into the saddle where he had a better view of the fighting.

His men remained clustered together, fighting back to back as they'd been trained, but the superior enemy force was closing in around them, swallowing them and blocking their way out. Frantic now, more terrified than he'd ever been during a battle over what he felt in the air, Octavian blew the horn again, hoping his people heard it over the din. A few of them looked in his direction, and they shouted to their comrades, but the fighting around them had grown thick and desperate. They wouldn't be able to get away quickly, and Octavian knew time was running out for every man on that field. When the magic building over the bluff released—Goddesses, his wildest imagination couldn't picture what would happen. It felt like it would rip the mountains up by their roots. He had to get his people to safety, and now, especially since the noble factions had begun their own retreats. Taking a page out of the other mage's book, Octavian heeled his horse's ribs, closed the distance, and knocked enemies out of the way with magical force and lightning.

As soon as he opened a channel, Octavian blew the horn again. "Retreat!" he screamed until his voice cracked. "Now! Turn and run! Goddesses, run!" He yanked his reins and spun the horse in a circle.

Everything seemed quiet and slow as he looked over his shoulder, hoping his people followed his signal. Something was coming—something big, bigger than he could comprehend—and he needed to get his men away from it. The Roses, as well as the allies they supported, rode hard to the east, trying to escape the fray as the gray clouds above them split open and fire-colored light shone through the fissure. Sparks spattered the ground like drizzle as an orange glow surrounded the mage on the outcropping. Octavian just wanted to get his people away from whatever was coming, and he blew the horn again as he waved with his arm.

Not only the Roses, but all the men loyal to the throne, retreated toward the Kanda River miles in the distance. The sky broke open, and a column of fire stretched from the firmament to the ground. A wave of heat and force roiled across the land, knocking men off their feet or out of their saddles. They no longer had to encourage the animals to run. The terrified horses whinnied and screamed, some of them tripping and breaking legs to get away from the fire falling from the heavens. Octavian couldn't stop to help. A fissure had opened in the sky, and fire poured down in sheets. Tongues of flame taller and wider than the horses swirled in a funnel. A white-hot wall stood in front of them, and ash rained down like snow, choking Octavian and filling his chest. Knowing he wouldn't survive much longer, he dropped his face to his horse's mane, covered the back of his head with his arms, and kicked the animal hard.

Intense heat enveloped him, stealing his breath and making his skin feel like it melted. He smelled his hair burning and tasted charcoal in his throat. It only took a few moments to pass through the fire, but Octavian felt like he'd emerged from the Shades' Abode. Balls of flame the size of boulders still rained down, the ground had been scorched black, and everything that could catch was on fire. The exodus was frantic and chaotic, with men who'd been fighting to the death only moments ago all running together, some on foot and others on horses. Octavian had no time to try to rally his people. They would know to return to the cairn. He only hoped he'd sounded the horn in time, that most of them had made it. Only a fool would expect all of them to reach safety when fire surrounded them and fell from the sky.

After a few miles of hard riding, Octavian and some of his people reached what looked like a farm. With fire still pouring down on them, some of the men broke through the iron gate to seek shelter in the buildings inside. Octavian kept riding, wanting only to reach the river, the blessed brown water and the bridge back to Rosecairn. He pushed the horse until he worried he'd kill the animal, silently promising it that it would lead a life of leisure in a paddock if it got him away from the carnage. Even after miles, smoke hung in the air and everything smelled of burned flesh and sulfur. Octavian didn't slow down until his saw the ancient stone columns marking the entrance to the Starlight Bridge.

To let the poor horse rest, Octavian stopped. The air here was crisp and clear and tasted of the river, but to the west, a swirling inferno that dwarfed L'Estrella Castle still burned bright against the black smoke rising like a giant mushroom. Octavian dismounted and pulled off his gloves. The minor burns on his hands and forearms weren't worth the magic they'd take to heal, so he turned his attention to the open wounds on his horse's snout, neck, and shoulders, using his arts to close them to satiny pink. The animal nickered and butted its nose against his shoulder. That horse had been a gift from the goddesses, and Octavian intended to keep his word and let her—he had the time now to notice she was a mare—live a life of luxury, maybe have a few foals.

Though his eyes stung, his throat felt torn to pieces, and he couldn't quite catch his breath, Octavian called out, "How many men here are Roses?"

Men—at least fifty of them—pushed their way through the throng. Karl came to the front of the group, his complexion as ashen as the debris falling from the sky. "Goddesses, Octavian. What was that?"

Octavian tried to fill his chest with air but couldn't quite do it. "Magic. More magic than I thought this world contained. Sisters, I—I cannot believe anyone would use that spell. It could have leveled an army five times that size. The bleeding dullard likely killed as many of his own men as he did enemies. Is—is this all of us?" Feeling suddenly dizzy, Octavian sat down in the snow and dropped his forehead into his hand. He didn't care what the others thought; he was just happy to be alive.

"Not all of our men came this way," Karl said. "When-when the fire started coming down, everyone scattered. Some of them went north, others south. It may take some time to make it home."

Octavian lifted his head and nodded. Scanning his filthy, bloody, and soot-covered men, he couldn't help noticing Breeze wasn't among them. He tried not to despair—Karl had told the truth about the messy retreat, and maybe Breeze had gone through the gate of the farm they'd passed—but Breeze was the best friend he had left, and he didn't know if he'd survive losing him.

"What should we do now?" one of the men asked.

Octavian got to his feet and closed his eyes until his head stopped spinning. Slowly, the clean air was clearing his head. "We must go back to the cairn. We've left it vulnerable. There, I'll attend to your wounds, and Lena can help. We'll see to our animals. Our men know the way home. All we can do is wait—and hope."

BACK AT the cairn, Octavian and Lena spent the next four days healing the men and horses. Octavian learned a great deal from her about caring for burns. Unlike cuts and other wounds, the flesh healed in unpredictable patterns, and while magic could be used to urge the skin and flesh to regrow, it couldn't replace tissue that had been destroyed. A few of the men would be forced into retirement, but most of them would come through with only some small scars.

Men trickled in over the next moon until about twenty were unaccounted for, Breeze among them. News also found its way to their gates through farmers who had been to market and traveling merchants. At what was now being called the Battle of the Starlight Bridge, the mage Yarroway L'Estrella, younger brother of the valen, had summoned fire from the sky and decided the skirmish. Taran Edercrest, leader of the traitors, had somehow died before the battle, and Agarick, king of Selindria, had been assassinated in his bed. His son, Garith, ascended to the throne and married Cothryn of Gaeltheon, creating a union between the two most powerful kingdoms in the known world. People were already calling it the Blessed Epoch and anticipating a long period of peace and prosperity. Octavian wasn't sure things were so simple, but he knew the young monarch owed him and his men a great deal of gold, and soon he'd ride to the royal estate in Meritage to collect.

Rumors, and some from reputable sources, circulated that the new king's highest priority was reclaiming the disputed territory along the river and solidifying his twin kingdoms. He certainly had the resources to accomplish it, with both Selindria and Gaeltheon behind him, and Octavian wondered what it would mean for Rosecairn. It didn't matter. Though they held no official claim to it, he and his men would defend the home they'd made. Too many had bled and died for Rosecairn to hand it over to an entitled, greenhorn king younger than Octavian. Garith and his knights would find their hands full if they tried drive the Roses away.

Even so, Octavian thought it might be prudent to bolster his ranks. He put out the news that he'd be recruiting, and he received an overwhelming response. Young hopefuls and seasoned veterans alike arrived at the gates almost every day. Octavian chose carefully and had soon augmented his force by nearly a hundred men, and between the outposts and the camp itself, he could support many more. Arranging shelter for them, assessing their skills, assigning missions, and training them filled much of his time, and Octavian was glad to have the distraction. Staying busy from dawn till dusk kept the worms at the edges of his thoughts mostly still, buried beneath more immediate concerns. If their crawling and wriggling to get to the front of his thoughts troubled him at night, he drowned them in wine.

Octavian hoped Breeze would be by his side as he faced the new challenges awaiting them, and so he waited. He waited through the springtime, manning the watchtowers overlooking the gates as often as he could, and through the summer moons. Day after day, he looked out over his lands, watching them turn from vibrant green to faded ochre, watching the sheep and goats wander across the windswept, rocky ground until their keepers moved them to stables for the cold part of the year, which waited just around the bend. When the first leaves began to color and curl on the branches and the air coming down from the mountains grew chilly at night, Octavian accepted that Breeze wouldn't be coming back. He used magic to inscribe Breeze's name into one of the stones of the cairn, and he mourned him with only slightly less wine than he'd had when he'd mourned Myrddin.

Chapter
Twenty-Six

AFTER THE Battle of the Starlight Bridge, Karl and many of the older warriors had chosen to retire. Quinn married, bought a small farm and a herd of goats, and discovered a buried passion for making gourmet cheeses. By late that summer, he'd already made a name for himself in their little northern corner of the world, tucked away in the shadow of the mountains, and finer inns and taverns proudly served his delicate cheeses and spreads. Karl had declared himself "too old for this nonsense," but he loved the home he'd built on the western side of the cairn, not far from the water, and so he offered to stay on and train some of the new recruits.

On his way to the watchtower, Octavian stopped for a few moments to observe their progress. They were quickly becoming skilled warriors, and soon enough, he'd be able to assign them to some of the less dangerous posts and let them get some combat experience under their belts. In the meantime, he needed to house them, and had ordered some of the men between jobs to begin construction of three large bunkhouses that would accommodate thirty men apiece. If his ranks continued to swell, he'd need more. Summer faded with each passing day, and the cold would descend on Rosecairn like a bird of prey. He couldn't have men sleeping in tents when the snow started.

Octavian reached the tower and ascended the steep steps. The sun beat down too bright and hot for this late in the year, and it washed the countryside to pale yellow dotted by blue-gray stone. The high grass looked almost like water as the wind rippled its surface in undulating waves. Octavian knew he should let some of the men move into Breeze's old house. It would sleep at least three or four men, and it did no one any good locked up and standing empty. Not even the most optimistic of fools would imagine Breeze would return at this point, not after nearly half a year. But letting someone else move into the house still felt too final, more of an end than inscribing his name on the stone. Myrddin had died in his arms, left him with irrefutable proof of his passing, but Breeze—maybe Breeze—Octavian swiped the heel of his hand across his eyes and wiped his nose on the back as he remembered working with his friend to construct the little stone cottage. Like Octavian, Breeze hadn't wanted anything fancy, just a comfortable place to enjoy a meal after a hard fight, a place to sit by the fire when he had to hang up his sword.

Goddesses, would any of them live to see old age? Octavian wasn't sure he desired that; he already felt worn thin, as if those damned insects in his head had chewed away everything that made him want to go on living and left him empty. When he'd visited his father's mill as a boy, he'd seen the burrows the termites had left in the wood and the sawdust on the floor beneath them. Sometimes he felt like all he held was sawdust—the chaff left behind when everything strong and pure had been chewed away. It was a silly poetic comparison, and Breeze or Sylvain would have teased him. Myrddin wouldn't, but if Myrddin still stood with him, he'd purse his lips and blow all the fetid debris away. Octavian felt more hollow than hurt, and he supposed that was a blessing. Besides, he commanded the Thorns of Rosecairn, and he had no time to feel sorry for himself.

The unseasonable heat continued for the next week, and Octavian spent most of his afternoons in the tower. The magical communication system would soon be more crucial than ever. He'd nearly figured it out, though even that victory left him underwhelmed. Closing his book, he returned his attention to staring out over his land. A few hours later, a lone figure approached the gate, and Octavian sat up straighter and leaned over the ledge for a better view. Sunlight glinted off metal, so Octavian assumed either a messenger or another hopeful approached. Something about the way the man moved seemed vaguely familiar, though the pronounced limp didn't. With the sun shining almost directly in his eyes, Octavian couldn't make out many details, even when the man stopped a few hundred feet away.

"Stop there," he called. "Announce yourself."

Breeze opened his hands and held them out to his sides. "Fabrezio Orvina d'Caelus. Not that you can pronounce it, you old bastard! Get your ass down here and let me in!"

"Goddesses," Octavian gasped, his eyes stinging. Everything frozen up and clogged inside him thawed in an instant and flooded his chest like the water rushing down the mountains in the springtime. The sawdust scattered and left him clean and exposed. He ran down the steps and directed his man at the other tower to open the gates, and as soon as he could, he flung himself into Breeze's arms, needing to feel him, know he was real, and that Octavian's mind hadn't finally crumbled. Goddesses, he was warm, his arms around Octavian were solid, and he smelled a little of sweat and the dirt of the road. It was wonderful, and Octavian pressed his face against Breeze's neck so he could taste the salt on his skin as he chuckled with relief. "Breeze, you slippery son of a bitch! We all thought you perished in the Battle of the Starlight Bridge. I'm glad to see we jumped to a premature conclusion. I should have known it would take more than a mad mage and the heavens raining fire to finish *Fabrezio Orvina d'Caelus*."

Though something about Breeze's expression looked both softer and wiser, he rolled his eyes, and it was as if they'd never been apart. Octavian couldn't stop smiling as he led the way back to his house. Lately he'd spent as little time—at least as little time sober—inside the cottage as he could. It was too full of ghosts. But with Breeze here and the light streaming in through the windows, ripe apples on the table, and bread rising on a shelf, it felt bright and clean, the home he'd intended when he'd built it. Breeze followed him into the kitchen, where they sat facing each other at the table beside an open bay window. "Tell me what happened to you," Octavian urged. "Were you hurt?"

They spent the next hour or so discussing what had befallen Breeze after the battle. He'd been badly burned and thought he was done for. He told Octavian he didn't remember anything after running through the gates of the farm they'd passed, hoping to seek shelter in a shed or a barn. Then, a moon later, he'd woken in a bed with his wounds bandaged and on their way to healing. Breeze's cheeks pinked a little, and his eyes glazed as he told Octavian about his savior: a vintner called Alain Lamont. Alain had taken Breeze into his home and cared fastidiously for his burns. Octavian knew very well what a gruesome job it could be to care for burns, and he inspected Breeze's skin. A wide patch of mottled flesh stretched from the corner of his jaw almost to his knee on the left side. The scars were severe and would probably be with Breeze all his life, but the care he'd received impressed Octavian. This vintner knew what to do and had clearly done it regularly. It was hardly a surprise Breeze held him in such high regard. Only a remarkable man could find the strength to endure the grisly treatment. It certainly wasn't for the faint of heart.

Octavian used his skills to ease the stiffness in Breeze's arm and leg, where he'd been burned down to the muscle and could no longer fully extend his limbs. Though it took more out of Octavian than he let on, he managed to coax the muscles to lengthen, and he gave some of his energy to Breeze to strengthen them. It exhausted him, but he managed to return full range of motion to Breeze's arm and leg. He regretted he'd be able to do little about the scarring, but Breeze didn't seem to mind. Odd. He'd been every bit as vain and as much of a sensualist as Octavian. Something about him seemed more content, but sad at the same time. As he spoke of Mountain Shadow Winery, Alain, his children, Courtenay and Fenn, and the work they'd done together, Octavian intuited what had happened while Breeze had been away. He wondered why Breeze had left when he'd fallen in love with the vintner, and he hoped it wasn't just loyalty. Octavian appreciated loyalty, but he didn't want to stand between Breeze and what might be Breeze's one chance at happiness—as Myrddin had been his.

He questioned Breeze carefully, and Breeze assured him he was glad to be home and ready to take up his sword again. He was a grown man and capable of making his own choices, so Octavian didn't argue. Maybe he was being selfish, but if Breeze wanted to stay, Octavian was glad to have him.

Soon they were laughing, gossiping, and catching each other up on the months they'd spent apart. Octavian told Breeze of the new king's plan, and Breeze asked him a favor.

"Alain took care of me for moons and moons and asked nothing in return. He's… a good man. A man with a lovely family. But he's been having some trouble with a merchant out of Felgard. Alain thinks it's over, but I know better. This hog-fucking piece of filth is only getting started, and Alain and his family, they don't deserve it. I was thinking maybe we could help them a little, pay back some of what he did for me."

"Who is this man who's threatening your friend?"

"Greasy pig, name of Wagonnier Almes."

Octavian curled his lip. "I know the man. He has tried to hire us on a few occasions, and I declined every time."

"Why? What jobs?"

"Mostly eliminating his competition—other merchants, and most of them honest. That's not the reputation I want for the Roses. I told him we're not assassins. That's not what you're asking me to do, is it, Breeze?"

"Pherara, Octavian. If that's what I wanted to do, I could do it myself. But no. Alain wouldn't want him killed. He'd be… disappointed. I only just convinced him we're not the same as the Cast-Down. No, I just want to pay him a visit, and I want you to come with me."

"Why?"

"Because you're Octavian Rose! If you tell him to keep away from Alain, he'll do it. I mean, if you want to threaten him a little…."

A wicked smile spread over Octavian's face. "I see. I owe your friend Alain a debt for looking after you and getting you back to me mostly whole, and besides, what you propose sounds like a great deal of fun. This man thinks too highly of himself. Someone should show him his gold doesn't make him untouchable, and it might as well be me. We'll ride for Felgard in two days, and we'll take a dozen of the men along."

"Octavian, this means a lot to me."

"It's good to have you back, Breeze. Just see I don't lose you for so long again."

IN THE weeks that followed their wildly successful and extremely satisfying "conversation" with Wagonnier Almes, Breeze grew more withdrawn until he was like a ghost haunting the edges of the camp when they weren't on a job. Even when fighting, he seemed distracted. Most evenings, instead of coming to the central fires, enjoying the warmest autumn Octavian could remember, drinking, brawling, and assessing the new young men on offer—all the things he'd claimed to miss—Breeze stayed on his porch or sat alone by the cairn, playing with a glass vial he always kept in a pocket. Octavian had him back… but not all of him. Breeze had left something behind, and Octavian knew where. Still, Breeze wanted to continue his career as a warrior, and Octavian would never turn such a skilled man away, friend or not.

Some wounds took years to heal, goddesses knew he understood that, and so he would give Breeze time.

But then, on what should have been a simple mission, one Octavian wouldn't have bothered with if the pay hadn't been so impressive, Breeze had been lost in his head, his heart somewhere other than the battle. If Octavian hadn't been quick to intervene, he would have been killed while he daydreamed. When they returned to the camp that night, Octavian knew he had to confront Breeze. He'd never ask him to leave, but he had to find out what he needed, how to fix him, and until he did, he couldn't let Breeze fight. His life might not be the only one lost if he couldn't concentrate. Octavian was Breeze's friend, but tonight he had to be his commander.

As usual, Octavian found Breeze on his porch, toying with his little vial. He quickly slid it into a pocket when he noticed Octavian approaching, and then showed Octavian such a sorry excuse for a smile that it broke Octavian's heart. He sat down next to Breeze and handed him a bottle of wine. "Probably not as good as you're used to now."

After taking a long pull from the bottle, Breeze wrinkled his face and forcibly swallowed before he muttered a few words of thanks to Octavian for sharing.

"Breeze, what in the Shades' happened today?" Octavian asked.

"Seems like we won," Breeze said, taking another swig from the bottle. The face he pulled this time didn't seem as pained.

"Goddesses." Octavian drank. "We're friends. I have never seen you so distracted in battle before. I have never seen you as you've been these past few weeks. Do you think I don't see you, sitting out by the cairn all day, staring off into the sky and playing with whatever you keep in that little bottle? Breeze, you're pining."

Breeze prickled. "Oh, fuck you, Octavian. I am not pining. Are you calling me a lovesick maiden?"

"Lovesick, maybe. Tell me I'm wrong. Tell me I have you back, all of you, that you didn't leave your heart and spirit on that vineyard. That was where your head was in the fight today, wasn't it? With your vintner."

"It won't happen again," Breeze said.

"I think it will," Octavian said.

"If you don't want me in this company, Octavian, just say so. If I'm not worthy of the Roses, I'll leave."

"No, friend, you misunderstand. Alain Lamont. Tell me about him."

Breeze chugged a few healthy gulps of the cheap wine. "Alain—goddesses. Beautiful. Fucking amazingly beautiful. White skin, quick to blush. Hair like sunlight, eyes like the sky. He hates to be teased. Sensitive, you know? He's… good. Puts everyone ahead of himself. Suffers so others will be happy. Just like when he took care of me. What he did for me—I don't know if I could have done it. I thought he was soft, pampered, but he's stronger than I am."

"And what do you want?" Octavian coaxed.

"I want him to be happy. Not have to worry so much." Breeze swallowed more of the bitter wine, drinking as if he competed with Octavian. Or maybe, like Octavian, he had something inside he wanted to wash away. "I-I want him to get to dance. He should dance every day. He should have someone he can always rely on. In celebration, or to cry against. He should have someone to protect him, someone he knows won't flinch no matter how ugly it gets. I—Goddesses. I want it to be me. I want him to know I'm the one who always has his back, who'll hold him up when he needs it. When he needs someone who'll never let him down, I want him to think my name. But I can't be that man."

"Why not?" Octavian asked.

"I'm not worthy of him, not good enough. Not for him and Courtenay and Fenn."

"Who says so, Breeze? Who says you're not good enough? Your Alain? I doubt it. It's the poison your parents planted in your head. I know it well."

"So what do I do? I'm a warrior. I don't know how to do anything else. This is home. Rosecairn is the first place I've ever felt useful."

"The first, but maybe not the only," Octavian said. "You are a fine fighter, and you'll always have a place by my side. But you're also my friend, and I love you, and if you'll be happier somewhere else, well, I'll be happy for you. Breeze, you do not seem happy here the way you once did."

He shook his head and rubbed his finger across his eyes. "It's just strange being back. I'll get over this." He forced a laugh. "What else? Can you honestly imagine me spending the rest of my life as a farmer?"

"I don't know. Can you?"

Breeze paused for a pregnant moment before barking out a chuckle. "No. I'd be out of my mind with boredom in a week."

Octavian took the wine from Breeze, drank, and said nothing.

"I mean, how common. I didn't learn to fight and make a name for myself to prune grapevines. It would be a waste of my skill and all I've worked to achieve."

"If you say so," Octavian said.

"Alain had this analogy about trimming the vines. You'll like it. It's poetic nonsense like most of what you say. He said you have to see the essence of the vine and then cut away everything else. Cut off everything but what's essential to it, and that makes it fight, makes it strong. Well, that's me as well. I'm a warrior. I just need to cull the rest."

"But surely you can cut too much," Octavian noted. "Take off all the leaves, and the plant will surely die. It needs enough to soak up the warmth of the sun and drink in the rain. It must be a very fine line between strengthening the vine and removing its ability to absorb everything good it needs to thrive."

Breeze nodded. "There's an art to it."

"Certainly. There's no beauty to a shriveled old vine with no green leaves. No sweet fruit can come from something like that, something dead."

"I can't imagine losing what I've made here."

"There is always loss," Octavian said. "We both lost something when we left our families. But sometimes, you need to cut away what's dead to make room for the new growth, just like with your burns. No good comes from holding on to something that's past its time. As you said, there's an art to knowing which is which."

"Well, I do know which is which," Breeze snapped, irritated, though Octavian couldn't fathom why. "I worked and bled to get where I am, and I'm happy with the life I've made. All of it. The gains as well as the losses. Now, did you come out here just to pester me and spout poetry?"

With a chuckle, Octavian stood and brushed his hand down the side of Breeze's hair. "Actually, I came to see if you might want me to warm your bed tonight, but I suspect the answer to that is no. You might want to ask yourself why that is." He leaned down and pressed a kiss to Breeze's forehead, but he sensed none of the reciprocated desire he had in the past. "Good night, Breeze."

Swinging the half-full bottle of wine beside him, Octavian considered making his way down to the fires. Quite a few handsome men had recently joined the company, and several of them looked at

Octavian in such a way that told him he could have them in his bed just by asking. A man or two, maybe even three, would take his mind off Breeze and his troubles for the night. But instead of going to the raucous noise coming from the lower portion of the camp, Octavian looked up at the sky and just let his feet move of their own accord. Soon he reached the cairn. It stood black against the crystal blue of the sky, ringed with stars like a crown, so covered in pungent blossoms that Octavian could barely see the stones. Though he couldn't make out the fat vines competing for space, twisting around one another, Octavian knew them from memory, and they recalled to him what he'd said to Breeze: *But sometimes, you need to cut away what's dead to make room for the new growth. No good comes from holding on to something that's past its time. There's an art to knowing which is which.*

Goddesses, it was easy to advise another, to see through the tangles another couldn't. Octavian sat in the dewy grass by the stone circle he'd built for Myrddin. It was much harder to take his own advice. It had been years. Myrddin was gone and he wasn't coming back. But Octavian held on even though he knew it made no sense. Sure, he found a man or two to entertain him now and then, but even as much as he loved Breeze, Breeze was a dear friend more than anything else. He enjoyed their time in bed, but he could tell Breeze didn't feel the way about him that he did about Alain Lamont. They were brothers-in-arms, and soon they wouldn't even be that. Shades, Octavian knew what he needed to cut away, but he couldn't do it. Not yet.

THREE DAYS later, the weather turned. Wind battered the buildings of the Rosecairn as cold air rushed down from the northern mountains. A little groggy from too much wine, Octavian curled beneath his blankets and furs. His fire had gone out during the night, but he dreaded the frigid floorboards, so he didn't get up to rebuild it. In the kitchen, the cat yowled as she batted something back and forth across the floor. Turning on his side and pulling the bedclothes over his head, Octavian decided to sleep for a few more hours. Maybe later the sun would drive away some of the cold and he could ride to the outposts to begin testing and implementing his magical communication system.

No sooner had he drifted off than pounding on his door startled him. Swearing, he sat up and swung his legs over the edge of the bed.

The floor felt like ice against his soles, but the person at the door persisted, so Octavian hurried to answer before they broke their hand. Grumbling, he opened the door. Breeze stood there in full armor with a heavy cloak overtop, a full pack draped over his shoulder, and the first winter snowflakes sparkling on his black eyelashes. He smiled, and Octavian's irritation melted away. He waved Breeze inside. "Have a seat, and I'll make us some breakfast."

Breeze wrestled away the iron skillet Octavian had picked up. "You sit down. Everyone knows your cooking is poison, and I have a long walk ahead of me. It'll be hard enough without the nuisance of leaky pipes."

Octavian couldn't argue, so he straddled a bench by the table as Breeze cut bacon and cracked eggs. Soon a wonderful aroma filled the kitchen, and the heat misted the windows. Octavian sliced bread and cheese and opened a bottle of wine while Breeze finished over the fire, and they sat down to enjoy what Octavian knew would be their last meal together.

"I've decided to go back to Lockhaven," Breeze said, as if it was necessary. "I can't stop thinking about Alain. I love him, Octavian. I—this is what I want. Are you sure I'm not letting you down?"

"No." Octavian reached across the table to pat the back of Breeze's hand, and he locked his gaze on Breeze's. "I know this is what you want, and I want you to be happy. This might be your chance, and you might not get another. I used to think we had all the time in the world, but it's an illusion, Breeze. Go after it while you can."

"I worry about you," Breeze said. "You're a bit like my Alain. You think you have to bear everything on your shoulders without any help. No man can be expected to do that."

"Well, your Alain will have you now. He's a lucky man."

"If he even wants me back."

"Would you even be going if you doubted that?" Octavian asked.

Breeze nodded. "I'm a stubborn prick, aren't I?"

"That you are. Breeze… you'll be happy on this vineyard, picking grapes and raising children?"

"Aye. I know it sounds dull, but I have missed it—and Alain—since the day I left. Octavian, will you be all right?"

"I'll carry on."

Breeze cleared his throat. "I've learned a lot about life and myself these past few months, and I know this: you have to recognize when it's time to move on. My time with the Roses was wonderful, and I'll never be able to repay you for taking a chance on me. But, my friend, you also have to know when to move on. You can't rule out the chance that you'll find someone special again."

"Breeze—"

Breeze held up his hand. "Just... just don't be obstinate if the opportunity arises. Don't kill it before it ever has the chance to bloom. You never know what life has in store. I passed out in a vineyard and found the love of my life. It's out there where you least expect to find it."

"I never would have figured you for such a romantic," Octavian teased.

Breeze kissed the back of his hand. "Things come along that change the way we see the world, I guess. Octavian, can I ask you one more favor?"

"Go on, then."

Breeze fished a small box out of his pack, opened it, and handed Octavian a perfect red-and-white rose from the cairn. "Courtenay, Alain's daughter—I told her the story of Rosecairn, and she made me promise to bring her a rose. But I'm going on foot, and I'm afraid this won't last until I make it back to Lockhaven. Anything you can do?"

Smiling, Octavian held his hand, fingers spread, above the flower. Soft white light enveloped it, and the drooping petals perked up. "It should last for at least several moons now. And if this girl is a mage, as you said, she'll feel my magic on it. I hope she'll feel how much I wish you and your new family a wonderful life. I will think of you often, Breeze. And you can always come back here. Bring your Alain someday. I would like to meet the man that captured your spirit so completely. He must be extraordinary."

"That he is." Breeze stood and leaned across the table to kiss Octavian. Their lips met, but no fire stoked in either of them. "But so are you. I won't forget you, Octavian."

"And I won't forget you. Can I walk you to the gate?"

"Of course."

It was late morning, chilly, clear, and still. The deep ochre leaves stood out in sharp contrast to the blue sky. The fall colors felt almost garish to Octavian when he wanted them somber—gray and soft and appropriate for a farewell. When they reached the gate, Breeze shielded his eyes with his hand and turned to take a last look at the camp. "I'll miss this place."

Octavian clapped him on the shoulder. "You'll only miss it until you're back beside Alain, in his bed. Then you'll forget all about this dump."

Breeze shook his head. "No, I won't do that. All jesting aside, I wouldn't be the man I am if not for this place, for you. You played a large part in the man I am, the man Alain could fall in love with. I'll always love you for that."

"I'll always love you for not letting me drink myself to death after I lost Myrddin," Octavian said. "The others—they might have given up on me if not for you."

"This is sinking into sloppy territory," Breeze said, though his eyes sparkled a little. "We're warriors, not girls in a parlor, aren't we?"

"I thought you were a farmer now," Octavian teased.

"Aye, a vintner, and proud of it. Give me a hug, you old bastard."

Octavian's breath stuttered a little as he held Breeze, but he tried to keep it to himself. Breeze didn't deserve to feel guilty for building a life with the man he loved. Octavian never wanted him to feel anything but happy about his decision. As they broke apart, Octavian took Breeze's cheeks in his hands and looked into his eyes. "I'm happy for you, happy you've found a life of contentment. Cherish it, Breeze. We're young and it seems like life will go on forever, but the world is a savage place. Unpredictable. Remember that. Don't dwell on it, and don't let it darken your days, but know every moment you have with your Alain and your children is a gift. Don't put off letting them know. Don't ever think you can always tell them later."

"Aye, I'll do that, Octavian. Same as I'll pray to Pherara every night you find someone to cherish again."

"Breeze—"

"Just shut the fuck up and let me do the preaching for once in your life, mate. There was a time when I thought you had all the answers. Don't get me wrong—you're still the cleverest son of a bitch I ever met, just not when it comes to yourself. Just try this. Try imagining what you'd say to me or someone else if I were you. What would you tell me to do? I'll make this real simple. You'd tell me to let go of things past their time. You'd tell me to live. You just did, actually. You told me to appreciate every moment."

Octavian shook his head, remembering something Sylvain had once said to him, even if he could no longer remember the exact inflection of Sylvain's voice or the tilt of his smile. Now, he more remembered how he'd described that in his journal than what he'd actually looked or sounded like. But he remembered what his archer had told him: "Maybe there are no second chances."

It surprised Octavian when Breeze threw his head back, held his belly, and laughed. "We're both living proof that's not true." He held up his finger and tapped them as he counted off. "Let's see, me—survived the journey from Espero when I could barely lift a sword, got accepted into the most prestigious mercenary company in the area, survived the bleeding sky catching on fire, and won the damned finest man in the light of the world. I'm on my fourth chance. And you? Lived through whatever earned you that ridiculous fucking knife you love so much. Defeated Brealon Lavock. Won the Rosecairn. Won the whole damned area."

"Maybe I've used them all up," Octavian said, sounding petulant even to his own ears.

Breeze punched him in the shoulder hard enough to make him stagger back a few steps. "The Octavian I knew made his own chances. He didn't wait for them to fall in his lap. He took them. Since you're clearly too thick to understand my subtle and artful poesy, I'll just say it, like the sell-sword I am. It's been years. You need to stop wallowing and be the man Myrddin looked at like he held the heavens in his hands."

That stung, and Octavian would have been angry if he hadn't known Breeze was right. But Breeze didn't completely understand. "No one will ever look at me like that again."

"Give them something to look at, something burning bright as you used to, and you might be surprised. Life—it's all kinds of fucked up, and you never know. You can't control much, the way I see it, but you can control the man you are. You're one of the best men I ever knew, and you just need to remember it. Now, I'm running out of sunlight, and it gets bloody cold at night."

"Just think of the warm bed waiting for you when you get back to Lockhaven," Octavian said with a wink. "Now, get on with you. And Breeze… the things you said just now, I needed to hear them. And once again, you had the bollocks to tell me. You are a true friend."

"Think about what I said," Breeze replied.

That was part of his problem. Octavian thought about everything, thought about it from every angle, cut it into tiny pieces in his head to get to the core of it, went without sleep until he did. But he just nodded and smiled at his friend. "I will. Now get going. I'll wager there's a man in Lockhaven who will be very pleased to see you show up at his door. Don't keep him waiting."

Breeze nodded. "Take care of yourself, or I'll come back and kick the shit out of you."

"I believe you." The gates opened, and Octavian sent Breeze on his way with a smack to the ass. He stood watching until Breeze disappeared over the crest in the road, and then he turned to go back to his house. He considered drinking a bottle of wine in honor of his friend's happiness, but he had too much to consider, and he needed a clear head. He'd take out his journal and try to make some sense of the tangled mess he'd been carrying around. He needed to crawl out from underneath it, and it had been too long in coming.

Chapter
Twenty-Seven

"ANOTHER GROUP of knights approaching, Octavian," said Ken, one of the young men in the watchtower. They'd quadrupled the guard at the entrance and added a few extra soldiers for good measure. "Looks like at least 120 mounted men, foot soldiers… the Warbler's Nest doesn't seem to know…. Bleeding Shades, I can't make sense of what they're trying to tell us." Squinting, the young man leaned closer to the piece of glass mounted on the wooden pedestal.

Octavian went to look at the glass over the soldier's shoulder. The communication system served them well, but it wasn't without small flaws. Worse yet, Octavian had concocted a structure too complex for some of the men, and he hadn't found the time to simplify it. Initially, he'd consider assigning each of his seventeen outposts with a number, but he'd worried numbers would be confusing when combined with reporting numbers of enemies. Besides, giving each station a name imbued it with an essence, an identity. Men were more likely to be proud of being a part of the Breezy Bluff, the Sunset Keep, or the Crag Sanctuary than Way Station Eleven. Pride translated to loyalty, especially for men who had never been a part of anything before.

Slivers of ironstone hewn from the holy peak, Starmont, powered the glass in each outpost. Octavian didn't know if he believed in the sacredness of Selindria's tallest mountain, but he had found ironstone held a magical charge better than any other material. Now he had to go to each station monthly and recharge the stone, but he hoped to soon devise a way to allow them to soak up magic without his direct involvement. To communicate with another station, a soldier dipped his finger in an oil Octavian had enchanted. He drew the symbol Octavian had assigned to his post, and then he waited for the shimmering lines and shifting hues to fade. The receiving station responded with their symbol, indicating they had seen the beacon. Octavian had tried to devise an easy-to-understand system, and he'd considered posting guides by each speaking glass, but he couldn't risk revealing their code if one of the fortresses was taken. Quite a few of the men struggled with what was, essentially, a new language.

Octavian patted his man on the shoulder. "You'll get used to it in time, so don't worry. It looks like the Warbler's Nest is reporting 120 knights and an unknown number of foot soldiers heading north. The Nest is our southernmost way station, which means the knights are probably sixty-five miles away. More than likely, one of the farms under our protection warned the Nest before the men there even spotted the knights, so they could be even farther south. We have at least two or three days before they reach the cairn."

The young soldier looked at Octavian over his shoulder, clearly worried. "Octavian, this is the second attack in a week. The young king is trying to wear us down. He's been after us since the snow melted enough for his men to use the roads. He's determined, that one. Determined to see an end to us."

"He won't succeed." Octavian didn't have to feign confidence. Garith had only been crowned a year and a half ago, and Octavian had been defending Rosecairn for more than eight years. "We might not have the resources of the crown, but we have loyal men willing to fight for their home, as well as the support of our neighbors for miles. No one will aid the knights against us—they want us here. And if that's not enough, I am much more clever than this whelp of a king.

"Here's what we'll do. Send a message to Wyrm's Eye, Wandering Wind, and Thirteen Arns. Tell them to send all the men they can spare to meet on the road near Archer's Regret. With the warriors in their new barracks, they should be able to muster at least a hundred men. That will give the king's lackeys pause. But just to be cautious, we'll lay a trap for them a little farther up the road. The men at Rose's Whisper recently dug a deep trench across the road. The heavy planks across it now will support horses, but if they change them out for saplings covered in dirt and leaves, at least a few of the knights will lose their mounts, if not more. Use the speaking glass and tell them to make it ready."

Octavian turned to leave.

"But—You mean for me to send these messages? All of them? Perhaps you should be the one to do it, Octavian."

Spinning on his heel, Octavian turned back to the young soldier and afforded him a smile. "I'd like you to send the messages. I'll stay to help you if you need it. I need men who can use the speaking glasses, and you're a good man, Ken. Don't be so nervous. You can do this. Go on, dip your fingers in the oil. You don't need very much. Good. Now, hail Wyrm's Eye. Draw a line with three humps and a circle; that's their symbol. Good! Now see there, they have responded with the symbol of the watchtower. Draw the symbol of Archer's Regret, the arrow, and write twenty-five, with a jagged line beneath the numeral. That way, they'll know twenty-five men is optional and not obligatory. See? They have responded with a triangle to tell you they understand. Can you send the messages to the rest of the posts?"

Ken looked a little astounded as he nodded. "I-I think so, tam. I'll do my best. But where are you going?"

"Me?" Octavian smiled savagely. "I'm going to gather about two hundred and fifty Roses and meet these knights. I have a few things I'd like to say to them face to face."

"I AM Octavian Rose, and this land belongs to me, my men, and the people who have made their livings and their homes on the land beyond our camp. We have not invited you here, and manners would dictate you leave. Next time, do us the courtesy of some advance notice if you are planning to visit. We would hate to be poor hosts."

The leader of the knights, a man whose face Octavian couldn't see due to his helmet, pointed his sword straight out in front of him. "You think this is a joke, you mercenary piece of filth?"

"As a matter of fact, I do." Octavian let his three hundred warriors—many of whom had refused to be left behind—his banners snapping in the wind, and his archers positioned on the bluffs surrounding the road say the rest.

In the manner of the deluded entitled, the knight commander ignored the reality around him as he railed against Octavian. "You have no claim to this territory! It belongs to His Majesty, King Garith of Selindria and Gaeltheon. You will leave the area and turn it over to its rightful owner, as ordained by the Thirteen Goddesses."

"And what will you do if we don't?"

The knight didn't answer. How could he, with his force outnumbered three to one?

"What will you do?" Octavian repeated, his voice ringing out across the limp, thawing grass and frosted rocks between them. No answer came, and he waited. "Answer me, turn around and leave this territory, or prepare to be driven out. I'm giving you a chance, and if you do not take it, I won't be gentle."

"We'll return with a greater force, and then we'll make you pay for your arrogance, sell-sword!"

"I look forward to that day," Octavian shouted. "I'd like to put the greenhorn king's forces to the test. Come back anytime. The Roses will be ready."

The knight commander turning around with his gaze on his horse's mane, signaling his men to follow, satisfied Octavian far more than a retort. The Roses hooted and shouted insults as the knights turned down the road, even their mounts looking dejected with their snouts pointed to the ground. Some of the local farmers had gathered to watch the exchange, and they sent the knights on their way amidst a hail of rotten vegetables and curses that made even Octavian blush.

He let them carry on a bit—it was good for morale—and then he lifted his hand. "Get back to your posts. We cannot afford to leave them unguarded. I don't trust the word of these blackguards."

Most of the men dispersed and rode off in different direction, but a handful remained: men whose counsel Octavian trusted, his unofficial generals. He directed his mount in a wide circle, turned around, and rode to meet with them. "I don't want to worry the others, but this situation is getting serious, and we need to figure something out."

One of the men huffed. "They don't stand a chance. A hundred men can hold the Rosecairn against a thousand."

"True," Octavian conceded. "The men at our outposts are not as secure, however. A group of knights that size could raze one of the way stations to the ground if they ambushed and surrounded it. Make no mistake—the king will resort to less honorable tactics when he realizes he cannot scare us away. We have built this territory up, and now that our mines are lucrative and the farmland is fertile, he wants to take it. He's had success reclaiming much of the disputed territory on the banks of the river, and it has gone to his head. Sure, we can defend our land when the whole company is available, but what will happen when half of the men or more are out on missions? As it stands, we cannot afford to leave our home unprotected, which means we cannot work. We need a permanent solution. I'll hear counsel."

For a long time, the men looked from side to side, toyed with their reins, and cleared their throats. The horses grew restless and nickered and pawed at the ground. Octavian took a firm grip on his skittish young stallion.

"Fine," said an older man with a thick black beard. "I won't dance around it. You're worried these knights are going to go further than trying to scare us? Well, we need to beat them to it."

A chill washed over Octavian, though a trickle of sweat wound down his spine. "What are you saying, exactly?"

"We have to make taking this land more trouble than it's worth. Shows of force and strong words are one thing, but we need this upstart king to see a loss. We… we need to start sending his men back to him in boxes. We need to make his efforts cost too much, so he'll abandon them. His forces are stretched thin along the Kanda. We need to make taking the Rosecairn too great an effort."

"Kill them?" Octavian chewed his bottom lip.

"Aye," said one of the other men. "I agree. Time for us to attack them instead of waiting for them to attack."

"It could backfire," Octavian mused, thinking, wishing he had something to write with so he could list the benefits and disadvantages, the results that could come from any action he took. "Right now, the knights are only threatening us. If we kill their comrades, they'll become more aggressive. We'll be making it personal to them."

"We'll stand against them," said another man. "There's not a man here who isn't worth twice one of those fancy, pampered knights. We can take them."

"But can the villagers and farmers in our shadow?" Octavian asked. "I would not put it past these people to retaliate against us by harming our neighbors. I don't want farms burned and country girls raped to force my hand. I don't want the simple people around here suffering because of their loyalty to us."

"We'll defend them."

Octavian shook his head. "That will spread our forces even thinner. We'll have to spare dozens of men, at least, to patrol the roads constantly. This damned king might not be able to take our land or drive us out, but he is going to drive us out of work as mercenaries if we cannot leave. I… go back to your posts. I'm going for a ride. Check on some of the local farmers. Maybe go by the mines."

"A few of us should go with you. Don't think these bastards don't know that killing you will be cutting the heart out of Rosecairn."

"I appreciate that, but I can take care of myself. Go back to your posts. I'd like to be alone."

Wind whipped through Octavian's hair and nipped his cheeks and the tips of his ears as he held the reins slack and just let his energetic young horse run. Spring had been late in coming, but the ground had finally thawed, and mud coated the stallion's legs and splattered Octavian's boots. The world smelled of possibility: rain and rich soil and green life struggling forth as it blurred by him in muted shades of gray, tan, and green.

Octavian had come to love this land, and he'd thought he'd do anything to defend it, until his warrior had suggested shooting men down on sight, killing them in cold blood. He lived by his sword, and sometimes that meant taking life. But these knights… so many of them were younger than he was. They had probably signed on in the hope of a better life, a living that might one day support a family. Not that it completely excused it, but they were following orders. They probably didn't see any shame in driving out a band of mercenaries and claiming the land for a king they were loyal to. Did they deserve to be shot in the back?

But then what about his people? What would become of the families at Rosecairn if the warriors could no longer support them? Goddesses, this boy-king might not be able to take their camp, but if he prevented them from working, he could starve them out. Were the lives of the women and children at Rosecairn worth more than the lives of those young knights? If he had no choice, didn't necessity dictate he side with his people?

Goddesses, Myrddin, what do I do? You were a knight. I don't want to kill good men. I don't want that weighing on my spirit. But my spirit must come second to hungry children, must it not? What a burden it is to lead, especially as alone as I am now. There must be a compromise, but I cannot see it. Perhaps I am not as clever as everyone thinks I am. Not as clever as I think I am.

Octavian let the horse run until he wore himself out. Foam speckled the stallion's breast, and its nostrils flared, so Octavian forced the horse to walk until he cooled down. They made their way to a small stream lined with big, round boulders. While the horse drank and nibbled at the newly emerged rushes, Octavian tossed pebbles into the water and watched the designs formed by the intersecting rings. They mirrored the overlapping of his thoughts, and the way his ideas formed, crystalized, and just as quickly wavered and faded.

"I cannot kill innocent men," he said. "That's not what I want the Roses to be. But I have to think of the people depending on me. Myrddin, what would you do? You wouldn't want to kill the knights, but you would want to protect Dirk's wife and his three children. How would you reconcile it? Goddesses, can this be reconciled?"

Octavian sat thinking and tossing rocks into the stream until the lack of light pulled him from his ruminations. He looked up to see his horse had wandered a few hundred yards away. Damn it. He'd been sitting here for hours, wasting the day away, and he was at least twenty miles from home. Stout as he was, Octavian didn't know if the stallion would make it home without something substantial to eat. Shades, what had he been thinking?

He took the horse's reins and began walking north. Cold set in quickly after the sun went down, and Octavian shivered without a cloak over his armor. He knew his horse would be cold without a blanket, but he could do nothing but make for home as quickly as possible. After a few hours of walking, the lights of a farm caught his attention. He recognized the house, so he left his horse tied to the fence and went to knock on the door.

Rol Billager answered, looking perplexed until he recognized Octavian. His wizened face broke into a smile. "Tam Octavian, what an honor. What can we do for you this evening, my friend?"

Octavian took the farmer's offered hand in both of his and clasped it tight. "I'm sorry to bother you. I'm afraid I was out riding and lost track of time. I also underestimated how cold it would get at dark. I hate to ask, but do you think you could spare some hay and water for my horse? Maybe a blanket?"

"You are never a bother, my friend," Rol said, standing aside so Octavian could enter. "You look frozen through. Come inside and sit down. Have some supper. I'll take your horse out to the barn, give 'im a rubdown and something to eat."

"That isn't necessary." Octavian hesitated on the threshold, looking between the cold night and the warm, orange, smoky light inside the small cottage. Before he could say anything further, an elderly woman with a rosy face, as wide as she was tall, took his hand and dragged him the few steps to the table. Casia, in an apron and muffin-style hat, washed the dishes in a wooden bucket by the hearth. She had put on a few pounds since Octavian had seen her last, and he greeted her when she smiled shyly over her shoulder.

"Those can wait," Casia's mother said. "See to our guest."

Casia dried her hands on her apron and took a clean bowl from a shelf. She filled it with stew from the cauldron over the fire while her mother sliced into a loaf of dark bread. Octavian took a seat on the bench at the table and started eating, at first only to avoid offending these good, simple people. The stew was delicious, though, and while he didn't go hungry at the cairn, he wasn't much of a cook, and his supper usually entailed whatever he had at hand to fry up and sometimes just cold ham and bread. He couldn't remember the last time he'd had such a wonderful meal—probably the last one Myrddin prepared for him.

"We have some ale," Casia offered. "Can I get you a mug?"

"If you'll sit with me and have one too," he said. Casia was one of the few people outside the cairn who knew of Octavian's inclinations. He had confessed to her one day so she wouldn't have to fear him—fear he would try to do to her what she'd come to expect from men. "We haven't seen each other in moons, with the roads so treacherous over the winter. Tell me how you've been."

As they drank, talked, and laughed, Octavian wondered what would happen to Casia. She was a tiny, timid woman, afraid to speak with anyone but him or her parents. And her parents were not young. What would happen to her when they were gone? Not only would she be unable to do all the farm chores on her own, she would have no one to protect her. Octavian clenched his fist beneath the table. He had to hold on to this territory; it was the only way to keep Casia and people like her safe. He didn't trust the knights any further than he trusted a gang of thugs when it came to a pretty young woman living alone.

Casia laid a hand as small as a child's on his forearm. "Octavian, what is it? You're troubled."

He didn't want to frighten or burden her, but so few people could read his moods. A burst of cold air struck his back as Rol came into the hut. "Your horse is all settled in, friend. Beautiful animal." He sat down at the table across from Octavian, took the ale his wife handed him, slurped a few gulps down, and sighed with contentment. "So how's the stew?"

"It's wonderful," Octavian said. "Best thing I've had in a long while."

Rol beamed at his daughter. "Well, you should marry Casia, and then you could eat it whenever you liked. It's high time you found yourself a good wife to look after you, lad."

Octavian actually considered. It wasn't a terrible idea. He had no more desire to lie with a woman than Casia did to lie with a man. They were friends. She could cook and mend his clothing, and they could talk in the evenings. He could keep her safe, and at least he wouldn't be coming back to a cold, empty house after his jobs, with no one to greet him but his rotten cat. And then she wouldn't be alone in this house after her parents went to the goddesses. "I will think about it."

"Well, the farm's no valenny, but it's profitable, and it would be all yours," Rol urged.

"Pa, enough," Casia said, blushing. "Now, Octavian, tell us what's bothering you."

"Have you seen the knights in the area lately? A year and a half ago, Garith of Selindria wed Cothryn of Gaeltheon and united the two kingdoms with the express purpose of reclaiming the disputed territory on both sides of the Kanda River. Most of it is held by mercenaries and warlords, and the young king has driven many of them out. Well, he's set his sights on Rosecairn now. I—this is my territory, ours. It is peaceful, safe, and fertile, good for everyone who lives here. I want to defend it, but I don't want to kill these knights in cold blood. That isn't what I want for the Roses. But as long as this threat is hanging over our heads, we cannot leave to do mercenary work. I can't devise a way to get these men to leave us alone for good without compromising our honor. I swore to my... I once made someone a promise that I wouldn't sacrifice my integrity for personal gain. But I should not trouble you with this."

Casia stood to refill all their mugs from the ale barrel in the corner.

"So what you need is a peaceful way to drive these knights from our home," Rol said.

Octavian slurped the thick head from his ale and nodded. "Yes, but I cannot conceive of one."

"You're trying too hard," Casia said, sitting down. "What do all men need to survive?"

"Food, water, shelter?" Octavian didn't understand her suggestion.

"Exactly. There's not a farm, a shop, a tavern, or an inn for probably a hundred miles that doesn't owe the Roses at least one favor. If we refuse to supply these men, well, it may not stop them, but it will certainly slow them down. They'll have to bring all their provisions with them, and they'll only be able to stay until they run out."

"Goddesses, maybe I should marry you. Casia, do you think the farmers and merchants will agree to this?"

She bumped her shoulder against his. "There's not a single person around these parts who wants to see you lot gone. They all know the custom they may lose from the knights will benefit them for years to come."

"Aye," Rol said. "I'll get the word out to our neighbors. You should speak with everyone you can. We might not be warriors like you, but if we all stand together, we can succeed."

Octavian was so relieved he wanted to cry. "Just deny them supplies," he said to himself. "No killing. We—we'll beat them with love and loyalty."

"That we will," said Rol's wife. "It's our way, isn't it?"

Octavian was overwhelmed. He held his empty mug out to Casia to refill. He hoped Myrddin could see this, see what they had made. "I hate to impose on you any further, but do you think I could spend the night? I'm reluctant to go back out in the cold, and being here with you has soothed my spirit more than I can express to you."

"Course you can, lad," Rol said, patting the back of Octavian's hand. "Our pleasure. My daughter makes as good a breakfast as she does a stew." He winked, and his wife shook her head.

"I'll get some blankets and furs, and you can bed down in front of the fire," she said.

They sat around the table and enjoyed a few more pints before Octavian retired to his comfortable bed on the floor and slept more peacefully than he had in years.

OVER THE next few weeks, the presence of the knights tapered off. As Casia had predicted, none of the local merchants would serve them. A few small parties attacked their outposts, but the Roses, well trained and well fed, made short work of them. None of the king's men made it more than ten or fifteen miles into their territory. Octavian stationed more warriors along the southern border of their territory, and he assigned patrols to make sure the farmers and shopkeepers who refused the knights service wouldn't suffer retaliation. A moon after he had spoken with Casia's family, it seemed the knights and their king had decided the Rosecairn was more bother than it was worth.

But then one warm day while Octavian sat in the watchtower writing in his journal, a message appeared on the speaking glass. Instead of adhering to the system he'd designed, the missive from the Warbler's Nest just said "Octavian. Come. Urgent."

He hurried to find a horse, and then he drove the poor animal hard, worried about the men at his most distant station. Reaching the Nest in the dead of night, it pleased him to find warriors on patrol, ready to stop him. They couldn't be too careful. Octavian dismounted and handed his horse's reins to a young recruit. "My animal will need a rubdown, then food and water." He turned to the man in command of the Nest. "Your message was rather cryptic. Why the urgency?"

"Please, tam, come with me. There are some knights here who want to speak with you. We didn't think we should allow them any farther into our territory, thought it better if you came to them."

Octavian patted the man's shoulder. "That was the right thing to do. Do you have any idea what these men wish to discuss?"

"No, tam. They say they'll only share their business with you."

"Take me to them," Octavian said.

He followed his warrior into the courtyard of the citadel. Warbler's Nest had been a ruin they'd built up—an ancient stronghold with a heavy outer wall around the fortress. Six knights waited within a rounded tower at the corner of the fortress. They leaned against the walls but sprang to attention as Octavian entered.

"What can I do for you?" he asked, crossing his arms over his chest.

"His Majesty, King Garith of Selindria and Gaeltheon, wishes to extend an offer to you, tam," one of the knights said.

"Is that so?" Octavian had little interest in the king's bargains.

"Yes, tam. King Garith is willing to grant you the land you now control if you and your people swear fealty to the throne. He'll make

Rosecairn a bairny of Gaeltheon, with you, Octavian Rose, as bairn. He's granting you a title and the legitimate right to this land, tam."

"Do not speak to me as if I am simple," Octavian snapped. "I hardly need it explained to me, though I do mistrust it. Are there papers, seals, anything to make this official? If your boy-king thinks I am a rustic fool, he is mistaken."

Another of the knights spoke up. "King Garith worried you might feel this way, Tam Octavian. He has invited you to come to his estate in Meritage and speak with him, if you doubt his offer."

Octavian turned on his heel and left the tower, pausing at the door. He remembered how these games were played. Without looking back at the men who had waited hours for his audience, he said, "You may tell your master I will meet with him in Meritage at the beginning of Diarana's Moon."

"But, tam, the king wishes to extend to you—"

"You have my answer," Octavian said, and then he left the citadel and found his horse. Goddesses, he hoped he remembered enough courtly protocol to deal with the upstart king. He wished he didn't have to face Garith alone, but other than some guards, he had no one he really trusted. As soon as he reached the path, he heeled his horse's ribs. He needed to get home to his book and plan what he would say to the most powerful man in the known world.

Chapter Twenty-Eight

THE KING'S riverside villa in Meritage didn't look much different from the buildings crowding it—sand-colored stone, red roof tiles, shutterless windows with pale wooden frames. Octavian rode down the path that merged from the cobbled street to the stables and handed his horse off to the servants. A quartet of knights waited to escort him to the king. Octavian nodded to the ten warriors who had accompanied him, indicating they should wait with the horses. He hoped they'd be offered food or at least something to drink, but he remembered only too well from his days as a wealthy merchant's son how ordinary men were treated by the privileged.

The king's soldiers, in their shiny plate that had probably never seen combat, led Octavian into the house and up the stairs to a library on the second floor. Though simple on the outside, the house was huge and lavish with polished stone floors, leaded glass in the windows, and heavy velvet curtains. Statues of the goddesses and vases of flowers adorned the alcoves in the hall, and portraits hung on the walls between them. The library itself was spacious but still cozy with fires in the hearths and sun spilling in through the windows next to the long table the men led Octavian to.

He sat down and got his first look at King Garith, who sat at the opposite end of the table. Octavian was twenty-seven years old, though he probably looked a little younger despite the lines the wind and the sun had carved into his skin and the scars reminding him of his battles. Garith couldn't have been more than twenty-two or twenty-three, but he had clearly led a life of luxury. He smiled easily, without pain hidden behind his dark eyes. He had yet to learn life could be cruel, and Octavian wondered if that would change. The young king favored his Esperon mother with his olive skin and black hair, and he was a handsome man, but not as handsome as the royal guard standing with his hand on the back of the king's chair, with his wild copper curls and large, sea-colored eyes. Octavian wondered if any of the other knights and advisors around the table noticed the way the king and his guard looked at each other. He thought they might want to be more discreet, but it wasn't his concern.

Garith showed Octavian that lazy smile and gestured toward the platters of bread, cheese, and fruit—enough to feed Octavian's entire camp. "Please help yourself to a little light refreshment, Tam Octavian Rose." The king waited while a pair of maidservants poured wine for everyone but the guards. "I appreciate you coming all this way to meet with me. Did you have a pleasant journey?"

Octavian hadn't known what to expect from this young monarch, but it wasn't to be treated as an equal, shown sincere gratitude. He had prepared himself for scorn and dismissal—which he noticed on the faces of some of the king's advisors—and he wasn't sure how to react when it didn't come from the king. "The journey was pleasant enough, Your Majesty. It has been quite some time since I have come so far south, or visited the Selindrian side of the river. The countryside is lovely this time of the year."

Garith sipped from his wine and leaned an elbow casually on the table. "I would have guessed, based upon your accent, that you are Selindrian. Where did you grow up?"

Though he bristled at that long-forgotten part of his life, a life that no longer even seemed to have belonged to him, Octavian understood courtly manners because of it. Before they could get to the matter at hand, they would have to talk about nothing like old friends who had all the time in the world, pretend to have the leisure to put off important business. "I moved about a great deal, Your Majesty."

"And how did you find yourself in a place as remote as Rosecairn?"

"Largely by chance," Octavian answered, careful to say plenty of words but reveal nothing significant. "I suppose I can only say I tried to take full advantage of those opportunities that presented themselves to me. As all men must."

"Well, by all accounts, you have prospered there."

"Thank you, Your Majesty. I have done the best I could. Your recognition means a great deal to me and my men. The others at Rosecairn will be quite pleased when I relay your gracious compliments."

"How do you find the climate?"

"Cold, Your Majesty, harsh much of the time, but it's my home now."

Garith raised an eyebrow. "One you are very reluctant to part with."

"Though you have no legitimate claim to it," an older man muttered.

"Peace, Tam Vartanan," Garith said. "Tam Octavian, let us talk as men. Offering you legitimate control and ownership of the Rosecairn and the lands surrounding it is not a decision I made lightly. It isn't something my father would have ever considered, and I did not do it because you proved your military might superior to mine. I need to make it clear to you that this is neither an act of concession nor desperation."

Their gazes met, and Octavian arched his brow this time. "Oh?"

"Indeed," the king said. "It is true that I did not want to lose my men, but I wouldn't hand lands and a title over to just anyone."

"I suppose I should take that as… some form of a compliment, Your Majesty," Octavian said.

"You should take it as a high one to even be sitting here in the presence of your king, mercenary," the dour advisor—Vartanan—said. "No matter what His Majesty claims, you should remember your place."

Garith raised a hand. "I intended it as a compliment, Tam Octavian. Your warriors are impressive. I fought beside them at the Battle of the Starlight Bridge. But what impressed me more was the loyalty of the people living under you. You nurture and protect them, and they respond with fierce loyalty. I respect that in a ruler. It's the sort of ruler I hope to be: a defender. A man who rules through love is much more powerful than one who rules through fear."

"I have always thought so, Your Majesty." The young king's insight and wisdom raised him a bit in Octavian's estimation.

"So, are you inclined to accept my offer?" Garith unrolled a piece of vellum and passed it to Octavian. "These are the lands that will belong to you, and to your heirs for as long as the goddesses allow. This will be recorded in both the Royal Archives and the temples of Vestrafori here in Meritage and at my father's fortress, and your livery will hang in the great hall of his castle back in Selindria, and everywhere else the heraldry of the noble families of Selindria and Gaeltheon are displayed."

The map illustrated the territory that would belong to Octavian, and it was at least double what he now held, extending probably another hundred miles south and around fifty to the east. A trill of excitement moved through Octavian's chest. This surpassed his wildest ambitions. Yet he knew it wasn't coming for free. "And what would you need from me? What will I have to do?"

"The same as my other vassals," Garith explained. "Pay a tithe of five percent of the profit from your lands and provide soldiers when they're required. You will be a part of my kingdom, however, and not outside of it. Which means if you and your people need aid, you can request it, and we'll do our best. You will be summoned occasionally to court and asked to provide counsel to me, something which I think will benefit me, all of us, coming from a man with your experience."

Octavian wanted to drum his fingers on the table, but he didn't want to display indecision or uncertainty. "I have several gainful mines on my land. Would you be agreeable to me paying what I owe to the crown from their proceeds? I am hesitant to tax my farmers, Your Majesty. Life in the north can be very hard, and many of these families need all the food they can harvest to survive."

"I'll agree to that," Garith said. He was much different than Octavian had expected. "I must insist, however, that you provide soldiers to aid our efforts to reclaim the rest of the disputed territory. As with any bairn, you'll be required to train, equip, and pay them. How large a force do you have?"

They spent the rest of the afternoon parsing the details, poring over official documents, signing and sealing. Octavian checked on his men and found them happily drinking in the barracks with Garith's soldiers. Then he followed a pair of serving girls to a room on the third floor, where a tub of hot water waited. After dismissing them and their enthusiastic offers to help him wash and dress, Octavian sat down on the edge of the bed and looked out the window at the river. The faltering sunlight turned its still surface to molten gold, and hundreds of boats clogged its banks.

"Can you believe it, Myrddin?" Octavian leaned his forehead against the warm glass. "Bairn of Rosecairn. A member of the landed nobility. I bet you wouldn't have predicted that when I walked into your camp all those years ago. Ah, life is strange, my friend. When I met you nine years ago, I didn't have enough copper to buy a loaf of bread. Now I have a copper mine, and I'm about to have dinner with the High King of Selindria and Gaeltheon. I couldn't have done it without you." He swiped at his eyes and sat for a few moments as cool lavender shadows replaced the waves of orange and gold. He traced patterns in the mist his breath had left on the glass and whispered, "I'd give it all up, go back to being that boy starving in obscurity, for another night with you, even an hour to sit beside the window in our house and talk." Then Octavian bathed and dressed, because soon he'd have to return to a life he never imagined he'd be part of again. He had to be ready.

OCTAVIAN ROSE'S Journal

Myrddin,

The world has changed a great deal in the two years since I became bairn. I scarcely know where to begin, and I'm sure something pertinent will slip my mind. A sea route has been discovered to the lands beyond the Lapir Mountains, to a place no one in living memory has set foot, until now. The culture in this land of Johmatra is wildly different from our own, and while trade is flourishing, so is conflict. The Johmatrans do not acknowledge the Thirteen Holy Sisters, and they believe only mages who can trace their lineage to the legendary sorcerer-emperor Fane should be permitted to practice magic. To prevent "common born" mages from using what they see as a limited supply of power, they kill them!

The island nation of Espero has been brutally attacked by these foreigners, with towns and villages destroyed down to the babes in their baskets. Nor has our own land been immune. Recently, invaders razed a temple of Fayelle to the ground and violated the priestesses within it. Predictably, it has led to war. The fighting has been worst along the southern coasts and to the east. I have had to send men from Rosecairn to help defend the kingdoms, and many of them have not returned. The names on the stones are increasing, as are the widows and orphans. I am realizing, more quickly than I'd like, the difference between mercenary work and actual war. What is happening in this land makes what we used to do look like boys playing with wooden swords. I cannot tell you how I long for what, in retrospect, I see as the simplicity of those days.

As I write this, there is a lull in the fighting, but I sense we are standing in the eye of the storm. The king has established a Royal Fleet, and along with the Emiri ships loyal to the Valen of the South Coast, our side achieved a decisive victory at the Bay of Blossoms, though the losses were great. No one doubts the enemy will return, and tomorrow morning, I'll ride for Garith's fortress of Eirion-Vale here in Gaeltheon to offer what counsel I can. Myrddin, I am afraid—less for myself than for the young men I will have no choice but to send to their deaths, and the families they will leave behind. As for me, I have achieved all I hoped to in life, and as often as not, life feels heavy on my shoulders. Casting it off might be a relief.

On a more personal note, let me inform you what has been happening in our bairny. I will never get used to saying that, as I'm sure you can imagine. And do not get a vision of me prancing around in velvets and lacy shirts, you old bastard! I am your same Octavian. Other things are different, though. My dear Lena has moved on. One day a merchant selling musical instruments came to the camp. He was a handsome man; I'd have gone after him myself if his gaze hadn't been glued to our healer. The man had a lovely singing voice. I'll miss Lena, and she taught me a great deal about easing pain and mending injuries, but I'm confident she'll be happy. She taught me to see through the eyes of others, imagine how they would feel. Those traits will serve her new family. Probably, she'll spend her days in her trader's caravan with a tribe of happy children and dozens of cats and dogs trailing along behind. Maybe even some mice and rats. Or a twirl-horn deer! That would be something to see.

So, aside from Karl, who occasionally trains my new recruits, none of the original members of our company are beside me. I have not found anyone, if you are wondering. I cannot say I don't occasionally find a man to warm my bed, and I enjoy it, usually, but it isn't like it was when we made love. I wonder if I'll find that again. Perhaps it's as Sylvain said, and each man only gets one great love in his life. I don't know, but if I will only get one, I'm glad it was you. I think of that alley cat of an archer more than I should. I hope he's happy. I think of Breeze, and I'm confident he's happy. He deserves it. I think of you, my love, and it still hurts. Here. I'm touching my belly. It's clenched up, and I still miss you fiercely. I hope the priestesses are right and we'll be together again one day.

Everyone leaves me. I cannot help but make the obvious deduction and think I am lacking. Have I ignored the needs of others in favor of my ambition? I have tried hard not to. Sisters, Myrddin, I hope I did not do that to you. I hope you knew I loved you. There's so much I'd like to say to you, things I should have said when I felt like we had all the time in the world.

As much as I'd like to expound upon my thoughts and fears across these pages, empty myself of the insects gnawing at my spirit, I must close this book, close it on the chapter of my life where I was Octavian Rose, mercenary commander. When I wake in the morning, I must be Octavian Rose, Bairn of Rosecairn, an aristocrat who sees men in numbers, who sacrifices them for the greater good of the kingdom.

Goddesses, I miss you. I miss the way you looked at me, the confidence those looks inspired. Without you, I am not whole. I am not whole, and yet I must ride out tomorrow to advise a king. Can this broken thing I am do any good, make any difference? Save even one man's life? For you, because you believed in me, I can only try.

Chapter Twenty-Nine

TWO WEEKS later, Octavian arrived at Eirion-Vale with his armor polished to mirror-sheen and his red cape trailing behind him. The servants took his horse and directed him to the throne room, but no one escorted him even though soldiers and harried servants clogged the halls. He tried to find his way through the huge, old fortress, following the movements of the servants with trays of food and the sound of voices. On his way to what he presumed was the meeting room, he encountered a very peculiar young man, one he wondered at being allowed inside the castle.

The strange man leaned against the wall, drinking wine directly from the bottle and smirking at passersby as they shied away from him and gave him a wide berth. Octavian could see why—the man looked as though he'd just staggered off a pirate ship. While he wore what had probably once been high-quality black leather armor, it had been torn in several places and patched haphazardly, if it all. Overtop, he wore several belts holding pouches but no weapons and a necklace made of seashells. His hair hung in white ropes almost to his waist, adorned with beads, more shells, string, and scraps of leather. Blue paint, permanent in the tradition of the seafaring Emiri race, wound down the left side of his face and neck in graceful, organic spirals that followed the contours of his flesh. Octavian sensed the magic swirling around the young man at the same time as he must have sensed Octavian's. He looked up and met Octavian's gaze with the palest blue eyes Octavian had ever seen. Something behind them made a line of sweat bead along Octavian's hairline and above his lip. He wanted to back away as the others had, but instead he cleared his throat and said, "Perhaps you can help me."

The man held out his bottle. "Care for a drink? I'd recommend it. Helps when dealing with these pretentious twats and their petty entitlements. I'll be glad when this is over and I can return to my valenny and my own people."

Octavian choked and nearly spit out the swallow of wine he'd gratefully accepted. "Your… *valenny*?"

The man smiled and shook his hand. "Sometimes I forget I'm not what people expect when they imagine an aristocrat. I've never been one for pomp and frills, though. I'm Yarroway L'Estrella, Valen of the Twenty-Nine."

"Octavian Rose, Bairn of Rosecairn."

"The mercenary my cousin Garith gave a title to?"

"That's right," Octavian said. "And you fought in the Battle of the Starlight Bridge."

"Something like that," Yarroway said. "So you earned your stature instead of getting it through an accident of birth. That makes you worth more than most of these fools, at least in my mind."

"I appreciate that," Octavian said. "It's a belief many of your comrades do not hold."

"They're hardly my comrades," Yarroway said. "I can assure you they don't hold me in any higher regard than they hold you. Their opinions do not matter to me, though. You shouldn't let them affect you either. They need us far more than we need them."

"I understand your words, Tam Yarroway, but the whispers and derisive stares do sting. It would be nice to be acknowledged rather than dismissed. I have worked and sacrificed for what I have gained, and I cannot pretend it doesn't matter."

"Yarrow. And don't let them dismiss you. All most of them know how to do is gossip and kiss my cousin's backside. They're only worth anything in their own minds."

"So were you summoned here for the war council as well?" Octavian asked.

Yarrow snorted. "I was *invited*. No one commands me. Even Garith isn't that deluded."

"How come you're not in there?"

"The hall is suffocating, and it smells. I'm not fond of places I can't see the sky from, or of having stone walls around me. I grow restless easily. Besides, I'm waiting for a friend. He had business of his own to attend to, and I'm eager to see him again."

"I don't know my way to the hall," Octavian admitted. "Will it bother you if I wait with you?"

Yarrow drank from the wine bottle and handed it back to Octavian. "No, you seem like my type."

A little flutter Octavian hadn't felt in a long time moved through his belly. "Is that so?"

Yarrow made a little hum. "I bet we have more in common than both being mages."

Octavian turned to face him and both of them pressed their shoulders against the wall.

Yarrow had thick, white eyelashes unlike anything Octavian had ever seen, and he batted them flirtatiously. "If we'd met a few years ago, I bet we could have had quite a good time."

"But not now?" Octavian asked.

"I'm spoken for," Yarrow said, "and while one of my companions wouldn't mind you joining the fun, the other certainly would."

"Unfortunate," Octavian said. "At least for me."

"Once I would have never imagined myself in such a situation, but it pleases me. Still, I'm always happy to meet another mage. I'll soon need as many mage friends as I can find."

"What for?"

"There are certain things only other mages can understand," Yarrow said. "The world is changing. Many of the assumptions it operated on are going to fall to pieces, and fall hard."

"Are you referring to Johmatra and the people there?"

"Other things. Far greater and more profound things. Things—" The other mage had grown excited, and as his eyes widened and glowed blue, the hair on Octavian's arms stood up, and he took a step away from Yarrow.

"Here you are," said a soft crisp voice that moved like a brush of velvet over Octavian's skin.

Octavian turned toward it and the air rushed from his chest when he saw a face he would never forget—a face from another lifetime. The other man's black eyes showed none of the surprise Octavian knew he wore on his face.

"Well, this is a surprise. Hello, Octavian Rose."

"Hello" was all Octavian could manage. The assassin who had helped him feign his death and escape his father's control looked much as Octavian remembered: rich dark skin, almond-shaped eyes framed with decadent black lashes, black hair that fell across his eye and cheek on one side, the most amazing mouth and fullest lips he'd ever seen. When they had met the first time, when neither of them had been fully into manhood, Octavian had thought the assassin was the most beautiful person in the world. In the subsequent years, he'd wondered if imagination had colored his recollections, but now he didn't think so. "I… I'm rather surprised you remember me."

"You remember me," the assassin said. "Don't you?"

"Yes, but you did something significant for me, something that changed the entire course of my life. Of course I remember. I didn't think it was as… as momentous for you."

"That's not entirely true. There was a lesson in it for me, even if I didn't know it at the time."

"You two know each other?" Yarrow asked. "How?"

"We met during one of my missions," the assassin said.

"How is he alive?" Yarrow teased.

The assassin narrowed his eyes and grinned. Something had changed in him; his eyes seemed more expressive, more alive. "He was not my target, obviously. This is not the place to discuss it."

"Will we discuss it later?" Yarrow looked between Octavian and the assassin, probably imagining all the things they hadn't said, and probably fairly accurately. Octavian's cheeks heated. Over the years, he had revisited their evening together in his fantasies.

"Perhaps," the assassin said.

Octavian turned to him. Even simple dark trousers and a gray doublet couldn't conceal the lean lines of his body and the power of his limbs. He'd earned a nasty scar on the side of his neck, and a fizzle of power—a dark magic—surrounded him. Octavian hadn't noticed that the last time they'd been together. It was a sinister, life-negating force unlike anything Octavian had ever experienced, and it disturbed him even more than Yarrow's chaotic magic, though he struggled not to let it show. He was truly happy to see this man again—his first advocate and lover. "It's taken ten years. Do I finally get to know your name?"

"Sasha. Did the dagger I gave you serve you well?"

"It still does," Octavian said. "I didn't expect to see you again. It pleases me."

"I wondered if you would survive," Sasha said. "You have done well for yourself. I made the right choice, it seems. Now, Garith and the others will be expecting us. We should go to the hall."

With a little whine, Yarrow said, "It's not necessary. I know what I need to do, and you have no real part in this. The three of us should go to the tavern for the day, trade stories. I'll fight to defend my lands when the time comes, but I see no benefit to listening to these pompous asses prattle on."

"We swore to Duncan, as well as your cousin, that we would be there," Sasha said to Yarrow in a gentle, indulgent tone Octavian didn't expect. "Besides, Octavian will be expected. A man with actual experience in combat will be a great asset to your cousin. Many of his advisors are pretenders at best, as we both know. Octavian is a man who understands doing what needs to be done."

"Very well," Yarrow said, and then, more brightly, "we can go to the tavern afterward!"

MEN FILLED every inch of the hall, the dozens of long wooden benches as well as the space along the walls. Octavian had expected King Garith to sit on a throne atop a dais, but he sat at a long table surrounded by the redheaded guard and some other men. As they wove through the throng, looking for a place to sit down, Yarrow leaned toward Octavian. He pointed to a handsome, dark-haired knight in well-worn armor and a yellow cloak. "That's Duncan, Bairn of Windwake, our other companion. Those are my brothers—Rayne, Valen of Lockhaven, and Rowan, Eyrle of Greyrclif." They resembled their youngest brother, but with dirty-blond hair, bluer eyes, and more traditional clothing.

A low thrum of magic came from the west side of the room, where a few dozen Esperons had gathered. Behind them sat the new sect of warriors who reported directly to the temple priestesses instead of the king: the Defenders of the Thirteen. A few priestesses sat with them. Yarrow chuckled. "Let's go and sit next to them. It will irritate them to no end."

Octavian wondered why, but he just followed the other mage, who for some reason had formed an instant attachment to him. It felt good to have at least one ally in a sea of men who considered Octavian some lower form of life because he hadn't been born to the nobility. As he followed his newest and oldest confidant, he wondered how the aristocrats would react to his actual lineage. The three of them found chairs in front of a window and sat down, the summer sun hot on their backs. For the next several hours, the gathered men discussed strategies and consulted maps. Octavian kept notes on what he heard in his new book. Some of the plans sounded better than others, and he hoped to explain the virtues and faults of each when he could analyze and articulate them. He hadn't known how desperate the situation had grown, especially in the south and along the Esperon coasts. The ambassadors from the island told horrible stories, and they made it clear they wanted to fight. To Octavian, it sounded as though few other options remained.

A big blond man called Bartoum Astir stood from the table. "Since the only route from Johmatra to Selindria and Gaeltheon is by sea, we should focus our efforts there. We need to add to the Royal Fleet. We need more ships, many more, if we're to stand a chance against these bastards."

"And as I have said upon so many occasions I am in danger of going mute, the gold for this endeavor must come from somewhere," Tam Vartanan bellowed.

"Tam, we're talking about defending our kingdoms against invasion," the king's redheaded guard said, color rising to his cheeks. "This must be our highest priority."

"Even so, Tam Lysander, coins do not fall from the sky, and the treasuries are running low."

Yarrow stood. "Not all of them, certainly. With the piles of gold in the temple coffers, we could build a thousand ships. Gold which has sat for hundreds of years without even a copper piece paid in tax. Why should the temples be immune from contributing, from helping to defend the kingdom? Why, when the kingdom's subjects die to protect them, should they offer nothing?"

A fat priestess in the rich purple robes of the Mother Goddess stood and pointed a finger at the mage. "The temples are providing well-equipped soldiers—"

"Soldiers who will swear no fealty to the king," Yarrow continued, blue light spilling from the corners of his eyes. "How stupid do you think we are? Those men are not allies, but an open threat to my cousin's rule. No one thinks otherwise. How dare you hoard your gold while you sit on your fat ass, safe in your temples, eating and drinking, while men defend your right to do so? While people—my people—die?"

"And what have you contributed to this effort, you blasphemous cur?" the woman shouted. "It is only your relationship to a very softhearted monarch that keeps you out of the dungeons, or the gallows!"

Yarrow shouted back, his voice breaking as he balled his fists and veins of azure light crackled over his skin. "What have I given? You can go to the Shades'! You cannot imagine what I have lost! And if you want to put me in the dungeon, I invite you to try it, you and your mindless puppet Defenders!"

A priestess of Vestrafori got to her feet. "The goddesses are the ones who will win this war for us, not mages or boats. We cannot hope to prevail without their blessing. You should remember that."

"What horseshit!" Yarrow shouted. At the table, his brothers looked mortified while the knight, Duncan, looked worried. Sasha smirked at him indulgently, almost with pride. People shouted accusations of sacrilege as the mages from Espero shifted uncomfortably. Likely they, like Octavian, felt the huge amount of chaotic power spiraling out from Yarrow. On his whim, he could level this entire wing of the castle, and he seemed rather unhinged at the moment. "If your precious goddesses give a damn what happens to any of us, then where are they? Why don't they appear and tell us what to do? Or better yet, why don't they come down from the sky and swipe the Johmatran ships from the surface of the sea? Where were they at the Bay of Blossoms?"

"Perhaps they're punishing this kingdom, and this king, for slights against them, for depravity!" the priestess of the Mother Goddess hollered. "Why not ask him what happened to my predecessor, a woman of holiness and virtue, when she questioned his decisions?"

The guard, Tam Lysander, stood, drew his sword, and pointed it at the women. "We might ask you what befell the team of scholars who dared to question your authority. Insult my king again and I will remove you from the hall and this castle, priestess or not."

Several of the Defenders also drew weapons, and soon men were shouting at each other until Octavian couldn't make out what was being said. Guards moved between the knights, mages, and Defenders to keep them from open confrontation. Yarrow seethed and sizzled with energy while Sasha looked ahead, his face an emotionless mask. Octavian couldn't believe what was happening. How could these people be arguing like this? Before taking time to consider his actions, he stood and strode to the front of the room. He stepped in front of the table and stood at the center. "Stop! Just stop it, you fools! We're facing a common enemy. We need to set aside our differences and stand together if we are to have any chance of victory. This pettiness and greed will assure the Johmatrans win!"

Some of the Esperons nodded, and a few of them even clapped. A man somewhere near the back of the room shouted, "That's a fine sentiment coming from a sell-sword dressed up as a bairn!"

Duncan stood. "This young man is right! We should be fighting the enemy, not each other. You should all be ashamed."

"We must devise a way to pool our resources," Octavian said, "and in the most efficient way. We have warriors, magic, and ships. We need to find the most effective way to combine and position them. May I?"

"Please," King Garith said. "I value good counsel no matter who it comes from, Bairn Octavian. You have given the most sensible advice I've heard so far. The rest of you, sit down. Now."

Octavian approached the table and pointed to the largest of the maps. "If I understand correctly, Your Majesty, our southern coasts are the most vulnerable. It will be impossible to guard so much territory, but between the ships we have, we can protect the most highly populated areas. Spells can help us defend the rest—wards to keep these invaders away."

One of the Esperons, a lanky young man in the loose trousers and a long sleeveless tunic traditional to the island, said, "Wards such as these have been in place in Espero for hundreds of years. Unfortunately, the Johmatrans have warriors trained to break through them, and we are not a nation of warriors."

"We are," Octavian said, seeing the pain in the man's liquid dark eyes. "We need to establish a force of mages and warriors. We need to learn to work together to counter the enemy. Mages must come here to fight alongside our soldiers, and we need to send knights to Espero." He focused his gaze on the priestesses and Defenders. "We must all contribute."

"I have been saying this all along," Tam Lysander said. "Bairn Octavian, as both a warrior and a mage, will you work with me to build this force?"

"Of course."

"I'll stay and fight," said the Esperon mage. "I-I'll do anything. I have nothing left back home. Life has taken a great deal from me."

Octavian met his gaze and saw his own pain reflected back at him. "And from me. From all of us. Which is why we need to stand together—so we don't lose even more."

OCTAVIAN WAS famished by the time the council broke up many hours later, but at least they'd gotten somewhere. Tam Lysander announced dinner would be served in an hour, but Yarrow grabbed Octavian's elbow and said, "Tavern. I'm in no mood to listen to those duplicitous nobles greasing each other's asses. The pickpockets and whores are more to my liking. At least they're sincere in their intentions."

Octavian couldn't help but agree. He'd had his fill of arrogance, veiled threats, and compliments that were really insults. He'd reached his limit and beyond with being tolerated and indulged by the hereditary nobility like a dull child whose feelings they didn't want to hurt even as they smirked and elbowed each other when they thought he wasn't looking. As he followed Yarrow, Sasha, and Duncan down the torchlit hall, he noticed the mage who had spoken earlier trailing several feet behind the group of his countrymen. Since they'd be working together, Octavian hurried to catch up with him. Unfortunately, he hadn't heard the man's name. He touched his arm, and the bare skin was warm and soft. The man turned to him with eyes the color of fertile loam, and Octavian could feel the pain flooding out of them. Still, the man managed a smile. "Bairn Octavian Rose, isn't it? Can I be of service?"

"I thought you might want a respite from all of this," Octavian said. "Some of us are going to avoid what will likely be a mirthless banquet and find a tavern. Would you care to join us? I… would enjoy your company."

The Esperon mage sighed like the prospect exhausted him, but he showed Octavian another weary smile. "I suppose I could use a little time away from thinking about the war. Me being in the castle will hardly keep the Johmatrans from attacking. Thank you for inviting me. I will enjoy your company as well."

Octavian took a step back to have a better look at the other man. He was slender, but lean cords of muscle showed on his arms. Waves of thick black hair fell over his shoulders. He had a long, oval face and heavy lids over his large dark eyes. His lips were beautiful: red-brown, shiny, full on the bottom, a pronounced bow on top. His smooth skin, darker even than Breeze's, spoke of a safe and leisurely life, but his tortured expression said otherwise. Up close, Octavian noticed the details of his clothing. His loose gauzy trousers were thin, almost transparent, as was the peacock-colored sleeveless tunic he wore overtop. Tiny glass beads, the colors shifting in the torch light, accented his lapels and the colorful, fringed sash around his waist. A mint green robe, sleeveless and edged in silver embroidery, trailed on the ground behind him.

Octavian squelched his sudden desire to run his finger along the edge of the man's thick eyelashes and cleared his throat. "I regret I have forgotten your name. With everything else going on in the council."

"Nothing to be ashamed of, friend. That meeting was an ordeal for all of us, I would wager. I'm D'Aurelian Ezperino Mezzacorfii. Now, shall we? A hot meal sounds a close second only to a cup of wine. Maybe a bottle."

"Goddesses, yes." Octavian and D'Aurelian followed the others out of the castle and into the heat and humidity of the summer night. The little village a mile or so down the road from the fortress was clean and quiet, wholesome. Octavian doubted Yarrow would find many whores or pickpockets to carouse with. Even in the tavern, they saw more shepherds and merchants than thugs. A few older men sat at the bar, laughing as they nursed large mugs of ale, and the five of them found a table near an open window where they could enjoy the evening breeze and the scent of promised rain it held.

As they ate and drank, Yarrow, Sasha, and Duncan leaned close and ignored everything in favor of what seemed a very serious conversation. Octavian reached across the table and grazed the back of D'Aurelian's hand with his fingertips. D'Aurelian looked up, and their gazes met, confirming much of what Octavian had suspected and hoped for. "It's stuffy and smoky in here," Octavian said. "Would you care to buy another bottle and take a walk with me?"

"That sounds nice, and I don't think the others will miss us."

Octavian nodded, stood, and went to the bar. He purchased the best bottle of wine the humble establishment offered and left a generous tip for the tired-looking gangly youth filling mugs. The boy gave them a smile and a nod as they left the tavern.

Outside, a rosy aura ringed the round moon. The streets were quiet except for the braying of some dogs in the distance as Octavian worked the cork out of the bottle, took a swig, and passed it to D'Aurelian. "Your Esperon clothing is probably comfortable in this heat," he said as he brushed sweat from his brow with the back of his hand.

"Actually, I'm freezing," D'Aurelian said. "Why would you wear a full set of armor like that to a council?"

"Appearances." Octavian took another swig from the bottle. "What I wear means more to many of those nobles than what I'm made of, what's inside. It's a game I must play now that I'm a bairn."

"And what are you made of?" D'Aurelian moved closer so their chests almost touched. They'd come to the outskirts of the little town, and the last small cottage stood a few hundred feet behind them. In front of them was nothing but a flat plain, high grass shimmering silver in the moonlight. Dew sparkled on the leaves of the bracken brushing against their legs.

"You aren't one for small talk, are you?" Octavian brushed the hair off D'Aurelian's cheek and pinned it behind his ear.

"I want to get to know you," D'Aurelian said, leaning in to Octavian's touch. "Once, I thought I had all the time in the world, but life has shown me otherwise. Once, I would have asked you what you liked to eat, what music you enjoyed, if you preferred the spring flowers or the autumn leaves. But those are details. Details I'd like to discover, but with this war, tonight might be all we get. I want to know the important parts. Forgive me if I'm moving too quickly, if I'm putting you off, but I sense there could be something here—something I didn't expect to find again. Maybe something we both need. You may stop me anytime you don't agree. If we're destined to be only friends, I'll accept it, of course."

They continued walking along the winding dirt lane until they'd left the village behind, and the stars burned brightly in the absence of the torches. Clusters of flowers—pale pink and white—exploded along the side of the road, their perfume heavy on the air and their lacy little petals bright in the darkness. "Who did you lose?" Octavian asked.

D'Aurelian sat on a fallen tree, and Octavian joined him. "Everyone. I lost everyone. I come from a small coastal village in

Espero, but my work took me often to the university in Pala Reapaza. I was away when the Johmatrans attacked. They killed everyone—my entire family, nieces, nephews, cousins, aunts and uncles, and... and the person special to me. A man. Such a man. The way he looked at me made me feel like something rare, something special. It's a hard thing to make another person understand. I didn't want to go on after I lost him. I just wanted to lie down and die. But then I found a reason to go on—to stop the Johmatrans, to make them pay for what they took from me, to make sure no one else had to hurt as I did. Fighting them is all I have now. I have one thing. That's the man I am. That's what you'll be getting if... I just thought you should know."

Octavian moved closer and put an arm around him, drawing D'Aurelian's head to his shoulder. Leaning his cheek against D'Aurelian's hair, he spoke. "You will get nothing better, if not less. I am... I'm broken inside. I lost someone too, years ago. Believe me, I can relate to everything you said. Since then, I've only had my Roses. It hasn't been enough. D'Aurelian, I can give you some of me, if you're sure you want it, but I can't give you all of me. A part of me will always be his."

"We understand each other," D'Aurelian said. "I can't offer you everything either. But for the first time, I feel like I might have something to share. Something more than a quick tumble. This is happening quickly, but... I don't want to be alone for whatever time I have left. I'll try if you will."

"What are you suggesting? We've only known each other half a day."

D'Aurelian kissed him softly, a slow sweep of lips and tongue and a gentle rub of cheeks. The warmth it sparked in Octavian was a subtle glow as opposed to the inferno of desire he'd felt in youth. Youth. He wasn't an old man yet, and he could move on. Maybe. Live. Find the courage to take this chance with this man. To try. D'Aurelian moved his lips along Octavian's jaw. "You're the first man who's made me want to take the risk. I don't know why. I don't care. I want to feel alive again, and you make me think it might be possible. Like I might find something in life to look forward to, instead of just enduring each day until it ends and dreading the next. I'm not a man to seek a night of pleasure, but if you think we could try for something more.... I don't know if it will work. But what have we got to lose?"

Goddesses, Octavian felt it. It made no sense after only a few hours, but he felt it—possibility, if nothing else. It tingled in his belly and raised the hair on the insides of his thighs. His balls knotted close to his body and his ass clenched—nothing he hadn't felt before. Yet the way his heart floundered and his fingertips numbed reminded him of how he'd felt when he'd first desired a man, felt something more than the need to empty his sac. But—"You deserve more than to be a last resort. More than something conveniently stumbled upon."

"Life is not perfect. If we can find some happiness together, why not try? I know we just met, and if you have doubts, I understand. But life is short and uncertain. Too short to be alone. I don't know what we might make together, but it will be better than being alone. Won't it?"

Octavian pulled away from him and dropped his head into his hands. "I don't know if I can love someone again and then lose them."

"Is it better not to take the chance? We might have days, we might have hours, or we might have years."

"You don't know me," Octavian protested weakly. "I've done things I'm not proud of."

"I am not interested in the past," D'Aurelian said. "The past is pain. The future might be pain too, but it might be a little easier with someone beside me. We can hold each other up. We might limp, but we can limp together."

"Goddesses." Octavian kissed him, harder this time, pushing his tongue past D'Aurelian's teeth to lick at the smooth insides of his cheeks and lap at the roof of his mouth. "Goddesses, yes. Let's try."

THEY STUMBLED through the door of the rented room in the tavern, kissing, Octavian holding D'Aurelian's face in his hands. He fell on his back on the narrow bed with his legs wrapped around D'Aurelian's waist. As D'Aurelian nipped up and down his neck, pulling at the skin with his lips, little lightning storms rolled over Octavian's body. He felt alive, part of the world, in the moment and not stymied in past regrets in a way he hadn't even known he'd missed. He brushed the green robe from D'Aurelian's shoulders and grasped his lean, firm arms below the globes of his shoulders. He moved his hands down until he could grasp D'Aurelian's hands and weave their fingers together, and then he held them beside his head as he rolled them over and pressed his knee between D'Aurelian's thighs. He looked down at him, his lips swollen and dark, his pupils dilated, and his dark hair fanning out on the white pillow.

"You're beautiful." The rain started, a soft, soothing, rhythmic tap against the window, as Octavian sat up and untied the sash around D'Aurelian's waist. He tossed it to the floor and opened the tiny pearlescent buttons down the front of his tunic until he exposed the other man's smooth olive chest. His nipples, the color of wet clay, beaded to hard buds, and a sparse patch of hair grew over his heart and meandered down his belly. "Are you still cold?"

"I'm not used to this clime." D'Aurelian tugged at one of the leather straps holding Octavian's breastplate. "I don't know how to get this off you."

Octavian had to close his eyes until the nostalgia passed. He could do this; he wanted this—to live in the present instead of the past. He shook off his memories and returned his attention to the beautiful man beneath him, the man looking up at him with dark eyes full of trust, desire, and promise for the future.

After leaning in to kiss him softly, savoring the warmth and slide of his lips and eager tongue, Octavian scooted to the edge of the bed and stood. With years of practice, he removed his armor and stacked it in the corner while D'Aurelian watched, enrapt, his erection tenting his gauzy trousers. Octavian stood naked. The way D'Aurelian looked at him....

"I… I'm not any kind of hero, D'Aurelian. I can't let you see something that isn't there."

D'Aurelian sat up and shrugged off his shirt. "What should I see, Octavian Rose?"

Octavian looked down at his chest and belly, the network of scars covering his skin, and his withering erection. Raised pink lines and whorls of gnarled flesh covered the fronts of his legs. "See what's really in front of you—a man who has made mistakes, who has tried and failed, who has been lucky a few times, but unlucky many more. Life has left its marks on me, and it is not pretty. I'm just a man who has done his best and stumbled through life."

D'Aurelian slid his trousers down his legs and toed off his strappy sandals. "That is what I see. A man who has lived, like me. Please, come here."

Octavian cast aside the last of his doubts as he draped himself over D'Aurelian and ran his fingers along the rungs of his ribs as he found his mouth, his tongue, with his own. Their cocks slid against each other as they rolled over the bed. Octavian stood facing a new road, one he couldn't see the end of, but maybe he didn't have to walk it alone.

Chapter Thirty

Octavian Rose's Journal

Myrddin,

Ten years of war. I am thirty-eight years old, and I know I don't look even a moon younger anymore. I feel a hundred. I am tired. Tired of losing men I care about. Tired of fighting. Tired of blood and death and struggling every moment to be able to spend a little more time in the light of the world. Tired, most of all, of never having the right thing within my sights, of having no honorable option, of compromising and losing a little more of myself each day. Do I dare believe it has finally come to an end? That there can be some peace in this world?

Am I still the man you looked at like I'd hung the stars twenty years ago? Goddesses, twenty years. If ever I harbored any delusions, any illusions that I, or my life, might be somehow special, singular, above or different from the lives of other men, this never-ending war has whisked them away like ash on the wind. I think my life reached its pinnacle the day I took the Rosecairn, or possibly the day I gained legitimate sovereignty over it, though that feels less significant, probably because you were not beside me. Everything that followed has felt diminished, with one exception. I know I am on the downward slope of my life. Is it entitled of me to feel I should get to enjoy it, that I have done enough to improve the state of what proves to be, over and over, a wretched and indifferent world where noble intentions are seldom rewarded?

Yet I continue to strive for nobility, because of the covenant I made with you at the cairn. I am still, and always, striving to be worthy of you. Because I said I would. Because you deserve it. I no longer know if I am the caliber of man who would do so of his own accord.

Necessity muddies those waters, sometimes irrevocably. I know you would argue if you were still here with me; in fact, I can almost imagine the words you would choose. You'd argue, but you'd forgive me of it, as you've always forgiven me everything. And then you'd make me smile. My smiles have been rare recently.

And yet life has not been completely bleak. In some ways, I am more fortunate than other men, for I've been allowed to experience love, not once, but twice. To indulge in poesy where no one can see it and taunt me, I would say my first love was summer—riots of color, lightning storms, heat and sweat and fire and frenzy…. My second is autumn and cozy comfort against the coming cold. Something to wrap around myself and hold tight, a quiet to sit inside while the storm rages outside. I hope this does not come across as unflattering. Nothing could be further from my intention. Nor do I mean to imply autumn is more beautiful, or even more mature, than that glorious summer. I mean only to say they are different, both special, both blessings I am not sure I have ever, or can ever be worthy of.

That storm, though. It pounds against the walls, rattles the windows. I have a hard time believing it is receding.

D'AURELIAN PINNED a stray lock of hair, streaked with gray and white now, behind Octavian's ear. Octavian looked up from his book at his lover of over a decade and smiled. Deep lines creased D'Aurelian's skin around his eyes and at the corners of his mouth, and the skin beneath his eyes had started to sag, but to Octavian, he was still beautiful—maybe the only thing he could still look at and smile— outside of his memories. He closed his battered old journal and lifted D'Aurelian's hand to his lips so he could kiss his knuckles. "My love, am I wrong to mistrust this truce?"

"It's better than nothing, isn't it?" D'Aurelian said. "It's at least a chance. Give it one, won't you?"

"I want it to end," Octavian said as he jostled on the padded velvet seat of the carriage. Ten years ago, he would have ridden to Agarick's ancient fortress in central Selindria atop a shining charger with his armor polished to the sheen of glass and his hair blowing in the wind, the personification of the storybook hero he'd once imagined himself, but exhaustion and the ache in his bones had finally trumped his pride. "I'm old. I've done enough fighting."

"You're thirty-eight," D'Aurelian teased gently. "And you'll be bored without your war, without something to conquer. However will we spend our days?" He brushed the hair off Octavian's neck to kiss the side of his throat, and Octavian's skin tingled.

"I'll find something to conquer, my love. You can still distract me, make me look forward to tomorrow. Thank you. I did not think it possible before I met you that night, all those years ago. I'm more thankful we didn't waste time than I am for almost anything. Not just any man could have compelled me to take that risk."

D'Aurelian grinned and pinched Octavian's nipple through his shirt and crimson doublet. "You make me look forward to tonight, old man. If this peace treaty pans out, there'll be quite a celebration."

Octavian hummed against D'Aurelian's temple. "A private one? You still want me after all this time?"

D'Aurelian lifted his head and met Octavian's gaze, looking serious. "I could tell you every day, and you still wouldn't believe me, would you?"

"I believe you." Octavian curled his fingers around his cheek—the bones felt sharper against his palm than before—and pressed his lips to D'Aurelian's forehead. "I just wanted to give you a better life."

"This is the life we've been given, and I like to imagine we made the most of it, Octavian. We were handed broken bits, and we made them into something at least functional. Didn't we?"

"Better than functional." Octavian sighed and raked his hair back from his brow. "We have drawn out all the beauty we could, patched the cracks with gold. But I want to rest now. Grow a garden. Maybe raise some kittens. Lie in our bed and listen to the rain for hours. I'm sick to my spirit of killing. But I don't know what else I'll be good for. Once, it meant so much to me for everyone to know my name, to show the world what I could do. But now I have to wonder if I have done anything of any value at all. Has it meant anything? Will it mean anything? Won't the world continue in its barbarity as if we were never here?"

"Stop. You're a healer and a mage. You can do a great deal of good. And besides, I thought you disliked cats."

"No, I respect cats, their independence, but more importantly.... The magic is drying up." It had been bothering

Octavian for the past couple of years, and he could no longer ignore it. "You must feel it too. Something is changing. Where's it all going? This world, everything, feels different. Foreign. As atrocious as it has all been, I fear this war is the least of it."

"A puzzle for another day, love. We've arrived at the fortress."

Inside the carriage house, servants came to take their things while others led them to the old fortress's cavernous hall. Hundreds of people filled the space, but Octavian noticed Yarrow's white hair near the dais toward the front. He and D'Aurelian took a seat near the back, at the top of the tiered benches. The king, when he appeared, looked like a child's toy soldier from their distance. Garith said a few words Octavian couldn't hear, and then he took his seat on his throne.

Dozens of young men and women in red robes—the garb of the war goddess Myint—flanked the platform and began singing, their strong, clear voices echoing through the hall and through Octavian's chest. He didn't know if he believed in the goddesses or their justice, but the music moved him. Music affected him that way, the same as poetry, and he wiped at his eyes. D'Aurelian clutched his hand, oblivious or uncaring of those who might notice and condemn them. They both seemed to acknowledge the world could take no more from them, and that every moment of happiness or comfort mattered, no matter what it cost.

The steady, solid pitch of the war dirge faded, and young men and women in white and purple robes—the colors of the Mother Goddess and Fayelle, Goddess of Purity, took their places. Their song was lilting and celebratory, a hymn of humility and hope. As the impossibly high notes of their voices dissipated on the autumn breeze coming through the spear-shaped windows, royal guards in shining golden armor came to stand in formation at the edges of the platform. Priestesses of all thirteen goddesses walked in a solemn procession down the aisle, followed by acolytes swinging smoking censers. Their prayers and speeches lasted for hours.

It was all a farce, Octavian knew. He'd been privy to enough councils to realize how thin the thread holding this peace truly was— almost translucent, like spider's silk. The Esperons wanted retribution for the innocent blood spilled by the Johmatrans. They wanted someone held accountable for their dead children. Octavian was one of the few outside the island who knew the mages had teams of spies in Johmatra, deeply ingrained and looking for anything they could use against the huge, powerful, and wealthy collection of city-states. If King Garith or the Johmatrans knew, none of them would be sitting here today.

Yarrow strongly—and vocally, and in language that would shame a sailor—opposed the truce. He had demanded, as a condition of peace, that the Johmatrans free their Emiri slaves, but he had been overruled. Still, as Valen of the South Coast, or what he called the Twenty-Nine— a vast region of islands at the mouth of the Kanda River and along the shores of both Selindria and Gaeltheon—he commanded a seafaring force—his Emiri—that rivaled anything the empires could muster if they combined every boat they had. He used it to defend his land and his people, only occasionally contributing to the greater effort, while the Emiri under his "rule" continued to raid up and down the coasts of both kingdoms. Predictably, the other nobles demanded his fealty to the king, his cousin, and the halt to the activities of the people he clearly had no desire to lead but would defend to his last breath. The man was a contradiction unlike anything Octavian had ever experienced. Yarrow clearly saw no value to politics and didn't seem to care if the kingdom dropped into the Shades' Abode, but if anyone so much as spoke against the pirate refugees living on his shores, he'd threaten them with death. No one had to be a scholar or a sage to see his "valenny" would not integrate into the rest of the kingdom, and Yarrow wouldn't abide the kingdom's rules imposed on it. He wouldn't allow even a single temple to the goddesses to be built in his lands.

Where would that lead?

And then there were the priestesses and their Defenders of the Thirteen—their army. Of course, their knights had fought alongside the monarchy's forces against the foreign invaders, but everyone with eyes and a mind knew of the animosity between Garith and the temples. What would happen when they no longer faced a common enemy? Experience told Octavian they'd renew their former feud. It could divide the kingdom, especially since the priestesses had been implying, subtly, that the war came as a result of the king's sins and lack of piety.

And no matter what they claimed, the Johmatrans would exploit any weakness they sensed; Octavian had no doubt. If that happened, they'd be back where they started. Where would Octavian and D'Aurelian, and the elite force of warriors and mages they'd spent a decade building, land if it came to a head? As a bairn, Octavian was obligated to stand with the crown, but D'Aurelian would side with

Espero, and no force in the world would make Octavian turn against him. On which side would he fall if Garith went to war against the priestesses and their Defenders? He'd have a hard time reconciling risking his life and his warriors for a religion that condemned men like him to the vilest pits. No matter how he'd led his life, the priestesses saw him as refuse because of who shared his bed. How could he fight for that? Yet at the moment, the priestesses controlled a superior force. What if Yarrow and his pirates rallied against the king, or the temples? Octavian didn't know if he could stand aside. Though he thought the other mage at least a little mad, Octavian respected Yarrow. He wasn't even sure why. Besides, he had a terrible feeling Yarrow could level the kingdom on his own if he dipped into the power he so tenuously held in check. But then Yarrow was dangerous, like a storm, as likely to decimate his allies as his enemies.

And what of Sasha and his… people? Octavian had no doubt he—*they*—had interests of their own and had been working toward the outcome they desired, but of course he was no confidant to their schemes, nor would he want to be.

But their actions would affect the course of the world; he had no doubt.

As the prayers droned on and on, words repeated so often they'd lost any sincerity, spoken by rote, Octavian attempted to plan for whichever conflict arose first. He scrunched his eyes closed and tried to predict which twig was weakest—which would snap first, and how he would react. He desperately wanted to be alone with D'Aurelian, who'd become both his conspirator and his conscience, his staunchest supporter and harshest critic, and plan for what he knew was coming. He wanted to take out his book and list every possible conflict and every response so he could choose the best—to the best of his ability— before more of his men died. Goddesses, even his mind felt old; it couldn't hold on to the details and subtle nuances the way it had twenty years ago. Octavian wasn't sure wisdom and experience were a fair trade for the reckless sharpness, the righteous certainty he'd felt at nineteen.

The hush in the hall snapped Octavian out of his musings. He lifted his gaze from his knees and focused on the aisle leading to the dais. Everyone—with the exception of Yarrow and some of the Esperon ambassadors—stood and waited with palpable anticipation.

Simultaneously, Octavian and D'Aurelian pressed their fists to their eyes at the sudden flood of magic. Octavian felt it surging in his veins until he thought they'd rupture. His eyeballs throbbed and his heart beat so fast it made him dizzy. Next to him, D'Aurelian gagged out, "They're doing this on purpose. How… how do they have access to so much magic?"

Through watering, stinging eyes, Octavian struggled to focus on the floor and aisle below him, tried to bring the grout between the square stones into focus. The other Esperon mages held their heads in their hands, while Yarrow stood, looking around, a vague impression of lightning blue wings furled around his shoulders. Octavian had seen it before, in battle, but today it unnerved him because it felt instinctive—magic reacting to magic.

Litters carried by Emiri slaves with shorn heads made their way up the aisle toward the king. The conveyances were built of supple, gilded wood, domed, and draped in crimson gauze with fringed and scalloped edges. Within, people reclined on nests of cushions. Octavian could only see the silhouettes of their bodies, but they looked… wrong, misshapen. He rose from his bench. Clutching D'Aurelian's sleeve to pull him along, he made his way, as clandestinely as he could, to the outer wall of the room and down the tiers toward the dais.

"What are you doing?" D'Aurelian whispered.

"I want to see them," Octavian responded. They had been told the potentates of the Johmatran city-states ruled through their claim of descent from the legendary mage-emperor Fane, descent they attempted to preserve through centuries of inbreeding that had led to grotesque deformities—and powerful sorcery. Despite all the fighting they'd done, Octavian had never encountered one of these Johmatran rulers. He wanted to know what he'd be dealing with if he ever faced one, and, as any man might be, he was filled with morbid curiosity. Together, he and D'Aurelian edged their way around the throng until they'd made it to the front row. The scarlet litter stood only a few hundred yards away.

D'Aurelian gasped as a slave lifted the translucent fabric from the front of the litter so the Johmatran emissary could address the king. Octavian winced. Deformities didn't come close to describing it. He didn't know whether the thing propped up on the embroidered pillows was male or female. It had a thin, bluish white body, prominent veins beneath the papery skin, and no muscle over the frail-looking bone. Layers of beads barely concealed the sagging tits. Its skull formed a cone, almost like a lady's headdress, and the eyes were too far apart, at the sides of its head, like a fish's. The nose was flat, the nostrils wide and prominent. It had no hair on its body, but swirling scars covered every visible inch of skin until a thin but ridiculously jeweled loincloth obscured the creature's—it hardly looked like a man or woman's—sagging groin. The bracelets it wore could have been shackles on its skeletal arms, and the long fingernails had been coated in gold and crusted in gems.

One of the Esperon mages stepped forward, a young woman with golden ringlets and big blue eyes that matched her functional vest and loose trousers. Little else covered her tanned skin, and her scant attire surely scandalized the ladies of Selindria and Gaeltheon—a fact of which she seemed proud as she held her chin high and jutted her bare belly out. A little golden stud with a blue gem dangled from her navel. "My name is Courtenay Jardine-Lamont, of Espero, Your Majesty. I will serve as translator for the Johmatran ambassador."

Octavian didn't miss the curl of her lips or the shake of her magnificent hair. Since the Johmatran lords couldn't grow their locks, all their people, including their Emiri slaves, were required to shave their heads. The young mage's small act of defiance wouldn't be lost on the foreign potentate, and Octavian found it glorious. He liked Courtenay Jardine-Lamont instantly.

"Thank you for your service," Garith said. He held his arms out to his sides and bent at the waist. "Selindria and Gaeltheon welcome the honored dignitaries from Johmatra. This is a momentous day for all of us—one that I pray will go down in history as the beginning of centuries of mutually beneficial friendship and peace."

Octavian expected nothing but a carefully rehearsed speech, but he leaned in to observe. Yarrow looked over his shoulder and met his gaze, his expression chaotic and unreadable to Octavian. All the arcane energy in the hall clashed and volleyed off itself, making it hard for him to concentrate. He wrapped an arm around D'Aurelian's waist, and they supported each other as they had since they'd met.

"The Johmatrans want all mages not descended from Fane, at least according to their records, killed as not to 'use up' the magic," D'Aurelian whispered to Octavian.

He nodded. "I know. But it was a concession of the peace treaty that our mages, and the Esperons, will be left alone. Foreign mages will even be safe to travel on the other side of the mountains without danger. They have sworn it."

"And do you think that will last? Their belief in some being worthy of sorcery and not others has been deeply ingrained in their culture—for thousands of years. Do you think they'll let it go?"

"No." Octavian leaned in, hoping to observe all he could, devise some way to stand against the Johmatrans when D'Aurelian's prediction proved accurate.

"Will you side with Yarroway L'Estrella, with Espero, when they show their colors?"

"I will side with you, D'Aurelian. Will it be mages against those without the gift, priestesses against the king, or just Yarrow against the world? He is the one we must watch. He is powerful."

"And unpredictable," D'Aurelian said. "And yet maybe our best gamble."

"Do you think?" Octavian asked.

D'Aurelian shrugged. "He wants a world where men take credit for their accomplishments and blame for their wrongdoings, without the pillowy excuse of the goddesses. That is something I can support. Forgive me, my love, but no goddess appeared to halt the Johmatrans killing Esperon babies in their baskets. Not even our Pherara. I trust things I can see and feel, and not abstracts others tell me to believe in."

"But you are the minority." Octavian shook his head. "Most find comfort in following the goddesses' law. It absolves them from personal responsibility. It's easier to be led than to decide, I suppose. That is something deeply ingrained in our culture. One can still be put to death for denying the existence of the goddesses."

"Quiet." D'Aurelian gripped Octavian's wrist as the thing in the litter spoke and the pretty young mage translated.

"Thank you for your kind welcome, High King Garith of Selindria and Gaeltheon. I am Lord Ky-Staahl Texes Duclembuis, descendant of Fane on both my mother and father's sides, ruler of the blue city of Roahb, in the north. I have the great honor of speaking for the rulers of the other city-states."

"And how do you find my kingdom?" Garith asked conversationally, though his pallor and the pinch of his lips belied his unease.

"To be honest," Courtenay translated, "we find it troubling and barbaric. We had never envisaged a place where common peasants are permitted to practice magic and the filthy refuse of the sea are permitted to wander freely and do as they like. We must admit we find it wicked."

"I find you wicked, you foul, twisted monstrosity," Yarrow yelled, getting to his feet.

"Cousin, you promised," Garith snapped desperately. "If you cannot hold your tongue, I will have you removed."

"I will remove myself!" Yarrow shouted. "I'll have no part of this—this travesty!" Courtenay had the good sense not to relay Yarrow's words, or the fragile peace might have shattered.

"Yarroway, by the goddesses, I am trying to save lives," Garith said. "Concessions were made on both sides."

"Do not speak to me of goddesses," Yarrow snarled, a blue light crackling around him, so bright it hurt Octavian's eyes and made him squint. "We fought these barbarians for ten years—ten years!—and saw no evidence of their presence, let alone their aid."

"Heresy!" a priestess yelled. "You should be thrown into prison!"

"Try it!" Yarrow shouted. "Try anything you think you can manage to stop me, but I will not sit here and grease these creatures' deformed asses, not after the mages they killed. Not after the horrors I have seen committed against the Emiri—the people of my valenny. If you are willing to sacrifice their lives for this peace, to let them continue to languish in unimaginable pain, you sleep at night thinking of it. What have they given us beyond a promise to stop killing Esperon babies?" He held up a hand to keep Garith from arguing. "I won't, cousin. I can't. Do as you must, but this peace does not extend to my valenny of the Twenty-Nine. We will offer no quarter to our enemies. I—we—have fought for you, bled. You cannot ask this of me."

"I can!" Garith shouted. "You hold that valenny at my bequest, and it is still a part of my kingdom. The Emiri are not my subjects, and as a part of this treaty, you will cease all attempts to liberate them from their rightful Johmatran masters. You will do this to stem the blood of Selindrian and Gaelthonic soldiers, and because I, as your king, command you to. You can be removed, and those lands can be granted to a loyal subject."

"Remove me, then, cousin. You know where to find me. I will be in the Twenty-Nine, surrounded by more than eight hundred Emiri ships."

An older man, Octavian thought he was a Gaelthonic noble, stood and pointed as Yarrow marched down the aisle, weaving around the crimson litters. "Your Majesty, your cousin is a traitor! It is high time we marched on his valenny—the *South Coast*—removed him, and drove the Emiri vermin from our shores."

"A matter for another time," the king said. "Today is a joyous occasion. A time for peace. I know that is what we all want. Please, all of you, before the opportunity is lost. Bring out the treaty so the priestess of Vestrafori can read the terms. Then we can all sign it and get to what promises to be a lovely banquet in the gardens."

Octavian and D'Aurelian leaned against the wall as the priestess read from the long scroll—for almost two hours. Since he knew everything that would be said, Octavian let his mind wander. Duncan, Yarrow's lover and the bairn of Windwake, watched the Defenders of the Thirteen. Sasha had not come to the ceremony, and Octavian wondered why and what he might be doing. It occurred to him that Yarrow had his Emiri force and the brethren of the Crimson Scythe in his corner, as well as his magic. If he really did match his force against his cousin's, it could make the war that had just ended look like a schoolyard wrestling match. Would Espero side with the fellow mage against their old enemy, the Johmatrans, or would they ally with the king who had—eventually—offered them aid? What of the priestesses' army? Would the holy women see Yarrow's heresy as a greater threat than Garith? Or would they stand by the wayside and conserve their power until the dust settled?

"This is not over," Octavian said to D'Aurelian when the meeting began to break up. "The peace is on paper, but there is too much animosity between too many parties."

"What do you plan to do?" D'Aurelian asked as they made their way down the long aisle toward the great double doors flanked by enormous statues of ancient warriors. Outside the castle, the air was bracing, the sky gray with clouds skidding rapidly across the firmament, crunchy brown leaves skittering across the cobbled lanes.

Octavian went to a stone bench and sat down. Standing so long had caused his right knee to act up, and he rubbed the cap. Goddesses, his armor and red cape had never felt so heavy upon his shoulders. His mind had never been so full of twisting things chewing at the edges of his thoughts. He didn't know what to do. Thank the heavens he sat next to a man he could admit that to. "We must keep the force we have built from your mages and my mercenaries strong. Increase our numbers if we can. This whole thing—it's like a dish that has been broken and pieced back together. It will break again, I just don't know where, or what blow will shatter it. Garith is… he is trying to be a good king. I understand why he caved to the Johmatran demands. I understand, and yet I understand it from Yarrow's perspective as well. D'Aurelian, who would you back, Yarrow or the king?"

"Do you think it will come to that?"

"If it does?"

"Couldn't the Roses stay out of it?"

"If we can't?" Octavian asked. "What would you do?"

D'Aurelian leaned his elbows on his knees and rubbed his eyes with his thumb and finger. "My loyalties are to you, the men we trained together, and Espero. In that order. I would try to do whatever I could to protect those parties."

"So… side with the likely victor regardless of principle?"

"Principle seems an extravagance these days. Not worth lives."

"I suppose."

"You disagree?"

"I don't know," Octavian admitted, looking out across the grounds, all brown and gray. "Once, I swore to do the right thing, the honorable thing, even if it went against my own interests. But that was so long ago. A different world. A different man than I am now. Goddesses, I long for the certainty of youth. Everything was black-and-white then. Good and evil. Now it's all so muddled. How can I separate the soil from the water when the mud is pouring in everywhere? To think I once wanted this."

D'Aurelian looked around to make sure they were alone before taking Octavian's hand and knitting their fingers together. "What did you want, once? What did you want when you still looked at the world and saw only possibility, back in the springtime of your life?"

Octavian laughed as he remembered the lad—even thinking that word still hurt—he'd been. "I was so ridiculous. I thought I could take over the world, make it virtuous and fair. Not that I was noble. I wanted glory. For others to know my name and respect it. This version of me I so carefully concocted. Mostly, I wanted to live life by my own terms.

I'm hardly doing that now. I feel like I'm at the mercy of everything. But what about you, love? What did you want as a young man?"

"Nothing so grand," D'Aurelian said. "To study, maybe publish a few books and papers. Make some small contribution to scholarship. A decent amount of wealth, enough to have girls so I didn't have to tidy my own house. I have always hated cleaning."

"Love?"

"I always imagined quiet companionship, another scholar to argue over points in ancient parchments, have dinner with, and go to bed early. Sort of a friend, more than anything. You?"

"I never thought I needed it, needed anyone. I even resented others' attempts to care for me. I have been a fool for many things. Hindsight, you know? I could have not survived the past ten years alone—without you."

"What's our next move? Shall we go to Espero to recruit more mages, or back home to Rosecairn?"

It warmed Octavian more than he would have imagined to hear D'Aurelian call Rosecairn home. He was getting sentimental in his old age, but he didn't mind showing it as he once had. He leaned over and kissed D'Aurelian's forehead, letting his lips linger on the lined, olive skin he knew as well as his own. "I love you, you know."

"And I love you. It makes everything else bearable. There are even moments of wonderful smattered about."

"There are," Octavian said, smiling. Of all the things he'd change in his past, the night he'd leaped off that cliff with this man wasn't one of them. D'Aurelian shuddered, and Octavian put an arm around his shoulder to pull him close. "Cold?"

"I can't get used to the northern climes. I fear I never will. Perhaps we should go to Espero."

"I've a better idea," Octavian said, leaping from the bench with a spark of the old excitement. "Why don't we take a detour to the Twenty-Nine?"

"Yarrow's valenny?" D'Aurelian narrowed his eyes with suspicion, but he smiled. "Why?"

"Just an inkling I have. I suspect Yarrow is up to more than freeing Emiri slaves from the Johmatrans. He's planning something bigger. Knowing what it is will give us a distinct advantage. As we both know, he's dangerous. More dangerous than the rest of them put together. We should keep an eye on him, gain his trust if we can, learn his plans. Then we can make counter plans if needs be. Or find a damned deep hole to crawl inside while everything else burns."

"And you think you can convince him to tell you?"

Octavian looked up at the sky. The clouds had pulled apart, letting a fissure of watery light bleed through. It fell across D'Aurelian, making his black hair shot with silver glisten and the beads of his heavy blue robe sparkle. His dark eyes glimmered between the wrinkled lids of his eyes. Maybe the world was not so hopeless, so worthless. Maybe it still held things worth fighting for.

"I can convince him, my love. We still have things to do, destinies to shape. Now is not the time to bow out. You're a great mage, D'Aurelian, and I… I am… I am still Octavian Rose."

Archer's Regret

Chapter One

To the east lay the river and the towns and settlements it supported. They meant whores, sellers of illicit goods, peddlers of the exotic, and muscular, sweaty sailors desperate for companionship—all things Sylvain enjoyed, or at least had until recently.

Amorous seamen had their charm, but Sylvain had exhausted it, and he felt no more pull toward it than he did toward the same meal eaten every night for a moon. Sustenance, surely, but boring enough it was hardly worth the bother. Almost better to go hungry than endure the monotony.

To the west was the Revenant Coast and the ghosts of those massacred on its shores. Nothing lived or grew along the sands and crags. No sane man would venture onto that cursed beach, and even Sylvain was not desperate enough for novelty to ride that way.

North—the way he had come from—held many good things: the brotherhood of the Rosecairn, the sweet and welcoming lips and limbs of his young Octavian, a place he belonged and where he was respected. But it had grown old, too safe and predictable, and so Sylvain had walked away. Despite all the benefits of Rosecairn and all Octavian's allure, something had been missing. Something had welled up in him and made him restless for adventure and the road. Something itched that he could not reach from his comfortable position by Octavian's side.

And here he was, at a crossroads astride his dappled gray gelding, looking down each winding dirt pathway as if he could see the destiny at its end. Which one led to something exceptional? Not even mages could discern what was to come. He knew only north was cold, west was haunted, and east was dull and well traveled. That left south, though he had avoided exploring the lush, hot areas of Selindria's peninsula for many years. Sylvain heeled his mount. Many things might await him in Elvara, and he could not deny it drew him as if it held him at the end of a rope. It hardly meant returning to what he had turned his back on so long ago, and with any luck, it would mean something bright and new that would fill the recent hollowness growing inside him.

Sylvain rode for days, stopping at night to camp or to take a room at an inn if he encountered one. This territory, while officially part of Selindria, lay far from the seat of power and beyond the scrupulous eyes of the king and his priestesses. Their customs differed vastly, but Sylvain was not afraid. He had been a feared warrior in the mercenary company at Rosecairn, and it took no false modesty to acknowledge himself as one of the finest archers beneath the goddesses' light. If need be, he could draw his bow, nock an arrow, and let it fly before his enemy had time to blink. That knowledge let him ride confidently through the wild and lawless territory in his snug leather armor and thick hood. Sylvain almost wished a band of brigands or a camp of thugs might ambush him. Someone worthy for a change. He could use the practice—and the distraction.

Anything to shift his focus from the parsing of past deeds and wishes. What good would it do to rake through the dust of abandoned things? Though he discovered only broken bits and tarnished baubles, he couldn't stop digging as the countryside around him grew hotter and greener. Moss hung thick from the branches of the ancient trees Sylvain rode beneath.

Sylvain needed something else to occupy his attention, something to enthrall him and captivate his senses until he considered neither past nor future. He needed something to engulf and absorb him until he lost the boundary between his identity and his pursuit, until there was only the game. The world, though, seemed turned upside down and emptied of anything new.

Octavian Rose had been that all-encompassing, pulling force. For a while. Until he grew strong and sure enough that he didn't need Sylvain anymore, and then the challenge had been lost. Sylvain dodged the revelations about himself that hurled at his face as he thought about Octavian, riding harder, faster, to escape the idea that he'd only desired Octavian when he had the upper hand, something Octavian needed. He valued Octavian beyond the impossible goals the young man set for himself—he had, and still adored "his treasure"—but part of him had been as drawn to the epic quest as to the man.

Was he really so pitiful and needy? He'd never been so before. He just needed something fresh, something to remind him of the wonder the world held if one was willing to seek it out. Then he would feel like his old self again.

To the Shades' with certain, comfortable things. He would leave them for common men, and that was one thing he had never considered himself, in any sense. He would let instinct, his sense for exquisite and uncommon things, guide him now as it had when he'd run away from his wealthy family's house.

Chapter Two

SYLVAIN RODE into Elvara half a moon later. The seaside community was much as he remembered it with its luxurious inns of white stone, sandy beaches to match, and tropical trees trimmed in garlands of glass baubles and shells. It smelled of the flowers growing in pots along the cobbled streets, the abundant variety of fruit for sale at stands lining them, and the sea in the distance. It was late afternoon, and people—most of them with the dark hair and complexions common to the southern region—made final purchases, congregated in front of taverns, or hurried home with full baskets.

Sylvain found a place to stable his horse and handed a few coppers to the stocky girl who led the animal away. He looked up and down the street at rows of lanterns hung between the buildings and arbors sagging beneath vines. When he had first come here from Foghollow in Gaeltheon, the cold, gray plain where he had grown up, he'd thought not even the goddesses' paradise could be as beautiful as this tiny town in Elvara. Now, though, he noticed the stray dogs gathered around the garbage bins, the too thin young prostitutes, and the makeup cracking over the wrinkles on the older whores' faces.

It seemed sad and desperate, people struggling to survive the same as anywhere else. Not the wanton, happy sex workers delighting in their lots. Nothing new—just men's greed and willingness to exploit the less fortunate. No paradise. It had likely never been any different, and Sylvain realized he had been the one that changed. He just couldn't pinpoint when, where, or how. Somewhere along the line, wonder had turned to ennui, and nothing seemed beautiful or enchanting anymore. He had thought Elvara, if anywhere, would rekindle that spark, and the fact that it hadn't terrified him. He didn't want to live out the rest of his days consumed by this emptiness. How could any man live without something to strive toward?

Sylvain considered leaving, trying his fortune elsewhere, but since his ass was sore from the saddle and his body stiff, he decided to stay at least a night. Most of the drinking in Elvara was done outdoors, in courtyards behind small taverns, ceilinged in flowering lattice and dotted with mismatched tables. He made his way to one, sat down, and ordered wine. If he remembered correctly, small dishes of free food would appear at a steady rate as long as he continued to buy drinks. The first platter contained octopus, lightly battered, fried, and served with a zesty sauce. Though he was hungry, Sylvain couldn't say he enjoyed it. Not even the thought of a night with three or four sublimely skilled brothel boys stirred much in him. He craved something fiercely, but it wasn't food, drink, or sex. What else was there in life? Adventure, gold, and glory—but even those did not call to him as they once had.

He poured more wine from the bottle and watched the thick burgundy liquid crawl slowly down the edge of the glass. What would his Octavian do if faced with this conundrum? Sylvain smiled as a serving girl set bread, cheese, and sausage on the table. Octavian would focus on his questions until the rest of the world crumbled and fell away around him. He'd take out that battered leather journal he always carried with him, list every possible solution and every possible consequence of each, and then he'd choose the best based on all available information. And then he would act; Octavian had never backed down nor run from an enemy in his life.

Sylvain knew his enemy. Until now, he just hadn't wanted to admit it. He shook his head as he imagined Octavian chuckling and teasing him for taking so long to come to the obvious conclusion.

Always reckless, Sylvain had walked away from wealth and a title simply because he was bored. Each time he started to establish himself and gained a measure of comfort and security, he'd turned his back to seek out something more exciting. By doing so, he'd lost recognition, loyal friends, and piles of gold, yet he had no regrets. He'd been certain of his moves every step of the way, with one exception. Only once had he doubted his decision, and that doubt had stayed with him, buried deep in his memories, dormant most of the time, only waking to flop and flounder if someone—most recently, Octavian— poked at it. But over the years, it had been burrowing its way toward the surface, chewing through his thoughts toward freedom no matter how hard he tried to push it down. It had broken out at last, and now he had to face it and cut the head off the thing. Then he could let it go to ground and return to the sweet things life offered without distraction.

Sylvain finished his wine, wrapped the bread, meat, and cheese in a cloth napkin and stowed it in a pouch for later, left a couple of coppers—payment for his drinks and a nice tip for the friendly serving girl—and stood to leave the courtyard tavern just as the sunset light began to gild the thick ivy and grapevines twisting over the stone partitions and latticed ceiling. He'd put an end to these doubts and regrets tonight and, goddesses willing, by morning he'd find himself drunk beneath a trio of lithe young men, all of them sated and covered in their sweat and fluids.

The solution to his problem posed no great challenge, but still Sylvain dreaded it. Walking determinedly down the pretty cobbled streets as lanterns and strings of tiny lights in colored glass orbs colored the spreading twilight, he vowed to be the warrior he'd pretended to be for the last fifteen years and face it head-on.

Chapter
Three

DOZENS OF white marble steps led to a building that would put most of the temples to the goddesses to shame. Towering columns supported the porch roof and the several arched entryways it protected. Two large golden statues, one male and one female—sculpted drapery concealing only the absolute necessities—stood seductive guard on either side of the main entrance. Potted plants decorated the terrace, and old and well-tended gardens with white stone paths that shone in the evening darkness surrounded the structure. Colored lanterns lined the paths and hung from the eaves, and musicians sat playing beneath cloth pavilions with scalloped edges.

From beneath a flowering tree across the street, Sylvain watched a steady stream of men and even a fair number of women entering and leaving the brothel. He smelled the sticks of incense the brothel servants lit nightly and poked into the soft soil of the hedges and potted plants, sweet, smoky tendrils drifting over to wind around him and beckon him closer. All the artifice had been designed and perfected to weave a fantastic illusion for potential patrons, and when Sylvain had been younger, it had worked. He knew he needed to break the spell of this place—and the one inside who had ensorcelled him so expertly— before he could regain his carefree life.

It should be simple enough. He would enter the whorehouse, and the fruits on the trays would be overripe and almost rotten. The flowers in the alcoves would be wilted. The beauty of the courtesans, he was sure he would discover, would be all in their elaborate jewelry and cosmetics, costumes designed to conceal and enhance—all gauze and illusion. Sylvain felt certain that like Elvara itself, all the beauty and magic belonged to his memory and the evils of imagination, and that the reality would disappoint him. Aeris would disappoint him even more than he already had. Instead of being the godlike ideal of Sylvain's dreams, the whore would show the truth of his greed, manipulation, and desperation. Sylvain doubted he would be anywhere near as gorgeous as he remembered, especially now. Years of selling himself would have taken their toll on Aeris, and he would likely be bitter, hard, and lined, all his artifice peeled away.

And as soon as Sylvain saw him, he could acknowledge he had done the right thing by turning his back on Aeris all those years ago. He could behead and bury his one doubt and continue reaping the sweet fruits of a selfish and independent life. Confident, he crossed the street and climbed the steep stairs. Then he handed the man in the loincloth the three gold pieces required for entry and went into the parlor.

The peeling paint on the erotic wall murals hardly surprised him. Neither did the heady incense burning to mask the smells of sweaty bodies, sex, and worse, and not quite succeeding. The watered-down wine a topless girl brought tasted as cheap and fake as everything else, and Sylvain left his goblet on a table as he wandered farther into the salon. As he had predicted, the artificial smiles of the brothel workers, their feigned caresses and flirtatious gestures, were as blatantly obvious as the scuff and stains on the scarlet rugs between the tables. No one here was truly happy or fulfilled—it was all an act, and not even a good one. It shamed him to imagine he had once fallen under the spell of this place. Now he saw it for what it was, and as soon as he saw Aeris and had evidence of his part in the falsehood, he could leave and find something fun to get up to.

Sylvain approached one of the large, shirtless men in snug leather trousers standing along the wall. "Can I be of service, tam?" the guard asked.

For good measure, Sylvain slipped a piece of gold into the man's massive, rough palm and offered him his most innocent smile, which he knew wasn't terribly innocent. "I'm interested in purchasing some companionship, and gold is no obstacle. I believe he is called Aeris, if I remember correctly. He was very skilled."

The big man with the close-cropped hair grinned and patted Sylvain on the shoulder. "Course I know Aeris. He's one of our most popular. Which means, I'm afraid, he doesn't start his evening's work this early. He's still at dinner, out with one of those rich old birds who don't want nothing but to be seen on his arm, if you know what I mean." The guard jabbed Sylvain's arm with his elbow, and Sylvain feigned a chuckle.

"I understand completely," Sylvain said, "but if it wouldn't be too much trouble, could you escort me to his quarters to wait? I am a man in a position… well, let's just say it would be better for me if I was not seen lingering here. I'm sure you understand."

"Hardly a unique request," the guard said with a wink. "Right this way, tam."

NOT SURPRISINGLY, Aeris lived in a much larger and finer room than he had when Sylvain had first met him. Situated at the northwestern corner of the complex, the huge suite boasted a private terrace overlooking some olive trees, with lanterns strung along the edge of the porch roof. Inside, flower petals drifted on the heated water of a central pool surrounded by upholstered benches, and a huge bed with an iron frame stood in a corner, with a pile of pillows and cushions in the corner opposite. Candelabras and lamps lit the space as bright as a hazy summer afternoon, all soft gold and fuzzy orange. Gold and marble statues of nude young men flanked the rooms, the firelight dancing along their smooth musculature.

Sylvain thanked the guard and tipped him another piece of silver, and the big but friendly man left and sealed the double doors with a resounding gong. After removing his bow and quiver from his back and stashing them in a corner, Sylvain began to look around, seeking the evidence of artifice and decay he'd seen in the brothel's parlor. He didn't have to look very hard to find flaking marble columns and slimy gray-green mold along the rock edges of the pool. All the linens and furs, though, smelled clean—of citrus soap and talc. The washing area and chamber pots were immaculate, as were the two ceramic bowls near the easternmost window. They sat on a little blue rug, and one held clear water, the other chunks of raw meat and fish that smelled fresh. Before long, a small brown cat with black stripes and a white muzzle pattered out from underneath the bed to lap at the water with a bright pink tongue extended out from black lips. The little creature paused in its drinking, looked up at Sylvain, noised a small *meerp*, licked its lips, and returned its attention to its bowls.

He watched the cat until it hopped up onto the bed, circled, and lay down with its striped tail over its nose, ignoring his presence. Sylvain continued to investigate the luxurious suite, looking for the signs of decay he had missed on his first visits here. The wine bottles on the rack were free of dust and the fruit in the carved wooden bowls was fresh. The spare sheets and blankets in a closet smelled pleasantly of lavender, and even the small chest holding faux penises carved from wood and stone seemed tidy and clean.

Still, Sylvain couldn't dismiss the filth that must underlie Aeris's life and profession, so he sat down on the edge of the bed, sure he would see it in the man's face, his eyes. He had himself so convinced Aeris couldn't be happy with his fate that when the man came through the doors, grinning and satisfied, toeing off his supple suede shoes to leave them on the mat by the door as he dropped his leather satchel on a stand, Sylvain couldn't reconcile his idea of his former lover with the reality. Aeris wasn't the shriveled and miserable husk he'd expected—needed—to see.

Both men were shocked by the presence of the other. Sylvain sprang to his feet from the edge of the bed while Aeris backed against the wall by the door. Slowly, they recognized each other, and Sylvain relaxed.

Aeris didn't. "What in the Shades' are you doing here, Sylvain? You said you'd never come back."

Cautiously, Sylvain took a few steps toward Aeris. Goddesses, his beauty enthralled Sylvain as it had the first time he had laid eyes on the man: his golden brown skin contrasting hard against the pale blond hair tumbling over his shoulders, light green-gold eyes shining, pink lips like pulpy, wet flowers, and a lithe body dusted in shimmering blond hair that more accentuated than hid his subtle musculature. Sylvain just wanted to back him against the wall and kiss him until neither of them could breathe, until their lips swelled and bled and they toppled together on the rug by the door. Just looking at Aeris filled the emptiness in Sylvain until it overflowed and burst his levees, tearing down all the structures he had built to defend himself against disaster. Stripped bare of all his armor, Sylvain lifted a hand in front of his face to shield himself. He had expected—wanted, and what in the Shades' did that say of him—an Aeris beaten down, haggard, pathetic, and leaching, a desperate creature wanting nothing but to siphon the life from him and any man he might enthrall.

But Aeris was no more a spider than his clean and comfortable quarters were a web meant to entrap the unsuspecting. Sylvain hoping to find something untoward here didn't make it manifest, and Aeris, in his brown trousers, white shirt, and blue tunic, could have been any man coming home from an evening at one of Elvara's acclaimed outdoor theaters. The lines around his eyes and the droop of jowls Sylvain had imagined were absent. He looked healthy, content, fit... more beautiful than the goddesses should allow.

"Are you here as a patron, Sylvain?" Aeris turned his back on Sylvain as he went to a table to pour himself a glass of water. "If that is the case, you should know my fees will be exorbitant, if I accept you as a client at all."

A hundred insults about Aeris being a whore and taking gold from anyone who offered it sprang to Sylvain's imagination, along with slights about the fortune Sylvain had already laid at his feet, back when he had been young and gullible. Instead of voicing any of them, though, Sylvain said, "No, I am not looking for that. I was passing through, and I thought I would check up on you, see if you are well." He didn't add that he'd hoped to find Aeris withering away without him, hopeless and miserable. How could he?

Without turning to face Sylvain, Aeris snorted. "I have not seen you in almost ten years, and yet you assume I need you looking out for me. You arrogant son of a heifer. You haven't changed at all. Just... leave. Get out of here, Sylvain."

Watching the severe lines and angles of Aeris's spine and shoulders, Sylvain wiped his damp palms down the front of his trousers and drew in a shaky breath. Again, he found himself looking down paths where he couldn't see to the ends and wondering where to put his feet, because the words he chose next would make all the difference.

"That's not what I meant to imply, Aeris. I... have been thinking about you. Something has been missing from my life, and, goddesses, I roamed over Selindria and Gaeltheon looking for it.... But I don't want to make this about me. I want to know how you are. Please, I just want to talk for a while if you can spare the time. I-I can pay. Make up the fees you'll lose—"

A ceramic cup flying through the air and shattering, showering Sylvain with terra-cotta shards, cut him off. Aeris spun and stomped up to him until only inches separated their chests. Stabbing a finger into

Sylvain's chest, Aeris shouted, "You conceited pig! You think I need your coin? I have more money than you, always have! Why do you always need to remind me I'm nothing but a whore? You think that just because I'm a whore, I can't love anything but gold? To the Shades' with you, Sylvain! I'm a man, and I have feelings, passion! Dreams of my own! Why can't you see—?"

Dusky rose spread over Aeris's cheeks and the bridge of his nose. His spittle hailed against Sylvain's face. Sylvain couldn't think. He grasped Aeris's wrists and held them next to Aeris's ears, pointing his elbows out like wings, staring into his gemlike, blazing eyes before he pressed their lips together. For a few moments, Aeris twisted and fought, but then the tension bled out of his body, and with a mewling groan, somewhere between irritation and desire, he curved against Sylvain and parted his lips to Sylvain's tongue.

Their kissing turned desperate, savage. Sylvain tore the lacings of Aeris's tunic and let it flutter to the floor as he nipped and suckled on the man's lips and tongue, feasting on his exotic yet familiar flavor. As soon as he released Aeris's hands, Aeris grabbed him by the back of the neck to hold him while he devoured Sylvain's mouth. Sylvain cupped the perfect crescents of Aeris's ass, then slid his hands up Aeris's back and around to the collar of his gauzy shirt. A tug rent it down the middle, and Sylvain pushed it off Aeris's shoulder and down his arms, frantic to get his mouth and hands on that sweet, soft, golden brown skin. He had just started dragging his lips down the man's long, graceful neck when Aeris grasped Sylvain's collarbones and shoved him back.

"Goddesses," Aeris said, looking down at the tattered white cloth on the intricate tile patterns of the floor. "That shirt cost a hundred gold."

"Sorry. I'll pay for it."

Aeris slapped him, his fingers striking Sylvain's tender lips just hard enough to sting and squelch Sylvain's arousal. "I don't need your fucking money. Do you really think you're the only man who comes here and offers me piles of gold?"

"No, you have always had many." After the smack, Sylvain couldn't resist the retort. "I suppose I cannot offer you anything more than dozens of others."

Aeris canted his head and batted his thick, gold eyelashes. "If you believe that, then you should go."

Sylvain tensed and balled his fists. "What do you expect? What in the Shades' do you want from me?"

Aeris walked around Sylvain, his hips swaying subtly. He sat on the bed and pulled a cylindrical cushion into his lap as he looked up at Sylvain. "You said you wanted to talk. Sit with me. Tell me your truth, and I will tell you mine. Can you afford that, my old friend?"

Though Sylvain wasn't sure he could, he sat down on the edge of the bed a few feet from Aeris, unbuckled his leather armor, and let it fall to the floor behind him. He knew this would cost him much more than gold.

Chapter Four

"I'LL GO first," Aeris said. "What made you come back here after all this time?"

Though he could have offered up any number of plausible excuses, Sylvain opted for the truth. "I have been restless. No matter what I do, I am not satisfied, and I have done great things, impossible feats. Yet the victories I achieved rang hollow, and I did not know why… not until I set eyes on you again. I have left this unfinished, Aeris, and it is gnawing at me."

"And how would you finish it?"

Sylvain arched a brow and tilted his head, a gesture that melted most men, left them malleable in his hands. Aeris only narrowed his eyes. "That is not how we agreed to play this game," Sylvain said. "I believe it is my turn to ask a question."

"Very well. Go on."

"Do you enjoy being a whore?"

Aeris raked his nimble fingers through his gold hair. "Enjoyment is a subjective term. It is better than farming, or laboring in a quarry, certainly. I like laying with men. I like giving pleasure and being pleasured. I like to come. I'm good at this work. Would I do it if I were a noble, independently wealthy? I cannot say, as I have never been in that situation."

"You must have almost as much gold hoarded away as most noble households," Sylvain argued. "So why do you carry on?"

Aeris shook his head. "My turn. Why me?"

"What do you mean?"

"Sylvain, how many men have you been with in the last decade? Hundreds? And for free? Why come back to me? I am not deluded enough to think I'm that special."

Sylvain looked at his glimmering eyes and bow-shaped lips. "Maybe I am deluded enough. Nothing since I left you has satisfied me like being with you. I'm hollow inside where you should be, and I assure you, I feel like a fool admitting it. I just can't live with the regret. If I cannot win you, I need to leave here knowing I gave all I had, that I let no chance for happiness slip by. Even then… fuck, Aeris. I have never felt the way I felt when we were together. You're good at what you do, but I know it was more than that. And I think that earns me a question. Why are you still selling yourself when you surely have enough gold stashed to retire like a king?"

Aeris stared down at the pillow in his lap, ruffling the braided gold fringe with his fingers.

"Aeris?"

"What do you want me to say? I'm good at this, and I have made a name for myself. What else makes me… *me*?"

"Goddesses." Sylvain pried Aeris's fingers loose from the pillow and closed his hands around them. "You do not have to define yourself as a whore. This isn't the only thing that makes you special. Fuck. To me… to me you're the sun and stars. Can you content yourself with one man adoring you instead of fifty or a hundred?"

"Ah, Sylvain. Can you?"

"What?"

Aeris shook his head. "You're no different. You see other men's situations clearly, but you cannot even see your own in shapes and shades. Goddesses, friend. Why the dangerous missions? Why move on as soon as things become secure? I ask this: Can you be content with one man thinking you are brave and can work miracles? Can that ever mean as much as a whole company speaking your name in awed whispers? Can you content yourself with one man pining away with his desire for you instead of an entire camp?"

"If it's you."

"I'd love to believe you," Aeris said. "But in time, you'll realize mine is only the opinion of a whore, of a man schooled to tell others what they want to hear. You'll doubt and resent me, and then where will I be?"

"You have enough gold to live without me," Sylvain protested, feeling confused, caught in a fog he couldn't stumble out of.

"Gold, sure. But… but men to tell me I'm beautiful? Worth anything? That will be harder to find as I grow older and my beauty fades."

"It will never fade in my eyes," Sylvain said, meaning it.

"The irony is you swear that while I am still beautiful," Aeris said. "I am not old and ugly. So the theory is impossible to test."

"Then you must trust me," Sylvain argued.

Aeris laughed. "Life has taught me that is a bad bet, friend. Can you disagree?"

Sylvain dropped his face into his hands. He couldn't stand looking at Aeris's eyes, peeled back, open, raw, and revealing his core. Could he flay himself apart for Aeris? Fuck, he had to try, had to expose his innards even if it meant leaving them a target for the other man.

Slowly, he stroked Aeris's agitated fingers with his thumbs. He looked at Aeris's eyes, hating the insecurity and doubt he normally masked so well with faux vanity and flirtation. "If I disagreed, would I have come here tonight, ripped my heart out and handed it to you bleeding, to nurture or destroy on your whim? You're the only man I have ever granted that awful power to, and yet here I am."

"You couldn't know, or even hope, I would walk away from my life for whatever you're offering." Aeris laughed. "I don't even know what you're offering."

"If I knew I wouldn't be hurt, that you would receive me, then I wouldn't need the trust. I didn't know, and yet I came."

Aeris slid a little closer to Sylvain, and his warmth soaked into Sylvain. He smelled as he always had: sandalwood oil on his skin, citrus and mint in his hair, his unique and tempting fragrance underneath. Subtle lines of kohl framed his arresting eyes; Sylvain hadn't noticed it until now, with Aeris only inches away. Fine gold dust glimmered in his hair and flaked onto his cheek when Sylvain raked his fingers through the blond locks. He guided Aeris's cheek to his shoulder and wrapped Aeris in his arms. Just having him close made Sylvain's fingers tremble in a way they hadn't since he'd touched his first man. Everything else— gold, glory, adventure, challenge, novelty—didn't seem to exist outside the sumptuous suite. Sylvain realized that, for the first time since leaving Octavian, or maybe even before, he was content. If he never worked another mission or defeated another clever enemy, he didn't care, as long as he could sit here and hold Aeris.

"I can't say I haven't missed you," Aeris said, running his fingertip along Sylvain's clavicle and up his throat and over his Adam's apple. "We certainly used to have fun."

"We can have fun again," Sylvain said, "but I want it to be as lovers, partners. Not a transaction. If you need to be told you're beautiful, I swear I'll tell you ten times a day. You'll get tired of hearing it before long, tired of me telling you that you are the most beautiful, perfect, and desirable man I have ever seen. You know me well. Could any less of a man entice me to give up having my choice of the eligible boys anytime I ride into a new town?"

"Goddesses, you're really serious. A whore learns early on to detect flattery and false promises. You really mean it… or at least you believe you do."

Sylvain stiffened. Among all his memories and fantasies of Aeris, he had forgotten the man's skill at dissecting another's motives and delivering a precision cut where it hurt the most. "You doubt my sincerity?"

"No. Only how well you know your own heart. Are you sure you don't want me only because I'm hard to win? One of the challenges that so captivate you? Will you be so intrigued when you have succeeded? Or will you, as you have done in every other aspect of your life, lose interest as soon as the struggle is gone? How many tales have you told me of how easily you become bored when things are easy and assured? Before you dispute it, remember the last place you stayed for any length of time, and remember why you left."

Goddesses, Sylvain couldn't deny it. He'd been absolutely enamored of Octavian Rose when Octavian had been penniless, untrained, and ready to take on the world. But when he'd secured the Rosecairn, the loyalty of the men there, and started a lucrative and respected mercenary company…. Sylvain hadn't felt needed anymore, and his feet had started to itch, and that hole inside him had gaped wider. Yet… "Not with you. Never with you."

"Ah, you say that now, and I'm sure it seems to you that your passion will never flag. But it will. It always does."

"So you're refusing me."

Lifting his head and meeting Sylvain's gaze, Aeris donned his artificial seductive smile and batted his painted eyelashes. "You're more than welcome to stay the night. I don't have any patrons scheduled, and I like the way you used to touch me, how you always took your time."

Sylvain pulled away from him and stood. "I—no. Goddesses, I can find a man to fuck in any tavern in this town."

"Not one as good as I am."

"No, but maybe one who will not treat me like work. I did the right thing leaving this place all those years ago. Thank you for helping me to see that. I will never bother you again." He gathered his armor and weapons, clutched them to his chest, and left without looking back at Aeris. He would have trouble enough scrubbing the man's face from his memories.

Chapter Five

SYLVAIN STOOD on the pier while the other sailors and workers finished stowing their gear and securing the ship's cargo. Since he had left most of his gold at a reputable establishment, all his worldly goods fit in his pack. The southern sun beat down hot, and sweat poured from his skin beneath his leathers. It had been almost a month since he'd left Aeris and the brothel, but the blow he had received there still gnawed at his gut, and nothing could completely relieve it, not even the idea of this voyage. Recently, a sea route to the exotic lands beyond the Lapir Mountains had been discovered, and though the way was perilous, those traders who braved it returned rich men. For Sylvain, the gold enthralled less than the idea of standing on ground where no man of Selindria or Gaeltheon had set foot in over a thousand years. For the first time since he had left Rosecairn, he felt the thrill of a challenge ahead.

They planned to set sail at first light. Now the sun had drowned in the western sea, leaving nothing but a few orange wisps reaching into the sky as it expired beneath the water. The sea birds stood out white against the wine-colored sky. Sylvain turned away from the rhythmic flapping of the sails and followed the men from his crew to a nearby tavern.

The pub was bright and busy, but a serving girl showed Sylvain and his party to a large table beside an open window overlooking the harbor. It smelled of fish and wet rope, but the evening breeze was pleasant. Soon food appeared, and Sylvain ate—mostly shellfish and bread—without caring much about what he was ingesting. The wine was piss-poor and the ale worse, so when one of the sailors brought out a jug and suggested they partake of the Emiri beverage *muri-ku*, Sylvain agreed. After three swigs from the jug, as apparently custom dictated it couldn't be poured into a glass, he faced the momentous decision between trying to stagger outside and risking a fall or just pissing in his trousers where he sat. Finally he decided soiling himself wouldn't gain him any favor in the eyes of the dark-haired seaman in the red bandana he hoped he might persuade to suck his cock later, so he stumbled through the throng and out into the hot, misty, fish-scented air.

Sylvain managed to make it into the alley alongside the tavern. He clumsily unlaced his trouser flap, leaned one hand against the slimy stones of the public house wall, and exhaled in relief as his piss rose in a steaming cloud. Afterward, he fumbled to get himself tucked away and laced up, and though he wasn't positive he'd accomplished it, he turned to head back into the tavern. His long leather tunic would cover anything he had done up less than properly.

"You son of a bitch, you owe me about a thousand gold."

Turning toward the voice, Sylvain drew his bow and nocked an arrow. Even at his drunkest, he could shoot the eye out of a Crypt Warbler, and tonight, well, luckily he was quick enough that he could stick an arrow in both of the shadowy silhouettes approaching him. One of them would be real.

"Put your damned bow down, you silly drunken bastard."

"Who—Aeris? No, you're a vision. I've had too much."

"I can see that," Aeris said, stepping into the torchlight coming from the tavern entrance. "But I'm here nonetheless. You gave me little choice."

"I—" Sylvain had never seen Aeris as he stood before him now, in a shirt, vest, and trousers so coarsely spun he worried they'd chafe Aeris's delicate skin. He'd tied his pale gold hair back in a leather loop, and stubble dusted his too pretty face. Sylvain had never seen him look more enticing, and he took a step forward, reaching out even though he still held his bow and an arrow. "I gave you no choice?"

"No, you prick." Aeris stepped back to deftly avoid Sylvain's inebriated reaching. "After you left, every time I tried to entertain one of my patrons, all I could think of was you saying you wanted someone who didn't consider you work. Damned if I don't want that too. I have never known sex as anything but a job—except with you. You ripped something open in me, and now it isn't enough. I want a lover. I want a man who wants only me. Fuck, I'm probably an idiot, but I want you."

Sylvain staggered over and draped himself drunkenly over Aeris. He smelled so fucking good. Goddesses, if this was a drunken hallucination, Sylvain hoped he was dead in the gutter so he'd never need to wake. He buried his face in Aeris's neck and nibbled wetly at the side of his throat. "You're all I want. All I ever wanted. Goddesses, can we get a room?"

"Not a moment too soon, if you ask me," Aeris said, petting Sylvain's hair indulgently.

Aeris must have ordered the room and paid for it, because Sylvain didn't remember doing so. He remembered Aeris helping him up the steps, even though he staggered and fell at least three or four times, and dragging him through the tiny, darkened cell and dropping him on the bed. Pulling his boots off. His trousers and pants.

He was naked from the waist down, and Aeris was naked on top of him, straddling him. The diffused light from the window lit his side as he rocked his hips down. Sylvain groped at his waist, trying to pull him closer, but Aeris wove his fingers into Sylvain's and guided Sylvain's hands next to his head on the pillow. "Stay there. Let me."

Sylvain grunted his acquiescence as Aeris palmed his cock, coating it in thick oil. His tip pressed against the tight gate of Aeris's opening, and then it broke through. Tight heat surrounded him, and Sylvain cried out. "Fuck, Aeris! It's you. It feels different when it's you." He thrust up toward Aeris, but Aeris grasped his hipbones to hold him in place.

"Because this is not just a job, Sylvain. It's not one of your convenient fucks either. This is us. You're not too drunk to realize that, are you? What this means?"

"No." He ran his fingers through the soft trail of hair on Aeris's belly and up between the muscles of his chest as Aeris's ass clenched around and pulled at him. "Aeris. I love you. Please kiss me."

Aeris fell forward. As their mouths met and their lips opened, tongues cresting against each other, Aeris began rocking his hips.

Though he restrained himself, Sylvain met him thrust for thrust, pushing up into him as Aeris pushed down. As his lips skimmed along the scratchy line of Aeris's jaw, Sylvain closed his eyes and let the other man's presence—his scent, texture, and heat—envelop him, curtain him away from the rest of the world. It was only them, their bodies moving together as if they'd been designed for nothing else, their heavy breaths filling each other's mouths. Sylvain crossed his arms over Aeris's lower back, not to restrain or control him, but just to have him close. Dropping his forehead against Sylvain's, Aeris cradled Sylvain's face in his hands as he rode him with short, hard jerks of his hips. "I'm putting everything I have on you. I love you. You're all I have now. Don't let me down."

"I won't." Sylvain held Aeris's waist as he flipped them and positioned Aeris beneath him. He hooked his hand below Aeris's knees and pushed them up and out, and then he looked down at Aeris's face, his pale eyes glimmering in the darkness, his full lips slack and his body pliant in absolute trust. Sylvain leaned in to kiss him, sliding their lips together and pressing his tongue gently past Aeris's teeth as he worked his cock back into Aeris in a slow, smooth glide. Aeris cried out and clenched his muscles as Sylvain buried himself to the hilt.

Their eyes met. "Come on, Sylvain," Aeris urged. "Fuck me. Fuck me, you mercenary son of a bitch. Show me you'll make up for all the others I left behind."

With a growl, Sylvain hooked Aeris's knees over his shoulders and plunged into him, hard and fast, driving Aeris's shoulders up the bed until they banged against the iron headboard and rattled the wall. "You're mine now, Aeris. My Aeris. Only mine. Nobody else gets to do this… gets your ass… any of you…."

"Prove it. Show me, Sylvain. Show me you only want me from now on."

Sylvain spread Aeris's legs wider, curling his spine, tilting him up so Sylvain could drive even deeper into him. Sylvain thrust, grunting with exertion and drizzling Aeris in his sweat, pounding into Aeris, and still Aeris begged for more. Sylvain pressed Aeris's knees together over Aeris's chest, folding him almost in half and giving all he had to satisfy the other man. Aeris sank his fingernails into Sylvain's forearms, and they screamed and groaned into each other's mouths, teeth scraping together, until Sylvain emptied himself into his Aeris until he felt drained to his core, as if he'd poured his spirit into the other man. He didn't care if he had. He didn't even care if he survived the night, because for the first time he could remember, he felt not only complete, but full to bursting. And if he died from being split asunder by too much happiness… well, then, plenty of men had it worse. And how many ever got to experience something like this?

Aeris bucked beneath him and came. Sylvain collapsed against him and pressed their cheeks together, grinning until his jaw hurt. Goddesses, he felt so young. He'd been with so many men, and he'd been with Aeris dozens of times, but this felt so new… sharing not only flesh but what hid behind it as well. It was… more. Just the experience he needed, and just the man he needed it with. Aeris. Had there ever been a time when Sylvain had not loved him?

"I love you, Aeris." Sylvain pulled reluctantly free of his clutching body, and Aeris groaned as Sylvain flopped onto the pillow beside him. "Everything I have been chasing… it's always been you. I just didn't know. I can be quite a fool sometimes."

Aeris pulled the blankets over them and rolled to rest his head on Sylvain's chest. "Shut up. You're still drunk. But, Sylvain, I love you too. It's possible I have loved you since the first night you bought me and spent all your time sucking my cock and licking my asshole. Telling me I was beautiful and paying for the privilege."

"No sane man would let such treasures slip through his fingers," Sylvain muttered, feeling exhausted. The cheap feather pillow molded around his face as he drew Aeris into his arms and held him against his chest, ignoring the sweat and mess smeared over both of them. "And if you want a repeat performance, my love, you need only ask. I'll suck your pretty cock and lick your ass every day and call it a blessing from the goddesses. I'll do it now, if you like." Sylvain swiped his hand over his mouth and nose. "Have a seat, my love."

Aeris swatted his forehead, then kissed his chin. "Idiot. Go to sleep. We're still set to sail at first light. We need to be ready."

"Aye," Sylvain said, sparing barely half a moment to wonder how Aeris had got himself onto the crew. Aeris… he could do anything. "To new worlds, then."

"To new worlds, together," Aeris said, kissing the bridge of Sylvain's nose.

Sylvain folded Aeris in his arms and held him as he drifted toward unconsciousness and dreams. "New worlds," he mumbled. "Goddesses help them, here we come!"

For the past few years Yarroway L'Estrella has lived in exile, gathering arcane power. But that power came at a price, and he carries the scars to prove it. Now he must do his duty: his uncle, the king, needs him to escort Prince Garith to his wedding, a union that will create an alliance between the two strongest countries in the known world. But Yarrow isn't the prince's only guard. A whole company of knights is assigned to the mission, and Yarrow's not sure he trusts their leader.

Knight Duncan Purefroy isn't sure he trusts Yarrow either, but after a bizarre occurrence during their travels, they have no choice but to work together—especially since the incident also reveals a disturbing secret, one that might threaten the entire kingdom.

The precarious alliance is strained further when a third member joins the cause for reasons of his own—reasons that may not be in the best interests of the prince or the kingdom. With enemies at every turn, no one left to trust, and the dark power within Yarrow pulling dangerously away from his control, the fragile bond the three of them have built may be all that stands between them and destruction.

www.dsppublications.com

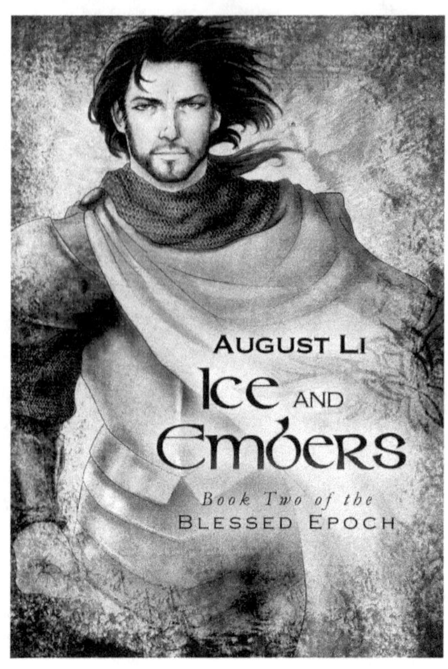

Despite their disparate natures, Yarrow, Duncan, and Sasha united against overwhelming odds to save Prince Garith's life. Now Garith is king and the three friends may be facing their undoing.

Distraught over Yarrow's departure to find the cure to his magical affliction, Duncan struggles with his new role as Bairn of Windwake, a realm left bankrupt and in turmoil by his predecessor. Many of Duncan's vassals conspire against him, and Sasha's unorthodox solutions to Duncan's problem have earned them the contempt of Garith's nobles.

When word reaches Duncan and Sasha that Yarrow is in danger, they want nothing more than to rush to his aid. But Duncan's absence could tip Windwake into the hands of his enemies. In addition, a near-mythic order of assassins wants Sasha dead. Without Yarrow, Duncan and Sasha can't take the fight to the assassins. They are stuck, entangled in a political world they don't understand. But finding Yarrow may cause more problems, and with his court divided, King Garith must strike a balance between supporting his friends and assuaging the nobles who want Duncan punished—and Sasha executed.

www.dsppublications.com

Sasha was born to, and has always defined himself by, the secret assassins' Order of the Crimson Scythe. He chose the love of Yarrow L'Estrella and Duncan Purefroy over his duty to his clan, forfeiting his last mission and allowing Prince Garith to live. Now, the order—previously Sasha's family—has branded him a traitor. He's marked, and that means the brethren of the Crimson Scythe won't stop until Sasha is dead.

Garith's twin kingdoms balance on the brink of war, and all three men have reasons to help the king, whether loyalty, duty, the interests of their own lands, or gold in their pockets. Still, Yarrow and Duncan are willing to abandon their reasons to seek out and destroy the assassins' order to keep Sasha safe. But Sasha isn't sure that's what he wants. Loyalties are strained by both foreign invaders and conspirators in their midst. It's hard to know which side to choose with threats piling up from every direction and war looming, inevitable, on the horizon. Their world teeters on the precipice of change, and Sasha, Duncan, and Yarrow can only hope the links they've forged will hold if Garith's kingdom is torn apart.

www.dsppublications.com

AUGUST LI is an author and artist. He's a lover of cats, foxes, books, video games, Asian ball-joint dolls, and all forms of creative expression. All of his extra time and money go toward traveling and exploring as much of the world as possible. Born in Hong Kong, he lives in Philadelphia, Pennsylvania, with two cats and many imaginary friends.

Blog: foxhatandfriends.wordpress.com

www.dsppublications.com

DSP PUBLICATIONS

visit us online.

WWW.DSPPUBLICATIONS.COM